# MARRYING THE VIRGIN NANNY

AND

# THE NANNY AND ME
BY
TERESA SOUTHWICK

D1448207

MILLS & BOON

**Teresa Southwick** lives with her husband in Las Vegas, the city that reinvents itself every day. An avid fan of romance novels, she is delighted to be living out her dream of writing for Mills & Boon.

# MARRYING THE VIRGIN NANNY

BY
TERESA SOUTHWICK

All the characters in this book have no existence outside the imagination of
the author, and have no relation whatsoever to anyone bearing the same name
or names. They are not even distantly inspired by any individual known or
unknown to the author, and all the incidents are pure invention.

First published in Great Britain 2010
Harlequin Mills & Boon Limited,
Eton House, 18-24 Paradise Road, Richmond, Surrey TW9 1SR

© Teresa Ann Southwick 2009

ISBN: 978 0 263 88838 6

23-1110

Harlequin Mills & Boon policy is to use papers that are natural, renewable
and recyclable products and made from wood grown in sustainable forests.
The logging and manufacturing processes conform to the legal environmental
regulations of the country of origin.

Printed and bound in Spain
by Litografia Rosés S.A., Barcelona

Dear Reader,

I love kids. From the time I was a little girl, if someone in the neighborhood had a baby I was glued to their side. I'm the middle child of six and helped with the younger ones, who were almost as big as me. These days, my definition of family isn't just those with whom I share DNA, it includes the people who touch my heart and become part of my life.

Maggie Shepherd, the heroine of *Marrying the Virgin Nanny*, was abandoned as a baby at the Good Shepherd Home for Children. The nuns and kids there became her family and she'd do anything to protect them, including marrying Jason Garrett, the wealthy boss who makes her an offer she can't refuse.

Jason has his own family problems. He needs a nanny and is dealing with a controlling father who keeps getting marriage wrong. When Jason meets Maggie, he'd do anything to make sure she's there for his infant son—anything except fall in love.

For me, the only thing better than holding a baby is writing about one, especially the littlest matchmaker who brings Jason and Maggie together. I hope you enjoy their story and look for the next two books in THE NANNY NETWORK series.

Happy reading!

*Teresa Southwick*

To Charles Griemsman,
who is simply a joy to work with. You're the best!

# Chapter One

Margaret Mary Shepherd had never been the sort of woman men undressed with their eyes.

But if Maggie had to pick someone for that particular job based solely on looks, Jason Garrett would be right at the top of her list. Dark curly hair and eyes the color of coal complemented the brooding look he no doubt used from the boardroom to the bedroom.

Standing in the doorway of his penthouse condo just off the Las Vegas Strip, Maggie listened to the wail of an infant and knew the exact moment the decibel level went up. The man winced, an expression that was perilously close to panic and put him on the fast track to fear. It also told her that what she looked like underneath her crisp denim jeans and blue turtleneck sweater wasn't even on his priority list.

"I very much hope that you're Ms. Shepherd from The Nanny Network," he said.

"I am."

"Thank God." He opened the door wider for her to enter. "Ginger Davis promised that you would be here within the hour."

"She said it was an emergency, Mr. Garrett."

He ran his fingers through his hair and from the looks of it, that wasn't the first time. Quite a tall man, he forced her to look up. His wrinkled white dress shirt with sleeves rolled up and recklessly loosened striped tie only added to his potent masculinity.

"I need a nanny," he said. Desperate need, judging by the ragged expression on his face. "Ginger assured me that infants are your specialty—"

An enraged, tiny-baby wail came from somewhere nearby. "Right on cue. That must be yours."

"My son, yes."

"I'll just go—"

"Wait." He glanced in the direction of the cry. "According to your employer you are the very best at what you do, but I'd like some confirmation."

The baby's distress was making Maggie want to tell him what he could do with his confirmation. "Isn't that why you contacted The Nanny Network? The agency has made its reputation by conducting thorough personnel background and qualification checks. Peace of mind is part of the service."

"I haven't had a chance to check out Ginger Davis and The Nanny Network the way I'd like. But I'm not hiring 'Ginger and Company.' You're the one who will be taking care of my son. The circumstances I find myself in—"

"What is your situation, Mr. Garrett?"

"I've had three nannies since my son was born and he's only a month old, born December eleventh. I need someone to care for him, someone I can trust."

The cry increased in pitch and urgency and Maggie couldn't stand it.

"Look, Mr. Garrett, I'm not sure what your problem is that

makes it a challenge for you to keep a nanny, but the job interview can wait." She turned in the direction of the crying.

"Hold on a second—"

"Not while that baby is upset."

As she hurried down the hall with the man hot on her heels, Maggie's impression of his home was understated sophistication and simple elegance that probably cost a bundle. The guy was loaded, some kind of genius developer sensation. And what did any of that matter to the tiny infant who was clearly distressed about something?

She found the nursery and hurried over to the crib. The infant was on his back, thank goodness. His little face was red and the desperate cry was constant, high pitched. His hands and feet were going a mile a minute and his little mouth quivered in the way babies did that could just break your heart.

Without hesitation, she reached in and scooped him into her arms. "Oh my goodness, sweetheart," she cooed. She lifted him against her chest and rubbed his back, making him feel as secure as possible. "It's going to be okay. I promise."

She pressed him close and gently swayed, the movement coming automatically. When he'd calmed enough, she settled him into the bend of her elbow, then took his tiny hand in hers and brushed his palm with her thumb. The intensity of the cries diminished until the sound was more like a cat's meow, one that was telling her off big time for letting the situation deteriorate to such a low.

"I know, sweetheart. You're absolutely right. The conditions here are deplorable and completely intolerable. But things are looking up." She glanced at Jason Garrett who was watching her through narrowed eyes.

"I wasn't finished talking to you." He wasn't accustomed to losing control of a situation.

"I was finished talking to you until this little one is sufficiently reassured that his needs will be met." She cuddled the child close. Smiling down she asked, "What's his name?"

"Brady." He moved close. "Brady Hunter Garrett." Tentatively brushing a finger over the downy dark fuzz on the child's head, he smiled.

Maggie's stomach quivered and pitched. He'd been all brooding darkness until he looked at his son. It was an expression so tender and loving her heart quivered and pitched, too.

"It's a good, strong name." She continued to caress the tiny palm as she said, "It's nice to meet you, Brady Hunter Garrett."

"Are you always so take-charge?" he asked.

"Are you always so long-winded?"

"What does that mean?" he demanded, the brooding look back.

"Brady's needs come before yours."

"Not when my need is to make sure he's safe," Garrett snapped.

"It's easy to see why you go through nannies like napkins at a car wash."

"I don't have to explain myself to you. I'm the employer; you're the employee."

"Not yet. If you can interview me, I should be extended the same courtesy to decide whether or not I want to work for you."

"Do you screen all potential employers?"

"This is the first time."

Maggie wasn't sure why she was doing it now except something was weird here. Her specialty was infants from birth to six weeks. Go in, stabilize the situation, so new mom could get her sea legs and some rest, get out before she, Maggie, fell in love with the child and couldn't leave without breaking her heart. Ginger Davis, owner of The Nanny Network, had always placed her in work situations with couples—husband and wife or man and woman living together in a committed relationship. Always she'd met the infant's mother first. Not this time.

"Where's Mrs. Garrett?" she asked.

"I'm not married."

"But Brady has a mom."

He frowned and his perpetual dark look grew positively black. "The woman who gave birth to him is not going to be a part of his life."

Was that his way of saying she'd passed away? If only there'd been time for Ginger to fully brief her on this position.

"Is she—I mean, was there a medical problem?"

"Nothing like that. All you need to know is that she won't be an issue." And the scowl on his face put an end to further questions on the subject.

She had news for him. A mother who disappeared from your life could be an even bigger issue. Maggie knew from firsthand experience.

"Now, if it's all right with you," he continued, "I have a few questions."

"I'm an open book," she said.

"May I see your references?"

"I didn't bring anything with me."

"Then you're the first who's arrived without them."

"I'm between assignments, Mr. Garrett, and was expecting to have several weeks off. Ginger said this was an emergency and I should come right away. She promised to messenger over whatever paperwork was required."

"I require it before you interact with my son."

"Then we have a problem."

She stared at the little boy in her arms who was sucking on his little fist and staring up at her with his father's dark eyes. There was a funny sort of tightness in her chest just before she felt a powerful tug on her heart. He was a beautiful child, but that wasn't a surprise because his father was an incredibly handsome man.

This was a first, too. She normally felt nothing but the

general nurturing instincts that babies always generated in her. This was different. Because there was no mother in the picture? Because she was one of a long line of nannies in his short little life? Because Jason Garrett clearly needed her? Or was it the man himself?

He was as compelling as any Gothic romance hero she'd ever read. He was Mr. Darcy, Heathcliff and Edward Rochester all rolled into one tall, muscular, attractive and dashing package.

She would be the first to admit that her hormones hadn't been out for a test drive in quite a while. But they were making up for lost time in a big way now. This father-son duo packed a powerful punch in the few minutes she'd been here. How much damage could they do if given half a chance? It was a disaster in the making.

"I don't think I can work for you, Mr. Garrett." She shifted the baby into his arms and the way he instantly stiffened told her he wasn't used to this.

She refused to let her sympathy cloud her better judgment and walked out of the room.

"Ms. Shepherd—" He caught up with her in the foyer. "Wait—"

Bracing herself, she turned to face him but could only raise her gaze to the collar of his shirt. "There's no point in wasting any more of your time."

"It's my time and I'm asking for just a few more minutes of yours."

"I don't think there's anything left to say."

"That's where you're wrong."

"I'm wrong?" she said, taking her purse from the table and sliding the strap over her shoulder.

The baby started to whimper and flail his fists and the just-this-side-of-panic look was back in his father's eyes. "Okay. Maybe I've been a little hasty in judgment. But look at it from my perspective."

"And what is that?"

It was a mistake to ask, but that wasn't her first one. Going soft when he all but admitted he was wrong was the number one slip-up.

"Nanny number one couldn't soothe him, and made some excuse about why it's all right to let babies cry during the night. When my son cries it's because he needs tending to and I'm in favor of feeding on demand as opposed to making him wait for a scheduled time."

"I agree." To her way of thinking babies always had a reason for crying and should not be ignored. The child came first. Period. The caretaker was always on call. "What happened to nanny number two?"

"A family emergency." He glanced at his son, a fiercely protective look. "Something I understand all too well."

She'd never had a family, at least not a traditional one. "That's not her fault."

"No, but now it's my problem. And I have to ask—you walked in and had him quiet in thirty seconds flat—how did you do that?"

She shrugged. "I'm good at what I do, Mr. Garrett."

"I couldn't say about babies in general," he said, a smile cutting through his uncompromising expression. The transformation was amazing. "But I saw for myself that with my son you're very skilled."

She wasn't the only one. Her skill was infants, his was flattery. At first he'd kept it securely under wraps, along with his seriously compelling charm. Now that he needed them, he pulled out both and set them on stun. "Brady is a beautiful child."

"He's more than that, Ms. Shepherd—"

"Maggie."

He nodded. "He's my son, Maggie. I'm a demanding boss. I'll admit that. And I don't know a lot about babies. I'll admit that, too. But most important for you to know is that I'm a protective father. It seems to me that when caring for a child there are some basic nonnegotiable principles."

"Such as?"

"Doing your job. When I arrived home from the office unexpectedly, I found nanny number three on the balcony with a glass of wine and Brady in his crib crying."

Maggie was shocked. "That's horrific."

"I thought so, too, and fired her on the spot."

"Good for you."

"So, you see, I find myself in a situation. I have a business to run."

"I've heard of it. Garrett Industries is developing that huge project just off the 15 freeway, the one monopolizing all the construction cranes in the Southwest." When he grinned again, her chest felt funny even before her pulse fluttered.

"There's nothing I'd like better than to stay home and care for my son, but I have obligations. People are counting on me and I'm counting on you. I'm in great need of your services."

"What about my references?"

"I understand that there's no way to measure a person's ability to do a good job, but it would reassure me to see something in writing that says you're qualified to care for children. But I'd like to hire you right now, references pending."

When Brady started to whimper harder, she really felt as if this was a father-son tag team. They were piling it on. His crying went from half-hearted to off the chart in a matter of seconds and Jason handed him back to her.

"Hey, sweetie," she soothed, and tried stroking his palm again. After several heaving sobs he started to quiet.

"I think I've just seen all the references necessary," Jason said. "He wouldn't stop crying for me and I offered him a thousand dollars. The interview is over, you're hired."

Maggie wasn't so sure this was a good idea, but she simply couldn't walk out on this child. "Okay."

\* \* \*

"Brady is asleep."

Jason looked up and saw Maggie in the doorway to his study. He'd been completely focused on the information in the envelope that Ginger Davis had messengered over. Reading about his new nanny was priority number one and he'd forgotten about asking her to join him when the baby was settled.

Sitting behind his flat oak desk in his home office, he held out a hand. "Have a seat."

She picked the left wingchair across from him, then folded her hands in her lap as she met his gaze.

"Is Brady all right?"

"He's an angel," she said, smiling for the first time. "He's bathed, fed and sleeping like a baby."

"Good." He nodded toward the stack of papers. "Ginger is very efficient."

"I've always found her to be a woman of her word."

Good to know because The Nanny Network charged a hefty amount of money for the service provided. Everything in life came with a price tag, but you didn't always know if it would be worth what you paid.

In the case of his son, he wasn't disappointed. He'd never known a love like he'd felt when he saw Brady for the first time. And the feeling had multiplied tenfold since he'd brought him home from the hospital. When Catherine had broken the news about the unplanned pregnancy, her next comment was that *it* would be history soon. Jason couldn't accept that his child would be removed as if it were nothing more than an inconvenience, an annoyance, a stain on the carpet.

After intense negotiation and a large settlement, he had a son whose mother received a bonus for signing off all rights to him. He'd have paid her far more than she'd happily taken, but that had been enough to finance plastic surgery or any other physical enhancement to further her acting ambitions.

What he hadn't counted on was how complicated finding competent child care would be.

"So you finally have my references?" Maggie asked.

Her voice pulled him back from the memories, and he glanced at her before again scanning the résumé that included very thorough background information. "You're an orphan?"

"That would assume my parents are dead. In fact, I don't know where they are. I never knew them at all. As an infant I was left on the steps of the Good Shepherd Home for Children where I was found by Sister Margaret and Sister Mary."

Her tone was so moderate and matter of fact it was several moments before the pieces formed a complete picture. She'd been no bigger than Brady when she was discarded, an annoyance, an inconvenience. "So Margaret Mary Shepherd—"

She nodded. "I was named after two nuns and a home for abandoned children."

It wasn't often that people surprised him, but he was surprised now. "Forgive me, I don't know what to say."

"That implies you pity me."

"No, I—"

"It's all right. I consider myself lucky. Everyone was good to me. No one turned me away when I asked for more gruel." She smiled at her reference to the famous scene in the dark Dickens book. "I had a roof over my head, a bed to sleep in and people who cared about me. I'm healthy and privileged to do a job I love. I didn't end up in a Dumpster or as a sensational, sad headline in the newspaper. It could so easily have been a story with a tragic ending, but someone cared enough to give me to the sisters."

Catherine hadn't cared, but for a price she'd given him Brady.

Maggie Shepherd met his gaze and her own was unapologetic, clear-eyed and proud. There was no sign that she intimidated her and he wasn't sure how he felt about that. Considering his recent nanny problems he'd have preferred a healthy dose of fear.

At first sight he'd thought her plain, although her wide dark-blue eyes that sort of tilted up at the corners were very unusual. Her brown hair was pulled back in a long ponytail. If worn long, it would spill over the shoulders of her turtle-neck sweater and down her back. For some reason, he wanted very much to see it loose, maybe so that she'd look older, less like a fourteen-year-old babysitter.

When she'd held his son and smiled, the mouth he'd thought a bit too wide was suddenly intriguing. The tender expression in her eyes when she looked at the baby made her beautiful. Not home-run-with-the-score-tied-in-the-ninth-inning exciting, or touchdown-to-take-the-lead-with-thirty-seconds-left-in-the-fourth-quarter stunning. But the individual features blended on a canvas of pale, flawless skin mixed with an air of sweetness and formed a pretty picture.

He folded his hands and settled them on the desk as he leaned forward. "Do you wonder about your parents?"

Her serene look didn't slip. "It's a waste of energy."

"But aren't you curious about anything?" He couldn't help wondering if Brady would have questions about where his mother was and why she'd disappeared from his life. The truth wasn't pretty, and Jason wasn't prepared to tell it. But at least he knew what the truth was. Maggie had no details about her parents and he wondered if that bothered her. "Do you ever think about where they are? What they're like? Why you are the way you are?"

She stared at him for a moment, then stood, serenity suddenly shattered. "If this is your way of saying you think I'm unsuitable for the nanny position…"

He stood, too, and noticed for the first time how small she was. Fragile, almost. He towered over her and now it made him feel like a bully until he remembered her fierce determination to comfort a distressed baby. She'd been like a force of nature.

"I didn't mean to pry," he said. "But I feel within my

rights as a father to know the woman in whose care I'm leaving my son."

"If you don't trust me, I'd appreciate it if you'd simply say so."

"There's nothing in your background, personal or professional, that made me change my mind about hiring you."

"Fine. Then, if it's all right with you, I'll go settle in while Brady is sleeping."

"Will you stay for another moment? I have just a few more questions."

She hesitated, then sat down again. "All right."

"When did you first become aware that you're a 'baby whisperer'?" he asked, rounding the desk to sit on the corner closest to her. "I'm just curious."

"I've always been around children. Everyone at the home was expected to help out, but it never felt like a chore to me. Then my first job while I worked my way through college was with a wealthy family who had four children, ranging in age from an infant to early twenties. He was in college." Her lips pressed together for a moment before she added, "I found I liked babies."

But she hadn't liked something. Jason wondered about that and also about what she did after college graduation. Her background information had only said that she'd spent time in the convent without taking final vows.

"Why did you decide to become a nun?"

"I admired the sisters and wanted to be like them. It was important to me to give back, help people the way I'd been helped." Her face was all innocence and sincerity that couldn't quite hide the shadows.

"There are many altruistic professions that don't require such a structured lifestyle," he said.

"I knew what I was leaving behind in the secular life."

So she'd dated and still chose to enter the convent. Or maybe dating drove her *into* the convent.

"You didn't find what you were looking for with the nuns?" He was pushing the boundaries of this interview and he knew it. But she stirred his curiosity.

She sighed and thought for several moments before answering, as if choosing her words carefully. "It wasn't a matter of not finding what I was looking for in the convent as much as I'm simply not good nun material."

The corners of his mouth curved up. "Oh?"

"When you're close to final vows, it's a time for reflection and honesty. I simply had too many doubts."

"About what?"

"Me." She shrugged. "There was an expectation of sacrifice and commitment that I wasn't sure of being able to sustain."

"I see," he said.

"And speaking of expectations—" she shifted in her chair, and met his gaze "—it's time we discussed what you expect of me."

"Take care of Brady. He's your only responsibility. I have a cleaning service and a cook who also runs the household. If you need anything let Linda know."

"Fine. But that's not what I meant." She blew out a breath. "It's obvious to me that you're not comfortable with Brady yet. Do you need me to teach you how to take care of him?"

"It's your job to do that."

"I'm not being sarcastic or judgmental," she added quickly. "It's just that this is different for me."

"How so?"

"You're a single father."

"Is that a problem?" he asked, thinking about her first job and the oldest son. Did she get hit on? The thought made him angry. "Like I said before, if I could care for my son, I'd do it in a heartbeat. But I have a large company and need to work."

"I understand. And are the people working for you entitled to scheduled time off?"

"Of course, but—"

"I require one day off a week. Saturday, until midday Sunday. That should be stipulated in the contract that arrived with the rest of the paperwork. Can you handle the baby for a day?" She met his gaze with a direct one of her own and when he hesitated, she said, "Since I've been with The Nanny Network it's never been a problem. But I've never worked in a home where there wasn't a father and a mother."

"Like I said, the woman who gave birth to Brady is a nonissue. I'm paying you to—"

"To be his mother?" she asked.

"No—" He'd paid a woman to bring him into the world and was going to pay Maggie to take care of him. There was no need to put a finer point on it. "Why does this matter?"

"Because you're a single father, it would make good sense for you to find a long-term situation. If I'd known that, I would have turned down the job."

"Why?"

"I only stay for six weeks, then—"

"What?"

"That's also in my contract. My assignments last no longer than that."

Jason didn't want a parade of strangers coming through. He didn't want a revolving door on Brady's care. Continuity and stability were the cornerstones of a well-adjusted child-hood and he'd do whatever was necessary to give his son the best cornerstone money could buy. He wanted long term now. He wanted Margaret Mary Shepherd.

She watched him carefully, gauging his reaction. "Ginger will find someone else—"

"What if I don't want someone else?"

From the moment she'd ignored everything but the need to protect a baby—his baby—she'd had him. No one else would do.

Shadows turned her eyes navy blue and she pulled her lips

tight for a moment. "I won't stay beyond what's stipulated in the agreement. It's important that you're aware of that up front."

"Are you already angling for a raise, Maggie?"

"This has nothing to do with money."

Right. And he was Mother Goose.

"Look," he said, rubbing the back of his neck. "This isn't something we need to decide tonight. When the time comes, we'll discuss new terms."

She stood up. "Six weeks, Mr. Garrett."

"Call me Jason."

"All right, Jason. But I'm not budging on my deadline. I won't stay more than six weeks."

He watched the unconsciously sexy sway of her slender hips as she walked out of his office after issuing what could only be construed as a challenge. Obviously Margaret Mary Shepherd had never negotiated with someone who was willing and able to pay whatever it cost to have her.

## Chapter Two

Maggie stretched the baby out on her thighs and curled his fingers around her thumbs. "Hey, big boy. Where's that smile? I know you've got one for me," she cooed to him. "Let's see it."

He wasn't five weeks old, and yet he was showing signs that he was on the verge of smiling. Would he look like his father? Her heart tripped up at the thought. This little guy wouldn't be in that heartthrob league yet. The lack of teeth thing could be an issue. But his dad was something else. Jason Garrett had a very nice, very potent smile when he chose to use it. And Brady showed every indication that he'd be the spitting image of his dad.

Stretching out, the baby pressed his little feet into her abdomen and she wondered, not for the first time, what it felt like when life moved inside you. This child was a beautiful miracle, one his mother had walked away from. Not unlike her own mother.

She liked to think lack of money and resources had factored

into the decision to abandon her. But Brady's father clearly had big bucks. The penthouse was understated elegance with recessed lighting, soft yellow paint on the walls, plush white sofas and dark wood tables. Walking on the thick beige carpet was like sinking to your knees in softness. Expertly lighted art hung on the walls and expensive glass pieces and figurines were scattered throughout. In fact, before her tenure here ended, she felt duty bound to remind him to put the pricey stuff up high when Brady got mobile. A toddler's oops in this place could cost way more than most people made in a month.

She glanced out the floor-to-ceiling windows with a spectacular view of the lights on the Las Vegas Strip and the valley beyond. Scenery like that didn't come cheap.

Jason had thoroughly checked her out, and she'd returned the favor, grilling Ginger for information. Her Nanny Network boss had assured her there were no sexual harassment or hostile work environment accusations against him. No hint of scandal or impropriety. Quite the opposite. Everyone who worked for him had only good things to say. Employee retention at his company was exceptionally high.

So why couldn't he retain the mother of his son? Maggie would really like to know the answer to that question.

As if he felt her attention drifting, Brady cooed his irresistible baby coo, and she smiled. "I wasn't ignoring you, sweetie pie. You're a charmer in training, that's what you are."

His mouth curved up at the corners as he happily kicked his feet. She laughed and a corresponding sound gurgled up from deep inside him in what could only have been a laugh.

It was a major "awww" moment, melting her heart like ice on a summer sidewalk. And that was cause for alarm. She didn't do the heart melty thing. That wasn't to say she didn't love babies, all babies. She did. But her thing was not to get attached. On her first day, this little guy had easily hurdled her defenses, then grabbed on to her emotions with both of his tiny hands and the sweetest disposition in the world. He was already starting to feel special and she had enough time left on her commitment for him to do a lot of damage.

Rubbing her thumbs across his tiny knuckles, she smiled. "You are too cute for words, Mr. Garrett."

"Thank you."

The familiar deep voice came from behind her and slid over her senses like warm chocolate and whiskey. Maggie had lost count, but this was the fourth or fifth time today Jason Garrett had dropped in unexpectedly. All that practice should have helped her get used to him. Unfortunately, she wasn't even close to comfortable with Sin City's most eligible bachelor and overachieving tycoon.

"Actually, I wasn't talking to you," she said. "I didn't know you were there. Just like a couple hours ago when you stealthily sneaked up behind me. And the time before that. And the time before—"

"Yeah." He came closer and set his suit jacket on the sofa back, then rested a hip beside it. He leaned forward and smiled at his son. "Hi, buddy," he said, then looked at her. "I get your drift."

"And I get yours."

"I'm not subtle?" he asked.

"Not even a little bit." From the moment they'd met, she'd figured out that he wasn't the most trusting of men. His behavior today was further confirmation. "You're checking up on me."

"Does it bother you?" he asked, not taking the trouble to deny it.

"No. Quite the opposite. I respect you for protecting your son. If every child in the world was cared for so well, it would be a much better place."

What she didn't say was that his defensive actions not only made her respect him, she liked him, too. That was a good thing, right? How come it didn't feel that way? All she felt was uneasy. The last time she'd liked a man this much the feelings had grown into love. He came with a family who liked her back and she'd felt as if she was getting everything she'd always wanted. Then it didn't work out, a major blow that had hurt a lot.

She chanced a glance up at Jason, and her stomach dropped like an airplane hitting turbulence. The sight of him in his rumpled white dress shirt and loosened red tie made it hard to breathe. It was much safer to look at the baby.

"Your daddy's home, Brady. For good this time? Or can we expect ongoing guerrilla warfare tactics this evening?"

"I'm in for the night. You can stand down."

"Good to know."

Jason leaned over again and stirred up the scent of him, something spicy and sexy and all male. Something that made it impossible for her senses to stand down. She felt tingly all over.

He reached out and loosely caught hold of a tiny foot. "Hey, buddy. How are you? Did you have a good day?"

The baby waved his arms and smiled. Jason laughed and the sound warmed her clear through. She was exceptionally good at resisting warm and fuzzy, but there it was again. As if she needed more proof, that double whammy convinced her the combined effect of the Garrett men was pretty potent and highly dangerous stuff. She scooped the baby into her arms, then stood and walked around the sofa.

"He's fed, bathed and in his jammies. All ready to spend some time with his daddy." She settled Brady in his arms and backed away.

This felt weird. After a year at The Nanny Network, Maggie had lots of assignments under her belt. When the man of the house returned from his day at work, Maggie faded discreetly away to give mom and dad couple- and family-bonding time. She waited in the background, ready to jump in and help if needed. The only couple here was father and son. She'd never been in this situation before and didn't quite know what to do with herself.

Jason smiled down at his child. "He smells good."

"Yeah. I don't think anything smells better than a freshly bathed baby."

He looked at her and something dark and dangerous glittered in his eyes for a split second before disappearing. "And he seems pretty happy."

"He's been an angel all day."

"I may be a new father, but I know this mood can disappear in a nanosecond. Before that happens, would you mind taking him while I get out of this suit?"

"Of course."

She took the handoff and tried not to think about him changing. The situation already felt too intimate. She walked around the living room, then into the kitchen. Never in her life had she seen such a beautiful, functional kitchen. Maple cupboards were topped by black granite and in the center was an island big enough for its own zip code. The appliances were stainless steel, including the Sub-Zero refrigerator and two ovens. A glass French door closed off the walk-in pantry that was tidy and organized. In her assignments, Maggie had seen lots of different houses and condos, but never anything as gorgeous as this.

It was past dinnertime and she'd already eaten, but the cook had left a plate for Jason. She felt the need to keep busy and settled Brady in the infant seat on the floor beside the glass-topped dinette. After spinning the toy strung in front of him, she watched him watch it until his interest kicked in. Then she took the plate of lasagna from the fridge, removed the plastic covering and stuck it in the microwave. There was also a salad that she tossed vigorously with Italian dressing.

When Jason returned in his worn jeans and powder-blue

pullover sweater, her insides got a vigorous tossing of their own. He looked as good in casual clothes as he did in slacks and tie. Maybe better, if possible.

She realized she'd been staring and to fill the awkward silence said the first thing that came to mind. "I'm warming up your dinner. You're probably hungry."

"I am." He had a funny sort of intense expression on his face. "If it's all right with you, I'll have a quick bite to eat before hanging out with Brady. Could you stick around?"

"Of course."

He glanced into the microwave. "Something smells good."

"Yeah." And she wasn't at all sure she meant the food. "Linda is a good cook. But you already know that."

"She's been with me for several years."

Stability. Since she never stayed more than six weeks, that was a foreign concept to her. She leaned over the infant carrier and nudged it with a finger, partly to keep nervous hands busy. Partly to rock the baby and stretch out this unpredictable contentment as long as possible.

"I can't help wondering what Linda's job interview was like," she said.

Jason glanced at her over one broad shoulder. "She had terrific references."

"Was there a test? Did she have to prepare pheasant under glass out of corn flakes and tofu?"

He laughed. "Are you implying I'm a demanding boss?"

"Heaven forbid."

"You'd be right. And I won't apologize for it." When the microwave beeped, he retrieved his plate and brought it to the table where his salad waited. "I don't demand more of anyone else than I'm willing to give. That said, working with food is relatively easy. Babies, not so much. Because I'm willing to give everything I've got."

"You're his father. That's the way it should be." She didn't have the right to give everything and had to hold part of herself back. Otherwise, leaving hurt too much.

Brady's snorts and grunts changed tone indicating that the grumpy portion of the evening was about to commence. She was grateful for the distraction because the words made her like Jason even more. "I'll take him into the other room so you can eat in peace."

"Stay." He put a hand on her arm and stared at it for a second before meeting her gaze. Shrugging, he added, "Peace is highly overrated. I haven't seen him all day."

"I beg to differ. What with the unannounced visitations."

"Let me rephrase. I haven't had a chance to spend quality time with him. Keep me company. It won't take long to wolf this down."

Her arm tingled from his touch and she felt strange, out of her element, which made her want to run and hide. But how could she refuse? Especially when he said it like that. Not to mention that he was the boss.

"Okay."

But when she tried to sit, the baby wasn't happy. She stood and her body automatically started a gentle swaying motion. She turned Brady so his back was against her chest and father and son could see each other. She caressed the baby's palm with her thumb because he seemed to like that.

"So, tell me," Jason said, "what did I miss today? What did you do?"

"Let me see," she started. "I changed diapers. Fed this little guy. Played with him. Sang songs—for your information, his favorites are 'Row, Row, Row Your Boat' and 'Rubber Ducky.'"

"He told you that?" Jason chewed as he studied her.

"Not in so many words. But in body language, he was rockin' out."

"Meaning he didn't have a meltdown during the performance?"

"Pretty much," she confirmed.

He laughed, then forked up a bite of salad. After chewing, he asked, "What else?"

She thought about the day. "He took two naps, during which I'm quite sure he had a significant growth spurt. I can feel the difference in density already."

"In one day?"

"Absolutely."

Singing his son's praises and giving the blow-by-blow of Brady's day made her feel more connected than she liked. And protective. She couldn't shake the sensation of wanting to go run interference for him because he was starting out life with one strike against him. Like her.

Jason smiled tenderly at the boy. "Way to go, buddy. Getting bigger is your job."

"Speaking of jobs," Maggie said. "What did you do today?"

Thoughtfully, he chewed a bite of lasagna and washed it down with water. "I had a great day. In between nanny surveillance, I closed a billion-dollar deal, which will net enough money to make a significant donation to a prestigious university. It's more than enough to ensure that my son will be accepted and get into whatever program he wants."

"So you bought him a way into college?"

He tilted his head thoughtfully. "Let's say I removed any doubt."

He was a man who had the means to get what he wanted.

Twenty-four hours ago Jason had said he wanted her, and here she was. The thought set off a powerful quivering in the pit of her stomach as she recalled the dark and determined look on his face when he'd made the pronouncement.

He *wanted* her.

That was a heady notion, a thought she refused to take any further.

After Jason finished eating, he set his dishes in the sink,

then took the baby from her. Murmuring tenderly, he settled Brady in the crook of his muscular arm, and Maggie barely managed to hold in a sigh.

Was there anything more appealing than the sight of a handsome man holding a tiny infant in his strong arms? If so, she'd never seen it.

She watched the two Garrett men walk away, although technically only one was walking. But that didn't change the fact that she was alone. Along with the solitude, common sense came pouring in. She'd never felt a pull on her heart like this. Was it because she was a stand-in mom, being the only female on the premises? Is that why she was feeling so connected to the single father and his motherless baby?

Whatever the reason, she had to stop. She was an employee, a very temporary one, nothing more. Soon she would be a nanny to another baby. And darned if the thought of leaving was about as appealing as a header off the top of the Stratosphere. It must have something to do with the fact that they were a family without a mom and she was a woman without a family.

This strong reaction, with five weeks and six days to go, made her wish she hadn't agreed to stay at all.

Jason wasn't accustomed to concentration problems when he worked—either at the office, or at his home office, which was where he was now. The baby had changed his life in so many ways, and could be a distraction, but that wasn't the problem. It had nothing to do with adjusting to his new situation and everything to do with the new nanny.

Maggie.

Margaret Mary Shepherd wasn't the sort of woman who would normally capture his notice. She wasn't classically beautiful nor did she have legs that went on forever. As a matter of fact, he'd never seen her legs except covered by denim, apparently the uniform of efficient nannies these days. Her appeal was all about character. She was dependable, efficient and sarcastically witty.

Admittedly, his taste in women left a lot to be desired. Case in point: his son's biological mother who had required a large sum of money to guarantee Brady's very existence.

Maggie wasn't like that. If she was, it would have been easier to put her out of his mind.

A soft knock sounded on his study door. It couldn't be Brady, so by process of elimination... His stomach tightened just a fraction with what felt like anticipation.

"Come in," he said.

And there was his distraction in the flesh, wearing jeans and a yellow sweater, looking a lot like a slice of sunshine.

"Maggie. Hi."

"Sorry to interrupt."

"Not a problem." He removed his glasses and turned off the computer, giving her his full attention—full, because she'd already had part of it since she arrived five days ago. "What can I do for you? Is Brady okay?"

"Fine. He was a little fussier than normal tonight. I hope he didn't disturb you."

"Never." Thoughts of her had disturbed him, but that wasn't her problem. Nor was it something he intended to share. "Any idea why he was restless?"

She stayed in the doorway. "Babies are a guessing game. He could have been overtired. Maybe gas. There's no way to know. You listen to the various cries—"

"It all sounds the same to me." Jason leaned back in his chair and linked his fingers over his abdomen. "They're different?"

"Very." She smiled. "There's a frantic edge to it when he's hungry. A sort of general dissatisfaction when he needs to be changed. Kind of a quiet mewling sound when he's telling you off because his need wasn't met in a timely fashion."

"Fascinating." As was the fact that she hadn't moved any closer to his desk. "Where are my manners? Come in and have a seat."

"Oh—I just wanted to remind you—"

He motioned her in and indicated one of the matching wing chairs in front of him. The smooth leather had gold buttons. Very pretentious. Very not her, but what could you do? "Please sit."

"Okay." She started to close the door the way it had been, then hesitated and opened it wide. "I need to listen for the baby."

"Of course." That was her job. She worked for him. At the office he didn't find it necessary to remind himself that any woman was his employee. But it was different with Maggie. Must have something to do with the intimacy of living under the same roof.

She sat in front of him and the movement brought the scent of her wafting to him. It was sweet, which suited her.

"I just wanted to remind you that tomorrow is Saturday— my day off. And I won't be back until noon on Sunday. You'll have to get up with Brady if he needs anything. Should I notify Ginger to send someone to fill in?"

He thought about it for a moment, then shook his head. "I'm looking forward to time with my son."

"Okay."

The smile she gave him was full of approval and he felt like he'd given the correct game-show answer that would make all his dreams come true. Her reaction shouldn't be that important to him.

"Do you have plans for the day?" he asked, mostly to distract himself from the unsettling thought.

"I'm going to do what I do every Saturday."

"And that is?"

"Volunteer at the Good Shepherd Home."

"I see." No shopping? Lunch with the girls? A manicure,

pedicure or facial? He was lying. He didn't see at all. "What do you do there?"

"I fill in for one of the staff who takes a day off. And to answer your question, I do whatever needs doing. Cooking. Cleaning. Playing with the kids. Talking to them. Tucking them in at night. It's important they know people care, that they're not leftovers. Throwaways."

"Is that how you felt?"

The question came out before he could stop it. His only excuse was that part of his mind was focused on her mouth, and its high sexiness factor. If she wasn't his son's nanny, he'd kiss her, take those unusually tempting lips out for a spin and see if they tasted as good as they looked. But she was the nanny and it wouldn't be smart. He couldn't think about himself when Brady needed her. And his son's needs came first.

He shook his head. "Forgive me for prying. That's really none of my business."

"It's all right." She sighed. "Probably wouldn't be normal for me not to have abandonment issues. Not letting that define your life is the challenge. My goal is to help the kids understand that message."

"You're a good person."

She shrugged and her gaze lowered to the hands clasped in her lap. "I'm just trying to give back."

"The home's gain is my loss," he said. Standing, he rounded the desk and rested one hip on the corner, just an arm's length from her. He wouldn't kiss her, but he wanted to get closer. Out of the frying pan into the fire. "Traditionally Saturday is date night. Your benevolence will put a speed bump in my social life."

"Speed bump?" She met his gaze and spirit sparkled in her eyes. "You probably beat the women back with a stick."

"Not lately." He laughed. "Now that I think about it, dating is tedious. Time consuming. Hectic and energy draining. Especially now when I need all the energy I have for Brady."

Again she gave him the approving smile. "Then you should think about settling down. Getting married. Did you know studies have shown that married men live longer?"

"I hadn't heard that."

"Oh, I know marriage takes energy." The earnest expression on her face was cute and incredibly appealing. "But a committed relationship is different. And the rewards make it worth the effort."

Not in his opinion. "And how do you know this? Have you been married?"

"Me?" She touched a hand to her chest. "No. But I've observed a lot of happy, contented couples who are united in their dedication to raising a family and making a life together."

"You get around."

She lifted her shoulders in a shrug. "Occupational hazard."

A subtle reminder that her time with him was finite. She didn't know it yet, but she wouldn't have to look for another job.

"From my perspective, marriage provides nothing but stress and discord," he said.

"Really?"

"Oh, yeah." *And then some,* he thought. "It doesn't work and inevitably leads to divorce and disillusionment or the demise of dreams. At the very least it causes bitterness and resentment."

She frowned. "May I ask what your perspective is?"

"My father. He's currently involved in financial negotiations in a divorce from wife number four and engaged to number five. I've had a front-row seat to discord and dying dreams."

The look she gave him was filled with pity. "I'm sorry."

"Don't be." His tone was more sharp than he'd intended. "It was and continues to be a good education. It's cost Dad a lot of money, a good portion of which goes to the army of accountants he employs to keep up with alimony payments."

"For what it's worth," she said, "I can see where that would give you pause. I might have abandonment issues, but at least I had stability. The nuns at Good Shepherd gave me that."

He didn't plan to debate the benefits and drawbacks of growing up in an orphanage versus the marriage-go-round of his own childhood. He had a thing about commitment; she had abandonment issues. That was information he would tuck away for another time.

He folded his arms over his chest. "Now that I'm a father, I can see where a case could be made for constancy. I'd be lying if I said it—marriage—hadn't crossed my mind."

"That's the spirit," she said.

He held up his hands. "Whoa. Finding someone to marry is a nice fantasy, but it's easier said than done."

"Are you one of those men who manufactures flaws in every woman he meets?"

"That's a loaded question."

"And probably none of my business. But you started it." She tilted her head to the side and her silky ponytail brushed the shoulder of her sweater making his fingers itch to do the same. "I just meant that some men find the smallest excuses to walk away from a relationship, not really trying to make it work."

"And you know this from firsthand experience?" Since he'd started the prying, what was the harm in a little more?

"Magazines. Articles in women's periodicals."

None of that was helpful information. "You don't date?"

"I have two problems with dating."

"Only two?" he asked.

She laughed. "Number one is lack of time. Between my job and working at the home, there's very little left over."

"What's number two?"

"Lack of men."

"Excuse me?"

"Think about it. My day revolves around infants. I go from job to job. It's pretty intense." She gave him a wry look. "And energy consuming. Besides, where am I going to meet someone?"

It was on the tip of his tongue to ask if he was chopped liver, but he figured that wasn't a place he was prepared to go for too many reasons to list. But right at the top was the fact that he was way too pleased she didn't meet men.

And suddenly the temptation to touch her was too much to resist when he was this close. And he didn't trust himself to only touch her. Straightening, he moved back around to the other side of his desk, putting distance between them.

"I'm the last person who should give you advice," he said.

"Actually, I think Sister Margaret and Sister Mary are the last ones to give advice on the dos and don'ts of dating."

He couldn't stop the grin. Wicked, witty sarcasm. It was incredibly intriguing. "Okay. Point taken."

She looked thoughtful. "For what it's worth, the most advantageous environment for Brady is one with positive male and female role models. That said, when you meet the right woman, you should snap her up."

"That's a challenge to do without Saturday nights. And make no mistake, it will take a lot of dating to get it right."

"I'm sorry I won't be around to watch."

"I should think your curiosity would be powerful motivation to stay," he said.

"There's only five weeks left on my contract and I can't extend it." Genuine regret darkened her eyes.

And she wasn't the only one. Unlike the other nannies he'd had, he actually liked Maggie. She was direct and didn't play games. On top of that she was incredibly good with his son. He couldn't imagine her being more loving, tender and nurturing if she'd actually given birth to the boy. In the nanny department, this time was indeed the charm. Did she really think he would let her get away without a fight?

Not so fast, Margaret Mary Shepherd. She hadn't seen his very best stuff yet.

## Chapter Three

"Good job on the bedtime prayers, Lyssa." Maggie pulled the sheet and blanket up, then leaned over and kissed the six-year-old's cheek.

In this wing of the home, the little girl was the youngest and the last of her ten charges to be tucked in. There were fifty children, from birth to eighteen, being cared for here and Maggie relieved one of the paid employees who took a much-needed day off. Her commitment to Good Shepherd Home for Children was unwavering because without this place, she wasn't sure what would have become of her. The nuns continued to protect and care for kids who desperately needed them and Maggie considered it a sacred honor to assist in any way she could.

"Maggie?"

She felt a small hand patting her arm and looked at the blue-eyed, blond cherub clutching a tattered blanket. "What is it, sweetie?"

"I asked God to bring my mommy back."

If Maggie had a dollar for every child who'd said that, she'd be a wealthy woman. The words never failed to tug at her heart because she knew exactly how the little girl felt. "I'm sure God will do His best to answer your prayer."

Lyssa rubbed a finger beneath her nose. "But I thought God can do anything."

She always hated this part. The children received religious instruction and were taught that the Lord is all powerful and merciful. The kids eventually came up with the same questions she had. If God loves me and takes care of me, then why don't I have a mom or dad? In Lyssa's case, her drugged-out mother and a boyfriend had abandoned the little girl at the bus station. There was no way this child would understand that God *had* taken care of her by making sure she was with the nuns here at Good Shepherd.

"God can do anything, sweetie."

"Why did He let her go away?"

She met the child's innocent gaze and wondered how to explain when she didn't understand it herself. "All I can tell you is that God always does things right, even if it seems wrong to us."

"Is it okay that I asked Him to bring Mommy back?"

"Of course." Maggie stroked the hair away from the small face. "Just remember that if you ask Him for something and you don't get it, you have to trust."

"Why?"

"Because you can be sure He'll give you what you need at the appropriate time. God can do anything He thinks is best."

"I think my mommy is best."

Maggie managed to smile even though the words hurt her heart. "And I think you're pretty special."

"I love you, Maggie."

"I love you, too, sweetheart."

When the little girl yawned and rolled to her side, Maggie let out a sigh of relief. For now she'd dodged the issue with Lyssa. But she couldn't help thinking about the infant in the luxurious penthouse in the center of Las Vegas who would one day be asking his father a similar version of the question: Why isn't my mother here with me? Why didn't she love me enough to stay? In Maggie's case, eventually the questions had hollowed out a place inside that became a need for someone to love her, someone who didn't have to because it was their job. Someone to love her just for herself. Now she channeled that need into the extra-special care she gave every child who came into her life.

After one final glance at the four other twin beds in the room, she was satisfied that everyone was sleeping soundly. She turned on the nightlight and left the door open in order to hear the children during the night.

The house was a big Victorian located on Water Street in the Old Henderson section. Rumor had it that there'd been a brothel here once upon a time. Then the church acquired the property and turned it into a children's home.

Maggie had spent a good portion of her life here and thought how different this place was from Jason's posh penthouse. At the bottom of the wooden stairs there was a living room on her right and dining room on the left. Neither functioned in that capacity. Worn furniture and toy boxes said loud and clear that this was a place for children.

Her steps echoed on the wooden floor as she headed to the kitchen in the back of the house. Cold in body and spirit, she thought a cup of coffee would hit the spot. When she entered the large room with rows of tables and benches, she saw Sister Margaret sitting by herself, deep in thought.

Maggie loved this woman—not just *like* a mother. Sister Margaret Connelly was the only mother she'd ever known. And she looked troubled.

"They're asleep," she said, moving farther into the room.

Sister looked up and smiled. "Thank you, Maggie."

"I was just going to pour myself a cup of coffee. Can I get one for you?"

"That would be nice, dear. I just made a pot."

Maggie knew that because Sister always made a pot for their catching-up chat, a cherished weekly ritual. She smiled as she walked over to the old white stove with the electric coffeemaker beside it. She reached up and opened the battered-oak cupboard door and pulled out a green mug for herself and a blue one for Sister. After pouring the steaming liquid and putting sugar and cream in each, she carried both to the long, picniclike table and sat down across from the nun.

Maggie wrapped her hands around the warm mug, which felt incredibly good on a cold January night, and studied the woman who'd raised her. The order she belonged to didn't wear habits and veils. That clothing was too restrictive for their active work with the children. She was in her usual uniform of striped cotton blouse, black slacks and thick, co-ordinating sweater. Blue-eyed, brown-haired Sister Margaret was in her early fifties with the spirit of a much younger woman. But tonight the years were showing and it had nothing to do with the silver strands in her hair.

"Is something wrong, Sister?"

"I was just savoring the quiet. It's such a rare occurrence in a house with so many children."

"You can say that again." There were times at Jason's, when Brady was sleeping soundly, that she experienced the quiet and missed the rowdy sounds of the kids. Loud and lively were normal to her.

"You must be tired, dear. That art project with the younger children must have worn you out. I can't believe you were up for using real paint."

Maggie nodded. "It was a little hectic. But the kids loved

it. And keeping them busy is the goal." On Saturday there was no school so channeling the energy was an ongoing challenge for her and the other volunteers.

"Speaking of keeping busy, didn't you just take on a new job?" Sister blew on her steaming mug. "Where are you working?"

"Spring Mountain Towers."

The nun's eyebrows rose. "That's some pricey property."

"No kidding. In the penthouse, no less. The infant is completely adorable. His name is Brady Garrett."

The nun took a sip of her coffee and studied Maggie over the rim. "And something's troubling you. What is it, dear?"

"I can't stop worrying about him when I'm not there."

"You've been coming to Good Shepherd on Saturday since you started working as a nanny and this is the first time you've ever expressed concern about the child in your care."

"This is the first time I've left the infant with a father and no mother."

"Where is his wife?"

"He doesn't have one." Maggie remembered him talking about dating and her vision of him with lots of women. The idea was oddly disturbing to her. "Jason—he's Jason Garrett—"

"The billionaire developer?"

"The very one. He only said that the baby's mother won't be an issue."

"If only," Sister said.

"Amen." Lyssa's bedtime prayer for God to bring her mother back still echoed in Maggie's heart. Jason had more money than he would ever need and couldn't give his son the one thing every child wanted most.

"What's he like?" Sister asked.

How did she describe Jason Garrett? Her pulse fluttered and skipped just thinking about him. "He's driven. Focused. He loves his son very much."

"You left out seriously cute," Sister added, blue eyes twinkling.

"I beg your pardon?" Maggie pretended to be shocked.

"I've seen his picture in the paper. And he was in that magazine's yearly issue of best-looking bachelors." Sister grinned. "I'm a nun, not dead."

"Clearly." Maggie laughed. "You're right. He's seriously cute—even better looking in person."

"So if he's devoted to his son, why are you worried about the baby?"

"What if Brady is upset and Jason can't quiet him? I showed him the five S's—" Sister slid her a blank look and she added, "The five S's of soothing a baby. I've taught the technique to the volunteers here who work with infants. It was developed by Dr. Harvey Karp at UCLA. Swaddling, side lying, swinging, shushing and sucking. You wrap him tightly in a receiving blanket to simulate the security of the womb, hold them on their side in your arms, swing gently back and forth and make a shushing noise."

"That seems simple enough."

"Maybe." She caught her bottom lip between her teeth. "But Jason builds big resorts. He's not a baby kind of guy. What if he can't handle it? What if he—"

"Needs you?"

"I know that sounds arrogant—"

Sister reached over and squeezed her hand. "Not at all, Maggie. It just shows how much you care. And I worry you'll get hurt because of that marshmallow heart of yours. You have to be careful."

The warning was too late, but Sister didn't know about that. Now there was no point in making both of them feel bad. "I'm a big girl now."

"That doesn't mean I don't still worry about you." Sister shook her head. "Some children never get over a deep anger and resentment about growing up in an orphanage, present company excepted. You were always a sweet child, loving easily and accepting without question."

That may have been true when she lived here, but that changed after she fell in love and then lost even more than her heart. She still cared deeply, especially about children, but now she had parameters in place for her own protection. That way she didn't have to hold part of herself back. But she was already more attached to Brady than she'd ever been to an infant and it had only been a week. That didn't bode well for her marshmallow heart.

"I'm older and wiser now, Sister."

"That sounds ominous."

"I just meant that as a working woman of the world I've acquired experience."

"You sound sad."

"No." Maggie shrugged. "I guess all the constant moving around in my job is making me restless. Making me yearn for stability."

Odd. It hadn't occurred to her when they talked, but that was something she and Jason had in common.

Sister's eyes filled with sympathy. "I didn't know you felt that way."

Maggie hadn't, until very recently.

"It's just that I haven't felt like I belonged since I left here at eighteen. When I entered the convent after college—" She ran her index finger around the rim of her mug. "I think I was looking for roots, like I had here at the home." Maggie saw the worry she'd noticed earlier in the nun's expression. "What is it, Sister?"

"It's not your problem—"

"So there is something."

Sister sighed. "The state has scheduled an inspection of this building."

"Isn't that standard procedure?"

"Yes. But we've been aware for some time that the home needs extensive and expensive repairs—starting with a roof and the plumbing and it's not in our operating budget. The diocese doesn't have the money, either." She shook her head. "We're hoping to get by just one more time, but if we don't, they could shut us down."

"But where will the children go?" Maggie couldn't imagine what would have happened to her without the love and support of Sister Margaret and everyone else here at Good Shepherd.

"We're looking into alternative placements, but the state is already burdened with more children than they can care for."

"Is there anything I can do to help?" Maggie asked.

Sister tried to smile. "That's very sweet of you, dear. But I don't think so. The Lord provides, and every day I ask Him to provide for us."

Maggie would pray, too. For Lyssa's sake, and all the rest of the kids at Good Shepherd, she hoped the volume of prayers would produce a miracle.

In his study, Jason looked at the computer screen to check his e-mail and rubbed his hands over his face, scraping his palms on the scruff of beard he hadn't had time to shave. He was bone tired. If he didn't know better, he'd swear a gravel truck had overturned in his eyes. Brady had been up every two hours during the night. The only way he'd napped was while being held and rocked. Jason had always thought building a resort was stressful, but that was before becoming a father. Right now he'd welcome budget woes, a spike in the cost of building materials and labor disputes.

And Maggie.

He'd take her in a heartbeat. As if his son heard that thought, the baby let out a cry. Just one. Just enough to say he'd need something soon.

"Brady," he groaned, rubbing his hands over his face again. There'd barely been time for a shower, let alone a shave. He looked at the gold clock on his desk. Thirty minutes until noon, when she was due back. If there was a God in heaven she was the punctual type.

He was walking past the foyer on his way to the nursery when the key sounded in the lock just before Maggie walked in. She was better than punctual; she was early.

"Hi," he said, casually lifting a hand in greeting.

"Hi. I'll check on Brady."

"Do you have X-ray hearing?"

"No. Why?" she asked, hurrying down the hall.

"You just opened the door." The baby had been quiet since that one dissatisfied cry. "How did you know he needed something?"

"Whether he did or not, I would have looked in on him. It has nothing to do with super hearing."

"I'm not so sure." He followed Maggie to her room where she set overnight bag on the floor and her purse on the bed. Then she went next door to the nursery. "It's like you're tuned in to his frequency."

"Hi, sweetheart." She lifted the baby out of the crib and cuddled him close. "I missed you."

"I bet you say that to all the boys."

Jason leaned a shoulder in the doorway and folded his arms over his chest as he looked at her. He'd expected a tart comeback to his comment, but there was only silence, which seemed out of character. What the heck did he know about what was or was not in character for a woman who'd come close to being a nun? He'd only known her a week. Still, she seemed like the spunky type and not inclined to overlook an opportunity for a retort.

He'd spent a lot of time in this room over the last few weeks, more than the entire eighteen months he'd lived here.

But he hadn't taken the time to notice what a good job the decorator he'd hired had done. The walls were a pale olive green with white baseboards, crown molding and doors. A changing table in maple stood on one wall with the matching crib beside it. The sheet, quilt and airplane mobile were in shades of green, yellow and pale blue. Stuffed animals filled every flat space and corner of the room. Satisfaction trickled through him that he could give his boy the best.

Including the best of care. Which was all about Maggie.

She kissed Brady's cheek and rubbed his back as her body went into the automatic swaying motion. In her worn jeans, sneakers and pullover red sweatshirt with the words *Good Shepherd* on the front, she was a sight for sore eyes. Weird that the gravel in them was gone now. And he felt as if he was seeing clearly for the first time in over twenty-four hours.

He'd felt her absence, and not because it had been too quiet without her. Brady had filled a lot of the silence with his outstanding pair of lungs. Now that she was here, he had a bad feeling that the deficiency he'd felt had nothing to do with taking care of the baby and that was unsettling.

"How was your day off?" he asked.

"I think he's hungry." She set Brady on the changing table. "When did he last have a bottle?"

Jason glanced at his watch. "About three hours ago."

"Just as I suspected. You're ready to eat." She undid his terrycloth sleeper and slid his legs out, grabbing one tiny foot and kissing the toes. "You have hollow legs, Brady Garrett. Yes, you do."

Jason was completely caught up in the tenderness that she lavished on the baby. And apparently he wasn't the only one. When she smiled down, Brady's tiny mouth curved up in response. His arms waved and legs kicked with genuine excitement rather than agitation. If that was anything to judge by, the little guy had missed her, too. No, not *too*. That would mean Jason had missed her and he refused to admit to anything but feeling her absence.

He was so caught up in that thought and watching her with his son, it took him several moments to realize she hadn't answered his question about her day off.

Now that he thought about it, she looked tired. There were circles beneath her eyes that made them look even bigger and more vulnerable.

"I'll get a bottle," he said.

"Thanks." She glanced at him for a moment, then finished changing the diaper.

Jason went to the kitchen and took from the fridge one of the formula-filled bottles she'd prepared before leaving yesterday and set it in the automatic warmer. When it was ready, he returned to the nursery where she sat in the glider with Brady.

"Did you have a good time with Daddy?" she said to the baby, holding him close.

As if talking back, the baby made a cooing sound that was new and Jason's chest tightened with tenderness. He'd never worked as hard in his life as he had taking care of his child. His only goal had been to make sure Brady was comfortable, happy and content. But it was nice just to be a spectator and watch, noting the milestones in his son that he'd been too busy to notice.

Maggie smiled at the cooing, and said, "I know, sweetheart. I bet you were an angel. Because you're just the best baby in the whole world. I'm so glad you have food and a place to sleep and a roof over your head."

Her eyes darkened and there was an edge to her voice. For the second time he remembered that she hadn't answered his question. "How was your day off, Maggie?"

She glanced up and held out her hand for the bottle. "See what Daddy brought, Brady?"

He handed it to her, then leaned a shoulder against the wall and watched while the boy latched on to the nipple and eagerly started to suck. Maggie smiled gently but it never chased the shadows from her eyes.

"What's wrong, Maggie?"

Her gaze lifted to his. "Excuse me?"

"How was your day off?"

"Same as always," she said. "I helped with the kids."

He didn't know if her reaction was the same because he had no basis for comparison. No one would accuse him of being the most observant guy on the planet, but even he could see that there was something eating her. "Are you always bothered after spending your day off there?"

"I'm not in the habit of discussing things with my employer."

"Look, I'm a businessman." He slid his fingers into the pockets of his jeans. "And the nature of your employment makes it necessary for you to live under my roof. The lines blur. As your friend *and* employer I ask again, what's wrong?"

She sighed as she set the bottle on the table beside her, then lifted the baby to her shoulder to gently rub his back. Within moments he burped, a sound that did a father proud. Instantly, he started squirming and whimpering, a sign he wasn't finished eating.

When she had Brady settled, Maggie looked up. "What's bothering me? Roofs."

"Would you care to elaborate?"

"Very soon the kids at Good Shepherd may not have one." She sighed. "Sister Margaret told me that the building needs repairs. If they're not done, the state could withhold or refuse to renew a certificate of occupancy, putting their license to operate in jeopardy."

"I see."

Her expression was ironic. "How could you possibly understand? You live in a castle in the clouds. That world is so far removed from your frame of reference."

He couldn't argue with that and decided not to try. "What are they going to do?"

"Sister says they're hoping for an extension that will give them time to come up with a plan. She's been there for a long time and if anyone can come up with a miracle, it's her." She glanced down at the baby who was limp and relaxed in her arms. "She told me not to worry."

"And it's obvious you're following that order."

"Trying to."

Maggie stood with Brady in her arms and looked around the room. "Where's the infant seat?"

"The other room."

She walked out of the nursery, down the hall and stopped dead in her tracks as she surveyed the living room. Jason had been so caught up in having her back that he'd forgotten this chaos. There were blankets, clothes, stuffed animals and toys everywhere. The infant swing, with a onesy hanging from it, stood in front of the sliding doors to the penthouse patio. It seemed a clash of cultures with the landmarks of Vegas just outside.

Numerous used baby bottles sat on the coffee and end tables as if Brady had invited over all his infant buddies and they'd had a blow-out party the night before.

Maggie looked up at him, then back at the clutter and chaos. "So, how did it go?"

"Good." The casual tone was forced. After glancing at the disorder he met her gaze and smiled. "Everything went fine."

"I can't believe you'd stand there and lie to my face when it looks like a gigantic baby store exploded in here."

"It's the truth," he protested. "By my definition of the word fine, that's how it went."

"Oh?"

"Yes. There are no casualties to report. Therefore things went fine."

"Has the cleaning staff seen this place yet?"

He shook his head. "They have the weekend off."

"Well, it won't be fine when they do damage assessment." The corners of her mouth turned up. The spunky comebacks she was firing off were more like the Maggie he knew.

As he watched her easily put the baby in the swing that he'd needed blueprints and specifications to operate, he breathed a sigh of relief. Now that she was back, all was right with his world.

"Maggie?"

She stood and put a finger to her lips as she walked over to him and drew him far enough away to not disturb the baby. "What?"

"Brady missed you."

"He told you that?" she asked, her mouth curving up in a smile.

"Pretty much."

Now that he was this close, he couldn't seem to stop staring at her mouth. "And I'm so glad you're back I could kiss you."

"Always nice to be appreciated."

It was more than that. But he ignored the pull of attraction and concentrated on what was best for Brady and, by extension, himself. After twenty-four hours without her, he never wanted the penthouse to be a Maggie-free zone.

The time had come to step up his campaign to change the terms of her employment.

## Chapter Four

Maggie's large, comfortable room in the Garrett penthouse was more like what she imagined a luxury hotel suite would look like, including its own bath. The walk-in closet was big enough to live in and the oak dresser, armoire, headboard and nightstands all matched. No garage sale or flea market stuff here. Brass lamps stood on either side of the king-size bed, which was covered in a beautiful Laura Ashley floral-print comforter. Accent pillows in shades of light pink and rose were piled high. A flat-screen TV was mounted on the wall in the sitting area complete with sofa, recliner and reading lamps.

Hands down, it was the most beautiful space she'd ever had in her life. But all of it paled in comparison to what she'd found on the dresser after settling Brady for the night.

She stared at the black-velvet jewelry box. It was not a very large box and she'd heard that good things come in small packages. Another in a list of gifts from Jason.

For the last four weeks he'd been doing thoughtful things

like this. Flowers. Candy. A generous bonus in her paycheck. All of that was wonderful, but didn't make her heart pound like it was now. She'd have to be deaf, dumb and blind not to know he was wooing her. Not in a romantic way. More of a loyalty retention, boss-employee appreciation sort of way.

But romantic things came in small packages, too. Hand shaking, she reached out and picked it up. In her whole life no one had ever offered her a small black-velvet jewelry box. She'd dreamed and fantasized about Jeff giving her an engagement ring—something that would fit in an elegant container like this. She hadn't thought it could, but her heart pounded even harder.

Even as she ran her index finger over the soft, curved lid, she had an uneasy feeling. Flowers were a sweet gesture. Candy was candy. And a bonus for exemplary work was not out of the ordinary. But this was... She wasn't sure what it was.

"Open it, you nit," she chided herself. Lifting the lid, she gasped when two large diamond-stud earrings winked and sparkled. "Oh, my—"

They were quite possibly the most beautiful things she'd ever seen. And she had to give them back. Right away. Before the idea of trying them on took hold.

If Jason's routine held true to form, this time of night with his son settled in sleep, he could be found working in his study. The door was ajar, with light trickling onto the plush hall carpet. She raised her hand to knock and took a deep breath before tapping lightly.

"Come in."

She pushed the door wide and met his gaze. "May I speak with you?"

"Of course," he said, pushing his glasses to the top of his head.

He'd changed out of his suit into jeans and a white cotton shirt, with sleeves rolled to just above his wrists. The missing power tie did nothing to diminish his power and one look tied her insides up in knots. That was so not how she wanted to feel for this conversation.

She walked in and set the jeweler's box on his desk. "I spent time in the convent, but that doesn't mean I'm stupid and naive."

He glanced down, then met her gaze. "I'm not sure what I did to make you believe I think that, but nothing could be further from the truth."

"You're trying to bribe me into changing my mind about staying as Brady's nanny."

"Bribe isn't an especially flattering word." He closed his laptop. "I prefer the word incentive."

She put her hands on her hips and lifted her chin toward the velvet box. "So you don't deny that's a shameless attempt to convince me to extend my contract?"

"No."

That took the wind out of her sails. "Oh."

"It was the latest in a string of attempts—flowers, candy and a very generous bonus." One dark eyebrow lifted. "All of which you accepted graciously."

"This is different."

"How so?"

Good question. It was personal? Not personal enough? "It just is," she said stubbornly. "I can't accept diamonds. It feels wrong."

"What if I told you they're cheap imitations?"

"Are they?"

"No."

"Then it's too expensive, extravagant and any other *ex* word you can think of," she said.

"Not for me." He smiled, but there was no warmth in it.

"Look, Jason, don't think I'm not grateful that you appreciate my work with Brady—"

"It doesn't look like work when you're with him."

*Doesn't feel like it, either,* she thought. No way would she tell him that and have him use it against her. "He's a sweetheart. But I can't stay any longer."

"Why?" There was an angry edge to his voice. "Look, Maggie, I'm not hitting on you."

"I didn't think that." Not really, even though a tiny part of her had hoped.

"Are you afraid I will if you stay? Did someone do that to you?"

"No." If only it had been that ugly. Self-righteous anger would have helped her get over her hurt.

"Then tell me why I can't alter the terms of this agreement and hire you permanently at an incredibly generous salary."

"Because money isn't everything. It doesn't buy happiness."

"It buys a hell of a lot of security."

"It doesn't buy an insurance policy against heartbreak."

"What are you talking about?"

The dark, angry expression on his face chipped away her resolve that her past was no one else's business. Maybe she did owe him an explanation.

She gripped the back of the chair in front of his desk until her knuckles turned white. "When I turned eighteen, I had to leave Good Shepherd because I aged out of the system."

"Aged out?"

"Too old for state funding."

"That stinks."

"Yeah," she agreed. "Fortunately I'd graduated from high school and I was determined to go to college. I had some scholarship money but still needed to work. My experience helping at the home came in handy. I got my first nanny job, which included room and board. I lived with a family and took care of the three minor children."

"Minors? That implies there was an adult child as well."

"The oldest son—Jeff Warren— This is the family I told you about." A vision of brown hair and blue eyes flashed through her mind. He was handsome, smart and sweet. And he broke her heart. "He had a bachelor's degree and was working on his master's."

"And he hit on you?"

"It wasn't like that. We dated."

"And then he hit on you?"

"You have to let that go."

She almost smiled at his tenacity. If she had any stars left in her eyes, she might believe Jason was jealous. But Jeff had taken all the twinkle out of her and left the hard reality in its place.

"What then?"

"We dated. The family liked me and approved of the relationship. We were engaged to be engaged."

"So it was all good?"

"Until Jeff's father got a promotion and was offered the opportunity to build a mega resort in Macau."

He frowned. "I guess he didn't want to commute?"

"No." She laughed and tried to keep the bitterness out of it, although without complete success. "Jeff's parents decided to move the family and gave him the option of finishing school here. He agonized over what to do, but eventually came to the conclusion that a classroom was no substitute for life experience. He moved with the family and we agreed that calls and e-mails would keep us connected. His parents said I was like a daughter to them and promised to keep in touch, too. It wasn't ideal, but we'd formed a bond and I finally had a family."

"But no happy ending?" He removed his glasses from the top of his head and tossed them on the desk. "Otherwise this wouldn't feel like a cautionary tale."

She didn't bother with a short affirmative answer. "He communicated at first, but it lessened over time and finally just stopped. When I called, he admitted that he'd met someone and was engaged."

"Son of a…"

Sadness welled up in her. It wasn't as acute, but still had the power to wound. "His parents eventually stopped communication, which was only natural under the circumstances. But natural didn't make it any easier to come to terms with. I gave them my loyalty, my heart, and I lost everything."

"That's a tough break, Maggie, but—"

"Don't tell me it will be different here. You have to do what's best for your family, and I'm not part of it."

"You're what's best for this family," he said.

"For now. But what if that changes? And don't tell me it won't. I know better." She rounded the chair and sat, gazing intently at him. "After I left the convent, Ginger placed me with a couple who'd just had a baby. Mom was on maternity leave and I helped out, staying on when she returned to work. That baby had me from day one and I gave everything I had because they said the situation was permanent. With my help she could have it all—a career and a baby."

"Don't tell me," he said. "No happy ending here, either."

"After six months she said it was too hard to be away from her child. She was missing too much and wanted to be a stay-at-home mom. So I lost everything again." It shamed her that the memory still brought tears to her eyes. "How could I even be mad? Having a mom is the ideal situation."

A hard look darkened his eyes. "Not if Mom didn't want you in the first place. Not if your own mother doesn't care enough to stick around."

"Is that personal experience talking?"

He shrugged, which neither confirmed nor denied, yet the expression on his face was anything but neutral. It made her curious about him and that was dangerous, another in a long list of reasons why she was right to stick to her time limit.

"It may not seem like a big deal to you, but I never want to go through that again. I've found that my time limit works for me. And Ginger has structured a marketing campaign around my skills and restrictions. I'm an expert at assisting inexperienced parents through the transition and adjustment of a new baby."

"What about my situation?" he asked angrily.

"Ginger has an impressive employee list. Many of them prefer long-term assignments—"

"That's not good enough." He ran his fingers through his hair. "I'm sorry you got hurt in the past. That happens when you wear your heart on your sleeve."

"Not anymore," she protested.

"That's where you're wrong. You still care. Maybe too much, but you can't help that. It's one of your most impressive qualifications. But now your caring has a short shelf life to keep you from getting hurt."

"I'm glad you understand." She stood. "I have a week left on my contract and then I'm leaving."

He stood, too, and towered over her. "Fair warning, Maggie. I'll find a way. Everyone has their price. If you put enough zeros on a check, it takes the sting out of life. However you want to say it, anyone can be convinced."

At the door, she chanced a look at him and felt a pull on her heart. "Not me."

Not with money. However, if he showed the slightest interest in her she wasn't sure the bravado would hold up. She'd walked into his office looking for a fight. Now she realized the reaction was out of proportion to his generous gesture. It was earrings. Big, expensive diamond earrings, but impersonal jewelry nonetheless.

The only reason she could come up with for her meltdown was that she'd half expected to see a ring in the black velvet box. It was stupid and naive, both of which she'd denied being, but that didn't change the truth.

She'd felt the sting of rejection once before, when she learned of Jeff's engagement. When she'd seen the earrings, it was even worse. She'd felt a lot like a mistress who was being appeased. And she'd been disappointed.

This was a sign as big as any on the Las Vegas Strip that she would be lucky if another week here with Jason Garrett didn't cost her as much, or more, than she'd lost in the past.

Maggie had finished packing her clean clothes and had the dirty ones in a laundry bag stashed by the half-opened door. On the tufted-silk bench at the foot of the bed she'd put out a pair of jeans and sweater for when she left in the morning. Ginger had a replacement coming. Jason had met and approved her, however ill-tempered and reluctant his attitude.

Now all she had to do was say goodbye to father and son.

Tears burned the backs of her eyes and her heart squeezed painfully at the thought of leaving. She caught her blurred reflection in the mirror over the dresser. It was going to hurt terribly when she walked out the door for the last time. A sob caught in her throat just before she heard a soft knock on her door.

Jason pushed it wide and stood there. With his tie loosened and the white shirt wrinkled from a long day at the office, he was incredibly appealing. For the last six weeks, it had grown increasingly difficult to keep from saying, "Hi, honey, how was your day?"

Quickly she turned her back to him, hiding the powerful reaction. Oh, God, not now. It was so not the time for her resolve to weaken. Leaving was the right thing for her.

"I'm sorry," she said, struggling to keep her voice steady. "Brady's already asleep. He was just worn out."

"It's all right. I wanted to talk to you anyway."

Too much to hope he wouldn't make one last push to change her mind. A man like him wouldn't be as successful as he was without a dynamic personality, a stubborn streak as wide as the Grand Canyon. Probably it worked for him with women, too. And she might even have changed her mind if her acute response to him just now hadn't convinced her she'd be safer away from him and Brady.

The thought of that sweet little boy punched a hole in the dam of her feelings and the tears she'd barely managed to hold back trickled out.

"There's nothing left to say, Jason." This time her voice broke.

"Are you crying?" He moved close and put his hands on her arms.

"No."

"If I haven't said it already, I will now. You're a lousy liar."

"It's not full-on crying. Just a tear or two." She sniffled and tried to step away.

His grip tightened and he turned her, pulling her into his arms and against his broad chest. Wrapped in his comforting embrace was probably the safest she'd ever felt in her life. How could that be when the things he made her feel were big and scary? The emotions swimming inside made her want to both run and stay.

He rubbed a hand up and down her back. "Don't cry, Maggie. Everything will be fine."

"I know. It's just—" A giant knot of emotion cut off her words.

"You're sad."

She nodded against his chest.

"You want to stay."

She nodded again.

"So don't go."

She shook her head, then permitted herself one last moment to savor the sweet, solid feel of him before stepping away. "I have to. Everything is all arranged."

"It can be unarranged. I'll call Ginger and cancel your replacement."

Brushing the moisture from her cheeks, she blew out a long breath. "Then what?"

"We go back to business as usual."

"And what happens two months from now if you change your mind? You find Ms. Right and don't need a nanny and kick me to the curb." She looked at him, the fiercely determined expression in his eyes. "What about me? That sounds incredibly selfish, but I—"

"I'll have a contract drawn up for any length of time you want. If my situation changes, I'll pay it out, no questions asked. I'll even add a rider for a bonus, proportional to time employed versus the amount of time left on the contract."

She realized he didn't get the emotional toll this was taking on her. "You think money can solve any problem?"

Without hesitation he said, "Yes."

"You're wrong, Jason. Money isn't the solution to everything."

"It doesn't necessarily buy happiness, but it can buy a way out of problems. And that may be as close to happy as a person can get."

"Money doesn't keep your heart from breaking," she protested.

"Do you love Brady?" He nudged her chin up with his knuckle, forcing her gaze to his. "Don't lie to me, Maggie. I'll know if you do. You're exceptionally bad at it."

"I guess I missed Deception 101 when I was in the convent."

"You're stalling. Do you love my son?"

Judging by the way her heart was breaking, the answer to that question was easy. "Yes."

"Then don't go. Stay and help him grow into the best person he can be."

She shook her head. "My mind is made up. There's nothing you can say to change it."

"There must be." A muscle in his jaw moved as his dark eyes turned almost black with frustration. "What if I asked you to marry me?"

She stared at him for several moments, not realizing she'd been holding her breath until she dragged air into her lungs. "That's a joke, and I'm not even going to dignify it with a response."

"Why not? I'm dead serious."

"Oh, please."

He rested his hands on lean hips, a challenging stance, as he met her gaze. There was a glitter in his eyes, as if he'd hit on the right button. "Marriage is a serious contract. It would protect your rights, something you never had in the past."

Her heart was pounding, yet it felt like all the blood had drained from her head. She couldn't think straight. He must be kidding, toying with her. And yet he looked completely determined.

"Marriage?" She held out her hands, a helpless gesture. "I don't even know how to respond to that."

"You need to come up with an answer, Maggie, because I still need one." They stared at each other and tension rolled off him in waves. "How much will it take? When you showed up, I couldn't help thinking I'd hit the jackpot. Nothing you've done has changed my opinion. I want to keep you. Name your price. How much will it take to convince you that I've never been more serious in my life? You're the answer to my prayers."

Prayer. She remembered another motherless child at Good Shepherd Home who prayed for a mother. That home was the only permanent one Maggie had ever known and it was still a haven for children. But not much longer unless Sister Margaret's prayers were getting results. She'd told Lyssa that God gives you what you need at the appropriate time.

The home needed money. A lot of it.

"Answer me, Maggie. What will it cost for you to marry me?"

She said the first thing that popped into her mind. "A million dollars."

"Done," he said without hesitation.

# Chapter Five

"I don't believe you'd give me a million dollars to marry you," Maggie said.

"You don't know me very well." He stared her down. "Believe it."

When he calculated a nine-month pregnancy as opposed to raising the child for an indefinite length of time, Jason figured it was a bargain. He'd paid Catherine as much just to bring Brady into the world and she'd been giddy at the number of zeros on the bonus check simply for staying out of their lives.

Not that he wanted that greedy, grasping, self-centered woman anywhere near his son, but when he'd made the deal, he hadn't counted on the complications of caring for and bringing up a child.

Maggie's protective instincts had kicked in before she even saw Brady. She'd refused to talk until the baby was comforted and content. After Brady's first nannies, her presence these

last few weeks had been like a cooling weather system from
the north taking the heat off a desert summer.

Not until Maggie had walked into his life had he understood what a difference the right woman could make, in terms
of child rearing. It would be stupid to let her get away, and he
hadn't taken the family company to a whole new level of
success by being stupid.

Maggie stared at him as if he had two heads. "I don't know
whether to laugh or be afraid."

"Why?"

*"Why?"* she repeated, her voice rising. "You just offered
me a large sum of money to marry you. It's like a scenario for
an outrageous reality show. Or *Punk'd.*" She looked up and
around the room's ceiling. "Do you have cameras on me right
now? Is this going on TV?"

"Don't be silly."

"Right back at you."

"On the contrary," he said, "this is the least silly idea I've
ever had. It makes complete sense."

"Not to me." She folded her arms over her chest, drawing
his attention there.

The only part of this idea that was silly had to do with his
level of attraction. Instead of decreasing with time as he'd
thought, the longer she stayed, the more appealing things he
noticed about her—the subtle curves of her body that jeans
only accentuated. Her high, firm breasts outlined by sweaters,
blouses and T-shirts. His escalating curiosity about how her
full lips would taste, how they'd feel against his own.

This was not a good time to let all that considerable appeal
distract him from negotiating with her.

"Nothing about this makes sense," she said.

"Can you be more specific?"

"In this day and age men don't pay women to marry them."

"That's where you're wrong." He held up three fingers. "Three words. Anna Nicole Smith."

"Oh, please. Completely different situation. The man was ninety-something and she was after his money."

"How do you know he wasn't looking for someone to nurture his children?"

"If I remember right, his son was in his fifties or sixties. The guy could take care of himself. By any stretch of the imagination she was a gold digger."

"Maybe he was interested in companionship and was willing to pay for it. Strictly a business deal. Not unlike what I've proposed."

"How do you know I'm not a gold digger?"

The idea that she could be manipulative and calculating made him smile. "The definition of a gold digger is someone who uses her feminine wiles for gifts or monetary gain. You haven't done that. And I will have my attorney draw up a prenuptial agreement to protect me from any possible challenge to my financial assets. It would just be a precaution. Something a smart man does."

"At this particular moment, I have some serious doubts about your intelligence level. A smart man wouldn't propose this in the first place."

"He would to do right by his son. What kind of father would I be if I didn't secure the best possible future for Brady?"

"You'd sacrifice your own future for his?"

That presupposed he had a romantic future. He didn't. No woman could get close because he wouldn't let them. "I'm not sacrificing anything, Maggie."

"Because you love him."

It wasn't a question, and that pleased him. "Yes."

"A father should love his son enough to do anything for him, but that doesn't mean you *should* do anything for him."

He took a step closer, near enough to reach out and touch

her. Something he badly wanted to do again after holding her in his arms. In the mirror behind her he could see her back, the trim, ramrod straight posture. Or it could be tension. This was a big step. It should give him pause, but the more he thought about it, the more right it felt.

"Tell me something," he said. "Do you need the money? Is there something you could do with it?"

She caught the corner of her bottom lip between her teeth. "Doesn't everyone need cash?"

He looked at her and smiled. "I don't."

"Okay." She slid her fingers into the pockets of her jeans. "But the average person could use a large sum of money. If not, Las Vegas would just be a tiny town in the desert. It's built on dreams of winning big."

"And I'm offering you an opportunity to do that. It's not a dream and there's no luck involved. All you have to do is say the word. And you didn't answer my question. Is there something you could use money for?"

"Yes." She looked down and her silky hair framed her face, teased her cheeks.

His heart lurched and his hands tingled with the urge to tunnel his fingers in all that shiny hair and cup her face. "Tell me what it is."

She met his gaze. "The Good Shepherd Home is in a bad way. I told you about the building being in disrepair. Sister Margaret and Sister Mary have done everything, talked to everyone they can think of. So far the money isn't pouring in. And I don't think bake sales and car washes will make a dent in what they need."

"I've just offered you the perfect solution."

The conflict raging within her shadowed her eyes. "It's not perfect."

"Nothing ever is. But we both get what we want." He took her hands. It seemed safe enough until he felt her doubts in the trembling and the softness of her skin. But he hung on and squeezed gently, reassuringly. "You're afraid of getting emotionally attached, then losing your position as nanny. I need someone I trust with my son. If you marry me, I get what I want and you'll have a guaranteed place in my household. Another plus is the money to bail out Good Shepherd. Call it a sign-on bonus."

"If it closes, the kids will lose their home. And each other. Some of them are the only family they've got."

Like her. He'd spent a lot of years resenting the revolving door of women through his father's life and the fact that his mother walked out when he was barely old enough to remember her. But he never forgot the grief and anguish of wondering what he'd done to drive her away. Still, he'd never had to worry about a roof over his head or where he was going to live. Or who would take care of him because his father had secured the best help money could buy.

"You have the power to make a difference, Maggie. All you have to do is say yes."

Her gaze jumped to his. "Why marriage, Jason? What if I just agree to stay?"

"I want a guarantee, too. Assurance that you *will* stay. That no one will hire you away." And another thought struck him, this one more disturbing. "What if you find Mr. Right? What if some guy swoops in, sweeps you off your feet and marries you himself? I need stability for my son, and marriage does that."

Jason stared at her hands, still in his. With his thumb, he brushed her left ring finger picturing another man putting an engagement ring there, the symbol of his promise to keep her forever. The idea didn't set well.

The same instincts that made him a successful businessman should have warned him to go slowly with this proposal. Unfortunately, he didn't have that luxury. He needed to seal this deal now, while she was off balance. Before she had a chance to sleep on it and say no in the morning. If that happened, she'd walk out on her own terms. And he needed her to stay on his.

"I have to have your answer, Maggie. What's it going to be? Will you marry me?"

She pulled her hands from his and folded her arms over her chest. "Jason, I just don't—"

"As soon as you say yes, I'll write a check to Good Shepherd with a lot of zeros on it."

"You could stop payment," she pointed out.

Clearly he wasn't the only one with trust issues. "If it will make you feel better, I'll set up an account. You can have an independent attorney look over the paperwork to make sure there's nothing funny going on. I'll jump through hoops if you want, but I need an answer now. Yes or no, Maggie?"

"It does feel a lot like God putting me in the right place at the right time," she hedged.

"I'd call it a sign," he agreed. "Are you in?"

Her beautiful eyes were full of doubt but she finally said the word he wanted to hear. "Yes."

He held out his hand and hers was shaking when she settled it into his palm, signifying the agreement.

"Is everything ready to sign?" Jason looked across the desk at his attorney.

Blake Decker of Decker and Associates had handled his father's third and fourth divorces, and was currently involved in financial negotiations for dissolution of property with the most recent, soon-to-be ex-wife.

"Of course it's all ready. But a lawyer's job is also to advise. They don't call me counselor for nothing. I need to ask if you know what you're doing." The guy was in his thirties, tall, black-haired and physically fit. What women today call a hottie. And one of the city's most notoriously marriage-phobic bachelors. "What are you thinking, man?"

"I'm marrying Maggie Shepherd. What's your point?"

Blake leaned forward in his chair. "You're making a legal commitment to the nanny. It's a hell of a step to take for continuity in child care."

"Then it's a good thing you're not taking it." Jason knew exactly what he was doing. "But you're entitled to your opinion."

"My opinion is that marriage is the worst possible risk. I've never seen one work out."

"With good reason. You're a divorce attorney."

"And I'm making an unbelievable amount of money doing what I do, which goes to what I just said. Getting married is a straight shot to legal, financial and emotional complications that you don't need. Trust me. I've been through it."

"That's because you, along with most of the rest of the population, go into marriage with starry eyes and unrealistic expectations."

"And you're not?"

"Strictly business. I need someone to care for Brady. Maggie is exceptionally good at it. She's already exceeded my expectations, and your job is to safeguard the financial part. Considering the fact that you negotiate so many breakups, I figured you were the perfect guy to draft a loophole-free prenup."

"If you insist on going through with this, she won't be able to touch your assets when it blows up in your face."

"That's not going to happen. Maggie isn't like that."

"That's what all starry-eyed grooms say," Blake pointed out.

"I've never had stars in my eyes." Just the opposite. Jason figured he was born a realist and life reinforced his basic nature.

"What about emotional fallout?"

"Not a problem. We're not in love." He liked and respected Maggie. She was smart, funny and pretty in a pure, innocent way that was incredibly appealing. But love? Jason knew better than to go there. "We both have good reasons that don't include a relationship. All the cards are on the table."

"So I can't talk you out of it?"

"No."

"Don't say I didn't try." Blake shook his head and leveled a "poor bastard" look at him, then opened the file. "I have the prenuptial agreement. And the paperwork is drawn up for a million-dollar trust. I'll be the administrator for the funds that go to the Good Shepherd Home for Children."

"Good."

"Then we're ready to get all the pertinent signatures." Blake pushed the intercom button and asked the receptionist to send Maggie in.

Jason had the strangest sensation of wanting to leave before any papers were signed, but he was his father's son, a witness over the years to the worst in relationship fallout that had shaped the man he was today. No way he'd take this step without safety measures in place because marriage was like sex with a condom—sometimes it breaks. He'd seen that happen, too, and Brady was the result.

But there was something inherently sweet and unspoiled about Maggie that he didn't want tainted or shattered. Seeing the lawyer had been all about protecting his son and himself. And now he couldn't shake the feeling of wanting to protect Maggie, too, from all the sordid and sleazy aspects of why they were here.

Still, she needed money. No matter how innocent she seemed, it was always good to have safeguards in place.

Maggie and Jason sat in the back of his town car with the baby strapped in between them sound asleep. His driver was taking them to the courthouse to get married.

Married.

Margaret Mary Shepherd, abandoned baby and almost a

nun, was going to marry one of Las Vegas's wealthiest and most eligible bachelors. It was absolutely and completely surreal. Long ago she'd rigidly and deliberately put any thoughts of a wedding day out of her mind. But when rogue dreams had managed to leak through, there had always been sunshine.

Not today on her actual wedding day. It was cloudy. The forecasters were predicting rain. In the desert. It never rained in the desert. Actually, it did, but when that happened flash floods were the result.

She swallowed any misgivings and reminded herself that there was a greater good here. The home was going to get the repairs so desperately needed, and she was going to be able to stay with the baby boy she'd fallen head over heels for.

And his father?

Jason was staring out the window at the buildings going by. His profile could have been carved from any one of the rocky mountains surrounding the Vegas valley. He hadn't said anything since leaving Blake Decker's office. His lawyer was a very handsome man—in her opinion not as good-looking as Jason, but they said beauty was in the eye of the beholder. If that was true, it pointed to her having a crush on her soon-to-be husband. She supposed that was better than not being able to stand him.

As far as the pros and cons in her decision to accept his proposal, all the checkmarks stacked up on the positive side. In a town with huge hotels and resorts that were built on losses, she was getting a legal commitment that would make her a winner. She couldn't get tossed out in the cold. But that didn't mean she wasn't nervous.

"Jason?"

He turned his head, his glance dropping on the baby first. His eyes softened and a heartbreakingly tender smile lessened the craggy angles of his face. "Hmm?"

"I thought Mr. Decker was very nice." She'd felt the need

to talk, but that was a lame thing to say. There was still time for him to back out. None of that paperwork meant a thing if there were no vows.

"Blake? Nice?" He met her gaze. "I'm not sure he'd think that was a compliment."

"Why?"

"Most attorneys wouldn't consider that adjective in keeping with their job description. And Blake Decker feels that way more than most."

"But it's just a job. I'm sure he's a very nice person."

Staring at her, he shook his head slightly. "Do you really believe that?"

"Of course." She clasped her hands together. "I know lawyers are called all kinds of unflattering names. Shark. Snake. Weasel."

"You forgot barracuda."

"That, too. But it doesn't define his true nature. It's his job to know the law and advise the rest of us who don't."

A guilty look flashed into his eyes, then disappeared. Working with kids at the home she'd seen the expression a lot and was pretty good at detecting it. Although what he had to feel uncomfortable about she couldn't say.

"Here we are," he said as the car slowed to a stop. Was that relief in his voice?

Jason opened the door as she unhooked the baby's car seat. He reached back inside for the handle and lifted Brady out without waking him.

Following him up the concrete steps outside the Clark County Courthouse, her heart started to race, and it wasn't about hurrying up steps or going through the metal detectors. The official atmosphere was crystallizing. It was one thing to discuss marriage and another thing to walk into the halls of justice to speak legally binding vows.

Their footsteps echoed on the marble floor as they made

their way to the elevator that took them to the clerk's office. He'd explained this to her. In Nevada, no blood test was required, but both parties wishing to marry had to appear before the county clerk for a marriage license. After proper identification was verified, a fee of fifty-five dollars in cash was paid and a certificate allowing them to marry exchanged. Her stomach lurched, not unlike the way it reacted in the elevator.

But everything went as he'd said it would. Then she followed Jason down the hall and into a room with generic plastic chairs lined up in the middle. Jason set the still-sleeping baby down on the floor by the first row. She'd always thought that if she married, it would happen in church. She'd have been wrong. Her wedding was happening in the same building where criminals went on trial and justice was meted out. It was best not to dwell on that.

Maggie sat and looked at the other couples waiting to get married. One girl who hardly looked old enough to be here wore a strapless, long white gown. Her husband-to-be didn't look like he shaved yet. A middle-aged woman, with the portly man of her dreams, was dressed in a black-and-white suit. Maggie's beige dress with matching jacket couldn't have been more unremarkable. This wasn't an especially good time to realize she'd wanted her wedding day to *be* remarkable.

Strapless-wedding-dress girl leaned across the chair separating them and smiled. "Your baby is so precious."

Maggie started to explain that he wasn't hers, then decided not to go there. "Yes, he is. Thank you."

"I'm going to have a baby," she confided.

"Congratulations," Maggie said.

"Thanks." She looked at Jason who was speaking with the clerk. "He's pretty cute, too."

Maggie studied the dashing figure he cut in his conservative navy suit, dark hair stylishly cut and her heart pitched and rolled. "I couldn't agree more."

"You guys are an awesome family."

Did that make her "awesome" by association? Before she could answer that question, Mr. Awesome returned. "We're all set," he said, picking up the car seat.

Maggie looked around at the couples who had been there when they walked in. "All these people are ahead of us."

"Blake pulled some strings. A justice of the peace he knows pretty well managed to get us in right away."

"Don't you get thrown out of amusement parks for taking cuts in line?"

He laughed. "I told you *nice* wasn't exactly the best adjective for my attorney."

"Still, it feels wrong. Shouldn't we wait our turn?"

One dark eyebrow lifted. "Are you stalling, Maggie? Maybe you're having second thoughts?"

Second. Third. Fourth. But God had given her the means to a miracle, and now she decided it best not to think at all. "I gave my word."

He nodded. "Then let's do this."

She sighed once, then squared her shoulders and followed him through a door. The room was an office, the man before them an officer of the court.

"Fred Knox," he said, shaking hands with Jason. Then he glanced at the baby. "Nice-looking fella."

"Thanks." Jason's voice was warm with pride.

"You're here to make this family official."

Jason met her gaze. "That's the idea."

"Let's do it, then." He opened a book and settled their marriage license on it. "Do you Jason Hunter Garrett take Margaret Mary Shepherd to be your wife for richer for poorer, in sickness and in health?"

"I do."

When he repeated the words to her, Maggie said, "I do."

"Do you have rings to exchange?"

Jason reached into his jacket pocket and produced a jeweler's black-velvet box with two gold bands inside and handed them over. He'd thought of everything.

The man said, "These rings signify that love is enduring, without beginning or end."

And sometimes it's nonexistent because this marriage wasn't about love. In spite of her sound logic and self-reassurances, the thought made her sad.

Jason slipped the band on her left ring finger and it fit perfectly. His large hand dwarfed hers as she did the same, using a little effort to slide the circle of gold over his knuckle.

"With the authority vested in me by the state of Nevada, I now pronounce you husband and wife. Congratulations, Mr. and Mrs. Garrett. You may kiss your bride."

Maggie's eyes widened as her gaze shot to Jason's. She was also aware that most business deals ended with a handshake, not a kiss. Her heart was pounding, but he seemed cool and in control. His hands on her arms were strong as he drew her against him. Then he lowered his lips to hers and her eyes drifted shut. The touch of his mouth was warm and soft. His hands slid down her arms and left heat in their wake. Her heart fluttered, quick and hard. Then he pulled away and she wasn't ready for it to be over.

"That's it then," he said softly.

Was that it? She looked at him and the intensity in his eyes made her shiver with a sort of excitement that was as new and different as her marital state. Before she had a chance to guess at what he was feeling, Jason glanced at his watch.

"It's getting late. We have to go."

After congratulations and goodbyes, he took the car seat and placed his hand at the small of her back to guide her outside and to the waiting car. When they were settled inside, he gave the driver instructions to drop him at his office and take Maggie and the baby home.

"You're going to work?" she asked.

"I'm late for a meeting," he explained.

Of course he was. This was just another day at the office to him. What had she expected?

That was the thing. Until she'd taken each step and realized otherwise, she hadn't been aware of having expectations. Getting married felt like a big deal to her, but to him it was simply the first business deal of the day.

She'd never expected to be sad and disappointed on her wedding day.

## Chapter Six

It was his wedding day.

"Night," Jason said to himself, something tightening inside him.

He tossed back the remainder of the Rémy Martin in his glass as he glanced around his study, noting that everything was the same. The lie echoed through him and collided with the heat that still lingered from kissing Maggie after their vows. The sensation was a lot like what happened when cold and hot air smashed together. Turbulence. Tornado.

All day he'd tried to get her off his mind. Some of it was about the bruised look in her eyes when his driver had left him at the office and Maggie realized her wedding day would be nothing out of the ordinary.

The devil of it was that there'd been nothing pressing workwise and he could have taken her someplace special for lunch. He hadn't because it was important to set a tone for the marriage. They were husband and wife in name only per their deal. What had seemed like a good idea at the time didn't look as rosy from this side of the marriage license.

Like every other night since she'd been his nanny, Maggie was bathing the baby and he was working in the study. He wanted to be with them but was keeping to his protocol of establishing a pattern. It seemed important until tension and heat ground through him.

He shot to his feet, grabbed his empty glass and went to the sideboard where he kept the cognac. After pouring another shot, he drank it down, glad for the burn in his throat and the scorching all the way to his gut. For that few seconds the scalding was all he could think about. When it subsided, there was still a vision of Maggie and the innocently seductive way she'd slid her tongue over her soft lips after he'd kissed her.

The phone rang and Jason was grateful for the distraction. "Yes?" he said into the receiver.

"Mr. Garrett, it's Peter Sexton."

The doorman. "What is it, Peter?"

"Sir, a Mr. Hunter Garrett is here to see you."

His father. "Send him up, Peter."

"Right away, sir."

The old man usually stopped by Garrett Industries corporate offices if he had something to say. This must be important. Jason had a pretty good idea what it was about.

When the bell rang, he opened the door. "Hi, Dad."

"Jason."

Hunter marched right in. "I need to talk to you."

"I figured." He shut the door. "Let's go in my study."

Jason led the way down the hall and held out a hand for his father to take one of the chairs in front of the desk. It occurred to him for the first time that the pretentious leather and gold buttons suited his father much better than his nanny. There was a resemblance between Hunter and himself, but he'd gotten his dark eyes and hair from the maternal DNA, not that he remembered much about the woman who'd birthed him. The few pictures he'd managed to find confirmed it.

The man who'd sired him was often called *distinguished* and that was fair. He was tall, and a personal trainer hammered him into fitness. Silver streaked his brown hair and his blue eyes, never brimming with warmth, were glacial at the moment.

"Would you care for a drink?" Jason asked him.

"Yes."

He poured another and set it down in front of his father before taking a chair on the other side of the desk. "How are you, Dad? How's Tracy?" Wife-to-be number five.

"Fine." The older man downed the contents of his glass, then leaned forward. "I didn't come to update you on me or my fiancée."

"Then why did you come?"

"What's going on, Jason?"

"Care to be more specific?"

"Don't be coy." For the first time Hunter's eyes were warm. Must have a lot to do with the glare. "There was a disturbing rumor on the news about the president of Garrett Industries at the Clark County Courthouse with an unidentified woman."

"I see." If his thoughts hadn't been so preoccupied with Maggie, he'd have seen this coming. Marriage licenses were public record and he didn't have an especially low profile. Someone was bound to notice. Call him perverse, but he was going to make his father work for this. He stared down the old man without saying more.

"I put in a call to Blake Decker."

"Oh?" What did that say about father-son communication that he called the attorney for information? "What did he say?"

"Nothing. He cited attorney-client privilege. That means he's your lawyer. Since when, Jason?"

"Today." Technically he'd had representation since making the call to draw up all the papers. But they'd been signed today. And he'd had his five-hundred-dollar-an-hour lecture on the potholes and pitfalls of ball-and-chain lane.

"Who's the woman?"

"Since I didn't see the news, I can't be sure who you're referring to."

Hunter's eyes narrowed. "The one at the courthouse. Who is she?"

"Her name is Margaret Mary Shepherd." Garrett, he added to himself.

"What is she to you?"

That was actually a very good question and something he'd been trying to figure out, what with the lopsided amount of time he'd been thinking about her. But he'd throw his dad a bone here. "She's Brady's nanny."

"Please don't tell me you're fooling around with the nanny."

"All right. I won't tell you."

Silver eyebrows drew together as he scowled. "Are you aware that the price of stock can rise and fall with even a hint of scandal? Hanky panky with your nanny is a very good way to get your name in the newspapers for all the wrong reasons."

His father should know. Marital escapades were his stock in trade. "Look, Dad, I'm in charge of the company now. You're chairman of the board of directors of Garrett Industries."

"I'm also your father."

"Yeah." By the tone he was assuming the old man felt the family connection gave him free rein over his life. "What's your point?"

"In this news item there was mention of a marriage license. So just why were you at the courthouse with her?"

"I married Maggie, Dad."

The old man wasn't often speechless and historically it didn't last long. "You're married? Legally?"

"Yes."

"At least you had the good sense to consult Blake."

"What? No congratulations?" Jason asked.

Without comment his father went on, "Did she sign a prenup?"

"She did." The rest of their terms were none of the old man's business.

"Good. If you made an honest woman of her there's no impropriety. No lawsuits for harassment."

"For what it's worth, the confidentiality agreement she originally signed is legally enforceable if breached. And The Nanny Network does thorough and extensive background checks on its employees."

"What is her background?"

Jason remembered Maggie's flare of temper when she assumed he was judging her for being abandoned at Good Shepherd. He decided to keep that part to himself and go with the later years. "Maggie was in the convent."

"She's a nun?" Hunter stared at him, again speechless.

"Not quite. She didn't take final vows." Jason finished the cognac in his glass.

The wheels were turning in Hunter's head and a crafty look slid into his eyes. "So she played hard to get." He nodded knowingly. "Marriage will put to rest any hint of impropriety while you fool around with her."

Anger knotted in Jason's gut. Fool around with Maggie? He wished he could say the thought never entered his mind, but since kissing her that's pretty much all he *had* thought about. And none of his thoughts were up for discussion, with his father or anyone else.

"Maggie isn't the kind of woman you fool around with, Dad."

"Maybe. But in my experience every woman has an agenda." Hunter nodded thoughtfully as he mulled that over. "Blake Decker is very good at his job, so even if she does, she can't take a chunk out of you financially in the divorce. Which is all you have to worry about." He smiled for the first time. "At least you're thinking with your head, along with other parts of your anatomy."

By association and genetics Jason felt slimy. He might think about it, but acting on impulse wasn't going to happen. He'd safeguarded his son's care and used Maggie to do it. No way would he compromise her further.

"Almost a nun." Hunter put his empty glass on the desk and stood. "I can understand the novelty. She's not your usual type."

"Yeah." And that worked both ways. He wasn't her type, either, not nearly good enough.

"Do yourself a favor, Jason." His father pointed a warning finger at him. "Don't make the mistake of falling in love."

Preaching to the choir, Jason thought. "Not a problem, Dad."

A sound in the doorway drew his attention and he saw Maggie standing there with the baby in her arms.

"You must be Maggie." Hunter studied her, then nodded his approval. "I'm Hunter Garrett."

"Jason's father." Then she looked at the baby who started to fuss. "And Brady's grandfather."

"Yes." He looked at Jason with a gleam in his eyes. "It's time for me to go. I'll leave you two alone."

He left with the same abruptness as his arrival. No congratulations or welcome to the family. No apology for dropping by on their wedding night, Jason thought darkly.

"I didn't mean to interrupt," Maggie said, staring at the closed front door. "Apparently he didn't come to see his grandson."

"That's Dad." A walking, talking cautionary role model. And his only family besides Brady.

"I brought the baby to spend time with you before he goes to bed."

"Thanks."

She settled the boy in his arms. "If he needs me, I'll be in my room."

It didn't escape his notice that she'd said if the baby needed anything. That specifically excluded Jason, which started a burning deep inside him. Why did the need for something crank up exponentially when you knew it was off-limits? He wanted her. As of this morning he had the right to have her in his bed. As his father had so indelicately put it—he could fool around with her and not worry about impropriety.

But he didn't dare touch her.

As she backed away, he noticed the same bruised look he'd seen a few minutes ago and knew she'd heard the last part of his conversation. The part where he acknowledged that he locked her into a legal relationship, confirmed that she wasn't his type and was adamant that he'd never have feelings for her. But why should it bother her? She was getting what she wanted out of the deal.

But he couldn't shake the feeling that he'd caged a butterfly. He'd never felt more like his father's son than he did now and he didn't like it one bit.

When Jason's driver dropped Maggie off in front of the home she saw Sister Margaret out front, pulling her black sweater tight against the wind. There was a truckload of— well, trucks—scattered on the property and along the street nearby. Pallets of roofing tiles and lumber waited on the cement driveway.

Maggie's footsteps crunched on the ground and the tall nun turned. Instantly a welcoming smile creased her worn face.

"Hi, Sister," she said with a wave.

"Maggie!" The nun opened her arms and gave her a big hug. "How are you?"

"Fine."

The fib was automatic, more like being economical with the truth. Mostly she was fine. Her body was functioning well, maybe a bit too well, especially when thoughts of Jason Garrett crept in and made her skin flush and her heart race. It

had been more than a week since he'd kissed her at their
wedding and the memory of his mouth on hers made her want
more of the same. The feel of his chest pressed against her
breasts made her hot and tingly all over, so her body was firing
on all cylinders.

But her spirit? Not so fine. After hearing Jason tell his
father that loving her was not part of his plan, her spirit had
pretty much imploded. Although that information was not
something she'd burden Sister Margaret with.

"How are you, Sister?"

"Excellent." She turned back to watch the workmen tearing
off the rundown roof. "We're getting this old building in shape
and the state granted us an extension for the work. The
children have a home and all's right with the world."

"I'm glad."

Sister looked down at her. "Without the generous donation
from your Mr. Garrett none of this would be possible."

Maggie opened her mouth to say he wasn't hers, but
decided more truthful economy was indicated. As far as the
state of Nevada was concerned, he *was* hers. Legally her
husband. At his luxurious penthouse, she would never be his
wife, only the nanny. As guilty as it made her feel to withhold
facts, Sister Margaret did not need to know she'd married
Jason for his donation. And he'd married her to ensure her
loyalty to his child.

She didn't want to see the disappointment in Sister's eyes
when she confessed to marrying the man for his money, no
matter how well intentioned she'd been.

"And there's more," Sister continued.

Maggie wasn't sure her guilty conscience could handle
more. She pulled her Windbreaker around her as a gust of cold
blasted her. With clouds covering the sun, it was very chilly.
Or maybe that was just the freeze in her heart.

"What else did Jason do?" she asked.

"He took care of getting bids on the renovations. I spoke with him myself and—"

"You talked to Jason?" *Oh, good Lord.* Did he say anything about their arrangement?

Sister nodded. "He's quite a charming man. Very nice phone voice."

He was even nicer to look at, Maggie thought, but kept the information to herself. And she knew all about that whiskey-and-chocolate voice. Somehow he'd used it to talk her into this arrangement. But if she was being honest, it had taken precious little effort on his part to convince her this arrangement would work.

"Jason is many things positive," she agreed.

"After helping us out with the donation I didn't want to take up his time with those details, but he insisted. He assured me that in his business dealings through Garrett Industries he has many contacts and finding the right company to do the work for us would be easier for him."

"He's built some pretty spectacular resorts here in Las Vegas."

"Does he talk about that?"

"We mostly talk about the baby." *His* baby, Maggie silently added. But every day Brady felt more like hers and she let herself go there. Because of the marriage, she wasn't going to lose him. "I've read about his work in the *Review Journal.* I read aloud to the baby." She shrugged. "It's never too early to start reading to a child."

"I can't argue with that. And speaking of arguing, when I tried to do that with Mr. Garrett, he asked whether or not I wanted to get the best quality construction for a rock-bottom price." Sister laughed. "Only an idiot would have said no to that."

"And you're one smart cookie, Sister," Maggie said.

"Before I knew it, the roofing company called and scheduled the job, and here they are. Next up are renovations to the plumbing. Also thanks to your Mr. Garrett. A crew will be available when this part of the project is complete. Which shouldn't be more than a week." She looked up at the threatening sky. "And with help from the good Lord, we will not get rain until after our brand-new roof is in place. Gus said that—"

"Gus?"

"The man in charge," Sister explained. "He said the job will take several days. Demolition—that's taking off the old roof—will be the most time-consuming part. Because of the weather they'll put plastic over it. But I'm thinking we might want to move the children in those upstairs rooms just to be safe."

"Okay. I'm here to help however you need me," Maggie assured her.

Sister draped an arm around her shoulders. "You're a blessing from God."

That was something Sister had said as far back as Maggie could remember, but now it felt different. She was glad that she'd been in the right place at the right time to make God's plan happen for this very special home. But she knew, as surely as she knew the thermometer would hit triple digits in July, that if Sister was aware of the facts behind this donation, she would not consider it a blessing. And that's why she could never find out.

Maggie would do anything to keep the smile on this woman's face. Including a lie of omission.

"We also have to keep the children inside and away from the workmen for their own safety."

"I understand."

"Sister Mary and another volunteer took a group of older kids to the movies. We received some free passes and the timing couldn't have been better. The little ones will be easier to look after inside."

"Okay." Maggie linked her arm through Sister's as they walked toward the house. "We'll keep them busy."

"You can read aloud from the newspaper," Sister teased.

"I promise you they'll love it," Maggie said.

"I'm sure they will. Sweetie, you could read the phone book and have them eating out of your hand. You've always had a way with the little ones." On the covered porch Sister Margaret stopped and took in the sight of the workmen. "It's so important to give them a positive start in life."

"I absolutely agree." Wasn't she doing that with Brady? She was grateful for the chance to give him all the tender, loving care he needed for a positive start in his little life.

"I want to do more, Maggie." Sister looked down at her. "This donation is so extraordinarily generous. With Mr. Garrett's help it will go further than just the repairs. There will be money left over for unexpected expenses. Or maybe a scholarship for someone who might not otherwise be able to go to college."

"That's wonderful, Sister." She'd struggled with money while getting her education. It would be fantastic to ease the way for an exceptional student with limited resources.

"It's a gift that will keep on giving."

Maggie looked at the woman beside her, the genuine happiness she felt at being given the means to smooth the way for others. Maybe even more good would come out of the deal she'd made. She'd always felt that she got a miracle the night the sisters found her on this very porch and took her in. Through The Nanny Network, God had put her in the right place, in Jason Garrett's path, so that she could pay her miracle forward.

She hoped so because personally this deal had landed her right in purgatory. It was a state of temporary misery where a soul could make up for past sins and earn a pass to heaven. She'd been taught that it was a condition where one could see what they were missing out on but not participate.

By that definition, she was definitely in purgatory. She had a front-row seat of what a family of her own could look like, a clear view of what she'd always wanted. But it wasn't actually hers.

She'd had a wedding, but no wedding night. And the more time she spent with Jason, the more her body felt the emptiness, the more she yearned to be his wife in every sense of the word.

He was a good man, a man she respected more every day. For the sake of the child he loved more than anything, he'd married a woman he could never love. Somehow she'd have to make peace with what she'd done.

She'd have to find a way to live with seeing what she wanted every single day, all the while knowing she couldn't ever really have it.

## Chapter Seven

Practically from the first moment Maggie had walked into his life Jason was aware of her in all the wrong ways. Tonight was no exception, unless you counted him wanting her more. That probably had something to do with feeling her absence. Not because flying solo with his son was an inconvenience. Just the opposite. He cleared his schedule without hesitation to make time for Brady. The more time he spent with him, the more confident he felt. But the penthouse had seemed so empty while she'd been gone doing her duty at the home.

That's the thing. He couldn't find a shred of a clue that she considered what she did a duty. Instead she only talked about what she got out of helping and felt selfish for getting anything at all. That purity of spirit was a big part of why he couldn't get her off his mind. He'd never known a woman like her.

With an almost soundly sleeping Brady pressed to his chest, Jason walked the floor in the living room as he looked at the bright lights of Las Vegas below him. Maggie had returned this afternoon. Normally she was perky and chatty and full of stories about the children and activities at Good Shepherd. Today she seemed troubled.

And how long had it been since he'd actually been aware of a woman's mood?

"Never." When Brady squirmed in his arms, Jason gently patted his back and made the shushing noise Maggie had taught him. "Sorry, pal," he said softly.

He continued to move until the baby completely relaxed, a sign that he was sound asleep. After walking down the hall into the nursery, he settled Brady on his back and gently brushed the dark hair from his forehead as tiny lips pursed and sucked in sleep.

A tenderness unlike any emotion he'd ever known welled up inside Jason as he pulled the blanket up to his child's waist. He wouldn't stay covered long because he was really moving around a lot, getting bigger every day. Maggie had informed him that soon Brady would be rolling from his back to his stomach. Amazing how much had changed since Maggie had come into their lives.

Including the fact that she was his wife, Jason thought.

His body went tight with need. Wasn't life ironic? He'd never been without a woman when he was a single man. Now that he had a baby and a wife, regular sex was a distant memory.

After sliding the baby monitor in the back pocket of his jeans, he walked out of the nursery. In the hallway, he heard sounds of the treadmill coming from his home gym. He'd bought an elliptical trainer, free weights and treadmill for the convenience of a home workout and not taking time away from his son. In the evening, while he and Brady hung out, it had become her habit to use the equipment.

Work waited in his study but he was too restless and distracted for spreadsheets and reports. Knowing it was probably a stupid move, he headed in the other direction.

The door was open and Maggie was walking briskly on the treadmill, her back to him. She was wearing a tank top and knit pants, both of which clung to the curves he'd been dreaming about, shifting his body into high gear. Instantly he had a mental picture of those shapely legs wrapped around his waist while he was buried deep inside her.

She was the one exerting herself, but sweat popped out on his forehead. He'd swear he hadn't made a sound, but only moments after he'd stopped in the doorway she looked over her shoulder and surprise registered in her expression.

"Jason?" She placed her feet on either side of the moving tread, then slid the speed lever to off so the machine slowed and finally stopped. "Is Brady all right?"

"Fine. He's asleep."

She grabbed the small towel draped over the handrail and wiped the moisture from her face.

The view from the front was just as good as the back, maybe better. The brief tank was moist and clung to her small, firm breasts. His skin felt too tight and his nerve endings were tingling. He was probably giving off some kind of electrical humming sound, which could explain how she'd known he was there. Or it could have been a moan, something he wouldn't have heard because of the blood rushing from his head to points south.

She blew out a breath and brushed the dark hair off her forehead. "This is early for him to go down. Maybe I better check to see if he's really settled."

"Take five. I've got the baby monitor. We'll know if sleep is a false alarm. My son isn't shy about letting his needs be known."

"I've noticed." The words were light and teasing, but her normal smile was missing in action.

"Is something wrong, Maggie?"

"No." Her gaze jumped to his. "Why?"

"You've been uncharacteristically quiet since you got back from Good Shepherd today. Did something happen?"

Turning away, she walked over to the elliptical machine and grabbed the sweatshirt hanging there. After pulling it over her head, she slid her arms in and pulled it down. The bulky garment hid even more of her skin and the curves that made his body tighten with need and ache to touch her. He very nearly reached out to tug the damn thing off, but resisted the urge, just barely, by sliding his fingers into the pockets of his jeans.

Maggie met his gaze. "There are lots of things happening at the home."

That didn't answer his question. "Define lots of things."

"Workmen were there ripping off the roof. Out with the old, in with the new."

"Good."

"Sister Margaret tells me when that job is finished, there's a plumbing crew waiting to make the necessary repairs and upgrades."

"Excellent."

"Yes, it is." She draped the towel around her neck.

"And yet you look as if there's something not right."

"Do I? Everything feels fine."

Not in his skin. But he wasn't about to share that. His household was in place and rocking the boat would be an incredibly dumb thing to do.

He reached out and brushed a dark strand of hair from her forehead, much as he'd done with Brady just a few minutes ago. "Really?"

She nodded, then swallowed hard. "It was very nice of you to get bids and line up building contractors for Sister Margaret."

*Very nice.* She thought his lawyer was nice. It wouldn't surprise him if she could find redeeming qualities in Attila the Hun. As far as adjectives, he'd have much preferred studly.

Athletic. Long lasting. And just like that his mind was right back in the sack.

He swallowed the need as best he could. "I know people. It wasn't a problem."

"Still, you're a busy man. Taking the time to help was very gracious of you."

*Very gracious?* More bland adjectives that made him feel sexless.

"The very least I could do to make sure no one took advantage."

"Sister Margaret wanted me to be sure and thank you. It's much appreciated. The kids and the nuns are incredibly grateful."

"What about you, Maggie?"

"Me?" She looked surprised, confused, doubtful. And incredibly beautiful. The pulse at the base of her throat fluttered wildly.

"Yes, you. Do the renovations meet with your approval?"

"If it means that the home will stay open, I absolutely approve of everything." Her chin lifted a notch as she met his gaze.

"I'm glad. Because truthfully, I've never met anyone at the home. When I made those phone calls to line up contractors, it was all about you."

"Me?"

"It's my way of thanking you for everything you've done."

"You put a million dollars in trust for something I care deeply about. We both got what we wanted. I don't understand why you went above and beyond to help."

That made two of them. He wasn't the only selfish bastard in the world, but definitely somewhere near the top. Having a child had shown him, for the first time in his life, what it was like to care about someone other than himself. And Maggie was important to his son. That's all it was about. That's all he'd let it be about. This was not a good time to have doubts about their business arrangement.

"Call it a bonus," he said. "To put the smile back on your face."

The corners of her mouth curved up and suddenly all the effort was worth it. "That wasn't necessary. But thank you."

"You're welcome."

She stared up at him, then blinked and moved toward the door. "I—I better go check on Brady. See if he needs me."

Jason needed her. Just to talk. To laugh. To fill up the emptiness inside him. Just a little longer.

He curved his fingers around her arm to stop her. "Wait, Maggie—"

She looked up at him, her eyes wide pools of innocence that drowned his willpower. He drew her against him, cupping her cheek in his hand.

"Maggie," he whispered again.

She opened her mouth to say something, but before she could he touched his mouth to hers. The soft sweetness of her lips was more intoxicating than the pricey liquor he kept in his office down the hall. Desire ground through him and knotted in his gut. He slid his hand beneath the bulky sweatshirt and settled it on her lower back, just above the curve of her butt, and pressed her more firmly against him.

Some vague instinct warned him to go slow and he fought the need to kiss her hard and possessively. He nibbled the corners of her mouth and felt her heart pounding against his own. Dropping small kisses on her cheek, then her chin and finally her neck, made her shiver and moan. When he stopped at a sensitive place just beneath her ear, she shuddered. Then he licked the responsive spot and blew softly until her groan echoed inside him. The sound sent arrows of need through him and his body tightened in response. Blood pounded in his veins and his chest felt like it would explode. The sound of Maggie's ragged breathing turned him on like he'd never been turned on before. She wanted him as much as he wanted her. For God's sake, she was his wife.

"I need you, Maggie," he whispered, his breath stirring her hair. His voice was ragged with desire.

He was about to scoop her into his arms when she pulled her mouth from his and stared at him, breathing hard. Something dark pushed the innocence from her eyes.

"What's wrong?" he asked.

"I don't want to be a novelty."

"Excuse me?" He was struggling to draw air into his lungs and that kiss blew his mind. There wasn't much left to take in and decipher a remark from out of left field.

"Your father said I was a novelty. 'Almost a nun' was different for you."

"Don't pay any attention to my father—"

"You mean the part where he was proud of you for protecting yourself financially? The part where he was pleased that you were thinking with your head as well as—other parts of your body? You planned ahead for a plaything. Offered marriage so stock prices wouldn't go down because of a scandal with the nanny."

"You know that's not how it was," he said, anger burning as hot as desire had only moments before.

"It's all about Brady, I know. But he's asleep now. Technically I'm off duty, or at least on a break. But you just kissed me."

"That's not breaking news." He couldn't deny it. Her lips were still moist from the touch of his own. But when a Garrett was backed into a corner he came out fighting. "I started it. And you kissed me back."

"It was a knee-jerk reaction." She stared at him for several moments, still breathing hard. "I'm not asking for love."

"You heard that, too?"

"Oh, yeah." Her frown pushed out any hint of sunshine, and it was his fault. "Just so we're clear, that's the last thing I'm looking for. But I will not be disrespected."

"That was never my intention," he assured her.

When he'd kissed her, he'd been thinking with his hormones, which were in perfect working order. Before she could argue that point, a sound came from his back pocket where he'd put the monitor.

"It's Brady. Break's over," she said. "I have to go to him."

"Right."

She hurried out of the room, and when she was gone, Jason felt her absence again. But this time it was all about the ache shooting through him.

He knew when it subsided he would be relieved that he hadn't taken Maggie to his bed. But right now he couldn't feel the blessing and struggled for logic.

Sleeping with her would have been a huge mistake. Sex was a complication that would destroy everything he'd so carefully put in place.

But he had to wonder what sin he'd committed. What transgression was so wicked that he was being punished by this gut-twisting desire for the one woman he didn't dare touch?

Masculine and sexy sat on Jason Garrett like a cloak and crown. Maggie had been enveloped in it last night and wanted more. She'd barely managed to break away before willingly becoming another one of his playthings. It made her wonder again about Brady's mother, but no matter how Jason had treated her, there was no way to reconcile abandoning her baby. If Brady was hers, Maggie knew there would be no walking away. He wasn't her biological child and she couldn't walk away. But there was also the small matter of the marriage to his father.

Although being driven around was a darn nice perk of the marriage, she thought, watching palm trees and buildings go by. Jason's driver had picked Maggie and Brady up from the penthouse. She sat in the back with the baby in his car seat, sound asleep beside her. The movement always did that to him. Jason had forgotten his briefcase and she'd needed the car for errands. She'd told his secretary she would swing by the office and drop it off while they were out. And, of course, the woman had said she was dying to see the baby.

Her heart seemed to expand in her chest when she smiled at the infant, probably the only person on the planet who could make her smile this morning. After what happened the night before, specifically THE KISS—all capital letters.

She wasn't so innocent that she didn't know he'd wanted her. If only the feeling wasn't mutual, but she'd be lying if she said that. Sleeping with Jason would complicate her already complicated life, but every part of her had tingled and begged to finally know what it felt like to be with a man. And not just any man.

Jason Garrett was the man she wanted. It couldn't be explained away by the fact that she hadn't been kissed in a very long time—before she'd entered the convent—by her disastrous first love. She hadn't slept with him and there'd been no one since. Technically that meant she'd saved herself for the man she married.

Silly her. When he'd dangled a million dollars in front of her, she hadn't inquired what he expected of her as his wife. Jason had been gone when she got up with Brady this morning. Now she had to face him for the first time after that kiss. In front of other people. Just goes to show that God had a sense of humor.

After exiting the 215 Beltway onto Green Valley Parkway, the car pulled into a business complex, then stopped in front of a multistoried building. As soon as the movement ceased, Brady's eyes popped open.

"This is it, Mrs. Garrett."

For a nanosecond, she thought the driver was talking to someone else. "Thanks, Martin. I'll only be a few minutes."

"Want to leave the little guy with me while you run the briefcase up to Mr. G?"

"I appreciate that, but his father wants to show him off."

Maggie had the baby in one hand and the briefcase in the other when she walked into the Garrett Industries building. Her sneakers squeaked on the lobby's marble floor as she headed for the elevator. After entering, she set both her burdens down and pushed the button for the eighth floor where Jason's office was located.

The elevator opened right into the reception area and a half-circle cherrywood desk that sat in the center of the room. Behind it was a redhead in her twenties wearing a headset for answering the phone.

When a muted ring sounded, she pushed a button and said, "Garrett Industries, Mr. Garrett's office. This is Chloe. How can I help you?" She listened for a moment and said, "Let me transfer you to customer service. Hold on, please."

Chloe De Witt. Jason's secretary. They'd talked just a little while ago.

Maggie stopped in front of the desk. "Hi. I'm—" She was going to say Margaret Mary Shepherd. But she wasn't anymore. She was Maggie Garrett, although she had no idea who Maggie Garrett was. With the very efficient secretary staring at her this was no time for an identity crisis. "I'm Maggie."

"Hi." Chloe flashed a professional smile, then disconnected her headset from the phone and came around the desk. She was wearing a snug gray pinstriped skirt and long-sleeved white blouse tucked into the waistband. The four-inch black spiked heels made her slender legs look a mile long. Her thick auburn hair was stylishly cut and brushed her silky collar. She was pretty enough to be a model. Or a show girl. Either or both of which were probably Jason's type.

After a quick glance at her own dark denim pants and red pullover sweater, Maggie felt like the peasant from Plainville, a drab and uninteresting dweeb.

Chloe saw the briefcase on the floor beside Brady's car seat. "You brought it. And this must be Jason's little guy."

"Brady."

When he heard his name, he flashed a wide smile and Chloe did a big "aww." "He is absolutely adorable."

"Yes, he is," Maggie agreed, smiling down at the incredibly cute little guy.

Could she be any more proud if he'd been her biological child? she wondered. That didn't seem possible. She was married to his father, but didn't have the right to claim him as her son. She was just the nanny.

Male voices drifted to them from down the hall. Before she saw him, Maggie heard Jason's voice.

"Chloe, do you have that paperwork yet?" The man who belonged to that familiar voice strode into the reception area with another man and spotted her. "That would be a yes. Hi, Maggie."

"Hi. I had some errands in The District, so I offered to drop off your briefcase." His cool, confident expression gave no clue how he felt about seeing her there.

"You met my secretary," he said, glancing between the two of them.

Chloe looked at him and it was clear from the adoring expression on her face that she had a serious crush on her boss. Maggie felt a tug of something unpleasant right in her midsection.

"Your son is just about the cutest thing I've ever seen," Chloe said.

Jason smiled down at the baby. "You'll get no argument from me."

"That's a first." It was the man with Jason. He was tall, about the same height, with dark hair and incredibly blue eyes. In a dark charcoal-gray suit, black shirt and geometric tie in shades of silver, he looked like a pirate, a modern-day corporate one—handsome and dashing, a scoundrel and a rogue. "But I haven't met the lady."

"Imagine that." Jason's words were laced with sarcasm and the tone squeezed out any hint of friendly banter. His eyes darkened to almost black as he frowned. "A woman in Las Vegas that you haven't met."

"What can I say?" The man's grin was unapologetic. "I'm a people person."

"Is that what you call it?" This semi-hostile Jason was a side he'd kept hidden.

"Women are people, too." He glanced at her. "Aren't you going to introduce me?"

"This is Maggie," Jason said grudgingly.

The stranger held out his hand. "I'm Nathaniel Gordon. Jason and I are working on a business deal together."

Maggie would bet Jason wasn't offering him a large sum of money to take care of his child. That was the only business deal she knew anything about. Of the four of them, five if you included Brady, she was the only one clueless about the business world. Taking that even further, she didn't have a whole lot of world experience in general. But one could never go wrong being polite.

"Nice to meet you," she said, putting her fingers in his. Brushing a strand of hair off her face, she saw that his gaze zeroed in on the plain gold band on her left ring finger. Jason noticed, too, if the muscle jerking in his taut jaw was anything to go by.

"The papers I needed are in here." He picked up the brief-case. "Let's go back to my office, Nate. I'm not finished getting the best of you yet."

"In your dreams, pal." He leveled an appreciative gaze in Maggie's direction. "It was a pleasure, Maggie."

Jason turned away. "Chloe, hold my calls for the next hour."

"An hour?" Nate followed him. "It won't take that long for me to get the upper hand in this negotiation."

Then the phone rang, and Chloe rounded the desk to plug herself back in. "Thanks for bringing the papers, Maggie. And the baby." She answered the call and waggled her fingers in a goodbye gesture.

Maggie stood by herself. This office and the professional atmosphere with its high-powered and attractive business players made her feel like she'd stepped into an alternate universe. This Jason was a man she'd seen before, driven and focused. He'd tried to be that way the first time they met, but concern for his infant son had stripped away the edges.

Here the edges were even sharper. He was cool, calm, in control. The boss. Last night, for the heart-stopping moments when his mouth had greedily taken hers, he'd been her husband.

Maggie took the elevator down, then walked to the car where Martin opened the door. She strapped the baby's car seat in and slid in beside him.

In the two months she'd known him, Jason had never forgotten the work he'd invariably brought home with him. Not ever. She wanted to believe today's anomaly happened because he'd been as bewildered by that kiss as she was. And although she desperately wanted to believe in miracles, she couldn't quite get herself to buy that one. It was easier to believe that his father was right and she was a novelty, a plaything.

The whole time she'd been in his office he'd only introduced her as Maggie and left out what she was to him. He'd never once called her his wife. She'd saved herself for the man she married, but up until that kiss she'd figured the man she married didn't want her as anything but the nanny.

Seeing him in his world, it was clear that she wouldn't fit in as anything *but* the nanny. He'd said part of the reason he insisted on marriage was to prevent another man from swooping in and marrying her.

She hadn't really bought into that, but he wasn't joking.

He didn't want her, but he didn't want anyone else to have her, either. This wasn't purgatory.

It was a deal with the devil.

## *Chapter Eight*

Jason loved this cabin in Lake Tahoe.

When he was about eight his father had bought the place with views of the water. Every year they came here during ski season and hung out—just the two of them. Because of the parade of women through Hunter's life, the Garretts didn't have many traditions. But this was one he wanted for himself and Brady.

And Maggie.

Out of nowhere that thought popped into his mind as he watched her play with the baby. The two of them were on the thick beige carpet in front of the fire in the big stone fireplace. Sitting on the overstuffed leather corner group, Jason smiled when she kissed the baby's belly and made him laugh. It was so incredibly normal, so amazingly down-to-earth. An unfamiliar and unexpected sensation of contentment swept over him, a warm feeling that expanded and chased out the emptiness. Loneliness was another name for it, but he never felt that way when he was with Maggie.

They'd slipped back into a relaxed give-and-take, for which he was grateful. That meant he hadn't screwed things up by kissing her. Clearly she hadn't held it against him. He wished he could keep from holding it against *her,* more important, forget about it. And he'd thought a change of scene might help. So far he'd been wrong about that, but they'd only arrived a couple hours ago. She hadn't said much.

"So what do you think?"

"About?"

"This change in scenery." His gaze settled on her mouth and he knew there'd been no progress in the ongoing battle to take his mind off kissing her.

"If you're asking about the ride in your Gulfstream, I think it was—" She hesitated, obviously struggling for an appropriate adjective. "It was pretty awesome."

"Yeah. It's good being me." He laughed when she made a face at him. "But that's not what I meant. How do you like the cabin?"

She met his gaze, then looked around. "Calling it a cabin is like saying that jet is an airplane. McMansion is more to the point."

"You think?" he asked, studying the log walls and high-beam ceiling. "It's only six thousand square feet."

"That much? Feels smaller," she murmured, then handed the baby a stuffed toy that went straight into his mouth.

"You don't like it?"

Her expression was wry. "It's fantastic, and I think you're just fishing for compliments."

"I didn't realize you knew me that well," he teased.

"This is a wonderful spot," she said, not commenting on understanding him. "It's too bad this trip is just a few days. Leaving will be hard." She crossed her legs Indian style and looked at him. "Speaking of this long weekend, I'm surprised you could get away from the office with a big business deal pending."

"Deal?" He was only half-listening, enjoying the sight of her with his son. It was almost bedtime and the little guy was bathed, in pajamas and ready for the sack. The idea of being just with Maggie sent anticipation buzzing through him.

"Aren't you the relaxed one?" she commented.

"Hmm?"

"You're not listening. Either your ears don't work in higher altitudes, or when you're this far from the office you go on autopilot." She tilted her head to the side and studied him. "Or both."

"Guilty. On both counts. This place seems to give me back my serenity." And then some. She looked extraordinarily beautiful with the glow of the fire behind her and his child at her knee. He slid his hands into the pockets of his jeans and stretched his long legs out in front of him. Trying to relax, though suddenly his whole body was tight and tense. Desire throbbed through him and the vibrations were like an electromagnetic pulse that short-circuited brain function. "I'm sorry. What were you saying?"

"That I was surprised you could get out of town with a deal in the works. The one you were involved in when I was there the other day to drop off your briefcase."

"Nate Gordon."

"Yes." She glanced at him, absently holding Brady's foot and rubbing her thumb across the bottom. "How's that going?"

Of all the people he did business with, why did she have to meet Nathaniel Gordon, entrepreneur and playboy? The guy discarded women like tissues. He'd asked a lot of questions about Maggie, and Jason hadn't been prepared for it. Every answer he gave just made Nate more curious about their connection. Finally, the remark about getting Maggie's phone number because she was a babe really got Jason steamed.

He'd blurted out that she was his wife, which led to more

interrogation. Like why he was keeping her under wraps. Why hadn't he received an invitation to the biggest society wedding of the year? He'd thought they were friends, etc.

Finally Jason put a lid on the whole thing with a question of his own. Did he want to do business or start a new career as a tabloid journalist?

"Jason?"

He looked at her. "Sorry. Altitude auditory malfunction again."

"Very funny." She smiled as he'd hoped. "How's that deal working for you?"

"It looks like we'll be merging into the largest development company in Las Vegas."

"Congratulations. That sounds pretty impressive."

"It's okay."

She tilted her head and studied him. "Not impressive?"

It might have been. Probably still was. But Jason's opinion of Nathaniel Gordon did a 180 when he showed an interest in Maggie. He didn't like the way Nate had looked at her. Like she was a ripe strawberry ready for picking.

"From a business perspective it will benefit both our companies."

When Brady started making unhappy noises because he'd dropped the stuffed toy, she handed him a brightly colored set of plastic keys, which he managed to grab and shove in his mouth.

"Really?"

"Stock prices will soar. It's a smart business deal."

"Then why do you look like someone stole your Black-Berry?"

He stared at her for a moment. Was she a mind reader? Strawberry? BlackBerry? He didn't like the idea of Nate poaching anything of his. He wondered if "almost a nun" meant that Maggie had a direct line to God. If so, he'd have to be careful because what he'd been thinking wasn't up for discussion with her.

But maybe this was an opportunity. "As far as business, there's no one sharper or more successful than Nate Gordon."

"Including you?"

"Except for me." He grinned and she returned it. "We met in college and hit it off. Our strengths and weaknesses complement each other and we'd make a formidable team in developing new projects."

"Then I'm not sure I understand the problem."

"It's personal." He folded his arms over his chest. "He's not the kind of guy who puts down roots."

"Is that a delicate way of saying he has commitment issues?"

"I wouldn't know about that. All I can tell you is that if you follow the trail of Las Vegas broken hearts it will lead straight to his door."

"So he's never been married?"

"Absolutely not."

"No children?"

"Not that I'm aware of," he said.

She put her hand on the baby's belly. "Until Brady, you just described yourself."

"That was a low blow," he said, indignant.

The little guy started to fuss. Instantly she picked him up and settled him to her shoulder, patting his back. "I'm just stating facts. Now you have a son, which forces you to plan ahead for your fun and maybe you're the tiniest bit jealous of Nate."

"You couldn't be more wrong." Anger curled through him. He might be jealous but it had nothing to do with his son.

"Then why did you marry me, Jason?" She held up a hand when he started to answer. "I know how the spin goes. It's for Brady. I was there, remember? I was also there for the father-son chat about appearances. Any hint of hanky panky and stock prices take a nose dive."

"What's your point?"

"How can business be affected by what you do when no one besides your father knows we're married?"

"Nate knows," he said, but didn't volunteer the circumstances of the interrogation that had dragged out the information.

"Does Chloe?" she challenged. When he didn't answer, she nodded. "I thought so. You told Nate because it was a territorial thing. Sort of a primal, Neanderthal, don't-take-what's-mine, pounding your chest kind of posturing."

"You're calling me a caveman?"

"So not the point," she said with a sigh. "We're married."

"I was there, remember?" He winced at how childish it was to throw her own words back at her.

"We have a legal commitment. But I'm trying to figure out what that means. All I am is Maggie. When I met your secretary, there was no qualification of what I am to you. I'm not sure what my life is anymore."

"Do you want out of the agreement?"

She stood with the baby in her arms and the fire's glow backlit her slender shape and womanly curves. It was a sight that knotted his gut and practically made him salivate. If he really was a Neanderthal, he'd carry her upstairs and have his way with her. His willpower was shaky, but he was trying to be noble here. She wasn't making it easy.

"What does that mean?"

"An annulment." Since there'd never been anything physical between them.

"The money you put in trust is already being spent. You know I can't afford to pay you back."

He wouldn't make her do that. To him it was chump change. A tax write-off. "Then what do you want?"

"I don't know." The baby started to cry in earnest and she pressed him closer to her, rubbing his back and brushing her palm over his head. "I want to go home."

Just a little while ago she'd thought this trip was too short and wanted to stay longer. He'd spoiled the mood, which made him feel like the caveman she'd accused him of being.

"We'll go back in the morning."

"Okay." Her tone said it couldn't be too soon for her and so did the troubled expression in her eyes when she met his gaze. A moment later she hurried past him and upstairs with the unhappy baby.

Jason brooded as he stared at the fire. This was a hell of a mess he'd gotten himself into.

Talk about not thinking it through. He'd been so focused on closing the deal and getting her to stay, he hadn't even considered the other things that marriage meant.

Companionship.

Intimacy.

Sex.

He stood and paced in front of the fire, feeling the warmth on his skin. The heat he felt inside was all for Maggie. He wanted her.

She was his wife, for God's sake. In some odd way thoughts of sex had made him mention *annulment*. To her, that was more ammunition to prove that he'd planned ahead to play her. The truth was he hadn't planned ahead for anything. He hadn't thought about her having a life, being a wife.

But he was thinking about it now. And not with his head.

Maggie stared out the window where the swiftly falling snow covered the road and piled up outside. Ordinarily she'd have been entranced by its beauty. Snow wasn't something a resident of Las Vegas saw every day. It got cold, but not usually cold enough to snow. The sight should have been magical. But when you wanted to escape back to the real world and Mother Nature decided to make the road to the airport too icy for travel, it felt like a cosmic joke at her expense. Be careful what you wish for, because now she had to spend another night in the romantic McMansion.

"It's a blizzard," she said, stating the obvious.

"I know." Jason's tone was grim.

Wasn't it amazing how much tension six thousand square feet could contain? After their angry words last night, the strain had been palpable all day as they went out of their way to avoid each other, all the while watching the snow falling faster, burying any hope of traveling home by tonight.

Fortunately baby Brady was blissfully unaware of the edginess in the adults around him. His routine of eating, playing, napping and now down for the night had remained unchanged, which made him the only happy camper in the cabin.

She glanced over her shoulder at Jason. "This is the beginning of April, for goodness' sake. How can there be weather-related travel delays in the beginning of April?"

He folded his arms over his chest. "Did you ever hear of the Donner Party?"

Eyes wide, she turned to face him full on. "There's no food here? Brady needs formula. And—"

"Don't panic." He held up his hands. "We have rations. I just meant that freak snowstorms happen in the mountains. If I'm not mistaken, the Donner Party got caught in October, which was early for winter. We're looking at spring and it's late in the season, but snow happens."

She cocked her thumb over her shoulder toward the window and visual proof. "I noticed."

"Obviously we're not going anywhere tonight. Might as well make the best of it. I think I'll open a bottle of wine." Without waiting for a comment, he walked away.

Maggie heard noise in the kitchen, the amazing kitchen with an oblong island big enough to land his Gulfstream. The sound of drawers and cupboards opening and closing drifted to her.

She didn't know what to do with herself. Wouldn't you

think a place this size would be big enough to lose yourself in? Growing up she'd always had to share a room with one or more girls. Then she did live-in child care and a room of her own came with the territory. Along with a broken heart. She'd never existed anywhere as spacious as Jason's penthouse and this beautiful, homey, woodsy cabin. Yet with him in it, she'd never experienced an area with less breathing room. Suddenly the walls seemed to close in on her and she opened the front door and stepped into the cold on the porch.

She moved to the edge, where she knew four steps descended to the yard and the lake that was normally visible through the trees. Now, the big, wet, white flakes hid everything, including the steps. The wind blew toward her and with it the snow, stinging her cheeks. She crossed her arms over her chest against the bitter cold and started to shiver. If she could stand it out here long enough, maybe Jason would be upstairs in the fabulous master bedroom and out of sight when she was forced to go in.

The front door creaked open behind her. "Maggie?"

"Nice out here," she murmured.

"It's a blizzard," he said, echoing her words.

"I've never seen a blizzard before."

"Watching it inside would be warmer and a much better environment from which to enjoy the view."

With him around there was no such thing as a bad view. And that was why she wanted to leave. This wasn't normal. Normal consisted of him going to work. Spending hours at the office, before coming home late and giving Brady his undivided attention until the baby went to bed and she could hide in her room. It was snatches of moments with him. Not this concentration of time where she was exposed to his powerful brand of magnetism. She'd made it clear to him that respect was important to her, but how could she respect herself when she'd chewed him out for kissing her at the same time she yearned for him to kiss her again?

"I'm fine," she lied. "Who knows when I'll get another chance to experience snow up close and personal?"

He moved right behind her, close enough for her to feel the heat of his body. With every fiber of her being she longed to lean into his warmth and not just because she was freezing her tuchas off. If she stayed out long enough, maybe the blizzard would numb her to the effects of prolonged exposure to Jason's appeal.

He put his hands on her arms. "You're shivering."

"I'm f-fine."

"The sound of your teeth chattering will wake Brady."

"Not likely. Must be something about the air and altitude. He's slept better up here than usual. Tonight is no exception. He's s-sound asleep."

"Come back inside before you catch cold." His warm breath stirred her hair and made clouds of vapor in the frigid night. "You don't want to get sick and pass it on to Brady."

He had her there. She sighed. "All r-right."

When the hot air inside collided with her cold body, she really started to shiver.

"I'll pour you a glass of wine. That will help."

On the coffee table in front of the fireplace, beside the baby monitor, there was a bottle of red wine and two glasses. He filled them both a quarter full and handed one to her. Nudging the bottom, he urged her to sip.

She wasn't much of a drinker, but the ruby-colored liquid went down smoothly. "That's good."

"I'm glad you like it." He didn't sound glad. He sounded annoyed, if the clipped tone of his voice was any indication.

"Okay, then. I think I-I'll go up—" A sudden violent shiver stopped her words.

"Oh, for Pete's sake—"

Jason put her empty glass on the table, then turned her and rubbed her arms. The fire was to her front and he was at her back. Close. So very close. She was surrounded by heat and not in purgatory anymore. She felt the proof in every stroke of his hands on her arms. She wasn't on the outside looking in.

This was heaven.

Funny how the paradise oxygen supply was so doggone short.

"Are you warmer now?" He hadn't touched a drop of liquor, but there was a whiskey-and-chocolate huskiness in his voice that stole even more of her breath.

Was she warm? If the liquid heat pooling inside her was anything to go by, her body temperature had shot up past normal as soon as he touched her.

"Y-Yeah. I'm fine."

"That makes one of us." His hands stopped moving and he squeezed her arms, gently drawing her against the solid length of his body.

"You're not fine? What's wrong, Jason?"

He turned her and stared down. A frown, dark and intense, made his expression forbidding. "Do you really not know how much I want you?"

How would she? What did she know about this sort of thing? All she knew was that she wanted him, too. She caught the corner of her lip between her teeth and saw his gaze settle on her mouth, his eyes darkening to the color of coal.

At the same time he lowered his mouth, his hands tightened on her arms and brought her to her tiptoes, to meet him. She braced for impact, but the touch was soft and gentle. The resulting firestorm inside her was anything but. Need tangled with the doubt, but it was no contest. Yearning, craving, longing swelled inside her and pushed out everything but this man.

She said against his mouth, "Do you really not know how much I want you?"

His hands tensed. "Are you sure? After this, there are no loopholes."

She couldn't think straight what with him playing her body

like a finely tuned violin. So the meaning didn't register. Right now she didn't care about anything, couldn't remember why this was a bad idea.

All she knew was that Jason was her husband. The one she'd saved herself for. Now, finally—*finally*—she would know the secret handshake. She would find out the mysteries and pleasures of being loved by a man.

She looked into his eyes and willed away the doubts. "I want this very much, Jason."

He dragged air into his lungs as he nodded. Then he took her hand and led her toward the stairs. Climbing them had never seemed to take so long, until now. But she'd waited far longer to give her virginity, and could manage a few more minutes. The hall light was on and trickled into the master bedroom.

Jason stopped beside the king-size, pine sleigh bed and turned to her. He cupped her face in his hands and kissed her deeply, then traced her lips with the tip of his tongue. Her mouth opened instinctively and he dipped inside, teasing, tasting, tempting.

Fire coiled in her belly, then spread outward and grew until she thought her insides would implode. His hands slid to her waist, then curved at her hips, drawing their lower bodies close. She knew the physical mechanics of sex and could feel that he seriously wanted her, which made her spirit soar.

He slid his palms up and beneath her sweater until his thumb brushed over the nipple on her left breast. It was as if Mother Nature had strung an electrical cord from that flash point to a place between her thighs. Her breasts ached for more as liquid heat pooled and settled between her thighs fueling the frantic need inside her.

"Oh, Jason," she whispered hoarsely. "I never—"

"Right there with you," he said, his own voice ragged and tight, as if his control was tenuous.

She'd done that to him. It was a heady feeling.

Jason took hold of the comforter and blanket, throwing both back in one powerful movement. Then he grabbed the hem of his flannel shirt and jerked it up and over his head, revealing the taut wedge of naked flesh and muscle just above the waistband of his jeans. Her palms itched to touch the contours of his chest and she lifted a hand without thinking.

When she hesitated, Jason smiled, a self-satisfied look that made her already pounding heart even more erratic. He gently took her wrist and settled her fingers on him, over his own hammering heart. Although she sensed his tension, he stood stone still while she explored the masculine expanse to her heart's content.

Sliding lower, she traced the skin just north of the button on his jeans and female satisfaction trickled through her when the touch made him draw in a quick breath.

"That's a dangerous game you're playing, Maggie."

She looked at his teasing expression. "I can handle it."

"Two can play," he warned, his voice a sexy growl that sent tingles dancing over her highly sensitized skin.

He took the hem of her sweater and tugged at the same time she lifted her arms to make it easier for him to undress her. Reaching behind her, he unhooked her bra and slid it down, letting it fall to the floor.

Maggie didn't have a chance to feel shy or embarrassed while he looked at her. Their eyes locked and his were as dark and mysterious as the sea during a storm. He pulled her into his arms and they were skin to skin from the waist up. Her bare breasts pressed into his chest and it was the most exquisite sensation she had ever known. He threaded his fingers in her hair and cupped the back of her head to hold her still for his kiss. As he thoroughly explored her mouth, the sound of his harsh breathing filled her, challenged her.

With an effort he pulled away and said, "I don't think I can

wait, Maggie… It's been a long time for me. I don't know—
if it's—" He shook his head. "I'll make it up to you next time."

She had no idea what he meant. All she knew was the need
consuming her was more than she could stand. And when he
reached out to unfasten her jeans, his hand was shaking. She
pushed it aside and unfastened her pants, then slid them down
and stepped out of them. No man had ever seen her completely naked. For reasons not really clear to her the fact that
he was her first time made her incredibly glad.

Nervous, but glad.

A satisfied look slid into his eyes as he let his gaze slide
over her from head to toe. "You are absolutely perfect."

The words chased away any lingering nerves and she
smiled. In the next instant he'd dropped his pants and let her
see him. His erection was impressive and started the nerves
buzzing inside her again. They threatened to immobilize her,
but Jason took charge. He lifted her in his arms and settled her
in the center of the big bed. The sheets were cold against her
back until he slid in beside her and warmed her with his body.

He kissed her deeply, their mouths meshing until everything disappeared except the two of them and the amazing
sensation of his strength enfolding her. Silky threads of
pleasure snapped inside her when he cupped her breast in his
hand. He lowered his head and took her nipple in his mouth,
flicking it with his tongue until the tension inside her grew
and her hips moved restlessly, her body instinctively asking
for what she didn't understand she wanted.

Jason's hand glided over her abdomen and between her
legs, nudging a finger inside her as if he understood what she
needed. Her body took over and she bore down on his hand,
needy and wanting as a moan slipped out from somewhere
deep inside her. The sound was to his breathing what kerosene
was to a campfire.

"I need you, Maggie," he said against her mouth. "Now—"

"Yes," she breathed. "Now…"

He shifted onto her, letting his forearms keep his weight from crushing her. "Wrap your legs around me," he urged.

She did as he asked and his hardness pushed against her. Then he probed gently into the tender folds of her femininity and felt him tense when he encountered resistance. He started to pull away and groaned when she tightened her legs around him.

He thrust again—harder—and the barrier gave way. There was a single sharp pain followed by the pleasurable sensation of him filling her. Suddenly his body went rigid and he groaned out his release.

But Maggie sensed tension still pumping through him and there was fury in the gaze he leveled at her. "Jason? What's wrong?"

"You didn't think it was important to tell me you're a virgin?"

## Chapter Nine

Jason didn't wait for an answer to his question but rolled away and disappeared into the bathroom. When he came out wearing nothing but sweatpants, Maggie was standing by the bed wearing nothing but his flannel shirt. It covered her top but left most of her legs bare. Next to naked, it was the sexiest look he could imagine. Damned if his body wasn't telling him in the strongest possible terms that he wanted her again. How was that possible when he was so furious? With himself and with her.

Minutes ago he'd completely lost any kind of restraint where she was concerned, so he stopped before crossing the empty space between them. If he reached out and touched her again, it would be a test of willpower he wasn't sure he could pass.

"You had a boyfriend. Engaged to be engaged, you said." It came out as an accusation.

"I did." She rested one bare foot over the other looking so impossibly young and incredibly innocent that it was a mystery how he'd missed the signs. "But that's different from sex."

"Not these days," he snapped. "Was he gay?"

"Not unless I turned him," she said, her chin lifting defensively.

"He never touched you?" That was hard to believe. Almost from the first moment Jason had itched to explore the taste and texture of her.

"I didn't say that."

Unfortunately he wasn't angry enough to miss the wounded look in her eyes. And that was *his* fault. Nothing like reminding her the jerk hadn't wanted her. Clearly the boyfriend was an idiot who was too stupid to know what he'd passed up. And Jason was handling this with all the sensitivity of a demented water buffalo.

He planted his feet wide apart and crossed his arms over his bare chest because he wanted so badly to hold her. If he touched her again it would just make a bad situation really, really bad.

"What *are* you saying?" he asked.

That was a dumb question and not really the one he wanted to ask. Maybe because he didn't really want to know why she hadn't stopped *him* before he'd gone beyond the point of no return. She'd made it clear from the beginning that she didn't get attached because she cared too much. He'd used that as leverage to make the situation permanent. But he hadn't *married* her, married her.

Until tonight.

Before he'd lost the capacity for coherent thought he'd even had the presence of mind to warn her about closing the annulment loophole. It had slammed shut a little while ago. But that wasn't what bothered him most.

"Maggie, why didn't you tell me you'd never had sex?"

"I didn't think it was important information."

"Trust me, it's important," he said.

There was a flash of something in her eyes, something that said "I did it and I'm not sorry." "Not anymore."

"Yeah." He ran his fingers through his hair. "I was there."

He'd also been there for her throaty little moans. Those were the sounds that had sent him over the edge, on his way to a mind-blowing finish. The man who prided himself on being in charge, the guy who never met a problem he couldn't fix with money had lost control and taken her virginity.

There was no fix for that.

He'd known she was innocent—almost a nun. The memory of his father's words kept crashing against the inside of his skull. A novelty. If he'd known the whole truth of it, he'd have taken better care.

"Why is it important? Would it have changed anything?" she asked, taking a step forward.

"Yeah. I might have stopped."

She moved closer, right in front of him now. "Why?"

She was so innocent she couldn't even understand why her innocence was an issue. "Never mind. It's not important now."

"It's important to me." Her eyes pleaded. "What would you have done differently if you'd known that I'd never had sex before?"

It was like she knew just the right thing to say to get his juices flowing again. The exact right button to push to work him up. He'd just about managed to get his libido under control and she had to go and ask a question like that.

"You don't really want to know, Maggie."

"If that were true, I wouldn't have asked. I told you once that I didn't meet men because of my job and responsibilities. That doesn't mean I'm not curious. It's one of the reasons I left the convent."

"To have sex?" he asked, trying not to be shocked.

"Sort of."

"Maggie—"

"Don't get your boxers in a bunch." She held up a hand. "It wasn't that defined for me. I just knew there was a lot I hadn't experienced in life and never would if I took final vows. I was curious. Mother Superior advised me to leave, live and pray on the problem."

He couldn't believe he'd just had sex and now they were discussing convents and talking to God. If there'd ever been any doubt about where he'd end up in the hereafter, it was gone now.

He was going to hell for sure. "It doesn't happen often, but I don't know what to say to that."

She smiled. "You could tell me why you're so put out that I didn't tell you I'd never done that before."

Now that she'd moved closer, into the light, he could see the soft pink staining her cheeks. The shyness in her expression in spite of her straightforward questions. Maybe if he explained, she'd let it go and back off.

"Okay." He let out a long breath. "I would have gone slower. Made sure you were ready—"

"How?" Her expression was honest and open, curious. Cute as could be.

And she had no idea what this was doing to him. "I'd have touched you differently." Before she could ask, he added, "A woman's body has places that are extremely vulnerable and sensitive to touch."

"I see." She nodded.

He knew she didn't have a clue. Sexual pleasure was one of those things that pictures and words couldn't define. There was no substitute for hands-on experience.

And this conversation was killing him. Time to end it. "If I'd known, I would have been able to make it less uncomfortable for you."

"It wasn't that bad. And you said next time would be better."

For God's sake, he'd actually told her there would be a next time? Mental forehead smack here. He remembered now. But he'd meant that because it had been so long for him, he wouldn't be able to last. And he wasn't going there. In fact this conversation should have been over a long time ago.

He looked at the sliding-glass window that opened onto the balcony overlooking the lake. The glow of the outside light showed that the snow had stopped.

"The blizzard is over," he pointed out.

She glanced over her shoulder, then back at him. "That's a relief."

For him, too. "We're going home in the morning. Go get some sleep."

"But—"

He held up a hand. "I'm tired, and it will be a long day."

"You're still upset. We should talk."

"That's the last thing I want."

"I really don't get why you're so put out about this," she said. "Some men would be—I don't know—*pleased* that they were first. What is your problem?"

"Up until a little while ago, I didn't have one."

She frowned as her fingers toyed with one of the buttons on his shirt. "Jason, please—"

He swallowed hard at the sight of her in that shirt, remembering all too vividly what was underneath, how her soft skin had felt, how perfectly her curves fit his hands. "Please go, Maggie."

He walked over to the window and looked out, not really seeing anything. But the darkness outside reflected her watching him before she turned to leave.

Stopping in the doorway, she said, "I'm not sorry it happened."

That made one of them.

And this was a hell of a time to think about birth control. She was too innocent to be on the pill and he'd been completely unprepared for how much he'd wanted her. Surely fate wouldn't nail him for the lapse. It was once. One time.

Her next time *would* be better, but it wouldn't be him. The thought made him crazier than trying to explain sex to an ex-nun. When she was gone, he let out a long breath, but there was little relief in it.

He remembered telling her that she was best for his family and she'd asked what would happen if that changed. He hadn't answered because he didn't have an answer. Until now.

Sex changed everything. Virgin sex changed everything times ten. He just found out that she'd waited all this time to give herself to a man and made the mistake of letting that man be him. He was one selfish bastard and what he'd done made him feel even more responsible for her at a point when he was already pushing back against any emotional connection.

Emotional connections didn't last. It's why he'd hired her to keep things professional. Now he had proof that she was too good for him. On top of everything else, he was a liar. He wouldn't give her a second time.

No way was he going to further risk the life he'd so carefully choreographed for his son.

It was nearly nine o'clock when Maggie heard Jason's key in the penthouse door. Brady had gone to sleep over an hour ago and she was in her room, trying to read an article from a women's magazine on how to revitalize marital intimacy. One of the problems, and there were many, was that the information was based on a normal relationship. Nothing about her situation fell anywhere within normal limits.

She listened to the sound of his movements through the penthouse. First he checked on his son. Then she heard him in the kitchen and finally he went into his office to work. In the week since they'd returned from the mountains, the man had barely said two words to her. Maybe it was the fact that she spent so many hours of every day with an infant, but Maggie felt an overwhelming need for adult conversation.

This was new for her. Normally after six weeks she went on to a new situation and interacted with either a couple and their new infant, or a family needing an extra pair of hands during that first month and a half. Interaction was the key word.

After seven days and nights of the silent treatment from Jason Garrett, she'd had it. She slid off the bed and checked her hair in the mirror over the dresser. Brady was the sweetest baby in the whole world, but after twelve hours of feeding, burping, changing diapers, walking, bouncing, shushing and patting, she looked like something the cat yakked up.

The way Jason had been acting, she really shouldn't give a rat's behind about her appearance, but she did. She marched down the hall to see him, determined to have her adult conversation no matter what she looked like.

The door to his office was half-closed and she peeked inside, expecting to see him doing computer work. Her expectation couldn't be more wrong. He was sitting behind his desk, but that's as professional as he got. There was a bottle of whiskey in front of him and he was just tossing back the contents of a tumbler when he noticed her.

"Maggie."

She walked in and stopped in front of his desk. "You're not even working."

"Excuse me?"

"Jason, I need to talk to you."

"Is Brady all right? I just looked in on him and he was sound asleep. Did he—"

"He's fine."

"Then I don't understand—"

"That makes two of us."

His dark eyebrows drew together in a frown. "Is something wrong?"

Where did she start? "I need to talk to a grown-up. Someone who can articulate sounds of more than one syllable that actually make sense. Don't get me wrong. Brady is a sweetheart. And I adore him. But he's not exactly a scintillating conversationalist. I'm sure some day he'll be glib and charming. He's got the charm thing going for him already. But I really want to have a dialogue with someone who can talk back."

"I see." He glanced at the chairs in front of his desk. "Would you like to sit down for this dialogue? Or is it something that needs to be said standing up?"

"No. Sitting is fine." She moved around the chair, then lowered herself into it.

They stared at each other for several moments and the corners of his mouth turned up. "Do you want to start?"

"Okay." Now that she was here, she didn't quite know what to say. Go for the cliché. "How was your day?"

"Besides the fact that there aren't enough hours in it?" He shrugged. "It was all right."

"Did you make a gazillion dollars and buy Brady a college of his very own?"

He laughed. "No. But I'm working toward a merger that will guarantee financial security for him and all his dependents ad infinitum."

"The deal with Nathaniel Gordon?"

He gripped the empty glass and slowly turned it. "Yes."

"How's that going?"

"Suffice it to say that the road to financial security is not without speed bumps."

"Even with friends?"

"Especially with friends," he confirmed.

"I'm sorry."

"Don't be." He met her gaze. "Tell me what Brady did today."

She tried to ignore the pang of hurt that he'd turned the thread of conversation to his son. After all, that's why she was here in his home. Except he'd made love to her. Remembering his lips kissing her everywhere, his hands touching her everywhere and the way he'd made her feel everywhere sent shivers through her. Since they'd returned home, he'd behaved like it never happened. If only she could do that.

This part needed to be said standing up, so she did, then put her hands on her hips as she stared down at him. "Why are you avoiding me?"

"I don't know what you mean."

"Oh, please." She pointed to his glass. "There might not be enough hours in the day, but you're not using all of them to secure Brady's future."

"I'm entitled to down time." There was a defensive edge to his voice.

"You call it down time. I call it hiding."

"What the hell are you talking about?"

"You're gone at the crack of dawn and home later every night. So late that you don't have to interact with me at all. Everything is different."

"I have a lot of work to do."

She looked pointedly at the whiskey bottle and empty tumbler on his desk. "I can see that."

"What's gotten into you?"

That was her point. "Jason, you've been steering clear of me since we made love."

There. She'd said it.

"You're imagining that." The words were automatic and the fact that he didn't quite meet her gaze was clear evidence that he didn't believe it any more than she did.

"I know caring for an infant isn't rocket science. Or multi-bazillion-dollar business. But I'm good at what I do. Well trained and intuitive. My intuition tells me that things are not the same between us since we got back from the cabin. If one is splitting hairs, everything turned upside down the night we were snowed in. I know it, and your actions since then prove it. Don't patronize me by denying it."

"I have the utmost respect for what you do. If I didn't, I wouldn't have married you."

Her very own personal lesson in the art of the deal. But the deal changed when he took her to his bed.

She sat down again on the edge of the chair. It was the perfect place since she was on an emotional edge.

"We were as close as a man and woman can be and I'd expected—" She gripped her hands together in her lap but refused to look away. "I'd hoped it meant we'd turned a corner in this relationship."

"There's no corner to turn."

"What does that mean?"

The tension in his expression was a lot like the one he wore during sex, but in all probability he wasn't finding pleasure this time. "Maggie, that night was a circumstance that I should have handled better. It's a biological fact that men have needs—"

"As do women." She remembered the need grinding through her while in his arms with the snow falling softly outside the window. It was magical and he was chalking it up to simple biology. "I had this talk with Sister Margaret when I was twelve." She glared at him and stood up again. "Just because I was still a virgin, doesn't mean I was raised on the moon."

"No one said you were."

"Then why are you acting as if I just fell off the rocket booster?"

He ran his fingers through his hair. "The truth is that I don't know how to act."

"If you'd tell me what's wrong, we could work on it together, like married couples should."

Now he stood. Agitation did that to a person and she ought to know. She'd never in her life been as agitated as she was now.

"That's the thing, Maggie. We're not a couple. Not really. What we have is a business arrangement."

The words shouldn't have hurt so much, but they did. "I

thought after that night—" She swallowed hard. "We made love, not business. That shifted everything. And it's not just a clash of testosterone and estrogen."

"This is exactly the reason I intended to keep things strictly business."

"Define *things*."

"You. Me. Brady—" A darkness slid into his eyes as he stared at her. "Sex complicates everything. It was my mistake, and I take full responsibility for what happened."

"Unfortunately you can't take it back, either."

"No." He blew out a breath. "I have been avoiding you. It's all I can do to try and go back to the way things were."

"You're kidding, right?" She did an internal head shake at the absurdity of the male thought process.

"I'm completely serious. The reality is that we have a business arrangement and it can never be more than that because my only concern must be my son. Emotional entanglements complicate a situation. Assumptions are made. People get hurt. I don't want to do that to you."

"So the reason you won't talk to me is all about me?"

"That's one way of putting it. For your sake I've been keeping to myself. I would never hurt you, Maggie. Brady needs you."

She hadn't realized how much she wanted him to say he needed her until he didn't. So much for not hurting her. It was an effort not to let him see how much he *was*. Way past time to shift the focus of this ill-advised conversation.

"Speaking of Brady, this situation isn't good for him."

"What do you mean?"

"By avoiding me, you're sacrificing time with him." Putting aside her bruised feelings, Maggie realized it was true. The tension between them was costing Brady his father. That was unacceptable. "I think you're right."

"I am?"

She nodded. "We have to go back to the way things were before. I know you have a company to run. But all your free time should be spent with your child. He has to be your priority. I'm completely fine with that."

He looked surprised. "Really?"

"Absolutely." She walked around the chair and stopped halfway to the door. "I'm glad we had this talk. To clear the air."

"Good. Me, too."

"So don't stay out too late tomorrow."

He saluted. "Yes, ma'am."

She couldn't manage a smile and concentrated on getting out of the room before any of the emotions swirling inside her slipped out. Her chest and throat felt tight from holding back. If only she could dislike him, but he was being noble. Hurtful, but noble. His motives were above reproach. It was all about Brady. She loved that baby, too, with all her heart. That was the only reason she would try and do the impossible. She would do her very best to pull off a miracle and go back to the way things were before making love with Jason.

That meant shutting off her feelings, and she just didn't know how to pull that off.

So much for her dialogue with someone who could talk back. She wished she could take back the conversation. Now that he'd spelled everything out, the air might be cleared, but the confusion? Not so much. And she hurt more than ever.

## *Chapter Ten*

Jason parked his Lexus SUV in the medical building lot on Green Valley Parkway where the pediatrician had his office. He saw his car and driver in another space and knew Maggie was still here with the baby. One glance at the Rolex on his wrist told him the appointment time was a half hour ago. He'd hear about it; she was direct that way. A man always knew where he stood and what was on her mind.

Like when she'd said in no uncertain terms that avoiding her was costing him moments with his son. It had been a week since they'd cleared the air. Yeah. Right. If that were true, he wouldn't feel like he wanted to put his fist through a wall. Or explode. Or both.

He hurried through the lot and into the landscaped court-yard with medical offices on either side. Rocks were artfully arranged as a dry lake bed with water-smart plants in orange, yellow, purple and red scattered around for splashes of color.

After locating Dr. Steven Case's office, he walked into what felt like an alternate universe.

The waiting room was packed with women and small children. Some of the women with small children looked like they were children themselves. Or maybe he was older than he'd realized. This was Brady's four-month checkup. Jason had missed the two-month and Maggie had made her disapproval clear.

He tried to tell himself not repeating the mistake wasn't about that, but about being there for his son. Which was true. Her approval didn't matter to him one way or the other, and he almost believed that.

The office was done in shades of light green, blue and brown with textured paper on the walls. Generic upholstered chairs with wooden arms and legs interspersed with faux leather benches that lined the walls and, in the center of the room, formed a conversation area, although no one was actually conversing. He wasn't the only guy, but was definitely in the minority. This was primarily an XX chromosome zone. Some harried mothers were attempting to control toddlers whose patience had been tested to the limit. Others were doing their best to pacify infants who were not happy.

Had his mother ever sat with him in the pediatrician's office before she walked out on him forever?

The thought popped into his mind out of nowhere because he hadn't thought about her for a long time. His father had advised him not to waste energy on unimportant things and he'd believed that to be the case until being on his own with Brady showed him how important parenting was. Then Maggie walked through his front door and put a finer point on the lesson by showing him how important a mother was.

With some difficulty, Jason finally spotted Maggie in a corner with the baby. He walked over and sat beside her on the bench.

Maggie studied him. "Are you all right?"

Except for that mental hiccup a few moments ago he was great. "I'm fine."

"I was beginning to wonder if you were going to make it," she said.

"Has Brady been seen yet?"

"No."

"Then in doctor time I'm punctual."

She smiled. "He's glad you're here."

"Yeah. I can tell." He looked at his son, peacefully sleeping in the infant seat. "How come you're sitting all by yourself over here?"

"Haven't you ever heard that doctor's waiting rooms are a breeding ground for germs?"

"I guess I missed that breaking news."

"Well, it's true." She angled her head toward the most congested part of the waiting area by the receptionist's check-in window. "I'm trying to shield Brady from those mini microorganism makers over there. And I don't mean that in a good way. Granted, they're cute as can be, but they want to kiss him and touch him and we don't know where those hands have been."

He glanced over and nodded. "I would never have thought of that."

"That's what I'm here for."

That's what he kept telling himself. Brady needed her and to make sure he had her, Jason needed to keep *his* hands to himself. Not so easy when all he could think about was touching her again.

A door to the back office was opened by a young woman wearing blue scrub pants and a top with cartoon characters. "Brady Garrett?"

Maggie stood, a grim expression on her face. "Man your battle stations. We're up."

Jason lifted the car seat and followed her past the germ

section and into the inner sanctum where they were led to an exam room.

"Hi, I'm Lisa." She smiled. "Mrs. Garrett, if you'll get Brady undressed, I'll be back in a few moments to weigh and measure him."

"Okay."

When they were alone, Jason glanced at her grim expression and wondered if it was about being addressed as his wife, or disturbing Brady from a perfectly good nap. Or both. He liked hearing her called Mrs. Garrett.

She squatted down and undid the straps around the baby, then lifted him out. He squeaked and stretched and let out a whimper.

"He's not going to like this," she said. "I hope he pees all over the exam table."

"Retribution tactics. Is that really something you want to encourage?" he teased.

"When he's in therapy and the repressed memory surfaces after hypnosis, I'll take responsibility for the coping strategy. But you just wait until after he gets his shots. We'll talk again then."

"Shots? You didn't tell me there would be shots." He watched her undress the baby, who started to cry.

She cooed to the unhappy little guy. "I know, sweetie. I don't like this any more than you. I really hate to say this, but it's for your own good, pal."

"What about the shots?" Jason demanded.

"Immunizations. Four of them. One for every month of his little life. If I'd said anything, would you have shown up?"

"Of course."

"Well, I wish I didn't have to. We can put a man on the moon and build a space station in orbit. Wouldn't you think someone could figure out a way to immunize innocent babies in a noninvasive way?"

Before he could answer that, Lisa returned. "Okay, let's get his stats. If you'll put him on the baby scale, please."

Maggie picked Brady up and settled him on the contraption that, mercifully, had something to shield tender baby skin from the cold, unforgiving metal. Then the young woman measured his length and head circumference. In Brady's chart, she plugged the information into his growth graph.

"He's in the ninety-fifth percentile on everything."

Jason couldn't stop the grin. "An overachiever. That's my boy."

When Maggie cuddled his boy to her and the unhappy sounds instantly stopped, Lisa nodded. "Someone's getting pampered. Dr. Case will be in shortly."

As she was leaving, a tall man wearing blue scrubs walked in. "Hi, I'm Steve Case."

"We met in the hospital after Brady was born," he said, shaking hands. He'd seen no reason to explain the baby's biological mother wanted nothing to do with him. Jason had only talked with the doctor about the baby.

"I remember," the doctor said. "Hi, Maggie. How are you?"

"Good," she said.

She'd handled all the well-baby visits and had developed a rapport with the pediatrician. She was Brady's mother in every way that counted.

Dr. Case washed his hands at the sink, and while drying them with a paper towel, studied the notes on the chart. "His numbers look good. Let's see what's going on with Mr. Brady. If you'll put him on the exam table on his tummy."

Maggie did as directed and stood by protectively, her hand on his back. The baby immediately lifted his head and rolled to his back.

"Good job, buddy," the doctor said. "His weight and growth are right on the money. Do you have any concerns about his eating or sleeping patterns?"

"Yes," Maggie said. "When should I introduce solid food?"

When he pressed the stethoscope to Brady's chest, the

baby waved his hands, reaching for the long tube. "Just what I wanted to see." As he talked, he ran his hands over the baby—back, trunk and legs. After nodding with satisfaction, he looked at Maggie. "Keep doing what you're doing. We'll talk about cereal at his six-month visit. And vitamins. Let's let his system develop further before rocking the boat."

"Okay," she agreed. When the doctor removed the stethoscope, the baby started to cry and Maggie picked him up.

"My nurse made a note here that you might be holding Brady too much."

Maggie met his gaze. "I believe the term she used was *pamper,* but what she meant was *spoil.*"

"It's all right to let him cry sometimes," Dr. Case pointed out.

"Sometimes we do. But it's my—" she met Jason's gaze, but he figured she was doing fine "—it's our philosophy that when he cries, he's got a good reason. Figuring out what that reason is and reassuring him is the way to build trust. To make sure he knows that his needs will be met." She glanced around the room, her gaze settling on the scale. "This is an unfamiliar environment to him. He's stripped naked and cold. Then he's poked and prodded and feeling pretty vulnerable. In my opinion, he's got a good reason to express his dissatisfaction with the situation. And I *will* comfort him."

The doctor grinned. "Good for you."

Jason seconded that. Everything he'd done, all the frustration he felt in not touching her, was worth it when he thought about her not being there at all for Brady. That was unacceptable.

Dr. Case looked at both of them. "Next time we'll talk about what to expect in the coming months, including baby-proofing Brady's environment."

"Okay," they said together.

"If you have any routine questions, we're here during office hours. For emergencies, one of four doctors in the group is on call, so don't hesitate. Brady is doing great. Keep up the good work. My nurse will be back in a minute." He shook hands again, then left the room.

Maggie looked up and said, "I really hate this next part."

"Way to make me feel better."

"You're a big boy. It's not you I'm concerned about—"

Before she could finish that thought, Lisa was back with several syringes on a metal tray. This time her look was sympathetic. "I know this is difficult. Do you want to hold him?"

"Yes," Maggie said without hesitation.

The nurse was good at her job and it was over quickly, but Jason was a wreck. If there was any way he could have taken the medicine instead, he'd have done it in a nanosecond. The first poke sent Brady into a fit of hysterical crying. Maggie cuddled and comforted the baby and didn't seem to notice that he peed on her instead of the exam table.

"I know, sweetie. I'm so sorry. But it's going to be okay. I promise," she cooed against his cheek as he snuggled against her with absolute trust that his needs would be met. "Oh, my goodness, the tears."

Brady wasn't the only one. Jason saw the tears in her eyes, too, and his chest pulled tight.

"You're right," he said to her. "This part sucks."

For a man of action, this was a tough place to be. He wanted to comfort Brady, but his son wanted her and she was handling the situation better than he ever could. She was strong and sexy at the same time and it blew him away. Her bottomless capacity for caring made her as beautiful on the inside as she was on the outside. He shouldn't be thinking about any of that at a time like this, but he could because Brady wanted her, not him.

He'd bought his son a mother but making Maggie his wife in every sense of the word was a step he couldn't take. It would make everything personal and destroy the stability he was striving to provide his son. A stability he'd never known in his own life.

If he hadn't slipped up and made love to her, maybe this problem would be easier. But he *had* slipped up and made everything more difficult.

He'd tasted her intoxicating innocence and knew how sweet it felt to have her in his arms. Resisting her now was his hell to pay, because resist her he must.

Somehow.

Maggie felt like roadkill.

Her head hurt. Her throat was raw. And if there was any part of her body that didn't ache, she wasn't aware of it. The tightness in her chest made it hard to breathe, although that was much improved since her visit to Mercy Medical Center's E.R. She'd rather die than give what she had to the baby, so keeping to herself in her room was the only solution. In bed propped up with pillows, she was trying to work up enough oomph to look at the book on her nightstand even though reading it would take more energy than she could rally.

Jason peeked in her half-open door. "You're awake."

"What was your first clue?" Her voice was hoarse.

"Your eyes are open and you're sitting up. That's an improvement."

"If you say so."

He walked over to the bed and put his hand on her forehead. "How do you feel?"

"Go away." She shrank away from him and put her palm over her nose and mouth. "I'm contagious."

"I've already been exposed."

"Maybe. But now you're tempting fate. I'm in quarantine."

"A maxi-microorganism maker?"

"Yes. And if I taught you anything it's to stay away from people like me."

"Because the strategy worked so well for you," he said wryly. "Obviously you caught this at the pediatrician's office."

She'd already guessed that. "Is Brady sick?"

"No. He's fine."

"So the strategy worked. I'm probably run down." Brady had been up a lot at night. Probably teething. She hadn't had a lot of sleep lately. "The microorganisms found a fertile environment and invited all their friends to the party."

"They must have been having a good time judging by how sick you are."

She ducked out of range when he reached his hand out again. "Go away. It's not just your health I'm concerned about. I'm out of commission, and Ginger couldn't send anyone over on such short notice. Brady needs you to be in tip-top shape."

"I'll take the risk."

He was so lying. If he was really a risk taker, he'd have agreed to open up about why he'd pulled back from her. He'd have agreed to work on making what they had a marriage instead of a business arrangement. When she glanced up he was staring at her, intensity tightening his features. Had she said all that out loud? Her head felt as if it was filled with cotton so thinking straight was a challenge.

The mattress dipped from his weight when he sat on the bed beside her. Their thighs nearly touched. This time she had nowhere to go and his cool palm settled on her hot forehead. The sensation was so heavenly, she couldn't quite hold in a sigh.

"How do you feel?" he asked.

"You tell me."

"I think you still have a fever. In the E.R. they clocked you at a hundred and two."

"I still say it wasn't necessary to take me to Mercy Medical Center."

"Breathing shouldn't be that difficult. I made an executive decision." He brushed his knuckles over her cheek. "For the record, the doctor agrees with me."

"Executive decisions are what executives do."

"Speaking of executives, Mitch Tenney—"

"Who?" she croaked.

"The doctor in the E.R. at Mercy Medical. His name is Mitch Tenney. His wife is a behavior-modification coach who works with executives on strategies to resolve conflict in the work place."

"Oh?" She didn't feel much like talking or listening, but she liked having him there and that response took the least amount of effort to encourage conversation.

"Yeah. I've been thinking about instituting a corporate program like that, and he had some interesting information. It seems that not long ago he was encouraged to get counseling. That's how he met his wife—Samantha Ryan. Her father is the administrator at Mercy Medical."

"I see." When her nose started to run, she grabbed a tissue from the box next to her and mopped up. Part of her wanted him to go away and leave her alone to look like the wrath of God. The part that wasn't sick wanted him to stay forever.

"They're expecting a baby—Sam and Mitch."

"I didn't realize the E.R. was the hottest place in town for a male-bonding experience."

He had the audacity to grin. "We bonded over Brady. The doctor was quite taken with him since he'll be a father soon. And I met Dr. Cal Westen, an E.R. pediatrician. He's the guy in the group who doesn't see anyone in the Mercy Medical E.R. over eighteen. I'm told that kids are not just small adults and need doctors who understand that."

"I hope Brady never needs them, but it's good to know they're there."

"I got a lot of information while waiting for you."

"I'm sorry it was so long. You should have taken Brady home."

"And left you there?"

"I could have called a cab," she said.

"Transportation wasn't my biggest concern at the time." His grin disappeared and a worried frown took its place. "You had to have several breathing treatments to open up your airways."

"Apparently you and Dr. Tenney bonded over medical stuff, too."

"You had an asthma attack, Maggie."

"Thanks for the newsflash." She pulled at the tissue still in her hands.

"Have you ever had one before?"

"Yeah. But not—" She started coughing. At least it wasn't the tight sound of an asthmatic cough. It was deep and chesty and flulike.

"Damn it." Jason stood and left the room.

For Brady's sake it really was for the best that he keep his distance, although she instantly missed him. It was sweet that he actually seemed concerned about her. Genuinely worried that she was okay. She sighed again.

How stupid was she? Jason Garrett was a decent guy. If there was one thing she knew about him it was that he tried to do the right thing. His instincts registered in the noble range on the humanity scale. His recent attention was not evidence that his feelings had changed. It probably meant only that he didn't want her to stop breathing on his watch. And she was pathetic for even allowing the thought to enter her mind that it could be anything more.

She closed her eyes when she felt a pain in her chest, not entirely sure it had very much to do with the flu.

"Maggie?"

Jason's voice was a whisper, but it got her attention and she looked at him. He was standing beside the bed with a glass in his hand. There was a flex straw in the liquid.

He held it out. "Drink this."

"I'm not thirsty."

"Mitch said you need to hydrate. That means lots of fluids."

"I know what it means. You tend to hear it a lot when you have asthma attacks on a regular basis."

"You do?"

"Not anymore. Not since I was about sixteen or seventeen. I think as I grew my lungs got bigger and it allowed me to compensate. But when I was having the attacks, it was long enough."

"For what?"

"To keep me from being adopted." She met his gaze and saw the pity there. "Good Shepherd encourages families in the community to take in kids. They work with one of the local TV stations, do pictures on the Internet and everything possible to find permanent homes for the kids. It's not that no one wanted me—"

"But?"

Apparently her thoughts had taken a turn for the pathetic. She wished she could take back the words, but now that she'd told him, he wasn't likely to let it pass. "I had a medical problem that adoptive parents just didn't want to take on. So that's why Good Shepherd was my permanent home until I was eighteen."

He set the glass on the nightstand and settled beside her on the bed. "I'm sorry, Maggie."

"You have nothing to be sorry for." Well, maybe he should be sorry he couldn't love her. Her weakened condition was the only excuse for letting that thought form.

"It's a lousy thing to go through."

"What doesn't kill you makes you stronger." She shrugged.

The cliché was meant to be spunky speak but it must have come out pretty high on the pity scale because he maneuvered himself beside her and slid his arm behind her back, pulling her against him as he leaned against the piled-up pillows.

She should have protested that proximity to her was dangerous because she was highly contagious. She could have believed that her weakened condition made resistance too much effort. The truth was that his shoulder was nice to lean an aching head against. Having his arms around her simply felt too wonderful. Staying put meant letting down her guard, but the reward was so worth the risk.

She sighed and let her eyes drift shut. For just a little while she didn't have to put up a brave front and be strong. She could leave it all to Jason. The concept of not being completely on her own was incredibly appealing and she could be forgiven for wanting it to go on forever. It was a perfectly normal reaction to wish things were different. That *she* was different, the type of woman he could be attracted to.

Her eyes drifted closed as the fuzziness in her head took over. "If only I was someone you could love even though your father doesn't want you to," she whispered.

Had she said that out loud?

Of course not. She wouldn't do that. It was just the flu talking, making her head fuzzy. She felt like roadkill, but if there was a silver lining, it was that finally she was in bed with her husband.

## *Chapter Eleven*

"Jason, you must have better things to do than come with me to Good Shepherd."

In the penthouse foyer, he picked up the baby in his car seat, then slung the diaper bag over his shoulder. "Not really."

"It's not that exciting. Lots of kids. Making meals. Doing crafts." She shrugged. "You'll probably be bored out of your mind."

"It's my mind." He smiled. "Boring sounds nice after all the excitement recently."

It had taken almost a week, but he noticed the shadows beneath her big blue eyes were finally fading and there was a little color in her cheeks. The well-worn jeans and Good Shepherd T-shirt tucked into the loose waistband showed that she'd lost weight during her illness. Definitely too much excitement. He liked order and stability and that didn't happen when Maggie wasn't in tip-top form. He wanted her strong and sassy and in his face about whatever was her current peeve.

When she tilted her head to the side, her dark, silky pony-tail brushed her thin shoulder. "But after a long work week, I thought you enjoyed time alone with Brady."

"We had lots of bonding time when you were sick."

And that was the reason he wasn't letting her do the volunteer shift by herself. A relapse wasn't happening on his watch. She hadn't been out of bed that long and he intended to make sure she didn't push herself too hard. He didn't ever want to be as scared as when he'd watched her struggle to draw air into her lungs. And she didn't know it yet, but she wasn't staying overnight.

"You're sure about this?" she asked.

"I've never been more sure of anything."

"Okay." Her tone filled in the part about it being his funeral.

He drove them in the Lexus with Maggie in the front passenger seat and Brady in the rear. This was the first time the three of them had gone anywhere without a driver. It felt so amazingly—normal. Father, son and…mother? Something shifted inside him and he wasn't at all comfortable with it.

Using Maggie as his GPS, Jason followed her instructions and within fifteen minutes they pulled up in front of the old Victorian with the sign out front that proclaimed Good Shepherd Home for Children. After exiting the SUV with the baby and his stuff, they waited on the porch after ringing the bell.

An older woman answered. "Maggie!"

Maggie hugged her. "Hi, Sister Margaret."

This was the woman who'd found her as an infant on this very porch. Jason wasn't sure what he'd expected, maybe wings and a halo. To him the nun looked pretty ordinary in her faded-black slacks, pink-, purple-and-white striped cotton blouse. Her hair was short, gray-streaked brown and her eyes pale blue.

When Maggie pulled out of the hug, she glanced at him and held out a hand indicating the baby, asleep in his car seat.

"That is Brady Hunter Garrett and this is his father. Jason, this is Sister Margaret Connelly."

He held out his hand. "It's a pleasure to meet you, Sister."

"Likewise." When she put her fingers in his the effects of hard work were evident.

She smiled approvingly at him. "Mr. Garrett, I don't know what Maggie said to prompt your generosity toward Good Shepherd, but I can't thank you enough. If not for you, the home would probably have been shut down by now."

"I'm glad I could help."

He glanced at Maggie. Since she was putting a lot of effort into avoiding his gaze after *not* introducing him as her husband, the look on her face could only be guilt. Obviously, she hadn't broadcast the news of their marriage to Sister Margaret. The details were something he didn't talk about, either, but he wasn't a snap to read. Maggie must have been one of the easy ones to raise. If she ever tried to pull a fast one, the evidence would be right there in her eyes. Innate honesty was just one more thing about her to like.

"Let me show you what we've been able to do with your donation," Sister Margaret said.

"I'm not here for an accounting of the funds," he assured her.

Sister laughed. "I didn't think you were. But it would mean a lot to me for you to see that the money has been well spent."

"All right then."

"I'll just go see the kids," Maggie said.

"Come with us, Maggie," Sister protested. "The older ones just started watching a movie. The little ones are napping. And I know you've been sick. Don't wear yourself out."

Jason liked the way this woman thought. "That's what I've been trying to tell her."

"Follow me," Sister said.

As she hurried ahead, Jason leaned down so only Maggie

could hear. "Someone's been fibbing to the nun. Is that like lying to God?"

"I didn't tell an untruth to anyone." Her eyes flashed indignantly.

"At the very least it's a lie of omission to conceal the fact that we're married."

The flash disappeared from her eyes, replaced by something that made him wish for indignance. "You can't have it both ways, Jason."

"What does that mean?"

"Being married when it suits you and not thinking about it the rest of the time." The baby picked that moment to wake up and cry. "We both know we're married in name only."

Except for that one time at the cabin a couple weeks ago. And she couldn't be more wrong. He thought about it a lot, then took a cold shower whenever possible.

Sister Margaret walked back to them and looked sympathetically at the crying infant. "I didn't mean to lose you. I'm so used to hurrying. There's always something waiting to be done."

"If it's all right with you, Sister, I'll stay here and feed Brady."

"Of course, dear." She looked up at him. "This way, Mr. Garrett."

"Jason, please."

"All right."

After taking him through the bathrooms and kitchen to proudly show off the new plumbing fixtures and appliances, she led him outside and pointed out the brand-new roof, red tiles that contrasted with the beige stucco and stood out against the clear blue sky. The house was situated on at least an acre of property in the older section of Henderson. There was a playground with swings, jungle gym and other pieces of equipment set up on the more forgiving rubberized ground instead of blacktop.

For the older kids there was a basketball court, volleyball nets and baseball backstop.

"This is quite a place you have, Sister."

"I wish there was no need for a home like this," she said. "Unfortunately Las Vegas needs even more. It bothers me that I can't help all the children who are disadvantaged and deprived."

"I'm glad you were here for Maggie." He hadn't meant to say so, no matter that it was true.

"I remember the night Sister Mary and I found her. It was freezing outside." She shook her head. "She was so tiny, and so quiet. She never cried. It's a miracle we found her out there. If we hadn't…"

He was glad she didn't finish the thought. It wasn't something he wanted to hear because he couldn't imagine a world without Maggie's sweetness in it. "She told me that her asthma kept her from being adopted."

"It's true. A couple came very close to taking her once, but money and medical insurance were an issue. After it didn't work out Maggie asked why they couldn't love her. The children can't understand financial or other considerations, so they personalize everything." Sister looked up. "It was a conversation that broke my heart. Maggie is very special and very easy to love."

The words and look made him squirm because he didn't believe in a love that would last forever. The only kind he understood was what he felt for Brady.

He glanced over his shoulder at the house. "We should find Maggie. See if she needs a break from the baby."

They walked back inside and went to the kitchen where Maggie was sitting on one of the long benches. An empty bottle of formula was on the wooden table beside her and she had Brady over her shoulder, patting his back to burp him.

"Hi. What do you think of the place?" she asked him.

"Very nice."

Sister looked proud. "Because of your help with the

building contractors, Jason, we had enough money left over from the absolutely necessary repairs to have the inside painted and start a scholarship fund."

"I'm glad to hear that." He made a mental note to pad that scholarship fund a little more. He looked down at Maggie and said, "You look tired. Let me take Brady."

"Okay." She kissed the boy's cheek before handing him up.

"Hey, buddy," Jason said, putting Brady over his shoulder. The boy let out a big belch and he laughed. "He begs your pardon, Sister, but it's a sound that does a father proud."

Sister smiled as she gazed at them. "You work well together. Like a regular family."

"In a way," he said, glancing at Maggie. He wasn't going to rat her out and tell Sister the terms of their agreement. "But we're not very traditional."

"Neither is this home, but we're a family nonetheless." Sister shrugged. "You can't change the hand you're dealt, but it's how you play the game that makes the difference. Family is what you make for yourself."

"Or don't make," he said, because he chose not to play at all.

Sister leaned a hip against the table as she frowned up at him. "Why would you do that? Why would you choose not to be part of a family?"

"It's safer." He and Maggie both understood that.

"Then you're shortchanging yourself." She took them both in with a look that suggested she could read minds. "The Bible teaches that faith, hope and love are virtues. And the greatest of these is love."

"If it's the greatest," he said, "then love has the most potential for pain."

"You're very cynical, Jason." She folded her arms over her chest. "What—or should I say who—made you that way?"

"My father," he answered. If anyone but Sister Margaret had asked, he would have shut them down. But she was a nun.

"Other than Brady, he's my only family. Whatever virtues I have—or don't have—are because of him."

And that's why he needed Maggie. His father had hammered home the fact that loving someone was the first step to losing them. He'd been raised on cynicism. She was sweetness and light to his darker side. Optimistic to his pessimistic. Loving to counterbalance his deliberate detachment. It was the only way he knew how to be and it wasn't good enough anymore because he wanted better for Brady.

Mental backspace and delete. Correction: his son needed Maggie. Jason wouldn't let himself need her or anyone else again.

Late at night when she tiptoed into the kitchen, Maggie noticed the dim light beneath the microwave was on. Jason must have forgotten to turn it off. She filled a mug with water and set it inside the appliance to heat. Maybe a cup of chamomile tea would help her to sleep.

"Is something wrong, Maggie?"

Heart pounding, she whirled at the unexpected sound of his voice. Jason was sitting at the dinette, which was shrouded in shadow.

"Good grief, you startled me." She pressed a hand to her chest. "I didn't see you there."

"Are you all right? Is Brady settled?"

"He's fine. I got him back to sleep a few minutes ago. I think he might be teething." While the microwave hummed beside her, she leaned against the counter.

"You think? Aren't you the baby expert?"

"Aside from the fact that babies are unpredictable and can't talk to tell us what's wrong," she said. "My area of expertise is birth to six weeks. After that I move on."

"Until I convinced you to stay," he said.

"Yes." They both knew why she was here and she didn't

want to talk about it. "What are you doing up? Did Brady's crying wake you? I tried to soothe him quietly but he—"

"It wasn't that." He lifted a small glass to his mouth and three guesses said it wasn't chamomile tea. "And thanks for taking care of him. Technically this is your night off."

But Brady had long ago stopped being a job. She loved him, and he'd needed her to comfort him. It was probably a good thing she'd let herself be talked out of staying at Good Shepherd.

"It was pretty underhanded of you to get Sister Margaret on your side. Two against one was not a fair way to keep me from staying the night as usual."

"You're stubborn and I needed a good wingman. Or nun," he said.

She laughed. "Sister Margaret would like that. The 'wing-nun.'"

"She's pretty cool. You were lucky to have her growing up."

"I know."

"She's got good instincts, and I think you picked up on that while you were at Good Shepherd."

Something in his voice bothered Maggie. The sandpaper edges were ragged and she didn't think it was about Brady teething.

She took her warm water from the microwave, put her teabag in it, then joined him at the table. The shadows in this corner were her friend since she was wearing an old Runnin' Rebels T-shirt with no bra underneath and a pair of plaid cotton pajama bottoms. The fashion police could just suck it up.

Jason wasn't dressed for bed, unless he slept in worn jeans and a long-sleeved white cotton shirt. With his long legs stretched out and crossed at the ankles, she noticed his feet were bare and wondered why she found that so incredibly intimate. And worse, so amazingly arousing.

She pulled out a chair at a right angle to him and sat. "What's wrong, Jason?"

He looked at her and a spark of amusement had his mouth curving up at the corners. "Aren't we Miss No-Nonsense tonight?"

"Like you said, I've learned from the best. Sister Margaret is the queen of no-nonsense. So don't try to change the subject. Something's bothering you or you'd be asleep."

He stared at her for so long it appeared he wasn't going to answer. Finally, he sighed. "It was something Sister said about the three virtues."

"I remember. The greatest of these is love." She met his gaze. "And when you said love provides the greatest potential for pain, I saw the look on your face."

"What look?" He didn't move, but the tension rolling off him was almost palpable. "What did you see?"

"That someone had hurt you badly. Who was it, Jason?"

"Do I have to pick?"

He was trying to make light of it, but she refused to be sidetracked. At least not without a fight. She had him on the ropes. Now was the time to ask what she most wanted to know. The question he was least likely to answer. "Have you ever been in love?"

"Yes."

For some reason that surprised her. Not just that he responded, but because he admitted he'd cared deeply. She knew he was capable. His deep feelings for Brady were proof. But caring for a woman seemed unexpected. "Who?"

"April Petersen."

She waited but more details were not forthcoming. He was going to make her work for it. "When?"

"My first year of college. I was almost nineteen."

By now she knew the only way she'd get this story was question by question. "What happened?"

"Why did something have to happen? Couldn't it just not have worked out?"

She shook her head. "That's not what the look on your face said. Definitely something went down and it wasn't happy."

"There was a third party involved."

"She cheated on you?" Maggie asked, outraged for him. He was Jason Garrett. Who in their right mind would jeopardize love and a beautiful future with him?

"No." He smiled, but there was no humor in it. "At least not that I know of."

"Then I don't understand. Why didn't it work out?"

"Because my father paid her a great deal of money to disappear from my life."

She blinked at him, waiting for the "gotcha." When he stared back, misery in his eyes, she knew he wasn't kidding. "That's just nuts," she said.

For the first time since joining him, a genuine smile touched his lips. "I'll be sure to tell Hunter you said that."

"I'd welcome the opportunity to ask him what the heck he was thinking."

"Heck?" One dark eyebrow rose. "I do believe that's a four-letter word coming from you."

"It's a four letter word, period," she scoffed. "And you're changing the subject. Why would your father do something like that? Couldn't he wait until the fire of young love burned itself out? That's what usually happens."

The guy she'd fallen for had proved that.

"My father found out that April and I were planning to elope."

"Okay." She nodded. "That's a little more serious and deserving of some fatherly intervention. But there's intervention and there's *intervention*. He couldn't have initiated a father-son dialogue to tell you it was a foolish, crazy idea?"

"That's not the way Hunter operates." He toyed with his glass. "He bought me friends, tutors and eventually admission to a college that supposedly had no openings. I learned that if you throw enough money at a problem, you can make it go away. And that's what he did with April."

Again she recalled his earlier words. Whatever virtues I have—or don't have—are because of him. Where was his mother? Too preoccupied by Jason's relationship with Brady's mother, Maggie couldn't remember if he'd ever mentioned the woman who'd brought him into the world. In for a penny, in for a pound. All he could do was tell her to mind her own business.

"What about your mother? Did she have any opinions on your elopement?"

"I wouldn't know. She left him when I was a kid."

Between the lines she heard that his mom left and didn't take him with her. But this was his mother. He must have some feelings about it but he didn't say more. A cold, unformed sort of dread seeped into her.

"Okay, so Hunter ran the show. But buying off your fiancée? Who does that?"

Irony was rife in the look he settled on her. "Isn't the better question—what kind of woman would go along with taking money to dump me?"

More coldness crept in. "She was young, too—"

"She swore to love me forever. She made declarations of unwavering faithfulness until my father put enough zeros on a check to get her attention. The next thing I knew she decided things wouldn't work out for us and walked away. Not long after, Hunter was only too happy to share the details."

Maggie rubbed her thumb on the handle of her mug. "Are you still in love with her?"

"April?"

"No. Barbarella," she teased. "Of course April."

He smiled. "No, I'm not still in love with her. And you're right. She was very young. So was I. That doesn't mean I wasn't ticked off at him for a very long time. And her." His hand tightened around the glass. "Anyway, to be honest, now that I have a son, I understand where my father was coming from."

"Where?"

"He was trying to prevent me from making a monumental mistake."

"Marriage is serious," she agreed. "But why did you feel the need to take that step? Why not just live together? I'm assuming you went away to college. You probably had a certain amount of freedom. Why take legal steps to make it permanent?" That time. As opposed to now with her and his need to ensure his son would have continuity of child care.

"Does it matter? That was a long time ago. She *was* young, but she couldn't cash that check fast enough. Obviously she never loved me as much as I—" He stopped, then tossed back the remainder of the liquid in his glass. "Forget it. I don't remember why I felt the need to get married." The look on his face said different. "Young and stupid. It's my story, and I'm sticking to it."

She nodded, knowing it was useless to push further no matter how much she wanted to understand why he kept her at a distance. "In general you're not especially chatty and in touch with your feminine side. That's more than I thought you'd say."

"Maybe I just knew resistance was futile because you learned from the best and I learned from…Hunter."

The cold feeling inside her chased away all the warmth. He'd learned from his father how to buy people off. In her case it was about securing permanent child care, but he'd paid for her services just the same. Clearly he didn't feel his father had been the best influence and didn't trust himself not to utilize the behavior he'd picked up in that environment. Who could blame Jason when his only role model was in financial negotiations with wife number four and already engaged to number five?

Jason refused to risk making the same mistakes and based

marriage on a business arrangement instead of emotions. He refused to open his heart, and that made her incredibly sad because she wanted very much for him to let her in.

Who would have guessed that an abandoned baby who grew up in an orphanage would be the lucky, well-adjusted one? He'd respected her instincts, but she wished for more worldly instincts that would help her heal his wounded soul. She hurt for his hurt and wanted to put her arms around him to take away his pain. She wished it were as easy and uncomplicated as soothing his son after immunizations.

But there was nothing simple and easy about the way she felt. With little or no effort she could fall head over heels in love with Jason Garrett.

And that was a problem, because he was right. If love is the greatest virtue, it *did* have the greatest potential for pain. Somehow, she had to stop feelings that were picking up momentum like a runaway train.

# Chapter Twelve

**M**aggie listened intently to Savannah Cartwright, the Mommy & Me instructor at Nooks & Nannies, The Nanny Network Child Care and Learning Center. Sitting cross-legged on the floor with Brady in front of her, she smiled down at him and rubbed his belly as directed. "Does that feel good, big guy?"

Brady smiled and laughed, vigorously moving his arms and legs in response. He babbled happily and the sound was so joyful it was almost impossible for Maggie to be sad. Almost, but not quite. It was hard learning to coexist with a man who made it clear he would never be part of a couple. A man she couldn't stop thinking about with his shirt, and everything else, off.

She'd tried to keep him out of her heart and then he'd been so sweet and solicitous when she was sick. Were those the actions of a man who didn't care? But then she'd found out that love had kicked him in the teeth. No wonder he wanted no part of it again.

Petite, blond and twentysomething, Savannah squatted on

the rug beside her, smiling down at Brady. "You're a happy fella, aren't you?"

His arms and legs stilled while he stuffed a chubby fist in his mouth, intently studying the stranger.

The instructor looked around at the other women interacting with their children and said, "Brady is responding appropriately to his environment and the situation. I'm unfamiliar. He's communicating that by ceasing the happy, carefree movements of moments ago. When he gets to know me, he'll smile with pleasure at a recognizable face, just like the rest of the babies who have been coming for a while."

There were eight in the class, sixteen if you counted the babies. Maggie's new normal was trying to get back her pre-sex mentality toward Jason. Now she knew more about his trust issues and that she needed to focus all her energy on growing Brady instead of growing a relationship with his father. She'd joined the class that morning and didn't feel the need for full public disclosure about the fact that she wasn't Brady's biological mother.

Savannah smiled at the baby, then continued coaching the group. "Remember, tummy time is about developing your baby's interest in the world through sensory perception. Just like the massage techniques we practiced earlier it's about giving your baby generous amounts of attention to make him or her feel comfortable, safe and secure. All the skills these babies are developing by turning toward sounds, looking at and tracking interesting sights facilitates learning and helps them connect with loved ones."

Like the other women there, Maggie rubbed, gently scratched, tickled and touched Brady's tummy, making him laugh as he rolled from side to side. She watched carefully for all the signs that he'd had enough and when the reactions to stimulation were less enthusiastic, she picked him up and cuddled him to her.

Savannah nodded approvingly. "Way to go, Maggie. Reading your baby is important. When the current activity is not energizing the child, it's time to stop. Too much of a good thing and all that."

Pride might be a sin, but Maggie couldn't help being pleased with herself. She'd never cared for a baby into this stage of life and to know her instincts were on target made her feel good. She remembered what Jason had said about getting her good intuition from Sister Margaret while growing up at Good Shepherd. The stab of unhappiness at remembering that conversation with him made her realize again how many memories she was making that would have him as the star.

Savannah looked at the clock on the wall, then at everyone on the floor. "Time is up for today, ladies. I'll look forward to seeing you all here next week."

Maggie settled Brady on the portable pad she'd brought and changed his diaper, then gathered all her things while the other women moved off to the side to chat. She felt like an outsider, and not just because she was the new kid on the block. To make friends she'd have to share part of herself and she just couldn't.

She walked out of the room and down the hall, on her way to the parking lot where the driver and car waited. As she passed an office, someone called to her. She poked her head in the room and saw Ginger Davis. An attractive woman with short blond hair sat in a visitor chair in front of her desk.

"Hi, Maggie."

Ginger had to be right around fifty, but hardly looked a day over thirty-nine. Her brown hair fell in layers to her shoulders and was fashionably highlighted.

She smiled at her former boss. "Ginger. I didn't know you'd be here."

"I had a meeting and here at the learning center was the most convenient place for it." She looked at the woman. "This is Casey Thomas. Casey, meet Maggie Shepherd. She used to work for The Nanny Network, until receiving an offer she couldn't refuse. She recently got married."

Casey smiled. "Congratulations."

"Thanks," Maggie answered, feeling like a fraud for impersonating a happily married woman.

"Casey came in for her yearly evaluation. She's retired from the military. The army's loss is The Nanny Network's gain."

"Wow," Maggie said. "Taking care of kids is really a big change for you."

Casey nodded. "In a good way."

"Don't let me interrupt you," Maggie said.

"I was just leaving." Casey stood and looked at Ginger. "Thanks for understanding where I'm coming from."

Her ex-boss nodded. "It's exactly what I need to know to match you with the right client. I appreciate your time and honesty, Casey."

"No problem." She passed Maggie in the doorway. "Nice to meet you."

"Same here."

When they were alone, Maggie walked into the office. Ginger stood and moved from behind the desk, resting a hip on the corner. In her olive-green crepe pantsuit and low-heeled pumps, she looked every inch the business woman, attractive and successful. But Maggie had heard bits and pieces of her personal history, not the complete background check the woman did on prospective employees, but enough to know her past hadn't been speed-bump free.

"Maggie, what are you doing here?"

"I brought Brady to the—" She hesitated, feeling weird even saying it.

"Mommy & Me?" Ginger asked.

"Yes." She sat in the visitor chair Casey had just vacated.

Ginger looked down at the baby in the car seat who was studying her with dark eyes very much like his father's. A wistful, painful expression flashed across her face, then disappeared. "He is an absolutely adorable baby."

"You'll get no argument from me." Again she remembered Jason saying the same thing.

"So, how's married life?"

Maggie smiled as widely as possible and it made her cheeks hurt. "Fantastic. Could not be more wonderful."

"And Jason?"

"He's pretty amazing."

At least that part wasn't a lie. The man was honorable, caring, handsome, sexy and out of reach. The fact that he'd married someone like her was pretty amazing. And then there was the sex....

"Really?" Ginger's brown eyes seemed to burrow inside her, as if she could see all that festered there. "You know, we never did have a chance to discuss your situation. It was all so sudden. Was it love at first sight?"

"Something like that."

"Is this fantastic, couldn't-be-more-wonderful marriage everything you thought it would be?"

"And more." And less, Maggie admitted only to herself.

Ginger shook her head, a clear indication she wasn't buying the act. "What's wrong? There's something you're not telling me."

Maggie sighed and shook her head. "Am I that easy to read?"

"What's going on?" Ginger asked.

"I was determined to leave Jason's after six weeks. I even told him the sad story of why my terms are in place. He ignored it all and proposed marriage, security for all of us. In exchange, he agreed to give the Good Shepherd Home the money to make the necessary building repairs so they could pass the state inspection."

"Oh, Maggie—" Ginger frowned. "He paid you money to marry him?"

"It sounds weird and cheap when you say it like that. But essentially—yes."

"What are your expectations from this marriage?"

"It would be easier if you asked what they were when I agreed to it."

"Okay." Ginger folded her arms over her chest. "Start there."

"All I could think about was Good Shepherd closing and what would happen to the kids. The system is already over-crowded and they'd have nowhere to go. I love that place," she said simply. "I had to do something and Jason gave me a solution. On top of that, I wanted to stay with Brady. Selfish, I admit, but true." She looked down at the now-sleeping infant and smiled tenderly. "Beyond that I wasn't thinking."

"That's obvious." Ginger studied her. "Also obvious is that you don't look happy."

"I'm just tired." More than usual, actually, which she couldn't entirely explain away by chalking it up to the energy drain of caring for an infant.

"This is me and I'm not buying that. There's more you're not saying." Ginger shook her head. "I can't believe this. I feel so responsible."

"But why?"

"I sent you to him. He had a crisis situation and you're the best under those circumstances. It never occurred to me that he'd make an indecent proposal."

"It wasn't indecent. He's the most decent man I've ever met. He's—"

"What?"

How did she answer that? How could she put into words what he was like now that she'd experienced the amazingness of being in his arms, of joining in the most personal way? She knew the incredible, profound bond a man and woman could share and it was magical. But she wanted more magic. She wanted him.

Ginger watched intently when she said, "Tell me, Maggie, do you want a real relationship with Jason?"

For one perfect evening she'd had it all, everything she'd ever yearned for. Remembering made her response simple. "A marriage in every sense of the word is exactly what I want."

"All right then." Ginger tapped her lip. "You need to let him know."

"I already tried that. We had a talk and he doesn't feel the same. He's pretty damaged from some stuff in his past."

"I knew his mother. And I've met his father. I can see where he'd have 'stuff.'" Ginger's expression was grim. "But really, Maggie, has your life been a fairy tale?"

"Of course not."

"Mine, either. But you have to move on and if there's an opportunity for happiness, you reach out and grab it or life passes you by." Ginger took a breath. "We're all damaged in one way or another. Get over it."

"So what are you saying?" Maggie asked.

"You have to fight for him."

"I told you, I already did—"

"That was conversation. I'm talking about fighting dirty."

Maggie blinked. "I don't know what you mean. Dirty? I'm not sure—"

"I'm saying use every weapon in your female arsenal. Candles. Wine. Lingerie."

"Seduce him?" Maggie blushed.

Ginger grinned. "That's the spirit."

She was being advised to seduce her husband, something Maggie couldn't imagine Sister Margaret telling her to do. Yet it didn't feel wrong. Jason had wanted her once or he wouldn't have taken her to his bed. The intense expression he wore ever since was identical to the way he'd looked that night. If it was anything to go by, he still wanted her.

What was wrong with helping the situation along?

\* \* \*

In the nursery glider chair, Jason moved slowly back and forth with his almost-asleep son cradled against him. A chubby little hand rested over his heart. The sight tapped into a deep well of tenderness that sometimes threatened to swamp him. He would do anything for this child, give him anything he wanted even though he knew from personal experience that indulgence and interference weren't the preferred parenting style. That's why he was counting on Maggie. In the future when he agreed to some outrageous excess Brady requested, Maggie would remind him to initiate a father-son dialogue to tell him it was a foolish, crazy idea.

Brady stirred and sighed, his little fingers clutching Jason's shirt. The time he spent with his son in the evening was the best part of his day. Tonight was even more special because normally at bedtime the baby wanted Maggie.

Jason wanted her at bedtime, too, in a grown-up way. And every night he fought against it. Her recent illness had scared the crap out of him and he'd had to hold her, just to reassure himself she was okay. But feeling her soft skin and even softer curves in his arms had tested the hell out of his willpower and pushed him to the edge of resistance. If she hadn't been sick he wouldn't have been able to stop himself.

She was something else, he thought. Strong and straight-forward. Like the night she'd confronted him about hiding from her. He still wasn't quite sure how she got him to admit she was right. The fact that his body told him he was ready for her made his declaration about wanting to go back to their pre-sex relationship all the more absurd.

It couldn't be more ironic that he'd had no trouble sleeping with women before he was married. Now that he'd tied the knot, sleeping with this particular woman was a major problem. His head was telling him hands off. His hands were in favor of ignoring his head. In fact, the majority of his physical components were rallying for sexual relief, which meant throwing out all the sensible and sane reasons for denying himself.

He rubbed Brady's back. "What's a dad to do, buddy?"

As the baby grew more limp in his arms, Jason figured it was time to see if he was deeply asleep. He stood and very gently set the boy on his back in the crib. Long, dark lashes fanned out just above his healthy round cheeks. After pulling up the blanket, he brushed the dark hair off Brady's forehead, then leaned down and kissed him.

"I love you, son."

The boy sighed in his sleep as if he'd heard and understood and Jason's heart swelled with feelings so big he had no words to describe them.

He turned on the night-light and grabbed the baby monitor as he left the room in search of Maggie. After giving her an update, he'd go hide in his study and try to get her out of his mind by concentrating on the work he'd brought home.

Next to the nursery, he found her bedroom empty, although looking at her neatly made bed filled him with the need to hold her again. Maybe she was busy in the kitchen. The thought was so completely normal a part of him ached for that to be true. But, in his life, he'd ached for a lot of things that couldn't happen.

"Maggie—" He poked his head in the kitchen and found it empty. Except for his memories. This was where he'd talked to her about the past—about April and his mother.

Maybe Maggie had decided to work out. The last time he'd found her there he'd kissed her. The memory fired his blood like a match within breathing distance of kerosene. Now that he knew what the woman looked like naked, seeing her in workout shorts and tank top would sorely tempt him to separate her from them.

Steeling his self-control for the sight of her on the treadmill, he opened the door. He wasn't sure whether the empty room or his frustration was more disturbing. Memories of her were everywhere. She'd certainly made her imprint on the penthouse, and quite possibly himself. The only place she hadn't left her mark was his bedroom and if he was smart, he'd go there now to hide. But he needed to let her know the baby was in for the night.

Where the heck was she?

This was different, and a niggling sense of unease trickled through him. He passed the empty living room, then glanced into his office where he saw flickering light. It took several moments to realize candles were lit. And Maggie was there, setting a bottle of wine and two glasses on his desk.

"Maggie?"

She whirled around, her hand to her chest. "Jason—you startled me."

Welcome to the club, he thought, staring at her. Over the faint vanilla scent of the candles, he smelled the floral fragrance that mixed with her skin and was uniquely Maggie. She was barefoot and wearing a strapless cotton sundress. It was a change from the jeans and T-shirt she'd worn at dinner. Her hair was loose, also different from her usual utilitarian ponytail. The dark, shiny, silken strands made his fingers itch to touch.

"I've been looking all over for you."

"You found me." She shrugged and the movement drew his attention to her bare, slender shoulders.

His mouth went dry and he was in serious danger of swallowing his tongue. His acute sexual awareness of her almost kept him from noticing that she looked ill at ease.

"Brady's asleep," he said, setting the baby monitor on his desk.

"He was really tired from our outing at Nooks & Nannies today."

"At the learning center."

She nodded and strands of hair caressed her shoulder. "A

class for babies. The stimulation is geared to this stage of his development to help him learn to feel comfortable, safe and secure in his environment."

One glance at the flimsy elastic holding up her dress sent Jason's environment into stimulation heaven. His brain was still functioning because he got the message loud and clear to escape while he still could.

"Okay, then. I just wanted to let you know he's in for the night and you're off duty." He backed up a step. "I'll say good-night—"

"Wait—" She swallowed and twisted her fingers together. "I mean—well, I was thinking that you might like some wine. With me. Maybe. We could share a glass. Actually, you could even have your own." She laughed nervously. "There's a whole bottle. I opened it just in case."

What was she up to? Stupid question because he had a pretty good idea. It wouldn't be the first time a woman had come on to him, but this was definitely the most inexperienced technique he'd ever encountered. And he found it disconcertingly charming. After the one and only time he'd made love to her, he'd wanted her again within minutes. Every minute since had only increased the need to have her. And this inept, innocent seduction made his need unbearable.

"What are you doing, Maggie?"

"I'm just trying to open the lines of communication between us."

"It won't work." His tone was harsher than he'd intended, but he was running out of places to hide from her. He needed to tap into his inner bastard because he was really starting to question the importance of common sense and nobility.

"The last time I checked, talking was pretty simple," she said.

"If talk was all you wanted, you'd be wearing clothes."

She looked down, then pressed her palms to her yellow-cotton covered midriff, just below her breasts. "These are clothes."

"Not for you. You're the jeans-and-T-shirts type."

"The weather's warmer."

It was definitely warm and not because of the weather. "It's not going to work. I'm not going to take you to bed."

"We're married," she pointed out. "And we've already been down that road. So why not again?"

"If I'd known you were a virgin I'd never have touched you."

"You've made that abundantly clear and it doesn't make any more sense to me now. It's like trying to restore computer data after hitting the Delete button."

"That would be a lot easier." He dragged his fingers through his hair. "Maybe it's a guy thing. But I can't forget that you waited all this time for the right man. That makes you a responsibility. Personal. What we have is strictly business."

"Maybe at first. But remember—as they say on children's programming—walk backward through your mind to the beginning. I fulfilled my part and took care of Brady."

"You do an outstanding job."

"I know. It's not a job because I love him." She smiled tenderly. "You're the one who drew a line in the sand. You're also the first one who crossed it. You kissed me and we tried to ignore that. You crossed your own line again and the kiss led to consummation of our understanding. To me that spells *pattern*. In a married kind of way. So I'm not buying it when you keep playing the business card."

He realized if she hadn't become a nanny, she'd have made a hell of a lawyer. It was imperative to get control of this conversation. "I deliberately structured the agreement to steer clear of emotional considerations. Believe it or not, I'm doing this for you."

"It doesn't feel that way," she said, a bleak expression in her eyes.

"I've tried to forget what happened. I don't want to take advantage of you."

"You didn't," she cried. "That was the best night of my life. The virgin card is off the table. It's no longer an issue."

If only that were true. It made everything even more complicated and she would never understand why. "Just trust me on this, Maggie. Never again. You. Me. Sex. Not happening."

"Wow. Okay. My mistake." If only the embarrassment and humiliation on her face wasn't so easy to read. "I'll just—"

"Maggie—"

She brushed past him and hurried out of the room but not before he saw a tear on her cheek.

"Son of a—" He went after her and caught her in the hall, curving his fingers around her upper arm to stop her. "Please don't cry."

Her back was to him but her shuddering breath was hard to miss. "I'm not crying. I'm not a crier. It's okay. Don't give it another thought. I'm not usually this emotional. Normally everything rolls off my back. I don't know what's wrong with me—"

A sob cut off her words, and he hated that he'd made her cry. He couldn't stand it. He turned her toward him and folded her into his arms. The gesture seemed to break down her control and she buried her face against his chest, her shoulders shaking.

"Don't. I'm not worth it, Maggie."

She looked up. "That's not true, Jason—"

One minute he was looking into her big eyes swimming with tears, the next his mouth was on hers. There was no conscious decision. A deep, primal need took over and he was powerless to resist.

He tasted surprise before her lips parted. His tongue swept inside and took control. The kiss went deeper and he did a quick slide into an all-consuming heat. All he could think about was sinking in further, free-falling with her.

She put her arms around his neck and her small sounds of pleasure made the blood roar in his ears. He scooped her into his arms and carried her down the hall to his bedroom, the last stronghold, the only place her presence hadn't touched.

He stopped by his big king-size, four-poster bed. The sliding-glass door opened onto the penthouse patio and a spectacular view of the lights on the Las Vegas Strip. The brilliance of the neon panorama was no match for the innocent beauty in his arms.

He dropped his arm and let her legs slide down his front. After throwing back the spread and blanket, he looked into her eyes.

He cupped her face in his hands and brushed away the traces of her tears with his thumbs "Are you sure about this, Maggie? Really sure?"

She smiled. "Yes."

That was all he needed to hear to start his heart pounding against the inside of his chest. He let his hands slide into her hair, down her neck and arms. Hooking his thumbs in the top of her dress, he slowly lowered it, revealing her small, perfect breasts.

Sucking in his breath, he held them in his shaking hands and smiled. He hoped he wouldn't wake up and find out, like so many times before, that this was just a dream. "I can't believe how beautiful you are."

She covered his hands with her own, making his touch more secure. "I'm glad you think so."

"I do." And just like that he couldn't wait to see the rest of her.

He tugged on the dress pooled at her waist and pulled it down and over her hips, delighted to learn there was nothing underneath. The rest of her seduction needed work, but she had the most important part down pat.

She reached out and started to unbutton his shirt, but he couldn't wait and brushed her hands aside. After yanking it over his head, he unbuckled his belt and pushed slacks and boxers off until he was as naked as she.

She stepped against him and wrapped her arms around his waist, pressing them skin to skin. The feeling was powerful, passionate and spiked his pulse into the stratosphere.

He backed her against the bed, then gently lowered her to the sheets, settling beside her to kiss her deeply. He trailed his lips down her neck, over her breasts, belly, the inside of her thigh and everywhere else he'd dreamed about.

Slipping a finger inside her, he found that she was wet and waiting and he couldn't hold back any longer. He reached into the nightstand for one of the condoms he kept there and put it on. Then he rose over her and nudged her legs apart with his knee before settling between her thighs.

She took him easily this time and lifted her hands to his chest. "Oh, Jason, you have no idea how much I've wanted this."

She was the one who had no idea. He laughed as he stroked her hair from her face. "Not me. I haven't given it a single thought."

Her innocent eyes went wide. "Really?"

"Only a thousand times a day." He nuzzled her neck. "I've dreamed about you so many times but I always woke with my arms empty."

"Really?" she said, this time with pleasure in her tone.

"Tell me I'm not dreaming now."

She wrapped her legs around his waist and said, "Does that feel like a dream?"

"No," he groaned.

Holding back after that was more than he could manage. He thrust in and pulled back, reaching between their bodies to find the nub of female nerve endings that would give her satisfaction. She sucked in a breath as he lavished attention on the spot. Her breathing became ragged as her hips silently begged for release. An instant later she went still just before her body pulsed with the pleasure pouring through her.

"Oh, my," she said dreamily. "That was the most amazing

feeling I've ever felt." She opened her eyes and smiled. "It was like shattering into a thousand points of light then coming back together."

"I told you the next time would be better," he said.

"And you were right."

She wore the expression of a thoroughly pleased woman and suddenly he couldn't wait to find his own release. He plunged, deeply and gently, over and over, until he felt like his head would explode. A groan came from somewhere deep in his chest and his climax ground through him.

It was the most incredibly satisfying sex he'd ever known, but she had only one experience to compare with. He hoped he'd made it better this time. "Are you okay?"

"I'm perfect." She smiled. "You sure know how to relax a girl."

And those were the words that brought him crashing back to reality. He'd tracked her down and told her to relax because Brady was asleep. Then he'd proceeded to take her to bed and break every vow he'd made to protect her.

She was right about a pattern forming. The thing was, he didn't like the picture it made. And if the future was going to include her being there for his son, he had to find a way to undo what he'd just done.

## Chapter Thirteen

"I apologize, Maggie. Hunter and I probably shouldn't have invited ourselves over." Tracy Larson, Hunter Garrett's fiancée, stood by the infant tub on the granite counter in the bathroom and looked over her shoulder. "But I wanted to see the baby."

"It's no problem," Maggie answered. "Brady should get to know his family."

While the men were having after-dinner drinks, the women were bathing Brady. Actually, Tracy was doing the honors under strict supervision and getting soaked when he happily splashed, which didn't seem to bother her. Maggie gave the petite, green-eyed redheaded thirtysomething points for that. She gently dragged a wet washcloth over the baby and, of course, he grabbed it and stuffed the thing in his mouth.

"Brady boo, that's not good for you," Tracy cooed to him. He laughed when she playfully tugged it away, then glanced over her shoulder. "So how's married life?"

Considering that she'd been married for several months,

had sex twice but never actually spent the night in the same bed with her husband, things were just dandy. Maggie's stomach tightened, making nausea that had gripped her the last couple days worse. But she suspected something more than an awkward question was responsible for it. Something that really made her want to throw up.

After making love to her a couple nights ago, Jason had left her alone in the huge four-poster bed and slept on the couch. They'd been as close as a man and woman could be. He'd taken her to a place she'd never gone before. One touch had made her come apart while his arms had kept her together. It had been the best night of her life, then suddenly he was gone, back in his shell and she was more hurt and confused than ever.

"Married life?" she said, tapping her index finger against her lip while leaning a hip against the bathroom vanity. "It's different from the convent."

Tracy laughed and the baby did, too, making them both smile. "Why didn't you take your final vows?"

"I had doubts that the life was right for me." She folded her arms over her chest. "The thought of not ever having a family of my own gave me pause, so Mother Superior advised me to take a leave and think things over."

"And now you're married with a family of your own."

That wasn't exactly true. She was married, but this family was no more hers than the first day she'd walked in the door. Worse, she couldn't imagine loving this baby more if she'd given birth. And Jason? Her feelings for him were complicated. Every time he walked in a room her heart pounded and she couldn't catch her breath. When he wasn't there, it was hard to think about anything but being with him.

"That's a pregnant silence if I ever heard one." Firmly holding on to the baby, Tracy glanced over her shoulder.

If she only knew. "I'm definitely married. And Brady is the sweetest baby in the whole world."

"They're all sweet," Tracy said, longing in her expression when she stared at Brady.

"It's pretty obvious that you like babies." That made Maggie like her. It also made her wonder what Tracy was doing engaged to Jason's father.

"I do love them. I want one desperately and I'm not getting any younger."

"Does Hunter know?"

"Yes." She held out a hand. "Where's the towel? I think the water is getting too cold."

Maggie put the fluffy terry cloth in her fingers, then watched as she put it against her chest and lifted the baby, wrapping him warmly. They walked into the nursery where Tracy diapered him, then massaged his body with cream before putting on a lightweight sleeper.

"Do you mind if I just hold him?" she asked.

"Of course not. And I've got his nighttime bottle ready if he starts to fuss. Feel free to use it."

"Twist my arm."

Tracy sat in the glider chair with Brady in her arms. Almost instantly he began to alternately yawn and whine. This was his routine and he was sticking to it. She offered the bottle and he eagerly took it.

"You seem surprised that I'm a baby person," Tracy observed.

"I guess I am." Maggie remembered the first time she met Hunter, and how he completely ignored his new grandson. It seemed an odd match.

"Did Jason tell you I'm the one who recommended The Nanny Network when he was having problems with reliable child care?"

"No." That was even more surprising.

"My friend Casey Thomas works there."

"We met the other day when I took Brady to a class."

Tracy glanced away from the baby for just a moment. "I

used to date her older brother. We broke up, but I got custody of Casey."

"She doesn't look like she needs taking care of," Maggie commented.

"Don't let that disciplined-soldier exterior fool you."

"Working for The Nanny Network seems like a big change from the army."

Tracy nodded. "She was wounded in Iraq and received a medical discharge. Now she works with kids ten and under."

Maggie thought about her own inclination to care for infants up to six weeks and wondered why Casey specialized in that particular age group. "One of the things I like best about Ginger is her willingness to accommodate an employee's preferences."

"That's Case's feeling, too." Tracy smiled when Brady curled his tiny hand around her finger. "So I sent Jason to Ginger who brought the two of you together. When you think about it, I'm kind of a matchmaker."

"I suppose." Maggie didn't want to answer any more questions about the state of her marriage and decided to change the subject. "So how did you and Hunter meet?"

"I'm a cocktail waitress at the Palms. The Ghost Bar. Hunter came in one night and sparks just flew. He was still married at the time." She looked uncomfortable, but got more points for being honest. "He said he was planning to end the marriage. I know what you're thinking—they all say that."

"My experience is so limited I have no idea what they all say. Actually I was thinking that I respect your honesty."

Tracy's smile was pleased before she grew serious. "Here's a little more for you. If he was still with his wife, I'd continue seeing him. Because I love him."

Maggie didn't know what to say. In her book, that was wrong and love was no excuse. Fortunately she didn't have to comment because the other woman filled in the silence.

"The thing is I do my best to be a realist. I've read the articles—if he cheats with you, he will cheat on you. So, when he proposed, I didn't accept it lightly. Clearly his marital track record makes him a bad risk, but I accept that."

"Why?" Maggie asked.

"Because he makes me happy. And I'll take as much as I can get for as long as I can get it."

"What about children? Does he want a baby?"

"I'm hoping he loves me enough to give me one."

"But what if he doesn't?" If anyone knew how the terms of an agreement changed, it was Maggie.

"I'm not sure. I'll have to cross that bridge when I come to it."

"But what if you're already married and the answer is one you can't live with?"

Tracy frowned before asking a question that actually answered her own. "Did you actually marry Jason expecting happy ever after, Maggie?"

She wasn't sure what to say. Confessing the truth was too awful. Humiliation had been hard enough after taking Ginger's suggestion to argue and fight for a legitimate marriage. Wine, candles and a cotton sundress with nothing underneath had won her an invitation to his bed. Ending up there alone showed her that winning his mind and heart were another story.

Maggie met the other woman's gaze. "My beginning on the steps of the Good Shepherd Home for Children as an infant showed me that there's no such thing as a happy ending."

"It's good you're a realist," Tracy agreed. "Because, like father, like son."

Maggie's chest felt tight. "What do you mean?"

"You shouldn't expect the sun, moon and stars from a man who paid a woman a lot of money not to get rid of his baby."

"What?" Maggie couldn't believe she'd heard right.

"From what Hunter told me Catherine didn't deliberately get pregnant. It was definitely an accident because she's ambitious and determined to make a career in the entertainment business. Pregnancy is good publicity once you're a star, but not so much when you're breaking in. Jason changed her mind with a good-size check."

"I see."

"That's not all. He gave her even more to stay out of Brady's life and not make custody claims later. Rumor has it she's 'having work done.' Eyes, nose, boobs."

So that's what he'd meant when he said Brady's mother wouldn't be an issue. "I'm speechless."

Fortunately Tracy wasn't. As she smiled down at a sleeping Brady, she said, "Can you imagine this precious little life not being here?"

"No."

"I admire Jason for what he did."

So did Maggie. This would all be so much easier if she didn't. She tried not to judge other people lest she be judged. But it was impossible for her to understand how a mother could abandon her child. She would never know what her own mother's reasons were but if Jason weren't rich, Brady wouldn't have had a chance at all.

He bought the baby's life.

He'd bought her life, too.

She'd never thought about it like that before because saving the children's home made her feel as if she was getting the best part of the bargain. But the bargain she'd made didn't work for her now because she wanted Jason's love, not his money.

Looking back, it had probably been love at first sight or she'd never have accepted his unconventional proposal. She'd married a man who understood the power of money but had no clue about people. He had no idea that the same reasons she'd left the convent were even more true now. She wanted a family that included him, Brady, and more children.

She settled her palm protectively against her abdomen and the new life she suspected was growing there. Something that should have been joyous and special made her afraid. He'd made love to her, but if she was pregnant as she suspected, the child hadn't been conceived in love. Jason's actions ever since had proved he meant what he'd told Sister. He wanted no part of a family unit.

He'd simply bought a way out of his child-care problems and was happy with that. But Maggie had never been more unhappy in her life.

Jason looked at his father from where he sat behind the desk in his own study. They were drinking a brandy together, but that didn't mean this wasn't a business meeting. Where Hunter Garrett was concerned, every meeting was business, even a face-to-face with his son. Jason had learned at an early age that it was the only interaction the man understood. No reason to expect anything different now. All he could do was make sure the relationship he had with his own son was different. With Maggie's help it would be.

"So, Dad, when are you and Tracy getting married?"

"I'm in no rush." Hunter took a healthy sip from his glass, then stared into it, frowning thoughtfully. "She wants a baby."

"I kind of figured. What with her wanting to see Brady being the reason for this visit."

"She says her biological clock is ticking."

"And how did you respond to that?" Jason asked.

"Said I didn't hear a thing. She wasn't amused." He shook his head. "I tried everything I can think of to talk her out of it. I'm too old. A baby would tie us down. Was it fair to bring a child into this world in a situation like that?"

"Did you get through to her?"

He sighed. "She said the yearning to have a baby is as strong for a woman as the urge for sex is in a man. That statement was followed by a question about how I'd feel if I couldn't have it ever again."

Jason resisted the urge to squirm. Obviously he knew where babies come from but didn't want the image in his head of Tracy and his father together. He was sorry he'd asked. Although now that he had he was curious.

"How do you feel about it?"

"How would you feel if your current wife wanted another one?" Hunter snapped.

A knot pulled tight in Jason's stomach, but no way was he telling his father about unprotected sex with Maggie. That's where babies come from, but it was only once. Surely his procreation karma couldn't be that messed up. And referring to Maggie as his "current wife" ticked him off.

"Are you planning to marry your *current* fiancée without clarifying the issue?"

Hunter's gaze lifted. "Did I hit a nerve?"

Jason was tempted to blow it off, smooth it over. But he wasn't a kid anymore with one parent left. He was a grown man and he didn't have to worry about what would happen to him if his father left, too.

"Maggie's my wife." She fit seamlessly into his son's life and that's the way he wanted it to stay. He didn't want to hear anything to the contrary. "*Current* implies that there are numerous marriages in my future. I'm not a chip off the old block. I'm not like you."

"Meaning?" Hunter's blue eyes narrowed.

"I don't intend to recycle her like old newspapers. She's one of a kind and I'd be lost without her."

"Don't you mean Brady would be lost?"

Did he? Somehow the line blurred between Brady's needs and how much Jason counted on her being there. "What my relationship is or isn't with Maggie is none of your concern. The point is that I'm happy to follow in your business footsteps. Personal? Not so much. I'd appreciate it if when you talk about my wife, simply use her given name."

*Given* was definitely the word. Sister Margaret had given her own name to the motherless infant abandoned at her door. She'd given a lot more, molding Maggie into the wonderful, generous, beautiful woman she was today. And Jason realized he could no longer imagine his world without her in it.

Hunter swallowed the remainder of the liquor in his glass, then set it on the desk and applauded. "That was a great speech, Jason. It's easy to make judgments from where you're sitting. For the record, I loved your mother. If she'd stayed, I'd still be with her. It was her idea to leave, not mine. She made the choice."

"Why did she go?" The question popped out and he realized he'd never asked before.

Hunter shrugged. "She gave me some song and dance about obsessive love and not being able to breathe. I gave everything it was in my power to give her and none of it was enough."

Shadows swirled in his father's eyes, stunning him with the implication. He'd thought Hunter Garrett incapable of a deep, lasting love. "I had no idea."

"Now you do." Hunter stood. "And a word to the wise— you may not want to be like me, but you can't escape DNA. I recognize that look."

"What are you talking about?" Jason stood, too, and met his father's gaze.

"You don't defend the nanny unless you have feelings for her. That's a problem, son. I don't want you to get hurt the way I was. Walk away first. Your mother taught me that. If a woman gets your heart, she'll hand it back to you just before setting foot out the door."

He was too surprised to say anything, especially because

the uncharacteristic fatherly advice had come just in time. Defending Maggie had come as easily to Jason as breathing, proof that his feelings for her were spiraling out of control. It was time to get a grip.

He heard female voices and no infant crying, which meant his son was probably asleep. "I think we should join the ladies."

"Okay." Hunter looked at the gold watch on his wrist. "For a minute. It's time for us to go."

Jason followed his father from the study and into the living room where Maggie and Tracy were standing in front of the sliding-glass door that looked out onto the lights of Las Vegas. The sight of his wife's trim back in her snug-fitting jeans and cotton blouse stirred his already unsettled emotions. He missed her when they weren't together and looked forward to seeing her every night when he came home. And sex had taken him to a new level of need.

Hunter stopped beside his fiancée and put his arm around her waist. "So, have you had your fill of the baby experience?"

"He's so adorable," she said, leaning into him.

"Would you like to peek in on him, Mr. Garrett?" Maggie asked.

"You're my son's wife, *Maggie*." His father glanced at him. "Call me Hunter."

"All right. Hunter." She looked uneasy. "Brady's asleep but I'm sure it wouldn't disturb him if you just—"

"We have to get going," the old man said.

Jason knew why he cut her off, but that didn't take the edge off his own feelings of dismissal and rejection. Brady was the son of his own son. He and Maggie thought the kid was pretty damn special, but the old man was running away from his own problem, one he couldn't buy his way out of. It occurred to Jason that every marriage since the first one to his mother had been about Hunter running away.

"Okay." Tracy frowned up at him but chose not to debate.

Her expression said loud and clear that they'd have words about it later. She leaned over and hugged Maggie. "Thanks for letting us drop by."

"Any time," she said warmly.

"Goodbye, Jason. Maggie." Hunter put his hand to Tracy's back, hurrying her to the front door. "I'll be in touch."

That's what Jason said to clients as he ushered them out the door. Damn DNA. Or maybe it was environment. Man, this was a hell of a fix. Without Maggie, he wasn't sure he could break the patterns of his own environment. But given the strong feelings for her he wrestled with day and night, he needed to do something.

When they were alone, he turned to her. "I need to talk to you."

She smiled up at him. "Tracy wants a baby."

"Dad told me."

"She loves him and hopes he loves her enough to give her the one thing she wants most."

Good luck with that, he thought. If Hunter was telling the truth, no woman would ever take his mother's place. He didn't want to find himself in the same position, where no one could replace Maggie.

"I really need to talk with you."

"I was going to make some tea. Would you like some?"

Jason needed something stronger than dried herbs in a bag, but needed to keep his mind clear. "No, thanks."

"Okay."

He followed her to the kitchen, heat radiating through him as he watched the unconsciously sexy sway of her hips. She flipped the lights on and moved confidently around the room, filling a mug with water, then adding the tea before setting it in the microwave. When it was ready, she joined him at the table, sitting at a right angle to him. Lifting her foot to cross her legs, she brushed his calf and he did his best to ignore the arc of electricity that buzzed through him.

"What's up?" she asked.

"It occurs to me that we need to clarify things."

Holding her mug, she blew on the hot water, dispersing the rising steam. "You might want to start with clarifying what you mean by 'things.'"

"Specifically I mean the duration of our arrangement."

Surprise darkened the already vivid blue of her eyes. "We're married. Doesn't that sort of automatically spell it out?"

Clearly she meant that in her world marriage was forever. In his world it didn't work that way and he had to protect himself and his son by making the parameters clear.

"I was thinking that until Brady's in school we should keep things status quo."

"Status quo?" She frowned. "You can't even say married?"

Sometimes her straightforward nature wasn't so appealing, but he'd opened this can of worms. There was no way to unopen it. "He'll be about six, which is about the same age I was when my mother left."

"So what's good for the father is good for the son?"

This was about Brady, not him and his father. "What doesn't kill you makes you stronger. I survived."

"Surviving isn't the same as living a full, rich life." Maggie set her tea on the table and stared at him. "What's wrong, Jason?"

"Who said anything's wrong?"

"Come on. Your father was here and you talked in your office. Now you want to define the duration of our agreement? It doesn't take a Ph.D. in psychology to figure out that he said something to make you go into fight-or-flight mode. Clearly you're choosing the latter."

Anger churned through him, mostly because she knew and understood him so well. How did that happen? When did it? A pointless question that didn't change the fact he wasn't happy about it. "I'm not running away. Just the opposite. It's best for both of us to know where we are with this whole thing."

"'This whole thing' is called marriage and family. You can't even call it what it is. Like they're dirty words." She stood up. "I know where I stand on it. I'm willing to give things between us a fighting chance, but you refuse to risk being happy."

"Maggie, I just want to say—"

"Haven't you already said enough? I've certainly heard enough. Good night, Jason."

When she was gone the kitchen echoed with the silence. It had never seemed so big and empty before Maggie. Would it feel bigger and emptier when "this whole thing" was over? The thought of *his* world without her sweetness in it made him unreasonably angry.

Instead of making things better, he had a very bad feeling that he'd just shot himself in the foot.

*Chapter Fourteen*

The Saturday following Hunter Garrett's visit, Maggie made a detour on her way to the Good Shepherd Home because a pregnancy test had confirmed her suspicions. If she didn't talk to someone about the situation a personal implosion was entirely possible. Ginger Davis had a penthouse suite in the Trump building located on Fashion Show Drive across from the mall, bordered by Las Vegas Boulevard and Industrial and Desert Inn Roads.

When Maggie drove down Industrial, it occurred to her that the juxtaposition of businesses—Elvis-a-Rama, Love Boutique, and Adult World—with the classy elegance of the tower bearing the famous developer's name was typical of Las Vegas. It was a blend of old and new, good and not so good, the best and worst of life. Right now her life couldn't get much worse.

She found a parking space, then walked into the elegant lobby with its circular marble pattern on the floors, glittery

chandeliers, round granite-topped artsy table, wood, glass
and mirrors. At the reception desk, she gave her name and was
cleared to take the elevator up to the floor where Ginger's suite
was located. After exiting, she found the number she was
looking for and rang the bell beside the white door with grace-
fully arched decorative molding.

Since they'd called up from the reception desk, Ginger
answered almost immediately. "Maggie, come in."

"Thanks."

She glanced around the foyer and realized she was running
out of adjectives. Again, the first word that came to mind was
elegant. The floor was beige stone, each tile fitted together
with barely a line showing. No grout. Textured paper covered
the walls in a seafoam green that was bordered by wide white
molding. A large table holding a vase of fresh, sweet-smelling
flowers sat in the center.

"Let's talk in the other room," Ginger said, extending her
hand.

"I'm sorry to drop in without notice." She followed the
other woman into an area with floor-to-ceiling windows and
a view of old downtown Vegas.

"Not a problem." Ginger sat on a white, overstuffed loveseat and indicated that Maggie should sit on the one at a right
angle, which she did. A rectangular glass-topped table completed the grouping. "What can I do for you?"

"So, you have an office here in your home, too?" Why
jump right into a horribly complicated problem when procras-
tination was so much easier?

"Yes. There's a study in the other room." Ginger glanced
around. "I do a lot of computer work here and get together
with prospective clients as well as employees. Having the two
locations for meetings is convenient for me, too."

"This is a lovely place for a home office."

"I like it very much. And I guess you couldn't help noticing the mall across the street?" Her brown eyes twinkled until the color was like warm maple syrup. "Makes retail therapy incredibly convenient."

Maggie had never been much of a shopper, but could appreciate location, location, location. "It's very beautiful."

"But you didn't come here for a tour. What's bothering you, Maggie?"

She started to question why her former boss would assume there was a problem, but figured that was a waste of time. She had never dropped in like this and any change in habit was a big clue.

"I'm pregnant."

"Congratulations," Ginger said. Then she studied Maggie and frowned. "You're happy about it, right?"

"What was your first clue?"

"It might be sooner than you and Jason planned, but it's the natural next step for a married couple." There was a slight emphasis on the word *married*.

"It couldn't be a worse step for me," Maggie protested.

"I'm sure that's just pregnancy hormones talking. Once you get used to the idea, you'll be ecstatic."

"Do you know how it feels? Have you ever been pregnant?"

A shadow drifted into Ginger's eyes and her smile faltered for a fraction of a second before she restored it. "I've done extensive reading on the subject," she said, not confirming or denying, which was out of character for the straightforward woman. "You love babies, Maggie. Your reputation and experience made you the nanny all new parents requested. There was a waiting list and it was a blow to lose you to Jason Garrett. How can you not want a baby of your own?"

"I never said I didn't want the baby. I've always wanted to be a mother. I just said it couldn't be a worse step for me. Personally. With Jason. Right now," Maggie finished, twisting her fingers together in her lap.

"I don't understand. The marriage was quick, but if anyone understands love at first sight, it's me. Jason isn't the kind of man to take the step without a deeper emotion guiding him."

"It *was* quick," Maggie admitted. "But falling in love? Not so much." At least not for him, but she couldn't say the same for herself. She'd fallen in love with her husband and she was certain of it. All she could think about was being with him. She adored Brady, but when she saw Jason, it was like a light going on in a pitch-black room.

"What's going on?" Ginger slid forward to sit on the edge of the loveseat. "What's the deal, Maggie?"

"Funny you should phrase it like that." She took a deep breath. "He's determined to stick to the finer points of our agreement. Nothing personal."

The other woman's eyes grew large, but she was speechless for several moments. "He's determined to maintain distance even after sleeping with you?"

"Yes. For Brady's sake."

"But you had sex. That's pretty personal. Unless…" If possible her eyes opened wider. "Is Jason the father?"

"What?"

"Did Jason father your baby?"

"Busted," Maggie said. "I picked up a guy while dancing topless at a gentlemen's club. You caught me." She would have laughed at that vision if she wasn't so upset.

"I'm sorry." Ginger shook her head. "This scenario has really thrown me and I'm having trouble wrapping my brain around it."

"Join the club. I was in the convent, for goodness' sake. Nearly a nun. A virgin until that night at the cabin with Jason."

"Let me make sure I understand, so there are no more stupid questions. The marriage was consummated a while ago, before I encouraged you to fight for him," Ginger said.

Maggie nodded. "Although he was trying to go back to the way things were. For the record, I took your advice and it worked out. Temporarily."

"What does that mean?"

"We made love. And then Jason slept on the couch."

"I don't get it." Ginger shook her head again. "He seems like a highly sexual man to me. Obviously he's attracted to you or there wouldn't be a baby."

"He's been hurt and doesn't want to compromise his son's security and stability by giving his heart. He will never let me be more than the nanny."

"Are you sure about that?"

"Very. He's already planning when to sever our relationship." She blew out a breath. "He decided that Brady starting school would be a good time to terminate the agreement and my services as his caregiver will no longer be required."

"He put a time limit on the marriage?" Ginger asked.

"Pretty much."

"Does he know about the baby?"

Maggie shook her head. "I suspected but hadn't confirmed it yet. And when he said we should keep things status quo until Brady's in school, I accused him of going into fight-or-flight mode. Right after that I sort of pointed out that he was afraid to take a chance on being happy."

Ginger nodded her approval. "Good for you."

"Not really. I was pretty harsh. Not that he didn't deserve it, but he's so wounded, Ginger. I just want to help him, and he won't let me."

"Maybe if you tell him about the baby."

"I'm afraid." She met the other woman's gaze. "He has Brady because his girlfriend was going to end her pregnancy and he paid her a lot of money not to do it."

"What does that have to do with you? You're planning to have this baby."

"He gave her a bonus to never darken his door again," Maggie confided. "What if—"

"No." Ginger stared, a fierce expression in her eyes. "This is completely different. I'm not saying there aren't a lot of speed bumps in the road ahead. But you're not that woman. And he married you. He needs to know you're going to have his child."

"I never considered not letting Jason know about the baby."

Ginger smiled. "Of course you didn't. Doing the right thing is your trademark, and Jason knows that, too."

"For what it's worth."

Ginger sighed. "I wish I could give you the magic words or snap my fingers and make everything perfect, but I can't."

Maggie shrugged. "Talking it through helped."

"I believe he cares deeply about you, Maggie. I'm a pretty good judge of character or I wouldn't be a successful businesswoman. If Jason didn't have feelings, he'd never have married you. The question is whether or not he can take a leap of faith and admit how much he cares."

"Jason is capable of great love," Maggie said. "And he's a terrific father. Why wouldn't he love another child, too?"

The bigger question was whether or not he could take a chance on loving her and making a future together. Or if he'd try to make her a nonissue as he'd done with Brady's mother.

Jason sat in a lounge chair on the balcony, the electronic monitor on the glass-topped patio table beside him while Brady was napping. It was a spectacular spring day. Everyone complained about the Vegas heat in July but no one said a bad word when the thermometer hovered just under eighty degrees and there wasn't a cloud in the sky.

His life, on the other hand, had clouds in great quantities and most of them were about Maggie. He looked at the Rolex on his wrist. It was eleven-thirty, which meant she would be walking in the door any minute. Punctuality was one of her best qualities, especially when he'd missed her like crazy. He didn't want to miss her, but couldn't seem to control it.

Even after he'd made such an ass of himself by spelling out the duration of their agreement. What the hell was status quo anyway? He had no idea what was going on with them. She'd called him on it, too. She knew right away it had something to do with his father. Jason could negotiate a business deal until an adversary screamed for mercy but when it came to Maggie he didn't know when to keep his mouth shut. Digging himself in deeper seemed to come naturally when she was around.

*You always hurt the ones you love?*

The message he grew up with made it tough to know what he was feeling and he'd taken that out on her. He couldn't blame her for walking away first. Even as the words poured out of his mouth, the thought of a life without her in it had his gut tied in knots. Maybe that's why he'd missed her more than usual after she'd left for the children's home yesterday. It also gave him a lot of time to think about how he'd screwed up.

Mostly he was hoping to figure out a strategy to fix things between them. She was trying, and he'd hurt her. He'd loved loving her. He'd loved it too much. And she'd been right when she said that some men would be pleased to be her first, but he'd rejected her.

His only defense was that growing up he'd had no positive role model for a couple's dynamic. He went into every relationship with an exit strategy in mind. It always involved him saying goodbye first, followed by delivery of a very expensive gift. That wouldn't work with Maggie because material things didn't matter to her—people mattered. *He* wanted to matter.

With the patio door opened, Jason heard her come in and felt excitement rush through him. He swung his legs to the side and stood, grabbing the monitor on his way inside.

"Maggie?" He glanced down the hall, toward Brady's room, because that was always her first stop after coming home. It was such a mom thing, he realized and something dark moved in his chest.

She came out of the nursery and pulled the door half-closed behind her. "He's sound asleep. Did everything go all right while I was gone?"

"Fine." Unless she meant his peace of mind. "How are things at Good Shepherd?"

"Oh, you know. Noisy. Chaotic. Wonderful." She twisted her fingers together.

There was a wary, deer-caught-in-headlights look on her face. He didn't like it, or the fact that there was no one to blame but himself. While alone he'd thought a lot about her innocent, awkward attempt at communication while wearing nothing but a simple yellow sundress. His whole body went tense and tight with need, urging him to take her in his arms, kiss her and let his body do the talking. To somehow convey the message that he didn't want her to ever go away again. But that would show weakness and he couldn't shake his core directive not to let her see how much he needed her.

He moved a couple of steps at the same time she did until their bodies were nearly touching. Reaching out, he took a silky strand of her dark hair between his thumb and forefinger.

"Maggie, it's been—"

"There's something I need—"

"Please, ladies first." He dropped his hand. "You go."

"On my way to Good Shepherd I stopped to see Ginger."

"Recruiting reinforcements?" he teased.

She didn't crack a smile, which was disturbing. "She's too busy with The Nanny Network for that."

"Then why did you go there? Looking for work?" The thought that she was planning her own exit strategy had familiar defenses dropping into place to deflect the pain.

"No. I just needed to talk."

He wasn't the poster boy for communication and he knew it. But that didn't keep him from saying, "What am I? Chopped liver?"

"I couldn't talk to you. Not about this."

But she hadn't gone to Sister Margaret. What was it that required a visit to Ginger?

He folded his arms over his chest. "Define *this*."

"I'm pregnant."

His stomach clenched and time stopped. "Pregnant? You're going to have a baby?"

"Yes."

She waited expectantly, but he was too stunned to speak. A baby? She was going to have his baby? He'd tried so hard to maintain stability and keep everything under control. That was laugh-out-loud stupid. With Maggie he'd never been *in* control. The money he'd invested in their agreement had given him the *illusion* of being in charge, but that's all it had been. Otherwise he'd have been able to form coherent thoughts instead of simply wanting her more than his next breath. He'd have been able to think about anything besides the overwhelming need to be with her. Anything including birth control.

Later the reality of what he'd done hit him, but he'd hoped that because it was one time without protection, maybe he wouldn't be punished for just once having what he wanted. This was a hell of a time to find out how high a price he had to pay for that mistake.

"Jason," she pleaded, "please talk to me."

He looked at her and steeled himself against the innocence and uncertainty darkening her eyes. "You're sure?"

She nodded. "I did the test. More than once. It was positive every time. It will be okay. You love Brady so much. I—I hoped you'd be happy about another child."

"Happy?" When he was in defensive mode, anger was his go-to emotion and it didn't fail him now. "That's not even close to what I'm feeling."

She flinched before her chin lifted to meet his gaze. "I know it's unexpected. And we're not what you might call a normal couple. But—"

"In my frame of reference there's no such thing as a 'normal couple.'" This complication was exactly what he'd been afraid of from the beginning.

"Maybe your frame of reference needs work."

He wasn't going there. "So you went to Ginger about this instead of coming to me?"

"Yes." Her look said she refused to apologize for it. "Can you blame me? Our last conversation was about ending this marriage when Brady starts school."

"That might have been a good time to share the news that you were having a baby."

"*We're* having a baby," she said, putting a finer point on the situation.

"What we have is an agreement, a plan, a deal." He saw the hurt in her eyes grow with each word but couldn't seem to stop himself. "That deal was all about you taking care of Brady. It never included giving him a sibling."

Disbelief mixed with distress until her eyes were dark pools of pain. She folded her arms protectively over her abdomen, an instinctively maternal gesture. Finally, without another word, she turned and walked down the hall, then quietly closed the door to her room.

Fuming, Jason walked outside onto the penthouse patio and turned his face into the wind as thoughts raced through his head. Once upon a time he'd craved isolation like this, but that had changed and it was Maggie's fault. Everything else was on him. He wasn't innocent and hadn't been for a very long time. He should have known better.

A baby. Another Brady. Or maybe a girl. Who looked like Maggie.

This was a bad time to realize that her innocence and capacity for caring—all that had attracted him in the first place—were the problem. She didn't understand the concept of the deal. She'd led with her heart. He'd led with his wallet. Until this moment he'd thought money would put him in control of the uncontrollable, the nebulous world of interpersonal relationships. He'd been so sure his "deal" would ensure that he could keep what he wanted most.

Too late he realized his behavior would secure him the highest place in the lowest level of hell. But he wasn't so sure that would be any worse than what he felt right now.

## Chapter Fifteen

At four-thirty the next day, Jason walked into the penthouse with his briefcase and a serious case of post-anger confusion. The situation with Maggie hadn't improved. The night before and this morning she'd cared for Brady in her usual tender-loving way. But she hadn't said another word to him. The cruelty of his own words echoed in his head and he'd give anything to be able to go back and delete. There were some things money couldn't buy, and the ability to concentrate while his personal life had gone in the dumper was one of them. Cutting short his day to sort things out seemed prudent.

But when he walked in the living room, Maggie wasn't there with Brady.

"Hello, Jason." Ginger Davis, wearing a navy crepe suit and matching high heels, was on the sofa with the baby in her lap. Brady was all smiles at the sight of him.

"What are you doing here? Where's Maggie?" He walked over and held out his arms for his son.

"Gone." She gave the baby a tender hug before handing him over. "And she called me to cover for her and make sure this little guy was well taken care of."

"Is she sick? She should have called me. I'd have come home to take care of her." He held Brady so close the baby started to squirm. "She knows that."

"Does she?" Ginger tucked a strand of brown hair behind her ear. "From what little she told me, I got the impression that she doesn't feel like she can count on you for anything."

"We've had some minor communication glitches," he hedged.

"Oh, please. It's a marriage, not a computer program."

When Brady fussed, Jason walked back and forth in front of the floor-to-ceiling windows. "Is Maggie all right?"

"Physically?" Ginger leaned back and crossed one trim leg over the other. "She's fine."

"When will she be back?"

"She's not coming back."

"You mean tonight." He nodded. "I'm home now to relieve you. Tomorrow she'll—"

"She's not coming back at all," Ginger clarified. "She quit."

"She can't quit. We're married."

Ginger tilted her head, studying him. "Don't you think it's a little too late to play the *M* card?"

He'd put his briefcase down in the foyer, but his case of confusion had compounded. Instead of answering he said, "When was Brady last changed?"

"I was just about to do that when you walked in."

He nodded, then turned away and carried the baby into the nursery. On the changing table, Brady grabbed the rattle Maggie always kept there to keep his little hands busy. "Hey, buddy. How was your day? I bet you're pretty mixed up. Join the club."

"Is it really that big a stunner, Jason?"

He glanced over his shoulder to see Ginger standing in the doorway. "Of course I'm surprised. I had nanny trouble when he was first born, which is why I hired your agency. It came highly recommended. Now I'm not so sure."

"Are you put out because you lost a nanny? Or is this shock and awe about your *wife* walking out on you? Pick one because you can't have it both ways."

It would be so much easier to make it about an employee. The first three nannies hadn't crossed his mind since he'd let them go. But Maggie hadn't been out of his mind since the first time he'd seen her.

He finished diapering Brady and snapping his overalls, then put his palm on the baby's belly to keep him secure as he faced the woman. "Do you know why she left?"

"Yes." Ginger folded her arms over her chest.

He waited but she didn't say more. "Are you going to tell me?"

"Do you really want to know?"

"Of course I do."

"Why?"

He picked Brady up and said the first thing that came to mind. "Because this is out of character for her. She takes responsibility seriously. She's organized and conscientious and she loves Brady. Why would she do this?"

"She loves that little boy more than her life, but the cost of loving you is her soul. Don't you think that's an awfully high price to pay?"

He was stunned. Maggie loved him? "She told you that?"

"Pretty much." Ginger's expression hardened. "And before you claim this is news to you, she also told me she's pregnant. And you were less than thrilled."

He put a thick quilt on the floor and set Brady down with toys. "Did she also mention that the Garrett men have a lousy track record with women?"

"She didn't have to. Your father makes the 'Vegas Confidential' column on a regular basis. And I knew your mother."

He straightened and stared at her. "When?"

"Right after she left your father." Ginger leaned against the baby's crib. "We both worked the registration desk at one of the Strip hotels. It was just one of her jobs. She was working three."

"Why?"

"Trying to earn enough money for the legal battle to get you back."

"But she walked out on me."

Ginger shook her head. "No. She walked out on your father when her life with him became intolerable. He refused to let her take you. She spent time with you when she could, but knew that with all Hunter's money, a court fight for custody would be a joke without a sizable bank account of her own."

"Did my dad know?" He'd certainly never shared the information if he did.

"I'm not sure. Your mom was a smart cookie and it wouldn't have been very intelligent to give him a heads-up." She looked down for a moment, sadness in her expression. "Unfortunately she was killed in a car accident before she could follow through on her plan."

"Dad told me about the accident, but not that she wanted me to go with her when she left." Something shifted in his chest. Something dark and heavy broke free and slipped away.

"I'm not surprised." She shrugged. "Your father isn't the sort of man who'd share how much your mother loved you. That wouldn't be a win for him."

"Yeah." He watched Brady roll from his tummy to his back and wave his arms. "I got the version about him giving her everything, including his love and it wasn't enough for her."

"She loved him once. And he probably loved her in his way," Ginger said. "But his way included holding on to her so tightly that he squeezed every last drop of love out of her. It was oppressive. He was so afraid of losing her, he all but pushed her out the door."

"And he keeps making the same mistakes."

"At least he's not shutting himself off."

Now she was defending Hunter? "You can't have it both ways, Ginger. Is he a bastard or not?"

"Your mother was the love of his life and your father's string of relationships are about looking for that feeling again." Ginger took a step forward. "He lost your mother because he held on too tightly. You lost Maggie because you won't hold on at all."

"Wait a minute—"

"Don't get me wrong. I'm the last one to defend Hunter Garrett, but at least your father isn't hiding under a rock. He keeps getting it wrong, but he hasn't given up. Unlike you."

She was comparing him to his father? Now she'd crossed a line.

"Hold it. You don't know me. What gives you the right to judge me? I'm not my father." He settled his hands on his hips. "Maggie and I have an understanding. I was honest with her, as straight with her as I know how to be. I gave her everything she needed—"

"Everything but what she needed most." Intensity darkened her eyes.

"What did she need that I didn't give?"

"Yourself." She put her hand on his arm. "Think about it, Jason. She married you to save the home that saved her and Good Shepherd became her family by default. All she's ever wanted was a family of her own, freely given because of love. Do you have any idea how precious that is to her?"

Her words were like pulling the plug on his anger and it all drained away, leaving him nowhere left to hide. "I don't want Maggie to go away. Do you know where she is?"

"Yes."

"Tell me. Please," he added.

"You want her to come back?" Ginger asked.

"Of course I do."

"Why?"

Hadn't they just been through this? What the hell was she doing? "Brady misses her."

Ginger actually smiled. "He told you that?"

"He didn't have to. She's the only mother he knows. Not having her here will confuse him."

"I think you and I know who's really confused. Trust me. I've been around the block a time or two. You'll feel a whole lot better if you just tell me why you want Maggie back."

For a man who thrived on fixing things, all this conversation seemed like a waste of time and energy. Every part of him vibrated with the need to see Maggie, to talk to *her*. To negotiate terms for her return, probably including an apology if he could find the right words. First he needed to know where she'd gone and to get that information he had to pass some test of Ginger's.

"Why do I want Maggie back?" He raked his fingers through his hair. "Because I need her. She makes everything better. She makes me better. I can't imagine my life without her in it. She's the best thing that ever happened to me."

"You love her."

"I care very much for her."

Ginger shook her head, pity in the gesture. "Why is it so hard to say the *L* word?"

"Because I don't want to screw things up like my father." He curled his fingers into his palms. "Where is she?"

"She's home. With her family."

*Good Shepherd. Of course.*

"I have to see her. Will you—"

"Stay with Brady?" She nodded. "You don't even have to ask. Go get his mother."

"Yes, ma'am."

She pointed at him. "Smile when you call me that."

He grinned before saluting, then raced out of the penthouse. Before seeing Maggie he had a stop to make. Until now, he'd always gone into a relationship with an exit strategy in mind. This time he needed an entrance plan. Until now, walking away included an expensive present. This time he needed something that would show Maggie he loved her and was in this relationship forever.

When the kids at the home had finished eating and the kitchen was tidied, Maggie went to the little room nearby that served as Sister Margaret's office. She knocked softly on the door and when she heard "come in," she did. Sister was behind her desk, reading glasses on the end of her nose as she squinted at a computer monitor.

"Sister Mary said you wanted to see me?"

"Yes." The nun smiled. "Sit down, Maggie."

There was a generic visitor's chair in front of the desk and she sat. "What's up?"

"You tell me."

"I don't understand."

"Yes, you do. While I personally don't believe a lie that small will keep you out of heaven, stalling is counterproductive." Sister removed her glasses and looked across the space with eyes that had never missed anything. "It's not Saturday. You take care of Jason's son the rest of the week. Who's watching him because you ran away?"

"He's in good hands," she said. "I needed a break."

"Why?"

Because Jason didn't want her or the baby they'd made together. Between the punch of that thought and the pain that always followed, there was a blessed numbness she tried desperately to hold on to. It lasted a nanosecond before tears burned the backs of her eyes. There was no point in pretending. She'd never been able to fool Sister Margaret.

"I'm pregnant."

Sister's eyes widened a fraction but it was the only indication that she was surprised. "I see. An out-of-wedlock pregnancy—"

"It's not out of wedlock." Maggie sat on the edge of the chair. "Jason and I are married."

This time Sister couldn't suppress her shock. "You're married? When?"

"Six weeks after I went to work for him. He didn't want me to leave."

"A man of action who fell in love and—"

"No." Maggie hated to destroy Sister's romantic fantasy. "He wanted me to take care of Brady. When I shared my reasons for limiting my stay, he offered marriage as a solution that would work for both of us."

"I see."

"That's not all."

"Good gracious, Margaret Mary. What more can there be?"

"I turned down his offer."

"But you say you're married." Sister Margaret looked confused. "I don't understand."

This part was the hardest because she didn't want Sister to blame herself in any way. "He—Jason—was raised by his father to believe that money buys a way out of problems. If you want something badly enough, you simply have to find the right number to put on a check."

"And?"

"When I told him Good Shepherd was in trouble because the building was in disrepair, he offered me a million dollars to marry him."

"Oh, Maggie, no—"

"It was a chance to give back when I'd received so much," she hurried to explain. The words kept rushing out. "I just couldn't stand the thought of Lyssa and the other kids losing their home. If not for Good Shepherd I'd have had no one, nothing. It felt like the right thing to do. At the time."

"And now?" Sister asked.

"Now everything is all wrong." Her lips trembled. "I thought he cared when we were—he seemed so caring when the two of us—you know."

"Made love?"

"Yes," she said, relieved that Sister said it for her.

"Does he know about the baby?"

"I told him."

"Since I know you so well, it's not necessary to ask if you have feelings for him. There wouldn't be a baby if you didn't. That means you're here because he doesn't have feelings for you. Is that right?"

"He won't let himself care." A single tear slipped down her cheek.

Sister stood and came around the desk, pulling Maggie to her feet for one of the comforting hugs she remembered. She hung on for all she was worth and let the tears come while Sister patted her back and murmured words of encouragement until Maggie pulled away, swiping at the moisture on her cheeks.

"Don't cry, Margaret Mary." Sister's expression was full of sympathetic wisdom. "I know it seems hopeless right at this moment. But remember what I used to tell you when you were a little girl? God always does things right, even if it seems wrong to us."

"But I don't know what I'm going to do."

"That's all right. You can be sure He will give you what you need at the appropriate time."

Maggie had told Lyssa the same thing, but right at this moment it was very hard to believe.

There was a knock on the door and Sister looked at Maggie, asking with a look if she was okay. Maggie nodded and she said, "Come in."

"Hi, Sister." It was Rachel, a slender, dark-haired sixteen-year-old who lived at the home. "Hey, Maggie. There's a guy at the door. Says he wants to see you."

Jason. She didn't know any other guy, let alone one who would look for her here. She couldn't face him like this. "Sister, I don't want to see him."

"You can't run away from this forever, Maggie." The nun glanced down at her flat abdomen.

"I know. And I won't. But I need a little time before I face him again." From the hall a man's familiar voice drifted through the open door. "Please run interference for me, Sister. I'm going in the other room."

"All right." Sister nodded and Maggie quickly slipped into the adjoining room. She heard the nun say, "Show the gentleman in."

With the connecting door open, Maggie could hear Jason as if he were standing in front of her. His deep, velvety voice wrapped around her like a warm blanket and raised tingles over her skin.

"Sister," he said, "it's nice to see you again."

"I wish I could say the same."

"Maggie told you?"

"Everything, yes."

"Where is she?" he asked. "I have to talk to her."

"She doesn't want to see you, Mr. Garrett. It's not an exaggeration to say that you didn't take the news of the pregnancy well."

"No."

In the brief silence Maggie pictured him raking his fingers through his wonderful thick hair as he always did when he was uncomfortable.

Jason cleared his throat. "I don't think anyone will argue when I say that I handled the situation with all the sensitivity of a water buffalo."

"At least you admit your failing."

"As lame as it sounds, I can only say in my own defense that the news about the baby came as a shock."

"That makes two of us," Sister said wryly, making Maggie squirm again.

"I hurt her. If I could, I'd take it back in a heartbeat. Hurting Maggie is the last thing in the world I would ever want to do. I need to see her. Tell me where she is."

"I can't," Sister said firmly.

"I have to make things right between us. She needs to know how wrong I was about everything. I have to apologize and somehow convince her to forgive me. Tell her I'm here. Please."

There was a note of intensity in his voice, bordering on desperation, Maggie thought. This didn't sound like the cool and controlled Jason she knew. This was more like the man who'd kissed her because he couldn't seem to help himself.

"I'm sorry, Mr. Garrett. She made it absolutely clear that she doesn't want to see you. When all is said and done, Maggie is a girl who believes in God, prayer and marriage forever. Apparently you don't share her convictions."

"What can I do to convince you that I'm not here to hurt her? I want to make it right."

"Why is it so important?"

"Because I'm in love with her."

Maggie stood up straight, away from the wall. She'd expected him to pull out his checkbook, so his declaration got her attention in a big way. There was what could only be described as a pregnant silence in the other room.

Finally, Sister said, "Maggie, come in here please."

With her stomach quivering in a way that had nothing to do with the baby and everything to do with Jason, Maggie stepped into the room. Jason looked uncharacteristically rumpled and completely wonderful with the long sleeves of his white dress shirt rolled up and his red tie loosened at the collar. Expertly tailored gray slacks hugged his flat abdomen and muscular legs. He was a sight for eyes aching from the tears she'd cried just moments ago.

"Hello," she said.

"Maggie, I—"

"I don't mind saying that this situation is beyond my sphere of expertise," Sister said. "I'm going to leave you to sort this out."

Before Maggie could protest, the door closed and she was alone with him. She said the first thing that popped into her head. "How's Brady?"

"Fine. He seems happy with Ginger. But not as happy as he is with you." He frowned. "It's not like you to run away from a situation. Why did you leave?"

"Because, as it turns out, I can't live up to the deal I made. I can't stay because my heart breaks a little more every day, knowing you'll never feel about me the way I do about you." She twisted her hands together. "I'll pay you back the money. Somehow. If you'll give me some time."

He shook his head as already dark eyes darkened even more. "The rest of my life won't be enough time."

"I know it's a lot of money, but—"

"You don't understand, Maggie." He moved forward and stood right in front of her without touching. "I love you. I'm in love with you. The rest of my life won't be enough time to make up for the hurt I've caused. I feel like I've waited an eternity for you and a lifetime isn't long enough to love you."

"I know it's a lot, but—"

He touched a finger to her lips. "The cost of having my son was losing my faith in people." He looked around the tiny office. "Repairs to Good Shepherd cost me a measly million. Falling in love with you is priceless."

She shook her head even as hope filled her heart. "Why should I believe you now? How do I know you want what I do? Like Sister said, I'm a girl who believes in God, the power of prayer and until-death-shall-part-us marriage. Ours is based on a cash transaction. All I am is an asset to you."

Jason shook his head. "One doesn't care about an asset the way I care about you. You don't miss the scent of an asset when she's gone. An asset doesn't determine whether every heartbeat will be full of joy or unbearable pain. No matter how hard I tried, I couldn't seem to make you an asset." A fierce intensity glowed in his eyes. "And I didn't know you were in the next room when I told Sister Margaret how I feel. If you don't believe anything else, you have to believe I'd never lie to a nun." He drew in a deep, shuddering breath. "And I'll never lie to you. The church's loss is my gain. I am incredibly grateful that you didn't become a nun."

"Jason, you're a good man. I know that, but—"

"No buts." He reached into his pocket and pulled out a small, black velvet jeweler's box, and flipped it open. "You're beautiful and good and the woman most likely not to get caught up in material things. But I'm hoping just this once you'll make an exception." Uncertainty trickled into his normally confident gaze. "Before you, I went into a relationship always formulating my strategy to get out first. I made mental notes to personalize the outrageously expensive gift that would take the sting out of breaking things off with a woman. Not this time."

She looked at the ring—a round diamond solitaire in a platinum band. "What does this mean?"

"I want a relationship with you for the rest of our lives. This is my entrance strategy." He got down on one knee. "Margaret Mary Shepherd, will you marry me?"

"But we're already married."

"Not in the church. We'll do it right this time." He cocked his thumb over his shoulder, indicating the home where she grew up. "We'll have a big wedding with your family there. I'll beg if I have to." He put his palm on her abdomen. "I want this baby. With you. There's nothing more important to me than family. And Brady needs you—his mom."

Joy filled her, making her lightheaded. It was hard to believe he was offering her everything she'd ever wanted.

She put her hands on his shoulders and stared into his eyes. The first time she'd met him he'd tried to conduct an interview and it was time to return the favor. "As it happens, I'm interviewing for a husband. I'd very much like to see your résumé. You can messenger it over."

He stood, grinning the grin that had stolen her heart the day she met him. Folding her in his arms, he said, "I can do better than that."

He lowered his mouth to hers and kissed her until her legs threatened to buckle. When he lifted his head, he met her gaze, his own filled with nobility, sincerity and love.

"I promise to be a good father and an exemplary husband. I love you," he said simply.

"You're hired," she said, "because I love you more."

"Not possible."

"Oh, yes it is." She stood on tiptoe, pressed her lips to his, savoring the sweetness of this negotiating technique.

No longer the virgin nanny, Maggie was happier than she'd ever thought to be. She was loved and in love with a wonderful man. She was a wife and mother with a family of her very own and it was everything she'd ever hoped for.

\* \* \* \* \*

Dear Reader,

The family dynamic is both complicated and emotional. When a relative dies, especially at a young age, the loss is deeper and more devastating, the "what ifs" more emotional, the "if onlys" more sad.

I grew up a middle child, one of six siblings. Like Blake Decker in *The Nanny and Me*, I lost my only sister to cancer when she was thirty-six years old. This shared loss brought my four brothers and I even closer, but there are certain things the guys will never understand the way my sister did. Like the vital importance of a gifted hairstylist. Or the critical need to keep a pedicure appointment.

No one can replace my sister, but through a shared love of storytelling I've been fortunate enough to meet bright, funny women who have become like sisters to me. And being part of the Mills & Boon family is an honor and privilege—not to mention a dream come true. I have the best job in the world thanks to you awesome readers.

Happy reading!

*Teresa Southwick*

For Taelor and Jensen Southwick,
who suggested the name for the dog in this story.
Girls, you're beautiful inside and out.

# THE NANNY AND ME

## BY
## TERESA SOUTHWICK

First published in Great Britain 2010
Harlequin Mills & Boon Limited,
Eton House, 18-24 Paradise Road, Richmond, Surrey TW9 1SR

© Teresa Ann Southwick 2009

ISBN: 978 0 263 88838 6

23-1110

Harlequin Mills & Boon policy is to use papers that are natural, renewable
and recyclable products and made from wood grown in sustainable forests.
The logging and manufacturing processes conform to the legal environmental
regulations of the country of origin.

Printed and bound in Spain
by Litografia Rosés S.A., Barcelona

*Chapter One*

No one liked to be made a fool of and Casey Thomas had reason to hate it more than most. The last time someone did it, her best friend had died.

The last thing she needed was manipulation from her boss.

And what a boss she was. Ginger Davis was a beautiful brunette who proved that fifty really was the new thirty and not just a marketing phrase. The president and CEO of the Las Vegas-based Nanny Network had to be on the far side of forty-nine but didn't look anywhere close to that. Apparently she thrived on the stress generated by managing the exclusive, expensive company specializing in child care for the rich and famous.

Casey glared across the glass-topped desk in her boss's home office. "This could have been handled over the phone, Ginger. You insisted I come here because you don't think I can tell you no to your face."

Ginger folded her hands, then rested them on a stack of files, her expression not the least bit apologetic. "I wanted you to meet Blake Decker and his *orphaned* niece and tell him no to *his* face."

If that wasn't blatant manipulation, Casey would eat her *Child Rearing for Dummies* handbook. The woman just had to get the word *orphaned* in there. It wasn't that Casey was unsympathetic. She'd lost her own mother when she was eleven. But as a nanny, she had rules—and good reasons for them.

She had the physical and emotional scars to prove that undoing a system of beliefs ingrained over many years was a losing proposition and a waste of time and energy. Army service had taught her that life was unpredictable and whatever time one had on this earth should not be squandered by spitting into the wind. If she was going to help a child, it would be in the child's formative years, before negative influences took hold.

"You know my focus is on children under ten years old."

Her boss nodded. "And you know that my job is to pair up my employees with clients who are a good fit. You're happy. The client is happy. Everyone is happy."

Casey wasn't feeling the love. "Is this where we link arms and sing 'Kumbaya'?"

"If that works for you." Ginger smiled. "Casey, I know what happened to you overseas while you were in the service. And I understand why you specialize in a certain age group. I've respected your boundaries without question since you joined the Nanny Network family."

Owing this woman was darned inconvenient. Ginger had taken her on after she'd been medically discharged from the army. Casey had received on-the-job training in the preschool Nooks and Nannies and was now working for the Nanny Network while taking early childhood development classes to finish up her elementary school teaching credential.

She was a live-in nanny, caring for children ten and under, giving them a stable base of operations and showing them how to be upstanding human beings through example, discipline and love. The career was incredibly rewarding. And she needed all the rewarding she could get to fill up her redemption jar. When a friend paid with their life because of you, going on with your own life wasn't easy.

Still, she was trying to make a difference as best she could. Why did Ginger have to put her on the spot? Why couldn't Ginger let her continue to do what she loved to do on her own terms?

"I'm already working for the Redmonds."

"You have a break for the next month, while they're in Europe with Heidi and Jack. I'll have a replacement when they return."

The truth was, Casey had been dreading having too much time on her hands to think. That didn't mean she was willing to bend her rules. "I have plans for my time off."

"And I need to ask you to cancel them as a favor to me. This little girl is twelve—only two years over your bottom line. She's a kid who needs a break."

Casey knew she was going to hate herself for asking but couldn't stop the words. "Why should I make an exception for Blake Decker and his orphaned niece?"

"See for yourself." Ginger hit her intercom and asked her assistant to send them in.

There was very little wiggle room between a rock and a hard place, and Casey hated that, too.

Moments after the summons a man came into the office with a young girl strolling behind him. He walked right up to Casey, who was still standing in front of Ginger's desk.

"Blake Decker," he said.

"Casey Thomas," she answered, shaking the hand he held out.

He looked at the girl beside him. "This is my niece Mia Decker."

"Nice to meet you, Mia."

"Yeah. Whatever."

The child barely made eye contact. In her threadbare jeans, multilayered T-shirts and zippered cardigan sweatshirt, which was hanging off her shoulders, she was the picture of bored indifference. She was also a beautiful little girl with long, wavy brown hair and huge eyes that were an unusual shade of blue-green, almost turquoise.

Apparently the remarkable Decker DNA was liberally spread around. Her uncle was an exceptionally good-looking man somewhere in his mid- to late thirties. Casey had seen her share of hunks in the army, but this guy's dark hair, blue eyes and square jaw could fill movie theater seats around the world.

The dark charcoal suit, red tie and white shirt fit his tall, lean body perfectly and looked expensive. Instinct told her that he could afford the Nanny Network's upscale price tag, but so far she hadn't seen any reason to make an exception to her personal rules. Not even the fact that he looked like he wanted to wring his niece's neck for her rudeness and attitude.

"I'm sorry for Mia's bad manners," he finally said.

"And I'm sorry you're such a dork," Mia shot back.

Ginger cleared her throat. "Why don't you both sit down and everyone can get better acquainted."

"What for?" Mia asked. "He's just going to dump me like everyone else."

Her uncle shifted uncomfortably. "Mia, I'm not going to dump you—"

"Define *everyone*," Casey said.

The girl stared angrily at her. "Why do you care?"

"I don't," Casey answered honestly. The last thing this kid

needed was an adult patronizing her. "I don't know you well enough to have an emotional investment in you."

"Then why are you asking questions?" Mia demanded.

"Call it curiosity."

"I'm not show-and-tell," the kid snapped. "This is all just stupid—"

"Mia—" Blake's cell phone rang and he pulled it from the case at his waist. After looking at the caller ID, he replaced the phone and let the call go to voice mail. He shot his niece a stern look as he stared down at her. "Miss Davis asked you to sit."

Mia glared defiantly for several moments, then apparently decided that arguing about this wasn't a hill she wanted to die on. Without a word she flopped into a chair, although her body language was anything but silent. The slouch and scowl said loud and clear that every adult in the room was a complete moron.

In spite of herself, Casey was getting sucked in, and apparently her boss knew and planned to capitalize on the weakness.

The first clue was when Ginger stood and said, "I'm going to let the three of you talk. I have some calls to make and I'll just step into the other room to do that."

Before Casey could protest, they were alone. She wanted to end this meeting and walk out, too, but the girl's words had struck a nerve. "You didn't answer my question, Mia. Who else dumped you?"

"My niece has had a tough time," Blake said for Mia. "My sister wasn't in a good place and never developed the instincts or skills to handle her. There's no point in going over all that."

Casey looked up at him, way up. "First of all, Mr. Decker, my question was directed to Mia." She glanced at the girl and noticed something in her eyes. It vanished almost instantly, but for just a moment interest had replaced the bored look. "Secondly, may I ask what you do for a living?"

"I'm an attorney."

"Family law?"

"Not exactly."

"What exactly?" Casey asked.

"Divorce." He met her gaze but it was impossible to tell what he was thinking.

"I see." She looked at the child. "Are you going to answer my question?"

"Do I have to?" Mia glared.

"Yes." Casey folded her arms and looked down, letting Mia know she was prepared to wait as long as necessary.

"I forgot what it was."

"Who else dumped you?" Casey repeated.

After several moments, Mia huffed out an exasperated breath. "My father split before I was born. My mother died. I stayed with his sister for a while but she didn't want me."

"It's not that black-and-white," her uncle said.

"Sure it is," Mia shot back, her beautiful eyes spitting anger and resentment. "No one wants me. Including you."

The words touched Casey somewhere deep inside and she looked at the girl. "Mia, would you mind waiting for your uncle in the other room?"

"Why?"

"Because I'd like to speak with him alone." Casey met the defiant gaze and said wryly, "What have you got to lose? This is all stupid, anyway. Right?"

Her full cupid's bow mouth pulled into a straight line before Mia snapped, "Whatever."

She stomped out of the room and slammed the door.

Casey leaned back against the glass-topped desk as she looked at the uncle. "If it's not black-and-white, there must be shades of gray, Mr. Decker. Tell me about your niece."

He unbuttoned his suit jacket and rested his hands on lean

hips. "It's an old story, Miss Thomas. My sister got involved with the wrong guy. She got pregnant. My parents threw her out and she disappeared. I was away at college and never heard from her. I didn't even know I had a niece until Child Protective Services recently contacted me. There's no one else to take her."

The kid was right. He didn't want her, either. "You could let her go into the state system."

"No."

"Why not?"

"That's a good question." His phone rang again, and when he looked at the number, he said, "Excuse me. I have to take this." Flipping the phone open, he snapped, "What?" After listening, he nodded. "I'll be there in a half hour. It's a deposition. They can wait." He ended the call and replaced the phone in its case, never taking his gaze from hers. "You want to know why I took her in and I wish I had an answer. It could be as simple as the fact that she's family, but it doesn't feel that way. She's a stranger. All I can tell you for sure is that she's not going to Child Protective Services."

Casey respected his honesty a lot more than she wanted to. She wished he were a complete jerk, which would make it easy to tell him to take a flying leap. Instead she asked, "Why do you need a nanny?"

"I have to work." He ran his fingers through his hair. "It's safe to say that I have no idea how to raise any child, let alone a girl. She's too young to leave unsupervised."

"There are after-school programs." Casey could feel her resolve weakening. *Darn Ginger.* She was right about telling him no to his face. The rock and the hard place were putting the squeeze on her. "I'd be happy to recommend activities that will give her supervision while you work."

"First of all, my workday is longer than your after-school

activities." He blew out a long breath. "Second, don't pretend that she's your average, normal twelve-year-old girl. She needs more than arts and crafts and a field trip to the zoo."

"What does she need?"

"You tell me. That's your area of expertise." He held his hands out in a helpless gesture that looked like it didn't fit, like it was foreign to him. "If you were a client wanting to dissolve your marriage, I would be the legal professional you'd consult."

"But I'm not." She'd never been married. Came close once, but it didn't happen. She wasn't marriage material. Marriage required trust and that was blasted out of her by a suicide bomber in Iraq.

He met her gaze and there was something almost desperate in his own. "My point is that a good lawyer knows when he is out of his depth and needs to consult an expert. Specifically, I need an expert on children. The Nanny Network comes highly recommended and Miss Davis tells me you're the expert I need to consult."

This man was asking her to intervene on behalf of an obviously troubled girl and she didn't want to go there again. Her judgment couldn't be trusted and it wasn't fair to either of them for her to agree to the arrangement.

"Did she also tell you that I don't accept clients over a certain age?"

"Yes. I asked her to prevail upon you to make an exception in Mia's case."

"I can't do that. I'm sorry." She straightened away from the desk. "Ginger has a lot of contacts. I'm sure she can help you find someone."

"She already found you and she tells me you're highly qualified for Mia's needs. I'd really like you to think it over," he said.

So she'd finally told him no to his face and he didn't under-stand the meaning of the word. Casey walked to the door and opened it. "I've already made up my mind."

She glanced around, expecting to see a hostile Mia slouched in a chair, with antagonism rolling off her like sound waves. Instead the room was empty.

Blake Decker needed this like a brain aneurysm. He had back-to-back appointments stacked up like planes waiting to land and was due in court after lunch for a high-profile celebrity client whose wife had been caught cheating by the paparazzi. Mia couldn't have picked a worse day to do a dis-appearing act.

In the elevator, he glanced down at Casey. "You don't need to help look for her."

"No. But two pairs of eyes are better than one."

When the elevator reached the ground floor, the doors whooshed open and he held out a hand, indicating she should precede him. They hurried across the lobby of the luxurious high-rise building and walked outside, then scanned up and down the sidewalk, looking for a glimpse of Mia.

"Do you see her?" he asked.

Casey stood on tiptoe, trying to see around the pedestrians strolling past. "That green sweatshirt she was wearing will stand out, but I don't see it."

Blake wondered how this day had gone so horribly wrong. Technically, things had started south when Mia came to live with him a couple weeks ago. Since then his days and nights had been a nightmare of calls from school regarding tardiness and skipped classes, of not knowing where the kid was half the time, and of wondering what she was doing while he was at work.

He was a lawyer. He was good at it and understood the law.

As his niece's legal guardian, he was responsible for her behavior and liable for her mistakes. The buck stopped here. His life hadn't been this screwed up since he caught his wife sleeping with his best friend.

He looked down at Casey. "I appreciate the gesture, but she's my problem. I'll find her."

"Don't look a gift horse in the mouth."

The gesture was definitely a gift, because she had turned down his offer of a job and wasn't on the clock. Another way his day had gone south. He wasn't accustomed to losing a negotiation.

He studied the shadows in her big hazel eyes. Casey was an attractive blonde with silky hair cut in choppy layers that skimmed her shoulders—messy, straight, sharp, sexy layers. And shoulders. The white sundress showed off bare arms that were as tanned and toned as her great legs. Her sandals revealed toes painted a vivid shade of red.

What he could see told him she kept in shape and that shape was better than good. But it was nothing compared to her mouth. He could hardly keep himself from staring at her full lips. They were no doubt a result of an amazing gift from her gene pool, because she didn't seem like the cosmetic injection type. And the deep dimples in her cheeks flashed when she was annoyed, which made him wonder how they'd look with a smile, which so far he hadn't seen. She was no-nonsense, no pretense, no games. No compunction about turning down his job offer. Yet here she was, pounding the pavement with him.

"Why do you feel the need to help?" he asked.

"I sent her out of the room. I feel responsible for her taking off. She's obviously upset—"

His cell phone rang and he recognized the office number. "Hi, Rita. I know I'm late." He listened to the list of appointments, although it was a waste of breath. He already knew his day was screwed thanks to Mia. "Look, something's come up. I need you to cancel my appointments and reschedule." He glanced at his watch. "With luck I'll make it to court. If not, I'll let you know so Leo can fill in. You're a lifesaver, Ree. Thanks."

"You're a busy man," Casey commented.

He nodded. "My niece picked the worst possible time to crank up the rebellion."

"Like I was saying," she said pointedly, "Mia's obviously upset."

"How can you tell? What you saw was normal for her. Since I took her in, sarcastic, abrasive and belligerent have been the full range of her disposition." He looked up and down the street without spotting the familiar green sweatshirt. "And I think it's safe to add unpredictable to that list."

"It's not really a surprise, given the instability in her life. We're all a product of our environment, Mr. Decker—"

"Call me Blake."

She nodded, then continued. "I sent her out of the room and that makes me feel a certain responsibility for her taking off. The least I can do is help you find her."

The seriously stubborn look on her face told him he couldn't talk her out of this, and truthfully, he was grateful for the company. "Okay. Thanks."

"You're welcome."

As they walked and talked, her gaze scanned left and right, as if they were on patrol. He remembered a detail of her résumé, one that made her come-and-get-me red-painted toes even more intriguing. "Miss Davis said you were in the army."

"That's right."

He waited for her to elaborate, but she didn't. "She thought your background would make you a good fit for Mia. Strong and smart enough to handle her."

"Ginger is wrong."

He studied the tension in her shoulders and mouth. He knew the basics of her military experience but had a feeling there was a sad story in there somewhere. She had the sexiest lips this side of heaven and the saddest eyes he'd ever seen. Sad stories and broken dreams were his stock-in-trade. He'd lived his own and made a fortune on other people's. This woman touched a nerve with him and that hadn't happened for a long time. It wasn't a good thing.

So maybe it was for the best that Casey had refused to work for him. On the other hand, the more time he spent with her, the more convinced he became that her boss was right about her being strong enough to deal with Mia.

Down the street from the corporate office of the Nanny Network, they stopped at a traffic light. Fashion Show Mall was across the street, and there was still no sign of Mia.

"Maybe we should call the police," Blake said.

"We will if we have to but let's keep looking."

"Any ideas where we should look?"

Casey looked at him, her expression part wryness, part pity. She nodded her head toward the upscale shopping center. "If I wanted to lose myself, that's where I'd go. Retail therapy works wonders."

He nodded. "I see the 'duh' look in your eyes. I believe I already confessed to knowing zero about a twelve-year-old girl."

"And what makes you think I do?"

"You were twelve once and you're female. That puts you one up on me." The look in her eyes said it was a long time ago. "Little girls are way beyond my range of experience."

"Big girls are more your style?"

"I like women, if that's what you're asking. But my style? I don't have one." He shook his head. "For the record, I don't think any man understands them. Young, old or anywhere in between, women are the eighth wonder of the world and as mysterious as the elusive commodity of luck in this town."

She put a hand to her forehead, shading her eyes from the sun. "I'm not sure how to respond to that, so I won't. But I say we go check out the mall."

"Okay."

After crossing at the light, they followed the sidewalk and entered the mall at the food court on the third level. He shadowed Casey when she headed for the escalator. That was when he realized she moved pretty fast for a woman who wasn't all that tall. She was maybe a couple inches over five feet. Blake was six feet two and had a long stride, but when they got off on a lower floor, she had no trouble keeping up with him. They marched past Nordstrom, Dillard's, Neiman Marcus, Saks Fifth Avenue and every small, upscale store in between. On the first level they did the same thing, without spotting Mia.

In the center of the mall he stopped to look around. "I think maybe it's time to call the police."

She was studying a graphic of the mall's layout. "Okay."

He started to pull out his cell when she took off. "I thought we were getting the cops involved."

"We are. In a manner of speaking."

Blake trailed after her to the mall security office. Inside there was a twentysomething guy in navy trousers and a light blue shirt with an official mall security patch on the sleeve. Blake saw a familiar girl in a green sweatshirt sitting by the desk.

"Mia." He let out a long breath, then explained that she was his niece and he was her legal guardian.

Rent-a-cop gave Mia an unsympathetic look. "She was caught stealing makeup."

The Bonnie Parker wannabe had been gone for what?

Twenty minutes? A half hour tops? It hadn't taken her long to get in trouble. Probably he should be grateful that she wasn't good enough at being bad to get away with it, but that was small comfort.

Blake knew the law, but everyone had a specialty and criminal law wasn't his. When all else failed, it couldn't hurt to bluff. "I'm guessing that pressing charges would be more costly and time-consuming than it's worth. What if I give you my word that you won't see her in here again?" He looked at Mia, who was trying to look sullen, but a little bit of fright leaked through. "And there will be consequences for her at home." That part was *really* a bluff, because he had no idea what those consequences would be.

"Okay." The security guy frowned at Blake's niece. "You got off easy, kid."

Blake nodded. "Thanks. I'll make sure she doesn't do anything like this again."

Right after he flapped his arms and landed on the moon, because he had no clue how to keep that promise.

With Mia between them, Blake and Casey walked back toward the mall entrance.

"I have to go to the bathroom," Mia said when they passed the restrooms.

Was this another escape attempt? Could he trust her not to take off again?

As if Casey could read his thoughts, she said, "I'll check it out."

She disappeared into the ladies' room and was back in a moment. "Clear," she said.

Mia did a dramatic eye roll but held back any sarcastic comment as she went in.

Blake studied the door that said Women. "Maybe I can get her one of those electronic surveillance devices for her ankle."

"You're not very good at this, are you?"

He sighed. "You have no idea how badly I'd like to say 'Duh.' That's what I've been trying to tell you. I freely admit that I need help. It's why I tried to hire you in the first place."

She nodded without saying anything, but it was almost as if he could see the conflict raging inside her. Doubts darted across her face and highlighted the uncertainty in her eyes, but finally she met his gaze.

"Do you still want me to work for you?" she asked.

"Is the pope Catholic? Do bears go anywhere they want in the woods?"

A half smile curved up the corners of her mouth. "Is that a yes?"

"That's as close to a yes as I can get without begging," he confirmed.

"Okay. I'll accept the position on a trial basis. If it doesn't work out—"

He touched a finger to her lips to silence her. "Think positive."

That was his plan and he wasn't an especially positive kind of guy. However, he was positive that brushing her lips just now had made him want to explore them even further. That was pretty stupid, after she'd finally agreed to work for him.

Still, considering his history with women, stupid was pretty much in character for him. Since his marriage imploded, he'd learned to expect the worst, because that way he never got blindsided.

Right now he chose to hope for the best with his new nanny, because he really needed her.

## Chapter Two

Casey stood at the door to Blake Decker's penthouse, located
at One Queensridge Place, and fervently wished for a decision
do-over. He'd said he specialized in divorce law, and judging
by his living arrangements, there was an obscene amount of
money in marriages gone bad. The lobby of this luxury building had all dark wood walls, crystal chandeliers and a grand
staircase with intricate wrought-iron railings. One look at the
expansive marble floor gave her the most wicked desire to slip
on a pair of Rollerblades and race through the building,
shouting "Cowabunga" at the top of her lungs.

She pressed the button beside the door, but Blake already
knew who was there because security at the front gate had
called to announce her.

"I'm glad to see you," he said after opening up.

"Hi." She wheeled her small weekend bag into the marble
foyer, which mirrored the elegance of the building's lobby.

He frowned at her luggage. "Where's the rest of your bags?"

"We agreed to a trial basis. If it doesn't work out, why waste time and energy moving a lot of stuff?"

"So much for the power of positive thinking."

Casey used to be an optimist, but not anymore. "Never test the depth of the water with both feet."

"Right." He picked up her suitcase. "I guess you want to see where you'll be staying."

"Okay." She couldn't help noticing how wide his shoulders were as she followed. Nice butt, too. "Where's Mia?"

"In her room." He glanced back. "Doing homework."

"She's in summer school." It wasn't a question. Casey was taking classes, too, trying to finish up her degree as quickly as possible.

"I met with a school counselor, who recommended it. To keep her busy and out of trouble. Albeit without much success. Also, because her educational background is a little sketchy, what with her unstable upbringing. They want to see where she is academically before the term starts in September."

"A good idea."

She followed him past a living room with light green walls and wide crown molding and furnished with several love seats and a couple of chairs arranged in a grouping designed to facilitate conversation. Next was the kitchen-family room combination. There was a built-in cherrywood entertainment center with a plasma TV almost large enough for a movie theater. An L-shaped, overstuffed couch sat in front of it. The floor-to-ceiling windows offered an expansive view of the Las Vegas Valley, including a golf course and several hotel-casino resorts nearby.

As they continued walking past rooms, Casey admired the penthouse's understated elegance, cloud-soft carpet and recessed lighting, which showed off every detail to perfection.

"How big is this place?" she asked.

"Six thousand square feet, not counting the terrace." He looked down at her and grinned. "Give or take a square foot or two."

"Do you provide a GPS unit to your employees?"

"If you're as smart as Ginger Davis says, you'll learn your way around in no time." He walked into a room at the farthest corner of the penthouse. "Welcome to your new home, sweet home. I think you'll be comfortable."

She looked around at the oak armoire and matching dresser with a multitude of drawers, large and small. A floral comforter and a plethora of pink, green and maroon throw pillows covered the bed. To the right was a dressing area with a walk-in closet and a bathroom, which technically made this a suite. Chalk up one for her boss, the divorce lawyer.

"What do you think?"

She nodded. "It'll do."

"Good." He set her single suitcase on the tufted bench at the end of the bed. "It won't take you long to unpack. So, if you don't mind, I'd like to talk to you. In my study."

"Okay."

They retraced their steps, and somewhere beyond the family room, he turned right and entered another room. The desk, computer, and built-in bookcases holding big, fat, boring-looking books clued her in to the fact that this must be his study. Looked like an office to her, but when you had enough money, it probably earned you the right to call it whatever you wanted.

"Have a seat," he said, indicating the two leather barrel-shaped chairs in front of the desk.

Casey picked the one on the right and sat. "First of all, you should know that I need two evenings a week off and an afternoon on the weekend."

"How about *one* weeknight?" He was still standing on

the other side of the desk. Maybe he was striking an intimidating pose.

The thought almost made Casey smile. A five-star general in the United States Army was intimidating. Blake Decker? Not so much. As long as she ignored the gleam of amusement in his blue eyes. Or the smokin' hot jawline, which could have been carved out of a rugged peak in Red Rock Canyon. He was wearing khaki shorts, a black T-shirt that highlighted impressive muscles in his chest and arms, and flip-flops that might have made him look like the dork Mia had accused him of being. But the kid would be way wrong.

Casey refused to be intimidated. All he had to do was give her even the ghost of a reason and she'd be so out of there.

She cleared her throat and didn't like the fact that to meet his gaze, her chin rose slightly. It made her look defiant instead of cool. And she so wanted to look cool. Frosty. Emotionally unengaged.

"I need two evenings off," she said. "I'm taking night classes. It's not negotiable."

"That's a challenge, since negotiating is what I do."

His slow, challenging grin actually made her world tilt, along with producing a shimmy and shake in her stomach. The reaction was a big, honkin' clue that she should exercise her escape clause and, well, escape.

"Look, Mr. Decker—"

"I asked you to call me Blake. Remember?"

*And how.* "Obviously you're good at what you do and it pays pretty well, or you wouldn't live in the Parthenon."

"Excuse me?" If anything, the gleam in his eyes intensified.

"This complex is like a Greek temple with fountains, archways, anatomically correct sculptures and Roman columns."

"You're mixing your civilizations," he pointed out.

"And you're splitting hairs to distract me," she countered.

"I've been working my tail off to get a teaching credential and I'm almost there. Two evenings a week for classes, and either a Saturday or Sunday afternoon, your choice which. Those are my terms. Take it or leave it."

When she started to stand, he held his palms out in a conciliatory gesture.

"Yes, ma'am. Understood." He saluted, then sat in the plush desk chair. "Your military is showing."

Casey pressed fingertips to her chest and the scars hidden beneath her sleeveless cotton blouse, souvenirs of her time in the army. They were both a warning and a reminder that trusting anyone was a dangerous proposition. She'd let the wrong person come close, and an IED—an improvised explosive device—had taken her best friend's life and left her two little kids motherless. Blake Decker had no idea how much military she would always carry around with her.

"Another thing," she said, ignoring his charm. The man had buckets of charm and her military training hadn't prepared her for that. The army was about discipline, chain of command, following orders. There was no handbook for how to remain impassive when you were attracted to the person giving the orders. You were simply expected to follow the command without question.

"Yes?"

"From what you told me about Mia's background and the behavior I observed—"

"What a nice way to say she's a shoplifter."

"You can only be grateful that she's not very good at it."

"That already occurred to me," he admitted.

"I've been thinking about it, and in my opinion the two of you could benefit from counseling. I can give you several recommendations of excellent family therapists—"

"No."

She stared at him for a moment. "Just like that?"

"Yes."

"But negotiating is what you do," she reminded him.

"It is. But some things aren't worth a compromise. And going toe-to-toe with a Dr. Phil wannabe is one of them."

Casey recognized the heat of anger in his cool blue eyes and wondered about the nerve she'd stumbled on. "Mia would get a lot out of talking to someone."

"Talk is cheap."

"Not at the prices they charge," she pointed out.

"It's not the cost I object to." But he stopped short of saying what he *did* have a problem with in regard to seeing a counselor. "You get two out of three, Casey. Two evenings and an afternoon off. Any of my social engagements can be scheduled around your commitments."

"You mean dates?" The words popped out before she even realized the thought had formed.

"Yes," he confirmed.

"Are you dating anyone?" She really hoped she hadn't said that out loud, but the way his mouth curved up told her she wasn't that lucky. That was twice in a matter of seconds that the words were out before going through a rational thought process. It wasn't something she wanted to make a habit of.

"The only steady woman in my life besides my mother and Mia is an ex-wife I'd rather forget about."

Her not-so-stealthy recon had produced interesting results. He'd been married. He wasn't now. And there was no permanent arm candy.

The fact was, that information made her want to smile, a big clue that taking this assignment was a very bad idea.

"And," he added, "I'm not in the market for a romantic relationship."

"That makes two of us."

His eyebrows rose slightly, the only indication that her agreement surprised him. She had good reason for feeling that way. A person needed to trust to be able to form intimate ties and Blake seemed to be lacking in that department. It was something they had in common. A bomb in Iraq had blown her trust to kingdom come, which meant she wouldn't be forming ties anytime soon, either.

A week later, Blake stared at the stack of completed paperwork on his desk and figured productivity was the happy by-product of having his habitat invaded by females. His new norm was barricading himself in his study, instead of sitting on the couch in front of the TV to watch sports or the news or engage in other mindless entertainment.

Not that he wasn't using his mental capacity for other things.

One of the reasons he was cutting himself off from the invading females was that Casey had invaded his mind as well as his environment. He stared at the two chairs on the other side of his desk. A week ago she'd sat there and teased him about the way wealthy people lived. Instead of taking offense, he'd been impressed by her sense of humor. She was smart. Still, he knew a lot of smart women and spent little or no time thinking about them.

And flirty ones activated his gold-digger sensors. Casey wasn't flirty. Just the opposite.

She was clear that she wasn't interested in anything but a boss-employee relationship. Period. That one intrigued him.

He'd done love once, and the end had been painful and ugly. As a divorce attorney, a successful one, he spent every day representing clients who were looking to end painful and ugly relationships. That made him cautious and determined *not* to open that door again.

But what was Casey's story? What had happened to turn her off to romance?

A soft knock on the study door pulled his thoughts back to the moment. "Come in," he said.

Casey stood in the doorway. "Dinner's ready."

No salutation, small talk or frivolous chatter. She was straightforward and to the point. The devil of it was that she couldn't be further from his type. Her white cotton capris and black sleeveless top were a far cry from the silk and sequins his dates wore. Casey Thomas was all button-down efficiency and he couldn't stop thinking about *unbuttoning* her. How stupid was that?

He was her employer and an attorney. Any move in that direction on his part would be inappropriate, not to mention it would open the door for a sexual-harassment lawsuit.

"Blake?"

He met her gaze. "Hmm?"

"I said dinner's ready. I'm going to get Mia."

His niece. The whole reason Casey was here. And since he'd hired her, there hadn't been a single phone call from the school or the police. That made him cautiously optimistic that the new nanny was the solution to the Mia problem. Another excellent reason to continue keeping his distance.

"You and Mia go ahead and eat without me. I have a lot of work to do."

Instead of backing out of the room, as she'd done every other evening, she advanced on him, and the look in her eyes could best be described as determined.

"We need to talk."

Four words a man never wanted to hear coming out of a woman's mouth. Especially when the mouth in question was as kissable as Casey's. There were about a million things he would rather do with it that didn't include conversation.

"We'll schedule a meeting. "I've got to get through this stack by tomorrow—"

"You're here. I'm here. By my definition it's a meeting." She sat down in one of the chairs across from him. "And what I have to say won't take long."

Definitely determined.

"I'm not going to beat around the bush."

He'd have been surprised if she did. "What's on your mind?" he asked.

"Work is not an acceptable excuse for avoidance."

She knew he was dodging her? Offense was always the best defense. "Six thousand square feet of high-end real estate doesn't come cheap. It takes billable hours. Keyword *hours*. I have to put in a lot of them to pay the rent."

"It's not about a roof over your head," she shot back. "This behavior appears to run in the family. Mia has inherited the evasion gene, too."

"What are you talking about?"

"She's hiding in her room, the same way you are here in your study."

"I'm glad to hear she's hitting the books," he said, trying to deflect some of the truth.

"How do you know that's what she's doing?"

"If she's in there, what else would she be up to?"

Her wry, pitying look was a clue that his remark was going to bite him in the backside. "She has a computer with Internet access, a cell phone, a house line and a TV. Those are the most obvious electronic devices. And this is a girl who everyone, including herself, admits has had a rocky go of things so far."

"And your point?"

"Do you seriously believe that a couple of weeks in your high-end real estate has turned her into a disciplined scholar focused on good grades and college goals?"

When she put it like that, he didn't. The truth was, he hadn't given Mia a lot of thought at all. Everything with his niece seemed to be under control. Casey was the one he'd spent too much time thinking about.

"You're saying she has distractions," he said.

"Yes."

"So tell me how dinner is going to change things. Especially a dinner with me there."

"A meal together isn't just nourishment for the body. It goes a long way toward feeding the soul."

He tilted his head and studied her serious expression. "Do you really believe that?"

"Completely."

"Why?"

"Your niece needs to feel stable and secure. A family unit around a dinner table is the best place to start."

"Why?" he said again.

"It shows you care."

"Right." He and his ex-wife, Debra, had eaten together a lot, and he'd found out how much she cared when he caught her in bed with his best friend. "Look, Casey, I appreciate your dedication above and beyond the call of duty, but—"

"That's not all," she interrupted. "It's an opportunity for you to find out what's going on with her."

He leaned forward and rested his forearms on the desk. "Just to be clear and make sure we're on the same page, you are talking about Mia Decker, my niece?"

"Yes."

"The same one whose default response is, 'Whatever'? The girl who thinks I'm the dork who's trying to dump her? That's the kid you're talking about?"

"Hostility is a defense mechanism."

"It's effective." He knew a thing or two about hostility.

"The thing is that if you show up and she gets used to you being there, eventually she'll start talking. Whether she means to or not, she'll give you clues about what's going on in her life, good and bad. But communication isn't all about talking. Listening is an important component. You can't do that if you're isolated in this room. For whatever reason."

His gaze snapped to hers. "So for Mia it's a defense mechanism, and I'm a head case?"

"That's not what I said—"

It was implied. "Look, Casey, you're a soldier slash nanny whose primary responsibility is being my niece's bodyguard."

"Blake, I—"

He held up his hand. "The point is that it's not your job to get into my head. Others have tried and failed."

"That's not what I'm doing." Anger flashed in her eyes as she scooted to the edge of her seat. "Mia has been neglected and left to fend for herself. An expensive roof over her head doesn't mean it's not still happening."

"I repeat, you were hired to keep her safe."

"I'm paid to do that, but you're her biological family. She tries to hide it, but like every other human being on the planet, she's looking for love and acceptance. The more you keep her at arm's length, the more you reinforce that she's not lovable. Blake, you have to—"

He held up a finger to silence her. "Don't tell me what I have to do. She has a place to live. It's your job to tell me what she needs—food, clothes, school supplies. It's my job to write the check."

Anger and something that looked a lot like disapproval swirled in her eyes, making the gold and green flecks that turned to hazel a lot darker. It was almost as if he could see the wheels in her head turning, words pressing to get out. Finally she stood and all but saluted when she snapped out a curt, "Yes, sir."

And then he was alone.

It should have been a relief, but it definitely wasn't. Verbal sparring with Casey was the most invigorating thing he'd done in a very long time. He should be mad as hell. In any other employee he'd call it impertinence. But her earnestness had come through loud and clear, erasing any hint of insolence. He believed she was genuinely trying to help, but he didn't need it. Mia was far better off than she'd ever been in her life and didn't need him meddling.

He'd made a mess of his own life. Who was he to tell Mia what to do? That was for the nanny. The one with a mouth made for kissing. And a body with curves in all the right places.

The one he couldn't stop thinking about.

And he wondered, not for the first time, if hiring Casey was as good in reality as it had looked on paper.

## Chapter Three

"Boring."

Casey glanced over at Mia, who was slouched in the front passenger seat of her Corolla. They'd just sat through a college class on Shakespeare's tragedies, and as tragic as the girl looked, it was quite possible she'd actually absorbed something.

"I'm shocked and appalled that studying Shakespeare doesn't make you do the happy dance."

The girl responded with a dramatic eye roll. Casey wished she'd had the luxury of sinking to that level when she confronted her boss about not showing up as agreed so that she could attend class without having to bring Mia along. Blake Decker could have been a bigger ass, but she wasn't sure how. Actually, that wasn't true. He was a bigger jerk when he'd told her his only responsibility to his niece was paying the bills.

Casey glanced over at Mia. "If I'm being honest, and I

always try, Shakespeare doesn't excite me much, either. But it's something I need for my degree and I've put it off as long as I can."

"You didn't have to drag me along with you. I don't need a babysitter. I can take care of myself."

*Three whole sentences,* Casey thought. *Must be a record. Or the kid is really ticked off.* "At least you had something to read."

Mia looked out the window at the Suncoast Hotel marquee as they turned right onto Alta Avenue.

"Is it a book you're reading for school?" Casey asked, trying to keep her talking.

"No."

"Wow. Reading for fun. What a concept."

No verbal response. The only answer was a shoulder lift.

"So," Casey said, "what's the book about? And before you shrug, sigh or roll your eyes, remember the polite thing would be to use words."

Mia glared. "It's some stupid teenage vampire romance trash."

"Hmm." Casey turned the car into the driveway leading to the One Queensridge Place complex and the guard waved as she drove by. "It looked to me like you're at least halfway through a book that's five or six hundred pages long. I'm going to guess that you didn't get that far into it during my hour-long class, so you've been at it awhile. Good for you. How did you pick it?"

"Some girls mentioned it."

"So you're making friends?" Casey asked.

"No. I heard them talking."

"Are you reaching out to the girls at school?"

"What's the point?" Mia looked at her as if she were as dumb as a rock. "I won't be there that long."

"Why not? You have a home now, Mia. It's okay to relax and put down roots. Make friends."

"He's going to dump me."

Her uncle. The same one taking jerk status to new and even lower levels. "That's not what he told me." This is where verbal acuity came in handy for creating spin. Casey parked the car and turned off the engine. "He said you'd always have a place to live." A slight exaggeration of that infuriating conversation.

"Right." Sarcasm was thick in Mia's voice. "Wow. I guess I should worship at the altar of Saint Uncle Blake. Except where was he when my mom needed help? Where were her parents?"

"Your grandparents," Casey said, putting a finer point on it. "Without knowing the facts, it's hard to comment on your family—"

"They're not my family. Families are supposed to be there for each other. These people weren't."

Casey wanted to sigh, glare, roll her eyes or lift a shoulder in reply, because she didn't know what to say to that. In a perfect world family *would* be a support system. But after her own mother died, her father had withdrawn from her. It had been like losing both parents at the same time.

"Family dynamics are complicated, Mia. Your uncle made it clear that you're to have whatever you need. Money is no object." That was the best way to spin what he'd said about it being her job to make the list and he'd write the check.

"Don't go Mary Poppins on me. You see what he's like. You had a deal with him. He was supposed to be home and take over, but he hung you out to dry. Mom said her family didn't want her. You do the math."

Before Casey could think of something reassuring, your basic lie, the girl was out of the car and walking toward the private elevator. Just as well, because Casey hated lies and she couldn't think of anything else to say. She used her key card to access the top floor and they rode up in silence.

Inside the penthouse Mia disappeared down the hall, and

her disappearance was followed closely by the sound of a door closing. Forcefully.

Anger that had simmered when Blake was a no-show earlier now came to a full boil. Casey tracked him down in the kitchen, where he was making a sandwich, and it looked like he hadn't been there long. The matching suit coat to the charcoal slacks was missing, but he was still wearing his wrinkled white dress shirt, with the sleeves rolled to mid-forearm. The gray-on-black silk tie was loosened, and the first shirt button undone. His dark hair was stylishly tousled or he'd run his fingers through it a lot. Either way, the look worked far too well and was a major distraction when she wanted to be nothing but furious.

She set her notebook and purse on the granite-topped island in the center of the room. "I see you're no longer missing in action."

"I knew where I was the whole time." The words were full of charm and might have distracted her if she weren't so angry.

"You know what I mean."

"This was the night of your class. My secretary said she relayed the message that I'd be late."

"You agreed to my terms," Casey challenged. "One of which was two nights a week you'd be here so I could go to my class."

"Something came up."

"Not good enough, Counselor."

His eyes widened and he set the sandwich on the white plate. He picked up the longneck bottle of beer beside it and took a drink. "It's all I've got. When the judge says, 'Be in court,' I show up."

"No one else in your office could have gone instead?"

A flicker in his eyes said the challenge hit the mark. "I told you up front that my hours are unpredictable. That's why I've got you."

"You did tell me that," she agreed. "But my schedule is predictable and you approved the arrangement to be here on specific days. You weren't here as promised, which means you broke your word."

"I apologize. Clearly you worked it out."

She waited, but he didn't add that it wouldn't happen again. Folding her arms over her chest, she rested a hip against the island as she stared across the expanse at her boss. He was as extraordinarily stubborn as he was handsome and that was saying a lot about the stubborn part.

"You know, the first rule of parenting is to do what you say," she said.

"Okay." He finished half his sandwich and wiped his mouth with a napkin that he'd grabbed from the chrome holder on the counter. "Is there more?"

"If consequences are clearly defined, when a kid decides to break a rule, there should be no surprises when punishment is swift and sure."

"Is there a point to this parenting protocols lecture?"

The gleam in his blue eyes sent a tsunami-sized tremble rolling through her, and something that big could never be good, but she took a deep breath and dove in. "I took this job on a trial basis."

"And I have to say that your work is exemplary. Mia is under control and your conscientious attention to detail is clearly getting results."

"You're the one on probation, Blake. And I have to tell you, I don't like what I'm seeing."

"Excuse me?" He took another sip of beer. "You're saying that I don't meet your standards?"

"Pretty much. I'd planned to take time off while getting these classes out of the way, but I agreed to work for you as a favor to Ginger. Now I see it was a mistake."

"Are you quitting?" he asked.

For a moment he wasn't a wealthy, confident, high-powered attorney, but a man without a clue about dealing with a preteen girl. She could also see that he didn't like not being in complete control. It was a characteristic shared by a lot of military men. But this wasn't the military and she could walk away without consequences.

Considering the way he affected her, that would be the smartest move. "Give me one good reason why I shouldn't resign."

"Mia needs you."

"She needs a family. That's you."

"I'm here."

"No. Your checkbook is here. You're in court. Or your office. Or the study here at home. Or wherever else you can find to avoid her." Casey drew in a deep breath. "She's asking questions, Blake. And I don't have the answers for her."

"What kind of questions?"

"Like where you and your parents were when her mother was in bad shape."

Casey wouldn't be human if she wasn't curious about that, too. But she didn't ask and he didn't volunteer.

"It wasn't the Decker family's finest hour," he admitted.

She held up her hands. "I don't need to know. I'm just saying that Mia does. She's bitter and angry."

"Isn't that a teenager's stock-in-trade?" One corner of his mouth curved up but the teasing comment did nothing to clear the shadows in his eyes.

"This is more than that." She traced the circular beige pattern in the granite countertop for a moment. "She's scared, confused and mad as hell. I say again, on the record, counseling could help with that."

"Is it a condition for getting you to stay?"

That was a nonanswer if she'd ever heard one. Which

made him a good attorney, but it wasn't especially helpful in figuring out why he was so resistive. One look around his pricey, spacious penthouse made it clear that money wasn't the problem. And he'd all but admitted screwing up with his sister, but she was the last person to judge anyone's past. In Iraq people had counted on her and she'd let them down. It felt pretty crappy. She wasn't about to do that to a kid who'd been let down enough in her very short life.

"No," she finally said. "It's not a condition for me to stay."

Now he did smile, a full-on, take-no-prisoners grin that made the hair at her nape prickle, signaling danger as surely as if she were on patrol in downtown Baghdad. What the hell? She used to be a soldier. Yeah, there were a lot of women in the military now, but she'd spent the majority of her time with men. Not once had she felt this way. Personal relationships had been discouraged and for good reason. They were a distraction none of them could afford in a war zone.

Somehow One Queensridge Place had turned into a theater of conflict, one that had nothing to do with rocket propelled grenades, IEDs, bombs or body armor. If only she could put on a bullet-proof vest to protect herself from whatever it was that she was feeling for Blake Decker, because it smacked of improper. Technically, she couldn't actually control it, and impropriety would only happen if she acted on it. That wasn't an option, mainly because she was already carrying around more than her fair share of guilt.

Blake took a sip of his beer, and the act was so incredibly masculine that it violated the spirit of conviction she'd had just moments before.

He looked at her, and the confident, charming gleam in his eyes was turned on full blast. "So, can I take that as a yes? You'll stick around and extend my period of probation? I promise not to let you down again."

If only that were true. Mia's words were still too fresh in her mind. He hung her out to dry. If Casey was smart, she'd retreat right now. But Mia didn't have anyone else in her corner.

"Yes, I'll stay."

Blake hit the down button on the TV remote's channel selector, wishing desperately for football season to start, but it was only the end of July. In a few more weeks the exhibition games would start, but not today. Today he still felt like a prisoner in his own home. Like he had a guest who would never leave and a second in command who'd deserted a sinking ship. And he was on probation, which meant he was here alone with Mia while Casey had the afternoon off.

Facing twelve jurors was less intimidating than dealing with a disgruntled twelve-year-old. Not that he'd seen her, because his niece had been in her room for hours. Should he go check on her? Was that a breach of privacy? How much privacy did a girl need, anyway? If Casey were here, he could ask her, but she wasn't.

At least she was coming back—soon he hoped. He'd nearly blown it with her. Calling her bluff on the terms of her time off wasn't his brightest move, and he wasn't even sure why he'd pushed the envelope. He could have gotten home in time for her to get to class without taking Mia. Maybe he'd wanted to show her who was in command. It might have been his way of pushing back against her dictating the terms of employment. He was used to coming and going without thinking about anyone but himself—and that was the way he liked it.

What he didn't like was the curve fate had thrown him. Karma was probably having a good laugh at his expense, what with making him responsible for a kid—a girl, no less. That was bad enough, but he'd gotten a glimpse of what it would be like to raise the kid without backup, a sneak peek of him and Mia without a referee. It hadn't been pretty.

Blake had hired Casey with every intention of dumping all the responsibility for his niece in her lap. She'd surprised him by pushing back, giving him things to think about, which he didn't much like. He could probably find another nanny but he wasn't keen on starting the process again. And no matter how hard he tried, he couldn't manage to forget what Casey had said about Mia needing a family. Although, with his legendary power of selective memory, he'd managed to put her pitch for counseling out of his mind. It hadn't worked for him and Debra. It hadn't prevented her cheating, which doomed their relationship.

This penthouse used to be his sanctuary; now there was a twelve-year-old stranger here. Should he go in and talk to her? Did he really want to bring up the past? Wasn't it enough that he'd given her a nice place to live and three square meals a day? Didn't he get sufficient points for taking her in?

"You look deep in thought." Casey stood in the family room doorway.

Blake was so glad to see her that he felt the most absurd urge to kiss her. Not actually that absurd, since his thoughts went there a lot. At the moment he also felt the burden that had been weighing him down just moments before suddenly lift.

"Hi." He hit the power button to turn off the TV.

"Hi." She lifted a hand in greeting. "I just wanted to let you know I'm back. I'll just go see—"

"Wait," he said.

"Is everything all right? Mia?"

"She's fine."

"Where is she?"

"In her room. Doing homework." That part was just a guess, but what else would she be doing in there all this time?

Casey tucked a strand of straight blond hair behind her ear. "Was there something you wanted?"

"Just wondering how your afternoon off was," he said, slipping his fingertips into the pockets of his khaki shorts.

"Fine."

While waiting for her to say more, he moved across the expansive room, suddenly needing to shrink the distance between them. When she didn't elaborate, he asked, "What did you do?"

"Does it matter?"

"Not unless you're moonlighting at a topless gentlemen's club," he teased. "I'm quite sure it says something in the parenting handbook about that not being a positive influence on a preteen girl."

As hoped for, Casey laughed. "No pole dancing for me, you'll be relieved to know. Just a visit home. Sunday family dinner with my father and three brothers."

"Three brothers?"

She nodded. "The youngest one is Bradley, named after the fighting vehicle. Middle brother is Colin, which came from General Colin Powell. And Norm—"

"Don't tell me. General Schwartzkopf?"

"That's the one." She laughed.

"I sense a theme. Where did the name Casey come from?"

"I'm not sure." She shrugged.

"Obviously the inspiration in naming your brothers came from the military. Didn't you ever ask?"

"I was too busy trying to figure out where I fit in the all male environment."

"I can't help noticing you didn't mention your mother," Blake said.

"She died when I was about Mia's age."

"I'm sorry." His parents wouldn't win any awards, but at

least he had them. He couldn't imagine what she, or Mia, for that matter, had gone through.

"It was a long time ago." Casey shrugged. "I'm all grown up now."

He'd definitely noticed that. Her denim capris and sleeveless white cotton shirt were not especially sexy, except that she was wearing them. And every time he was this close to her, heat was an issue. It was July and hot enough to cook an egg on the sidewalk, but that didn't explain his acute reaction to the nanny.

"Obviously you missed your mother," Blake said.

"Why obviously?"

"Just an impression, I guess. What you said about fitting into an all-male world."

She pressed her lips together for a moment as shadows flitted through her eyes. "It's not easy for a girl to grow up without a female around."

"Did that factor into your decision to accept this job? Or was it completely a favor to Ginger?"

One slender shoulder lifted in a careless movement, but the intensity in her expression was anything but casual. "Mia's background, the loss of her mother, I'll admit that had something to do with my decision."

"Is your father a military man?"

"What was your first clue?"

"You mean besides naming your youngest brother after a tank?"

"Yeah."

Her mouth curved up at the corners and amusement made her eyes sparkle. It would be so easy to forget she was the nanny, but if he did, he'd be at the mercy of his testosterone. That would make him ready, willing and able to act on the impulse to explore his fascination for her contradictions. She was, after all, the most feminine soldier he could imagine.

"My dad was a career army man," she admitted. "He is retired now and works in engineering and maintenance at the Bellagio hotel."

"Did your brothers all serve in the military?"

She shook her head. "None of them joined up."

That was a surprise. "And you did? The only girl in the group?"

"Go figure."

"It's hard for me to imagine you in camouflage, carrying a rifle." He shrugged. "Call me a sexist pig—"

"You're a sexist pig."

The words were teasing, but the shadows were back in her eyes, and he kicked himself for putting them there. She had peddled the benefits of counseling to him more than once, but a shrink would have a field day with her.

"Seriously, Casey, what made you join the army?"

"What made you want to be a lawyer?" she shot back.

*Whoa.* That had touched a nerve. "I'm sorry. I didn't mean to pry. Military men and women sacrifice a lot to keep this country safe, and I'd never belittle that. You're a natural with Mia and it seems a contradiction—"

"I don't want to talk about it."

Her tension was visible and he wondered what was troubling her. She hadn't reacted this way when she'd mentioned the family dinner, and she'd seemed sincere when she said her mother's passing wasn't a current tragedy. By a process of elimination, he realized it was his inquiries about the military that had triggered this reaction.

"I didn't mean to offend you. But now that I have, maybe talking about whatever's bothering you might help. You're the counseling queen—"

"Don't knock it till you've tried it."

"Have you?"

"What if I have?"

Not an answer, he noticed. At best it was an evasive maneuver. *Your Honor, permission to treat this witness as hostile.* That wasn't exactly the right word. *Wounded* was the one that popped into his mind when he stared into her big hazel eyes. He remembered thinking after knowing her for less than an hour that she had the sexiest mouth this side of heaven and the saddest eyes he'd ever seen. Something had happened to her when she was in the army. He'd bet his very successful law practice on it.

"If you have had counseling," he said, "I mean, I'd advise you to get your money back, because there are clearly some unresolved issues that need dealing with. I'm not especially insightful, but I am pretty fluent in body language, and yours says that you'd rather have dental implants without Novocain than talk about this."

Full-blown distress was apparent in her expression, and she looked ready to cut and run. It was his fault. In his own defense, he wasn't used to a woman's wounded looks. His ex had looked alternately angry and frustrated when he didn't drop everything in the universe for a broken fingernail. Just before everything hit the fan, she'd simply looked bored.

And then she'd taken up with his best friend. Also an ex. One ex plus one ex equals two exes, algebraically speaking.

But this wasn't about him. He was trying to help Casey and he had the most insane desire to pull her into his arms. He reached out his hand and curved his fingers around her upper arm, simply to touch her and offer comfort for the as yet un-talked-about something making her look as if she'd lost her only friend.

Her skin was soft and silky and warm. She felt delicate, so very vulnerable, and again he had trouble seeing her as a combat soldier. She was a woman, a desirable woman. A really desirable woman who looked in desperate need of a hug.

Blake stared into her eyes as his pulse rate continued to head upward, and in the next moment he was pulling her against him. "Casey—"

Her eyes widened and she backed away from him as surprise pushed the sadness from her eyes. "I have to go check on Mia."

"Of course. Yeah. Right." He curled his fingers into his palm. "That's a good idea."

In a nanosecond she was gone, and he walked over to the floor-to-ceiling windows and a spectacular view of the setting sun. The gold, orange, pink and purple in the sky were Mother Nature's palette and a fitting backdrop against which to kick himself for what he'd almost done.

Casey was his employee and he owed her nothing but a paycheck. If she had personal problems, she had a support system to lean on. Ginger. Her father and brothers. Probably girlfriends. Even if it was about man trouble, something that didn't set well with him, it was still none of his business. In the reflection in the windows, he saw Casey walk back into the room.

"Where's Mia?" she asked.

He turned. "I already told you she's in her room."

"I just looked. She's not there. When did you last see her?"

He'd seen her at breakfast and when Casey had said goodbye. "After you left, I was in the study working for a few hours."

"What about after that?"

"I've been in here watching TV ever since," he hedged.

"So you didn't check on her at all?"

When she put it like that, he felt like the biggest jerk on the planet. Especially because he'd been relieved that his niece hadn't demanded his time. "I figured she was studying."

"For six hours?" She shook her head, and the pitying expression was back, laced with worry. "Obviously she sneaked out and there's no telling how long ago. We have to look for her."

"There's a mall not too far away," he offered. "Boca Park is pretty upscale. She might have gone there."

"We have to start somewhere. She told me she's not bothering to make friends at school, because it's a waste of time since you're only going to dump her."

If that remark was meant to make him feel guilty, it came dangerously close to being successful. Before he could grab his keys, the phone rang and he picked up the extension in the kitchen. "Hello?"

"Blake?"

"Hi, Dad."

"Mia is at the door and your mother is furious. This is not how it was supposed to go."

"I'm on my way."

Blake was used to drama, but it mostly happened in his office. His last thought before dashing out the door was one of gratitude that he had Casey in his corner.

## Chapter Four

Casey sat in the front passenger seat of Blake's Mercedes sedan. She was unaccustomed to being surrounded by luxury, and the softness of the leather surprised her. She wished Mia's unpredictability surprised her, too, but it didn't. Even if Blake hadn't clued her in right after they'd met, she'd seen it for herself the first time Mia took off and disappeared at the Fashion Show Mall.

Now that she knew the girl was safe, relatively speaking—a pun, considering she'd turned up with her grandparents—Casey could admit to herself that the disappearing act was a relief. It took the heat off her.

Blake's cross-examination about her family background had stirred up memories that she'd rather not revisit. He'd gotten on every nerve she had. In all fairness he hadn't touched on what had happened in Iraq, but only because he didn't know about it. And he never would, because it was one more thing she'd rather leave alone.

What she needed to deal with was her current predicament. She didn't want to care about another kid who would let her down, another child who was playing her. And Mia's behavior tonight was cause for concern. When she'd seen the empty room and realized the girl was gone, fear had immediately set in. That didn't happen when her feelings were idling in neutral.

And speaking of neutral, it hadn't escaped her notice that Blake had planned to kiss her. If only she could have been disinterested, but she'd been far *too* interested. Stepping away from him had taken discipline, and she wasn't sure where it had come from or whether she could manage to find it again. Should the need arise, which she prayed didn't happen.

"We're almost there," Blake said, slowing as he steered the car through a set of open guard gates.

His voice pulled her away from the disturbing thoughts and she studied the large entrance. "King Kong gates," she commented.

"Excuse me?"

"Didn't you ever see the nineteen thirties movie with Fay Wray? The big ape looks over this gate like it's a speed bump. Those big iron gates into the neighborhood remind me of that—tall and strong to keep out the big, hairy riffraff."

He laughed. "I have to face the folks and deal with Mia fallout. Under the circumstances I didn't think anyone could make me laugh. Thanks for coming along, Casey."

"You're welcome." Then his words sank in. "Mia fallout? What does that mean?"

Without answering, he pulled up in front of an imposing house with impressive columns in front. "Showtime."

"This looks like Tara," she said, studying the grand house.

"Another movie reference?"

She nodded. *"Gone with the Wind."*

"A Civil War reference." He looked at her. "You're about to find out how appropriate that is."

Just what Casey needed—another war zone. Not. But Mia was clearly feeling the effects of being ignored, and it was understandable. Casey was ready to roll and go to the kid's defense.

She followed Blake into the house. He didn't knock and the front door was unlocked.

They heard voices and Blake said, "They're in the sitting room."

"Because Tara doesn't have a family room," she muttered.

It turned out that the room was right off the entryway and had a fireplace, as well as two hunter green floral love seats facing each other at a right angle to it. A big coffee table and two wing chairs completed the conversation area, but no one was sitting there. Although there was talking, right now Mia was doing most of it.

Blake's father was a handsome, tall, silver-haired man, a preview of what his son would look like in his later years. A brunette, his mother was in her sixties and was still beautiful. Casey had seen shell shock and knew the older woman was feeling it now.

"My mother was pregnant," Mia shouted. "You guys threw her away like a piece of trash. Over a baby. It's not a crime to have a baby."

"Blake. Thank God you're here," his mother said.

"What in the blazes is going on?" his father demanded. He looked at Casey. "Who are you?"

"Casey Thomas." She walked up to him with her hand extended and he shook it.

"Lincoln Decker," he said. "My wife, Patricia."

Casey shook the woman's hand and, before Blake's parents could ask, said, "I'm your granddaughter's nanny."

"This hooligan?" Lincoln said. "She barged in unannounced and has been accusing us of atrocities ever since."

"Why don't we all sit?" Blake suggested. "We can get acquainted."

"Why?" the older man demanded.

"That goes double for me." Mia's comment was a clear indication that she was not taking responsibility for setting this scenario in motion.

"Blake, you've hired a nanny. How long has Mia been with you?" his mother whispered.

"Not that long," Blake hedged.

"Long enough for you to hire a nanny, but not long enough for you to tell us about Mia?" Patricia's expression was accusatory.

"Dad knew," Blake said. "Children's services contacted him first."

"And you didn't tell me about her?" Patricia turned the heat of her expression on her husband.

"I was protecting you," Lincoln said.

"From what?" Patricia demanded.

"That would be me," Mia interjected. "Delinquent in training."

The conversation deteriorated from there. As an objective observer without an equal emotional investment, Casey watched the three adults and one child, who all were doing a lot of talking and very little listening. She couldn't help but notice the family resemblance. A glare here, an angry gesture there. Stubborn chin. The shape of the face. Even to the untrained eye, it was obvious that these people shared DNA, if not harmony. But they were getting nowhere fast.

Casey decided to play UN peacekeeping force. "Time-out," she said. When no one paid any attention to her, she whistled, a shrill sound that never failed to get her noticed. "Listen up. Everyone needs to sit down."

Lincoln stared, his displeasure obvious. "Just a moment—"

"Excuse me, sir, but I'm taking control."

"What gives you the right?" Lincoln demanded.

"Because I'm a calm, impartial spectator, and you've had a shock."

"I'm not a shock," Mia said, outraged.

"That's not what your grandmother said," Casey pointed out, shooting a questioning look at Blake.

"Mom, I was going to explain, but—"

"No buts," his mother said. "This is one of those situations that don't call for a but. You should have said something to me. Both of you. I had a right to know. Sooner or later I'd have to know. I can't believe she's been here and neither of you said a word to me—"

"Our daughter ran off and broke your heart," her husband said. "I was protecting you."

"Everyone please sit," Casey ordered, when the older woman started to protest.

Four pairs of eyes blinked at her and she stared them down until everyone found a seat. The elder Deckers sat side by side on a love seat, with Blake across from them. Mia was by herself on a wing chair that faced the fireplace.

"This situation could have been handled more diplomatically." Still standing, Casey gave Mia a look, but the girl wouldn't meet her gaze. "I think everyone needs to take a step back and let reality sink in."

"The reality is they're dorks," Mia said. "Old ones."

"I feel so special," Blake said sarcastically. "I fall into the young dork category."

"Not helping," Casey told him. "Be Switzerland."

"What?"

"Neutral," Casey explained. "After a cooling-off period, a mutually agreeable time for a mediation should be selected."

Lincoln looked at his son. "You took responsibility for her. That means you must not let her run wild. You have to control her, Blake."

"Right. Like you did with April," Blake shot back. "Or is this a 'do as I say, not as I do' situation?"

"Accusations are counterproductive," Casey said. "Until you can get along—"

"Not holding my breath," Mia mumbled.

Casey knew how it felt to be an outsider and sympathized with the kid. It was hard not taking her side, but that would most likely result in a resumption of hostilities. It would be detrimental to the peace process.

"Mia," Casey said in a firm, "listen up, or else" tone. "Please wait for us in the car."

"But—"

"As your grandmother said, no buts. That's an order. Orders are meant to be followed without discussion."

"This is sooo stupid."

"I think you need another *o* in there so we know how you really feel," Blake said.

Casey shook her head. "You're the adult. Focus. Mia?"

The girl glared for several moments, then presumably did as she'd been told—following a slam of the front door.

Lincoln stared after her for several moments, then looked at Casey. "Well done, young woman."

"Thank you, sir." *Not my job to judge these people, who are strangers,* Casey thought. But how could they fail to acknowledge the child of their child? All the facts were not in evidence, and that was for another time. "As I was saying, take a break. Talk again soon."

Lincoln nodded. "I like you, Casey. You've got spunk."

"You're very wise for one so young," Patricia said.

"Yeah, chalk one up for the young dorks," Blake muttered.

Casey looked at him and sighed. "I think it's time for us to go."

"You'll get no argument from me." Blake stood and walked to the doorway.

Casey said goodbye to the older couple and followed Blake out onto the front porch. She glanced at the Mercedes and saw Mia slouching against it, and relief flooded her that the girl hadn't taken off. This was the second time and Casey didn't trust her to stay put. Again, it was hard not to blame her when she'd had confirmation that her grandfather knew about her and didn't want her.

As they walked down the steps to the car, Blake said, "You really earned your paycheck tonight."

"I should get hazard pay for dealing with your family."

"Amen."

"So how did I earn my paycheck?" she asked, unable to stop the glow his praise was generating inside her.

"My dad approves of you. You've got spunk."

"Hoo-yah," she said.

Casey walked from Mia's bedroom, past her own and into the family room. She glanced outside and spotted Blake on the terrace, staring out at the carpet of light that was the Las Vegas Valley. He had a drink in his hand and she couldn't blame him. It had been a hell of a night. She was sorry if he wanted to be alone, but she was about to disturb his solitude.

After opening the slider, she went out, instantly feeling the desert heat mix with the cool air from inside. Because this was the top floor of the building, there was room for a pool, and the lights at the bottom illuminated the immediate surrounding area. There was also a fire pit, patio tables, chairs and chaise longues scattered around. It was surreal and magical.

Casey had the most absurd desire to pinch herself, as a reminder that she wasn't Dorothy, that this wasn't Kansas *or* Oz. She wasn't off to see the wizard, but she and Blake needed to talk.

"Mia's asleep."

"That was fast." He glanced over his shoulder.

"She's exhausted." It was warm outside, but considering the daytime temperature had topped out at over one hundred and ten, the breeze made the outside almost comfortable. "It takes a lot of energy to maintain that level of anger."

"And mobility." He drained the liquor in his glass and set it on a table. "Did she tell you how she managed to find her way to my parents?"

"She found out where they live from your address book on your computer. Then she took a cab."

"Do I want to know how she paid for it?"

"Your dad coughed up the fare."

His dark eyebrows rose in surprise. "Someone feels guilty."

"As well he should." Casey leaned her elbows on the metal railing that capped the clear glass separating luxury from certain death if one fell. "I know he's your dad and you love him, blah, blah. But I can't believe he knew about Mia and not only didn't make an effort to know her, but kept it all from your mom."

A sizzle of heat flashed through her when he rested his forearms beside hers and their shoulders brushed. "Any questions you may have regarding my dysfunctional tendencies should all be answered after meeting Lincoln and Patricia Decker."

"Some," she admitted, laughing. "But not all. I got the feeling your mother was a little peeved at him."

A ghost of a grin curved up the corners of his wonderful lips. "You're a quick study of human nature."

"Not really." And not when it counted the most. If she were, two little kids would still have their mom, and she'd have her best friend when she needed her most.

"You're right," he said. "Dad is in for a rough time. I'd say he'll be sleeping on the couch, but you saw the size of that place."

"Yeah. I'm guessing he'll have his choice of Tara's ten or twelve extra bedrooms when he's in the doghouse." Only a slight exaggeration.

"Give or take," he agreed. "Is there any chance that Mia didn't understand?"

"You mean the part where her grandfather didn't want to have anything to do with her, then kept it from his wife to protect the family?"

"Yeah, that."

"Nope. She understood perfectly."

"That pretty much sucks." The silver glow from a nearly full moon highlighted his frown and the tension in his shoulders.

"Yeah. Mia would like him put to sleep. That's a direct quote."

"That's a little harsh, although I can see where she's coming from."

Casey straightened and leaned a hip against the railing as she studied him. "Speaking of dysfunctional—"

"Uh-oh." He half turned toward her and met her gaze, folding his arms over his chest. "I'm not going to like this, am I?"

"You didn't the first two times I brought it up, but maybe the third time's the charm."

"Ever the optimist," he said dryly.

"Just call me the bluebird of happiness."

He laughed, then took a deep breath. "Okay. Get it over with."

"Counseling." The single word had tension running through him. She was close enough to feel it.

"Casey, we've been through this."

"I take it the third time is *not* the charm."

"And you're like a dog that won't let loose of a favorite bone."

"Because," she said, "I think it's important. You told me to make the list and you'd write the check. So on top of vitamins, a training bra and supplies for that time of the month—"

He started humming and covered his ears. "This is me not listening to that. And shame on you for mentioning it."

She laughed. It was such a guy reaction and said more about his feelings than even he realized. But this was serious and important. There was only one way she could think of to get him to listen and understand that she meant business.

She pushed his hands down. "You're hilarious."

"Thank you."

"It wasn't a compliment. Blake, I'm making counseling a condition of my continuing to be Mia's nanny."

If only she could give him an ultimatum about toning down his sex appeal, her life would be far less complicated.

He didn't look surprised. "Is that a card you really want to play?"

"It might be overstepping, but I feel very strongly about this, and I'm willing to take the risk."

"Really? I couldn't tell."

"Stop being charming—"

"You think I'm charming?"

"That's not the point."

He grinned a very self-satisfied male grin. "I'll take that as a yes."

"You're changing the subject." And she was blushing, which she desperately hoped he couldn't see. The heat wasn't only in her cheeks. It was everywhere, and her heart fluttered against the inside of her chest like a caged bird struggling for freedom. "I'm very serious about this."

"I don't have a lot of faith in counseling," he said seriously.

"Have you ever tried it?"

"What if I have?" he shot back, defiant and defensive in equal parts.

She remembered saying the same thing to him. Just because a few sessions with an army shrink hadn't squeegeed the guilt from her conscience didn't mean he and Mia wouldn't benefit from talking to someone. His presence alone could go a long way toward convincing the girl he cared. And one didn't need credentials to see she desperately wanted someone to care. Casey knew how that felt.

"Look, Blake, you're a good man—"

"Says who?"

"Oh, please. Cut the tough guy act. If you weren't a decent person, Mia wouldn't be here now."

"Neither would you," he said, a gleam stealing into his eyes.

He was right about that. If the child was in the state's custody, he'd have no need for nanny services. Life would be easier, but maybe her life wasn't meant to be easy. Maybe she was here for a reason.

"The thing is, I am here and you have to deal with me. Because I'm here, I have an obligation to that little girl asleep inside. You *are* a good man, or you'd have let the state of Nevada worry about her."

"I'm not so sure."

She decided to ignore that. His actions spoke louder than her words. "Now that you've taken her in, don't let it just be about a place to live. Go the extra mile and really help her. Make a difference in her life."

In her earnestness to convince him, Casey put a hand on his arm and felt the strength beneath the warm skin. The contact with him made her heart race again. "You'll feel good about yourself."

"Okay, sign me up." His voice was husky and deep and scraped along her nerve endings.

He reached for her and pulled her to him. It felt like slow motion but happened at the speed of light. She was in his arms and it was better than anything her imagination had dreamed up. He was all hard muscles and coiled strength before he lowered his mouth to hers. It was as if she'd been holding her breath for this since the moment she'd met him, and she couldn't stop the sigh of contentment. It was as if she'd waited all her life to feel Blake Decker's chiseled lips take hers, tasting like Southern Comfort and sin.

Her breasts were crushed to his chest as he held her against him with one hand, the fingers of his other hand snarled in her hair, angling her head to make the contact firmer, deeper, better.

He made a sound in his throat, part groan, part growl, but all male. She breathed in the spicy scent of his skin combined with the warm breeze off the desert, and the exotic mixture was like a drug coursing through her system. Discipline where he was concerned was a pipe dream. Soft sounds of approval drifted between them, and she was vaguely amazed that they were coming from her. But she couldn't seem to help it, because his mouth was doing delicious things to her mouth, her face, her ears, her neck. Good Lord, it was like a jolt of the best kind of electricity arcing through her.

They were both breathing hard, and she felt as if the heat was melting her from the inside out, fusing her body to his in the most wonderful way. She wanted to be even closer, needed to be nearer.

Just as she was praying it would never end, it ended. He seemed to freeze, then dropped his hands as if they suddenly burned.

"Casey…" He took a deep breath and ran a shaky hand through his hair. "That was my fault."

*Fault?* That meant that what quite possibly was the best kiss she'd ever had was wrong. Or he believed it was wrong, which was right. This *was* wrong because it was confusing and so very not right. If there was anything positive about what was happening, it was that none of those words came out of her mouth as she blinked up at him.

He moved back, far enough that he couldn't touch her. "That was inappropriate. You're my employee. I know better. I'm sorry."

He stared at her a moment longer, something dark and unreadable in his eyes. Abruptly he turned away and disappeared through one of the sliding glass doors to the penthouse master bedroom.

Casey touched trembling fingers to her lips, still moist from his kiss. He'd been right, of course, to stop. But, God help her, the distance he'd put between them didn't stop her from wanting him. And she couldn't decide which was more humiliating—that he'd put an end to it or that he was sorry he'd done it at all. It was fate or something that he'd finished what he'd started earlier.

Maybe it had been calculated to distract her. The plan had worked brilliantly, because she still didn't know why the Decker men had felt the need to protect Patricia from her daughter's child.

Even with suspicions running rampant, Casey was missing the warmth of just moments ago. It was still hot outside, but she was cold all the way through because she felt empty inside.

As wrong as it was, she still wanted him, just one more item in the long list of her sins.

## *Chapter Five*

While Mia was in talking to the counselor, Casey sat in the waiting room—waiting for Blake. This was your standard issue area for hanging out. The chairs had a tweed seat on an oak frame and were arranged around the perimeter of the room. Walls painted in a serene shade of blue surrounded her, with generic seascapes hung here and there. A receptionist huddled behind a sliding glass window, probably looking at her watch every ten seconds to see if it was time to go home yet.

This was the last appointment of the day and Casey had called in reinforcements to set it up. Ginger Davis knew a lot of people in Las Vegas, and the counselor had worked them in two days after Mia's last disappearing act. Which also happened to be the same night Blake had kissed Casey on the terrace of his penthouse. *Kiss* and *penthouse* were two words she'd never expected to use in the same sentence regarding herself, but there it was.

Casey looked at her watch and noted that Blake was now officially a half hour late. She couldn't help wondering if his tardiness had anything to do with what had happened on said terrace, because she'd seen very little of him ever since. He was back to leaving early and coming home late. But he knew about this meeting with the counselor. Casey had called his secretary, who'd promised to remind him it was the last appointment of the day, making it easier for him to get here. And yet he wasn't here.

She'd tried calling his cell, but the call had gone to voice mail. Was he screening his calls? Because of that kiss? Or was it the fact that she'd drawn a line in the sand and made his presence here a condition of her continued employment? His not showing up would have to go under the heading of calling her bluff.

After exactly sixty minutes the door beside the reception window opened and Mia walked into the waiting room with Lillian Duff. The counselor was a small woman in her early to mid-fifties, with light brown hair and eyes. She wore square, black-framed glasses and looked as serene as the blue on her walls.

Casey stood and forced a smile. "So, how'd it go?"

"We got acquainted."

"Yeah, right." Mia rolled her eyes. "This is sooo lame."

"Feelings are good." Casey tried to put an optimistic expression on her face when she looked at the counselor. "It's best not to sugarcoat it, right? It's best to tell how you really feel."

Casey refused to pretend everything was fine. If that were the case, they wouldn't be here. If everything was hunky-dory, Blake would have made the effort to show up at the penthouse and take Mia to counseling, just the two of them, instead of standing his niece up.

"I have nothing to say." Mia flopped in a chair and folded her arms over her chest.

"Would you look at that open body language," Casey said.

"Bite me." The kid huffed out a breath.

"That's funny. When you ran away the other night and showed up at your grandparents, you had quite a bit to say. I'm thinking counseling is a good place to focus on what you'd really like to tell them."

"Dorks," she muttered.

Casey looked apologetically at Lillian. "She has issues."

"I noticed. Most kids who come to see me do." The counselor looked at her watch. "I see Mr. Decker wasn't able to join us."

"No." Multiple excuses flitted through Casey's mind, but she didn't say anything. It wasn't her job to monitor Blake or put a positive spin on his AWOL status. She glanced at Mia, who was putting a lot of energy into looking mad. "I'd like to make another appointment."

Lillian nodded. "For Mia and Mr. Decker?"

"Just Mia."

Casey set her anger on simmer. Blake was going to get his session, but it would be with her instead of the counselor. He was writing checks to both of them, so what the heck? Coming from her, it wouldn't be quite as politically correct.

Casey set up an appointment for the same time next week. Then she and Mia walked into the carpeted hall and headed for the elevator to the parking structure. She pushed the elevator button, and Mia turned away, slouching against the wall. The silence was deafening, worse than shrugs, eye rolling or name calling. It really fried her that all Blake had had to do was show up. He hadn't even had to say anything profound, because just being here would have said that he was invested in this child that no one wanted.

In all fairness, the Deckers were caught in a vicious cycle. Mia's inappropriate behavior was a cry for attention, but it made her hard to like and gave her uncle an excuse to push her away.

The elevator opened and Casey took a step forward so the doors wouldn't close. "Come on, Mia."

With the kid's back to her, all Casey could see was that she lifted a hand to her cheek.

"Hey, kiddo, we need to go."

Mia's thin shoulders hunched forward and she made a noise that sounded suspiciously like a sniffle. Casey held in a groan, but this was one more in a long list of reasons for her decision to specialize in the ten and under crowd. There was a world of difference between nine and Mia, who was going on thirteen. Hormones and feelings. Trauma and drama happened in that time and if a kid was at risk, this was when the behavior was most likely to show up.

Casey was used to dealing with kids pre-trauma and drama, when she could impact them in a positive way and head off the things that would send them down the wrong path. A path of destruction, like the one chosen by a kid she'd befriended in Baghdad. The seeds for his anger and frustration had been sown long before Casey met him, and dealing with Mia felt a lot like that.

But right here, right now, it was just the two of them and she had to do something. The question was what.

"Mia?" No answer. She waited, hoping the kid would blink first, but the standoff continued. "Are you crying?"

"No."

Casey moved away from the elevator and, when the doors closed, let it go. She walked over to the girl and stood there, but Mia didn't turn around.

"Hey, kiddo, talk to me."

There was no response, but the body language was dejected and unhappy.

Casey drew in a deep breath as she stuck her keys back in her purse and settled the strap more securely on her shoulder. She put her hands on Mia's thin shoulders and tried gently to turn her, but the kid resisted.

"I'm here for you."

"So?"

Casey was trying to pick up signals, but Mia didn't make it easy. It was hard to read between the lines when it was a single-syllable, one-word response, but Casey heard frustration, anger, hostility and, most of all, hurt. Maybe it would help if she could coax Mia to talk about it.

"Look, I think you know that your uncle is a busy lawyer. I'm sure something came up." Something like he absolutely had to make sure a married couple's relationship was severed between 5:00 and 6:00 p.m. today.

"Who cares about him?"

"Not me," Casey said, except maybe the part of her that felt guilty if the kiss she'd shared with him had in any way factored into his absentee status.

She should have stuck to her guns and not taken this job when her instantaneous attraction to him was off the charts. He'd kissed her, and she wished she could say she hadn't seen it coming. In hindsight she should have said her piece and walked away. In hindsight she wondered if deep down, she'd wanted him to kiss her. And now Mia was paying the price for her weakness.

"Look, Mia, I'll go out on a limb here and say that you obviously care about being stood up."

"You're wrong. I didn't want to talk to him, anyway."

"Okay. But wouldn't you have liked to *not* talk to him to his face?"

Casey turned the girl toward her, and the kid's eyes looked even more turquoise, because they were red rimmed. She had to do something to comfort this child. It was always easy to do that for the under-ten group. A hug. Kiss the boo-boo and put on a Band-Aid and off they went. She was winging it with Mia and felt as if she was skydiving and her chute hadn't opened.

Still, she figured a hug couldn't hurt and tugged the girl awkwardly into her arms. Mia stiffened and tried to jerk away, but Casey hung on, refusing to let go. Somehow Mia was going to get the message that someone in this world gave enough of a damn about her to acknowledge by comforting her that this situation sucked a lot.

The battle of wills persisted for another thirty seconds, which seemed like forever. Finally Mia relaxed into her and buried her face in Casey's shoulder. The girl was only a couple inches shorter, but a whole lot more lost, and the tug on Casey's heart didn't go unnoticed. She was officially sliding out of neutral and into the deep doo-doo of the affection zone. This wasn't how it was supposed to go. *Darn it.*

"I'm here," Casey crooned, patting the shaking shoulders. "It's okay. You're not alone, kiddo. And just so you know…" She paused for dramatic emphasis, to make sure Mia was listening. "You're right. Your uncle is a dork."

There was a muffled giggle before the girl looked up. "Told you so."

Casey pulled a tissue from her purse and handed it over. "Are you ready to go now?"

"I guess." Misery still coated her from head to toe.

Casey couldn't remember wanting so badly to see a kid smile. "How about on the way home I buy you anything you want?"

An unmistakable spark of interest appeared in Mia's eyes, for just a moment chasing away the indifference she wore like a favorite sweatshirt. "Anything?"

"Within reason." She put her arm around the girl's shoulders and led her back to the elevator. "Is there something you've always wanted?"

"A dog."

*Holy Mother of God.* But the more Casey thought about it, the more she liked the idea. A grin started slowly, then grew wider as Mia smiled, too.

"A man's best friend," Casey said as the elevator doors closed.

It was nearly nine when Blake rode the private elevator to his penthouse. He couldn't remember the last time he'd been this tired, but that was Casey's fault, which was his last thought before walking into his foyer where he found her standing. Kissing her had single-handedly sabotaged any restful sleep ever since, so it seemed somehow fitting that she looked ready to do battle.

And that was when he remembered that today was the counseling appointment he'd agreed to.

"Hi," he said, setting his briefcase on the floor. "How did the counseling go?"

Surprise flickered briefly in her eyes. "How do you know it took place? Maybe something came up and we forgot."

Along with the anger sparking in her eyes was a gleam of intelligence. Dealing with her would be much easier if she weren't so bright. But not nearly as entertaining.

"You don't forget anything," he said. "There's no doubt in my mind that you and Mia were there. And I wasn't."

"You're not even going to pretend it slipped your mind?"

He shook his head. "I was in mediation for a client whose financial settlement has been dragging on for close to a year. There was a breakthrough. Ending the session could have stalled things when we were on a roll."

"I see."

Her tone and the look on her face said that she didn't see

at all and that he was lower than the lowest life form. "Look, Casey, I know I—"

He heard something that sounded a lot like a throaty, deep bark just before a big yellow dog galumphed into the foyer. There was a clicking sound from its nails, which he knew couldn't be good for the expensive marble floor. Seconds later the animal peed on a leg of the table in the foyer, leaving a dark stain on the rug underneath. Just then Mia came racing in and skidded to a stop when she saw Blake, uncertainty in her big eyes.

He glanced from her to Casey as shock, surprise and anger rolled through him—in that order. "If I lived in the suburbs, I could see where it might be possible for Old Yeller to end up in my house. But this is the top floor and without opposable thumbs, I'm pretty sure it couldn't use the key card in the elevator."

"She's not an 'it.' Blake, meet Francesca. Frankie," Casey said to the dog, "meet Blake, your new dad."

"You brought this beast into my home?"

"It's Mia's home, too." Determined, Casey lifted her chin slightly. "She followed the rules and went to counseling, even though it was lame, dorky and sooo stupid. She was there in good faith, so I thought a reward was in order. She's always wanted a dog. Did you know that?"

"No."

"Well, it's true. So I agreed."

"I don't and I'm reversing that decision."

"No, Uncle Blake. Please let me keep her." Mia went down on one knee and put her arms around the dog, which nuzzled her cheek. "I promise she won't be any trouble."

"Too late." He looked at the dark spot on the rug. "She has to go. I mean leave."

"You can't do that," Mia cried.

"I already did," he said.

"Mia," Casey moved to the two of them and scratched the dog's head. "It would be best if you let me talk to your uncle. Show Frankie her bed in the laundry room."

"But—"

"Now," Casey said. "Make her comfortable, secure and accepted in her new environment."

Blake was pretty sure there was a message in those words for him, but he refused to feel guilty. He lived here, too, and last time he checked, the money for all this came out of his bank account.

He walked through the foyer, into the family room and straight to the kitchen, where he grabbed a beer from the refrigerator. After twisting off the cap, he took a long drink and let the cold, bubbly bite slide down his throat to his empty stomach. *Damn the torpedoes and let the chips fall where they may.* Fireworks were imminent, because Casey was right behind him.

"There's no way I'm telling that child she has to give up the dog."

He looked down at her. "You don't have to. I already did."

"Reversing *that* decision is the least you can do to make up for being such an ass."

He set his beer on the kitchen island and stared at her. "Excuse me, but I could have sworn you called me an ass."

"If that's your way of giving me a diplomatic out for what I said, forget it. I stand by the words and will say them again. You're an ass. The dog stays. And, if I have to, I'll take you on."

"You'll take me on?" His eyes narrowed on her, and damned if the thought didn't flash through his mind that she was beautiful when she was angry. "I'm a lot bigger. No way you can take me."

"Don't forget, I've had hand-to-hand combat training. I

know three hundred ways to incapacitate or kill an opponent with my pinkie."

"Right." His mouth twitched, but he refused to give in to the amusement. He was being ambushed in his own home. First Mia and now a dog? "The thing is, I've got the law on my side since I'm the boss."

"There's the law and then there's human decency." She put her hands on her hips and stared at him, anger rolling off her in waves while her chest rose and fell. "I'm fully aware that you sign my paycheck. I agreed to take this job, but you were present and accounted for when I made it clear, more than once, I might add, that you're the one on probation. If you're not willing to put the time in for your niece, give me one good reason why I should."

"Listen, Casey—"

"No," she said, pointing at him. "You listen. Oh, wait. You weren't there to see or listen when she tried to hide the fact that she was crying because you couldn't be bothered to show up."

He didn't like the guilt her words dredged up and went on the offensive. "So you let her bring Lassie here? That fixes everything."

"At least the dog will stick by her. It's more than she can count on from you."

"When Francesca can pay room and board, we'll talk."

"What about establishing a relationship with your niece? Your sister's child?"

Stirring up the past was throwing salt in the wound and he really didn't like that. "I have a job to do. Clients are counting on me."

"Taking cover behind the profession won't hide the fact that you're anti-relationship. A lone wolf doing his best to keep from bonding. You're so anti that even your career choice is all about ripping relationships to pieces."

"You've never been married. Otherwise you'd realize that I don't bring marriages down. But when they fail, each party has the obligation and prerogative to have their rights protected."

"Maybe. But there are a lot of demanding professions that don't get in the way of family responsibilities. You put in an awful lot of hours—or it could be that's just an excuse to dodge the hard work at home." She shook her head, and anger turned to pity on her face. "No wonder your marriage didn't work out."

"My marriage didn't work out because my wife cheated on me with my best friend." The memory of that still had the power to enrage him and it was fueled further by the fact that it did.

She looked momentarily startled. "I'm sorry."

The same two words he'd said to her the other night, after crossing the invisible line and kissing her. He'd decided the best course of action was to forget it had ever happened. *Yeah, right.* But maybe they should talk about it and clear the air.

"Look, I'm sensing a little hostility, and if it has anything to do with what happened the other night—"

"What happened?" She blinked. "Is that the correct legal term for a kiss?"

Okay, so maybe bringing it up wasn't the brightest idea he'd ever had. "Look, I've already apologized for that. I was hoping we could move ahead and forget about it."

"Is this some kind of strategy they taught you in law school? When you're sinking like the *Titanic,* create a distraction, and maybe no one will notice you just plowed into an iceberg?"

For a hotshot attorney who used words like Old West gunslingers used six-guns, this conversation, which he'd initiated, was going badly. His only defense was that he couldn't get that kiss off his mind. The taste and texture of her lips were pretty spectacular and made him want to do it again. And again. Frankly, memories of that kiss made him want to do far more than kiss, which was a formula for disaster.

"Casey, I promise you it will never happen again."

"You promise?" Her face had *skeptical* written all over it. "Is that like the promise you made to give me time off for my class?" She tapped her lip as her eyebrows pulled together in mock thoughtfulness. "Or maybe this is like the promise you made to go to counseling with Mia."

He had no defense. If she was a jury of his peers, he was guilty as charged. "I give up."

"There's a surprise."

"What does that mean?" he asked.

"It means you haven't even tried. It means relationships take work, and so far I haven't seen you work at anything but lip service. It means that if you're not willing to make an effort, Mia would be better off in the system."

"That's fairly heartless. If that's how you truly feel—"

"What? You'll fire me?" She pressed her lips together and stared at him as if coming to a decision. "I will not stick around and watch the hurt in that little girl's eyes over and over again when the only person she has in the whole world can't put her first even once. You can't fire me, Blake. What you can do is find yourself another nanny—because I quit."

## Chapter Six

When Casey turned and left the kitchen, she was shaking, but it wasn't all about being angry. All the while she was busting Blake about broken promises because he'd vowed not to kiss her again, her female parts were hoping he'd forget about that decision not to kiss her again. And didn't that just make her the world's biggest hypocrite? It was also a very good reason to go far, fast.

"Casey, wait—"

She wanted to ignore the request. For God's sake, she'd quit thirty seconds ago. Her insides were doing an energetic high five. All except her heart. The problem was that when she let her heart rule, bad stuff happened. She kept walking.

"Casey, please, I need to talk to you."

*Damn. Damn. Double damn.*

She stopped and turned to face him in the hall just outside

her room. Behind the closed door next to it, she could hear Mia talking to Frankie.

She met Blake's gaze. "We got her from the animal shelter."

"Who?"

"Frankie. If no one claimed her, she was going to be put down. It was Mia's idea to rescue a dog no one wanted, instead of getting a designer pet. Her words."

"I see."

"She's crying out, sure. But she's a good kid with a good heart. If you spent any time with her, you'd know that. But as long as I'm the nanny and you sign my paycheck, the odds are slim to none that that will happen. So I'm leaving."

"Without two weeks' notice?"

"Yes. So sue me. You're a lawyer." She turned away, fully intending to walk into her room.

"And if I promise to get to know her?" The look she shot him when she glanced over her shoulder must have contained sufficient sarcasm, because he added, "I know my track record doesn't inspire trust. And you're right about me taking advantage of your being here to shirk my responsibility to my niece. But I can change."

She turned and folded her arms over her chest. "Why should I believe that?"

"Because I got a reminder of what it's like to be in this on my own, and it scared the crap out of me."

What got her attention was the fact that he'd admitted to being scared. It was a clear violation of some macho code known only to men, where it was a major show of weakness to actually declare out loud to a woman that you were anything but in complete control.

She narrowed her gaze. "You're lying."

"Why would you say that?" Indignation shone in his blue

eyes, turning them to an intense shade that was almost navy. He settled his hands on lean hips, which made her notice how perfectly his wrinkled white dress shirt fit his flat abdomen and broad chest. The long sleeves were rolled up to reveal wide wrists and strong arms dusted with dark hair. It wasn't the breach in the macho rules she noticed now, but her all-too-female response to his masculinity.

"Why would you accuse me of lying?"

Because she wanted an ironclad reason, one without perceptible wiggle room, to stick to her guns and quit. "It's what lawyers do. Only you call it strategy. Or spin. Or reasonable doubt."

He nodded, but the dark look didn't budge. "I can't force you to believe me, but I can ask for another chance to show you I'm sincere. I'd like you to stay."

It was on the tip of her tongue to say no, but the hum of Mia's voice made her remember the kid's valiant attempt to hide how hurt she'd been at being abandoned at counseling—before she dissolved into tears. The good news was she could still cry, which was more than Casey could say for herself. The other good news was that the behavior was a sign—a sign that it wasn't too late to do some good. And that had been Casey's vow, to help her make sense of the mess she'd made in Iraq. She'd promised to dedicate her life to helping kids find the right path.

She needed to put up or shut up.

"Okay. I'll stay if the dog can stay." She pointed at him. "And you're still on big-time probation."

"I'll agree to be on probation if the dog is, too," he agreed.

"You're such a lawyer."

"Negotiation is one of my best skills." He let out a long breath. "And in the spirit of new beginnings, I'm sorry I missed the counseling session. I'll tell Mia the same thing."

"Good." She shot him a sympathetic look. "And you think I've been hard on you. Brace yourself."

"Okay. So we have a deal?"

"We do. Let's give this one more try." She sighed. "And if you can be magnanimous, how can I do less? I'm sorry I called you an ass."

"Apology accepted."

He grinned, and her heart was high-fiving, while her gut twisted with disapproval that she'd caved. There was little question in her mind who the ass was now.

A few days after she did a one-eighty on her decision to leave, life in the penthouse settled into a routine of summer school and doggy chaos without another major meltdown. Blake had been on his best behavior: he'd made it home for dinner each evening and he'd attended the rescheduled counseling session, which Mia had pronounced "lame." It was the new norm, and so far Casey was happy she'd decided to stay.

She was puttering around the kitchen while Mia surfed the Net, learning about canine care, when the phone rang.

"Hello," she said after picking it up.

"It's Pete with building security. There's a lady here who says she's Mr. Decker's mother, Patricia. Shall I send her up?"

Shock was Casey's best and only explanation for giving the okay. So much had happened since the night Mia had run away that Casey hadn't given much thought to Blake's parents. She was trying to figure out how to tell Mia that her grandmother was here when the bell rang and Frankie raced to the door and started barking.

"Who's there?" Mia asked, kneeling down on one knee to hold her dog.

"Your grandmother." Before the girl could comment, Casey opened the door. "Mrs. Decker, won't you come in?"

"Thank you, Casey."

"It's nice to see you again." Casey closed the door and let out a long breath. "This is a surprise."

They say clothes make the man, and if there truly were equality of the sexes, that would apply to women, as well. Patricia Decker was wearing a copper-colored shell, slacks and a matching jacket in a style that Casey recognized immediately. It was a brand touted as being able to hold up during travel. You could practically double knot the material, throw the garment in a suitcase and fly around the world, and it would look like it had just been pulled from the closet. The woman wearing it was another story.

Blake's mother looked ill at ease. And the dark circles beneath eyes the same turquoise color as Mia's clearly indicated that she'd been to hell and back. Still, every brunette strand of her shiny bob was perfectly in place. Diamond studs, which were almost certainly the real thing, twinkled in her ears.

Casey held out her hand. "Let's go sit in the living room."

"Do we have to?"

So much for a cooling-off period. Mia's antagonism seemed to roll off her in waves. A few minutes ago she'd been carefree and happy, trying to do the right thing by her dog. The change back to angry and hostile was startling.

Casey tried to be über-polite to compensate. "Mrs. Decker, why don't we—"

"Call me Patricia, please."

"All right." Casey held out her hand to indicate they should sit down. "Can I get you a cold drink?"

"Don't be nice to her," Mia protested. "She didn't give a crap about whether or not my mom and I were thirsty. Or cold. Or hungry."

Patricia's lips compressed into a straight line before she took in a shuddering breath. She looked at her granddaughter and said in a voice just above a whisper, "You look just like your mother."

"Is that supposed to make me like you?" the girl said.

"I didn't know you were here—"

"Before or after you threw my mother out and then she died?"

"Mia, that's enough," Casey admonished.

The girl glared at them. "Why should I believe she didn't know I was with Uncle Blake?"

"For what it's worth, Mia, I don't agree with what your grandfather did."

"He's not my grandfather."

"Technically speaking, he is." The older woman sighed. "He's your mother's father."

"Not after he threw her out. And I don't believe you didn't know about me," the girl said. She was hugging her dog as if the animal were her lifeline.

Casey sympathized with Mia, but that was no excuse for bad behavior. "Mia, you're being rude and that's not acceptable. The fact that your grandmother is here says a lot."

"She's here because she wants something."

"Whatever her reasons, I expect you to treat her with courtesy and respect," Casey shot back. "If you can't do that, a time-out is in your immediate future."

"You're sending me to my room?" the girl said doubtfully. "Like a little kid?"

"That's the way you're behaving," Casey agreed. "It's the way you'll be treated until you learn good manners."

"Lincoln was right. You do have spunk," Patricia said.

"I picked it up when I was a little girl with older brothers." And why the heck would she share that with Blake's mother? She must be more nervous than she'd realized. The woman wasn't here to see her. "Mia, I'd like you to apologize to your grandmother."

"It's all right." Patricia had been staring down at the girl, but the words got her attention. "The fact is, she's right. I do want something."

"I knew it," Mia said smugly.

Casey shot her a look. "What can we do for you?"

"I'd like to invite you to dinner," Patricia replied.

The statement was directed to Casey and she didn't know what to say. So she used the technique she'd learned from Blake. Distraction. "Do you think enough time has passed to qualify for a cooling-off period? It's not really a mediation if all the parties involved aren't present."

"It's not about arbitration. Mia has every right to be displeased. Just so you know, we didn't throw your mother out. We disapproved of her boyfriend and she ran away."

"My father?"

"Yes."

"He's a dork, too."

Patricia nodded. "I was heartbroken at losing my child and went into a deep depression. Then we learned she'd passed away and you'd gone to live with distant relatives. I struggled again, coming to terms with the fact that I'd never be able to make things right with my daughter. It took me a long time to come around. Your grandfather was trying to spare me from another episode."

"Doesn't make it right," Mia said.

"No, it doesn't. He was wrong to keep you from me, but I understand why he did."

"Whatever."

"Obviously, talk is cheap and won't change the past," Patricia said. "All I'm asking is that the three of you come to dinner."

Casey was pretty sure that meant her, not the dog. "That's very kind of you."

"It's not kind."

"No kidding," Mia interjected.

Instead of being aggravated, Patricia smiled. "Again she's right. My motivation is selfish. Whether you believe me or not, I simply would like to get to know you. Will you come?"

"I'll let Blake know about the invitation and have him call you," Casey answered.

"Fair enough." Patricia looked from Casey to her grand-daughter. "Thank you for seeing me and I'll say goodbye."

Moments later she was gone, but definitely not forgotten.

"Old bat," Mia mumbled before going to her room, with Frankie trotting eagerly after her.

Casey's head was spinning. Didn't that just figure? Today no one had run away from home or neglected to show up for an agreed-upon counseling session. Her boss hadn't kissed her or in any way indicated that he thought of her as anything but the hired help. It had been a trauma-free day in the child-care business, but heaven forbid that there should be any peace.

Blake had given his secretary strict orders to schedule his day so that he could be home in time for dinner at 6:30. Today was a close call, but he hadn't missed an evening meal with Mia since Casey had almost quit.

He wasn't ready to slap a "success" sticker on the arrangement yet, but he was even less prepared not to find Casey in the penthouse with his niece. The thought of her waiting for him sent a vibration through his system that was part awareness, part anticipation. And all heat.

Mia's nanny was an incredibly interesting woman. Alternately tough and tender. Glib and gorgeous. It was saying a lot that he appreciated her way with words more than the awesome way she filled out a pair of jeans. When she was around, he found himself watching the graceful movement of her body and waiting to see what she'd say next. On top of that, by some miracle, she seemed to be able to keep his niece under control. He'd be a fool to give Casey any reason to quit again, including, but not limited to, kissing her. Again.

In the lobby of his building, he slid his key card into the private elevator slot and rode the elevator to the penthouse, suddenly eager to be home. And when he walked in the door, Mia, Casey and the dog were all waiting. They started talking, and barking, all at once, and he was able to hear only the words *mother, dinner, witch, poison* and *no way.* The last words were followed by a bark from Frankie.

Blake held up his hands. "Time-out."

"I won't do it," Mia said. "You can't make me."

"Take a time-out?" he asked. "If you don't, I won't even hear what I can't make you do."

"She's an old witch who's trying to buy my goodwill. I'm not falling for her act."

"Careful, Mia," Casey cautioned. "She's your uncle's mother."

"So we're talking about your grandmother," he said to his niece.

The girl folded her arms over her chest and glared defiantly at him. "No way."

"Way." Blake shrugged. "Biologically she is your mother's mother, which makes her your grandmother."

Mia started to argue the irrefutable, and the thought crossed Blake's mind that she might make a good attorney someday. But not today. When Casey jumped into the fray, he held up his hands again.

"One at a time, you two. I have no idea what's going on." He pointed to Casey. "You first. Sorry, kid, but age has its privileges," he added when the girl opened her mouth to protest.

"Mia's grandmother stopped by today." Casey shot the

girl a "zip it" look when she made disapproving noises. "She came with olive branch in hand."

"I'd rather eat an olive branch raw than have dinner at the dork's house."

Blake set his briefcase by the door and Frankie trotted over to sniff it. Warily Blake grabbed the handle and set the briefcase on the foyer table. The dog gave him a "drop dead, bastard" look that reminded him of his niece. Then he focused back on the conversation. He was guessing "the dork's house" was his parents' place.

"Start at the beginning," he advised. Being a divorce lawyer and listening to two people with opposite points of view were good training for everyday power struggles. He looked at Casey. "Again, you go first."

"Figures," Mia mumbled.

To her credit, Casey refused to engage and ignored the comment. "As I said, your mother stopped by today. Without calling."

He was curious why she added that. Was it a problem for her? But that would only delay the exchange of information, so he said, "Go on."

"She invited us to dinner. Including me," Casey added. "I'm not sure why."

"My dad thinks you're spunky." Blake figured he and his dad had something in common. They both liked Casey.

"I won't go." Mia glared at him. "If she thinks I can be bought for the price of a rice grain and a dry crust of bread, she's wrong."

"Very dramatic. I don't suppose it would do any good to point out that there are children in the world who would consider that a feast."

Mia huffed out a breath and rolled her eyes.

"I didn't think so," he said. "Maybe the dorks want to get to know you."

"If the old guy did," Mia answered, "he wouldn't have pretended I don't exist."

"He didn't do that. Children's services contacted him about you first and he turned the matter over to me."

"He gave them a big no and said nothing to my...to her."

"We didn't think it through," Blake admitted.

"I get it," Mia said. "He didn't want Lady Dork to get her panties in a twist. And that will make me want to see them why?"

"You're family," Casey said. "This could be the beginning of a meaningful bond."

"Right." Mia's voice dripped sarcasm. "They're probably in trouble with the charity police and look bad for ignoring a grandkid."

Blake folded his arms over his chest. "Maybe they haven't handled this whole thing in the best way, but they're reaching out now."

"So?"

"So," Casey joined in. "I think it's safe to say that you've blown through your share of relatives because, frankly, you're not all that easy to get along with. Can you really afford not to at least accept their dinner invitation?"

"They're your mother's parents," Blake said.

The girl looked at them, standing side by side and presenting a united front. "Yeah, I get it," she finally said. "That makes them Grandma and Grandpa. Biologically. But they don't act like it."

Blake watched Mia and a feeling of déjà vu swept over him. He remembered his younger sister, the rebellious girl who had questioned everything. She'd been difficult, but also smart, funny, beautiful. He'd loved her and now she was gone. The only part of her left was this child, who was resisting a relationship with the people who, in her opinion, wronged both her mother and her.

Part of him couldn't blame her. The folks had handled this badly. He didn't know what had happened with them and his sister, but current and past history convinced him that what transpired had most likely been handled with the finesse and sensitivity of a herd of water buffalo. But Casey was right. The kid didn't make it easy to like her.

"Look, Mia," he said seriously, "my guess is that your grandparents want to get to know their only grandchild. Maybe they miss their daughter." He wouldn't be surprised. He missed his sister.

"I'm not going to take her place," the girl argued.

"No one expects that," Casey told her. "They're just reaching out."

"So what? It's too little, too late."

When Frankie bumped her nose on Casey's leg, Casey absently rubbed the dog's head. A minute later she stopped and Frankie nudged her hand, indicating she wasn't yet finished being rubbed.

"It's too late for your mother," Casey pointed out, her tone sympathetic. "But not for you. You don't want to look back and wish you'd given them a chance when there was time. They'd probably like to go back and change how they acted and what happened with your mom. None of us get through life without regrets about things we've done."

Blake was watching Casey and noticed the shadows that slid into her hazel eyes, turning the gold flecks to brown. It didn't take a PhD in psychology or expert credentials in body language to see that she had regrets in a very big way. He wondered what could possibly have happened to make her look like that, so sad and guilty. Casey was talking to Mia with the voice of experience, but the kid's next words showed that she wasn't getting the message.

"I don't like them."

"You don't even *know* them," Casey pointed out. "Get acquainted, and then you're allowed to have an opinion on whether or not they're worthy of your respect and affection."

"They won't like me." Mia's unhappy expression spoke volumes.

Casey got it, too. "I see we're getting to the real reason behind your behavior. Fear of rejection."

"I'm not afraid—"

Casey held up her hand. "It was just an observation. I don't blame you. But you have to take some responsibility for your behavior. I said before, and I'm not being mean, you don't make it easy to care about you. If you're rude and mouthy, it gives people a reason to brush you off that isn't about rejecting you as a person."

Blake had some experience with rejection as a person. His wife had turned to another guy, and not just anyone. His closest friend had ended up in her bed. He'd done his best to give her what she wanted and it hadn't been enough.

"There's a lot of truth to what Casey is saying." Blake knew the kid didn't like hearing that. "And you've got plenty of reasons to feel the way you do."

"Then I don't have to go—"

"I didn't say that." He held up his hand. "I want to talk to Casey about this before I make up my mind."

"Mia, why don't you take Frankie out for a walk?" Casey met his gaze. "You probably aren't aware of this, but there's a dog run in the complex. And Pete with building security will keep an eye on them."

"Okay." Blake looked at his niece. "You heard Casey."

The kid wanted to object, but apparently the safety-in-numbers rule applied, because she looked at the two adults, who stood shoulder to shoulder, then wordlessly got the dog's leash and left with the animal.

Blake ran his fingers through his hair. "What do you think?"

"You get to make the decision. I'm the hired help. You're the man of the house."

The fact that he was a man was never far from his mind when he looked at her. Right now he couldn't take his eyes off her mouth, and his hands itched to discover every part of her. He wanted to explore the lips he had only touched for seconds yet couldn't manage to forget. The depth of her appeal was uncharted and the effort to keep from charting it was taking a toll on his willpower.

"Still," he managed to say, "I'd like your opinion. Will dinner with my folks help or hurt Mia?"

Casey shook her head. "I don't have my crystal ball on me at the moment. The fact is, not even an expert in child psychology could answer that question. Best guess?"

He'd take her best guess over expert opinion any day. "Absolutely."

"I think Mia is protesting too much. She's the one who started this scenario in motion by showing up at her grandparents. Her actions are saying, 'Notice me.' But her defiance is about protecting her feelings. If they don't like her, she can say she was right. She told us so."

"Then we should call her bluff and meet the folks halfway?"

She nodded. "If for no other reason than it covers your backside."

"Excuse me?"

"I'd give your mother a call and accept the invitation so that in the future Mia can't blame you for keeping her from her family."

Casey ran her tongue over her lips and he couldn't see

anything except himself kissing her. Suddenly it seemed like the blood from his brain headed to points south of his belt and all coherent thought stalled.

"Point taken," he managed to say. "And I agree."

When Casey smiled, he was far too happy that she'd approved of his answer. And when he managed to use his brain for rational reflection again, he would try and figure out why that was so important.

## Chapter Seven

Dinner at the Deckers' could be more awkward and uncomfortable, but Casey wasn't sure how. Blake was doing his best to keep the conversation going, but Mia was sullen and uncooperative and wouldn't engage, even though the older couple had fixed a kid favorite, burgers and fries. Lincoln and Patricia would probably need a triple dose of cholesterol-lowering meds after serving fat-heavy foods to thaw their granddaughter's cold feelings.

Clearly that had been Patricia's intent when she'd come by the penthouse to issue the invitation. Even Lincoln was on his best behavior, conciliatory and subdued compared to the last time Casey had been here. His wife had probably given him a talking-to and he'd gotten the message.

The five of them were sitting around a dining room table long enough to land a jumbo jet, and the dark wood looked sturdy enough to hold the weight. A matching breakfront and buffet took up a lot of space in the big room. Delicate china, silver and crystal looked beautiful and dignified on a light green linen tablecloth. The formal setting seemed at odds with the menu, but it convinced Casey that the older couple was trying. So far the kid wasn't cutting them any slack.

"That was one of the best burgers I've had in a long time." Casey glanced from one end of the table to the other, at their host and hostess. "Do you barbecue often, Lincoln?"

"We have a housekeeper who does all the cooking," Patricia answered. "I gave her the night off so it would just be family."

Her husband set his cloth napkin on the table. "I forgot how much I enjoy it."

After yet another uncomfortable silence Blake cleared his throat. "I don't grill anymore, either. And I used to be pretty good at it."

"You've been able to get home for dinner more often lately," Casey said, meeting his gaze across the expanse of table. "You should try it again."

"Maybe I will." Blake glanced at his niece, to Casey's left. "What do you think, Mia? Steak or chicken?"

"Whatever." She slouched lower in her chair.

Casey noted with amusement that she'd eaten a good-size burger and an impressive number of fries for a kid who couldn't be bought with a grain of rice and a dry bread crust. Maybe the fact that she'd enjoyed the food served by the very people she'd vowed to hate was partly the reason for more attitude than usual.

"Let Mia and me help you clean up," Casey offered.

"That's very kind of you." There was a strain in the smile Patricia settled on everyone around the table. "Dessert, anyone? I have the makings for ice cream sundaes."

Casey knew that was one of Mia's favorites and looked to

her left for a reaction. Eagerness gleamed in the girl's eyes for a moment; then it disappeared, replaced by a deliberate mask of bored indifference.

"Mia?" Patricia looked at her granddaughter. "Do you like ice cream?"

"Not much."

"Oh." Disappointment clouded the older woman's expression. "I thought it would go best with a casual dinner. Probably I should have asked what you preferred."

Casey was starting to feel sorry for the Deckers. They had made a lot of mistakes, no question about that. But the fact that this couple, who were probably more the pheasant-underglass type, had served burgers and fries seemed like an obvious sign that they wanted to make amends. It didn't appear that Mia planned to bend anytime soon, so maybe a little help in that direction would be in order.

"Patricia, do you have pictures of Mia's mom?" Casey could feel the glare from the girl and the startled look from Blake. She ignored both.

"Yes." The older woman looked grateful, then glanced at Mia. "Would you like to see them?"

Before the kid could snap out an abrasive response, Casey said, "That's a great idea."

"I'll go get them." Patricia pushed her chair back and stood.

"Let me help," Lincoln offered.

Casey caught Blake's eye and said, "Why don't you give your folks a hand? Mia and I will clear the table."

Blake looked doubtful but said, "Okay."

When they'd carried a load of dishes to the kitchen, Mia said, "This is so lame."

"Including the food?" Casey set the plates in the sink, with Mia's empty one on top. "Let's go get the rest."

Mia did as asked, but if she'd moved any slower, she'd have gone backward. When they had the table cleaned off and the dishes arranged in the dishwasher, Casey leaned back against the cupboard.

"Do you want to talk about it?"

Mia glared. "I can't believe you made me come here."

"Technically, it was your uncle who made the decision." Casey remembered the expression on Blake's face when she'd said he was the man of the house. Even now the hungry look in his eyes made her shiver. But that wasn't something to deal with now. "He thought it was important for you to know your family."

"This is so wrong." Mia slumped against the island, elbows on the top, and rested her chin in her hands.

"I know you're angry and you have every right to be," Casey said. "But they can give you something no one else can."

"What? Nothing?"

"No. Memories of your mom." Sadness and regret rolled through her. "Take it from me that's something you're going to want."

"What do you know about it?" The misery in her expression took away the hostility in her words.

"When I was just about your age, my mother died of cancer. Just like your mom."

Mia's eyes filled with pain. "Do you still miss her?"

"Very much. And photos are all I have of her." This child didn't need to know that Casey's father had withdrawn and hadn't even shared himself after her mom died. "Your grandparents are reaching out. You don't have to let them off the hook. It's okay to make them accountable, but don't cut off your nose to spite your face."

Mia's mouth curved up just a fraction. "What does that even mean?"

Casey laughed. "Old expression. It just means that refusing to look at pictures of your mother will just punish *you* in the long run."

Mia stared at her for so long that Casey thought she'd refuse. Finally she nodded. When they turned, Blake was standing in the doorway with a bemused expression on his face.

"You did this to me," Mia said as she walked past him.

Casey looked at him and shrugged. "No good deed goes unpunished."

"Tell me about it." He rubbed the back of his neck as he stared after his niece. "I heard what you said."

"I figured."

"Have you ever heard the saying that people come into our lives for a season and a reason? Or something like that."

"Yeah."

"I can't help feeling that way about you."

"Oh?" Her heart started to pound. *Darn it.*

"Yeah. I'm fairly sure there are other nannies with strong child-care credentials and an impressive skill set. But your background gives you an empathy someone else might not have."

"Yeah."

She remembered thinking something similar at their first meeting, when her heart had gone out to the motherless girl. What she hadn't realized then was how the rest of her female parts would respond to her boss. It didn't make the assignment impossible, but it certainly challenged her in ways she'd never been challenged before. And the way he was looking at her now didn't help.

"You're a remarkable woman, Casey." He folded his arms over his chest. "You're good with Mia and not afraid of my parents. That's quite a combination."

The intense expression in his eyes wasn't exactly employer-employee relationship-friendly. It was more approachable, and then some, tearing down any obstacles that stood between. She didn't claim to be an expert in the field, but even she could see it was similar to the way he'd looked before kissing her.

And how he could kiss. But since then she'd found out his wife had cheated on him with his best friend. She'd been warned.

She knew why he didn't do personal relationships, why he wouldn't commit. That was important for her to know in case she was tempted to kiss him again. Like now. They were just beginning to make headway with Mia. Why jeopardize it by pursuing something doomed to go nowhere?

He stuck his fingertips in the pockets of his worn jeans. "I just want you to know that I've noticed."

*Right back at you,* she thought. But probably what she had noticed wasn't what he meant. "Speaking of your parents and Mia, we should probably go see what's going on."

"You mean be Switzerland?"

She smiled. "Just in case."

In the sitting room there was a big stack of albums on the coffee table. Patricia was sitting on a love seat in front of the fireplace, with Mia beside her and Lincoln resting on an arm.

"Here's one of your mother at just about your age," Patricia was saying.

The girl pointed to the picture. "Is that Uncle Blake by the pool?"

"Yes." The older woman laughed. "This was snapped just before April pushed him in."

Mia glanced up and grinned at Blake. "You were beaten by a girl."

He walked over and sat on the other arm of the love seat, the one closest to Mia, so he could see the photo. "I remember that. She caught me by surprise."

"Yeah. Right," Mia said.

"She was such a mischievous child," Patricia said wistfully. She glanced at the girl beside her. "You look a lot like her, Mia."

"You said that before."

"And now you can look at the pictures and decide for yourself." Patricia turned the page. "Here's another one of April and I swear it could be you. There's a very strong resemblance."

"I guess." Mia turned the page. "How old was she when this one was taken?"

Casey watched the Deckers pore over the family photos and felt good. Really good. Maybe Blake was right about her coming into their lives at just the right time. She'd wanted to turn down the job, not break her personal rule about kids of a certain age. But this was a good day with a positive outcome. She'd convinced Mia to meet them halfway for this moment in time. Would another nanny have been able to connect? She would never know.

Just like she would never know what connecting with Blake would be like. He wouldn't go there. And if he did, she'd be a fool to go there with him.

Blake opened one of the sliding glass doors connecting his bedroom to the terrace and stepped outside. It was a beautiful August night and the breeze that skipped over the lighted pool water picked up a little coolness. It was after midnight and he had a busy schedule the next day. Nowadays he had to cram the same work into fewer hours in order to make it home for dinner. He should get some sleep. If he could, he would, but thoughts of Casey wouldn't leave him alone long enough to rest.

There was a movement from one of the sliding glass doors on the other side of the terrace, near the room where she slept. And suddenly there she was. *Casey. Speak of the devil...* Although the way the moonlight turned her blond hair silver made her look more like an angel.

She was wearing pink cotton pajama bottoms and a thin-strapped, very un-angel-like white knit top that clung to her small breasts like a lover's hands. The image was sexy as hell—and not one he'd ever expected to have of a nanny.

But that was before he'd hired Casey.

She moved farther onto the terrace and stopped by one of the green wrought-iron patio tables, resting a hand on one of the matching chairs. Staring out at the lights of the suburbs intersecting with the glitz of hotel-casinos, she let out a deep, sad sigh. He wasn't sure what made him characterize it as sad, except that her shoulders slumped and she was frowning. He'd grown accustomed to her smile, spirit and sass, and missed them now. This introspective side of her made him even more curious.

If Blake was as smart as everyone thought, he'd go back inside before she realized she wasn't alone. When he took a step out of the shadows and into the bright moonlight, some part of him knew his brain wasn't the organ responsible for the decision.

"Casey?"

She gasped and pressed a hand to her chest as her gaze swung in his direction. "Blake. Good grief, you startled me."

"Sorry."

She stared at him for several moments, catching her breath. "I didn't mean to wake you."

He shook his head. "You didn't. I just couldn't sleep. What's your excuse?"

"Same."

"Insomnia epidemic." He stood beside her, the sleeve of his T-shirt brushing her bare skin. "I was thinking about my folks. And Mia." That was partly true. "I really appreciate what you did tonight."

"It was nothing."

"On the contrary. Like the song says, you were a bridge over troubled water."

"That's why you're still awake. Can't get the tune out of your head," she teased.

"Nope. Not the reason." When their gazes connected and held for a moment, a spark of sexual awareness passed between them and her eyes widened slightly, telling him she'd felt it, too.

She leaned away, as far as she could without taking a step. *Never show weakness.* "I'm glad you're happy with my work, Blake, but don't make more out of it than I deserve."

"You orchestrated a photo marathon with my family and I'd say that deserves quite a bit of praise. Although, for the record, I could have done without the photographic history of my geek stage, and I plan to initiate a covert op at my earliest convenience to search out and destroy all evidence of it."

She didn't laugh, which was a surprise. Normally she got his sense of humor. "In my opinion you never had a geek stage, like the rest of the human race."

"Right." He was glad she didn't think so, which meant her opinion mattered more than it should. "The thing is that somehow you convinced Mia to look at those albums with her sworn enemies. It was a miracle."

"Not a miracle. I'm no saint," she argued, self-incrimination lacing her voice. "Far from it."

The vehemence in her protest was sincere and forceful and out of proportion to the woman he'd come to know, which meant there was something about this woman he didn't know. "Why so hard on yourself?"

"I don't think I am. Just keeping it real. About myself and the job. To do it to the best of my ability, I need to achieve a level of emotional distance."

He could use some of that emotional distance right now,

because the sight of her toned arms and smooth skin was tying him in knots. She was a striking woman. She was pretending that the commitment and drive she focused on Mia were just part of the job. But he didn't buy it. She cared deeply, and that made her even more beautiful to him. The length of her neck, the curve of her cheek, her turned-up, freckle-splashed nose all tempted him to do what he'd promised not to do. More than taking his next breath, he wanted to kiss her—and somehow he had to distract himself.

What had she just said? *Oh, right.*

"Uh-huh," he said. "You were very objective and unemotional when you got my niece a dog. You could have fooled me."

"Not being fooled is the goal." There was a far-off expression on her face, as if she were halfway around the world. "Observation. Evaluation. Objectivity. Don't get sucked in. I learned the lesson well in the army…" Her voice broke and she turned away.

"Casey?" Blake put his hands on the bare flesh of her arms and felt her trembling. "What is it?"

"Nothing." But she was still shaking.

It wasn't like her to bring up that time in the military. Was it his teasing remark about a covert op? He'd been exaggerating, but she'd gotten specific.

"What happened in the army?" he asked.

She bent her head, and though he couldn't see her face, the movement was fraught with emotion and defeat.

"Nothing."

"I can tell by the way you're trembling that it's not nothing. Talk to me."

"There's nothing to talk about. I'm fine. Just tired. I'll be able to sleep now…" She tried to pull away, but he wouldn't let her go.

He turned her and the single tear coursing down her cheek shone silver in the moonlight. "You're crying."

"No, really—"

"Don't." He cupped her face in his hands and brushed his thumb over her cheek. "I know tears when I see them."

Misery was stark in her eyes. The longing to take away her pain joined with the need to taste her, and suddenly he couldn't fight it anymore. Blake lowered his mouth to hers. The light touch was hot enough, but what really sent nuclear blast-type heat billowing through him was Casey's soft sounds of pleasure and surrender.

A heartbeat later his ability to draw in air went from zero to not enough oxygen in the universe, and Casey was breathless, too. He thought about stopping, was working up to it when she put her hands on his chest, but the feel of her touching him decimated his willpower and took rational thought with it.

He curved his palms on her hips and drew her close as he kissed her lips, cheeks, jaw and neck. He nibbled a spot just beneath her ear as he brushed the tiny straps of her shirt out of the way and down her arms. The top pooled at her waist and—*thank you, God!*—she wasn't wearing a bra. His fingers ached to touch her and in a nanosecond the soft flesh of her breasts was in his hands.

He bent his head and drew her left nipple into his mouth and heard her sharp intake of breath as he sucked her deeper. Her breathy little moans heated his blood and sent it pounding through him, roaring in his ears. As he kissed her, they turned toward the moonlight, mining all the romance from the night. He wanted to see her in the glow of Mother Nature's glory and lifted his head.

And that was when he saw the red puckered scars that marred her midriff and disappeared beneath the waistband of her cotton pants. The sight was more horrifying because it was completely unexpected. He knew she felt his shock, because she tensed and a heartbeat later pulled out of his arms and turned away. Quickly she slid her arms through the straps and righted her shirt to cover herself.

"What happened to you?" he whispered, his voice hoarse and harsh. "Don't tell me nothing."

"I don't want to talk about it."

"Maybe you should," he said.

She turned back and shook her head. "I made a bad call. Like now."

He ran his fingers through his hair and blew out a long breath. "A slip in judgment. A broken promise."

"Yeah." She met his gaze and there was hurt in her eyes. "Not completely your fault. I'm a big girl. I can take care of myself. Been doing it for a long time."

"I didn't plan for it to happen."

"Don't worry. I know it wasn't like that. I'd never accuse you of anything."

"That's not what I'm worried about. It's just…" He didn't know how to say what was on his mind. "I don't want to take advantage of you."

"I remember. You're anti-relationship and a woman shouldn't expect a commitment."

"You make it sound like a tagline." He settled his hands on his hips. "Just so we're clear, I didn't pick a career based on ripping relationships apart. I was happily married, or so I thought. I was good at negotiating settlements—assets, money, alimony, visitation agreements, kids, even dogs. Not once did anyone ever talk about the love. It's all animosity and lots of it. The thing is, if the bitterness is that big, the love must have been, too, but no one tells you where it went. My wife struck the first blow when she slept with my best friend, but the love took a long time to die."

"Look, Blake, I'm not asking why. You don't owe me an explanation. You have a past and so do I. This isn't a good idea for so many reasons. The most important one being Mia."

"Oh?" His head was so messed up, he wasn't exactly sure what his niece had to do with anything.

"She's making strides. Maybe that's too ambitious. Baby steps. But I see progress and it's not a good idea to do anything to upset that. We need to channel all our energy into her."

"Right. Okay." He nodded a little too willingly.

She cocked her thumb over her shoulder in the direction of her bedroom. "I'm going in now. Good night."

Moments ago he had been in heaven, but now it pretty much was hell. And he blamed himself, the lust he'd let get out of control, what with his lack of a personal life. He'd been telling himself that would get better when everything with his niece stabilized.

He wanted to believe that what just happened was no big deal, but he'd also wanted to believe that his wife hadn't cheated on him. He'd especially wanted to believe that his best friend hadn't been involved. He'd been wrong then and he was afraid he was wrong now. But that didn't put the brakes on his lust. Or his curiosity.

The scars were evidence that something had happened to Casey, and he couldn't shake the feeling that the damage inside her was far worse than what he could see. But she'd refused to give up her past.

If there was one thing a divorce attorney saw over and over, it was that secrets had a way of not staying secret.

## Chapter Eight

The day after kissing Blake, Casey continued to be appalled at how easily he'd gotten past her defenses. She had faced danger every day in Iraq and had the scars to prove it, but the fact that he could make her forget everything, including those scars while he exposed them, really scared her.

"I miss Frankie."

Casey glanced over at Mia in the passenger seat of her car. After she had picked Mia up from summer school, the two of them had gone to lunch, then stopped at an office supply store for Mia's project paraphernalia. The class would be over soon and the final assignment was a good portion of the grade. So they'd decided to dazzle the teacher with materials and color. Browsing every aisle of the warehouse-size store had been time-consuming. It was nip and tuck whether or not they would beat Blake home for dinner.

"I'm sure Frankie misses you, too," Casey assured her.

"Yeah." Mia looked worried. "But when she's alone too long, she gets into trouble."

"Not unlike someone else I know," Casey teased.

The girl rolled her eyes. "I never got in the trash and dragged it all over the place."

"True." Casey signaled a left turn into the luxury condominium complex. "And I don't believe you've ever grabbed grapes from the bowl on the kitchen counter and eaten them off the floor."

"But she had consequences," Mia pointed out. "Her tummy was upset, because dogs aren't supposed to eat that stuff."

"Who do you think really suffered?" Casey glanced over. "Frankie did not keep that gas to herself."

"No, it was pretty stinky." Mia giggled, a happy and age-appropriate sound not heard as often as it should be.

*God bless that dog,* Casey thought.

After pulling into the complex and parking, Casey noted that Blake's car wasn't there yet. Then Mia grabbed the white plastic bags with school supplies from the backseat and they rode the elevator up to the top floor. Even before Casey fit her key into the front door, the dog was barking a welcome on the other side of it.

"She knows we're home," Mia said happily.

Casey wasn't so sure. Could be the dog thought they were breaking in. But when the door opened, Frankie was right there, looking up at Mia with adoring brown eyes. The girl dropped to one knee and gave her pet a hug.

"Hi, Frankie. Did you miss me? Were you a good girl while we were gone?"

Casey gave them a moment and walked through the foyer and into the family room. It was hard not to gasp at the sight of Blake's open laptop computer lying haphazardly on the carpet, with the keyboard letters scattered around. She looked closer and the damage indicated that the dog had repeatedly pawed the fragile electronic device until the keys came off. After her initial thought that this wouldn't go over well with Blake, her next was that he didn't usually leave the thing out. He normally used it in his study.

Her third realization came when she heard the front door open and close. It was unfortunate that they'd spent so long picking out Post-it colors, because there might have been time to hide the evidence and break the bad news to him more gently than the visual he was going to get.

"Hi, Mia," she heard him say. The dog must have jumped on him, because his next words were, "Frankie, get down."

Casey quickly scooped up the plastic keys and tried to push the wounded computer under the coffee table. She heard footsteps on the marble floor behind her and sighed.

"What the hell happened?" Blake's question confirmed that her efforts were too little too late.

She looked up from where she was kneeling in the ruins of what had once been a state-of-the-art portable computer. Now it was little more than a dog toy. Before she could answer the question, the doggy perp ran into the room and pawed at what remained of the keyboard.

Mia followed and flopped on the floor, throwing her arms around the dog. "It's not her fault."

"That's what all the doggy delinquents say." Blake looked furious. "That excuse is followed closely by accusations of abuse and neglect."

"Maybe it can be fixed," Casey said, her heart sinking when she looked at the keys in her hand—Tab, Caps Lock, Shift and Control.

"Fixed?" Blake asked incredulously. "There's a better chance of negotiating a lasting peace in the Middle East." His voice was deadly calm, too dead and too calm. He looked at Mia. "Why is it out here?"

"I saw it here this morning. You must have been working last night and left it here," Mia said.

Casey watched the muscle in his tight jaw jerk and wondered what was going through his mind. Memories of kissing him last night had been looping through hers all day. But he was a guy and probably hadn't given it another thought.

"It belongs in the study," he said, neither confirming nor denying. "How did she get the thing open?"

"She's smart?" Mia said, part statement, part question.

Casey stood and met Blake's gaze. "Obviously it was left open."

"No." All statement, no question.

It left no room for debate, but Casey didn't take the hint. "We've had this conversation before. Unless Frankie grew opposable thumbs, her canine abilities are severely limited. There's no way the dog opened the laptop."

"You left it open," Mia accused him.

"I don't do that," Blake responded just as stubbornly, and the glares between uncle and niece were almost identical.

"I bet when you were growing up and did bad stuff, you always blamed it on my mom."

"I have no independent recollection of that," he said.

"Look at it this way," Casey suggested. "When you're in court and you need an excuse for the judge, you can tell him the dog ate your computer."

"Not funny."

"I thought it was," Mia said, unsmiling, as she stared at him. "You're going to make Frankie leave."

"It's crossing my mind as we speak," he confirmed.

"You can't do that," she cried.

Casey agreed with her but had a feeling their reasons were very different.

"She's a good watchdog," Mia said.

"Who's going to watch *her?*" he shot back.

Mia thought for a moment. "She helps the housekeeper."

"What?"

Mia's chin lifted defiantly. "Crumbs on the floor. She cleans them up. Better than the vacuum."

"It's true," Casey agreed.

"The nanny isn't supposed to take sides," he reminded her.

"I'm not doing that," Casey lied. "Just being a witness to the truth. Frankie waits for someone to drop food and it barely touches the floor before it's gone. Environmentally she's a benefit."

"Right," he said, his voice dripping sarcasm. "No taking sides there."

"She's good to talk to," Mia continued. "She always listens and doesn't argue or talk back."

He folded his arms over his chest. "So she's a good role model for you?"

"Yes," Mia said. Then it sank in. "I don't argue or talk back. Anymore," she added.

"Except now," he pointed out.

Mia's eyes were suspiciously bright as she rubbed a finger underneath her nose. "She just wants to love you."

"You mean she wants to love *you.*" Blake shook his head and blew out a long breath. The anger seemed to drain out of him. "This can't happen again."

The girl's expression turned eager. "It won't. I swear, Uncle Blake."

"Why should I believe you?"

"If she does anything wrong, you can ground me for the rest of my life."

Casey saw his mouth twitch and noted the way he brushed his hand over the lower half of his face to hide the fact that he wanted to smile.

"Please don't make her go away," Mia begged.

"Okay, but here's the deal," he said. "She's your responsibility. That means if you want to keep her, you have to walk her, feed her, care for her and not let her destroy stuff."

"I promise." Mia stood and slid her fingers under the dog's collar to lead her down the hall. "You won't be sorry."

"Wait. There's more," he said.

She stopped and looked warily at him. "What?"

"You need to attend your grandparents' anniversary party in a couple of weeks."

"This is blackmail," Mia protested.

"I know." He grinned. "And you've done a really good job of making a case for the dog to stay. You might want to consider a career in law."

"If I consider it, will you let Frankie stay and not make me go to the party?"

"Not a chance, kid." He was enjoying this. "This is the deal. Not only will you voluntarily go to the party, but you will be gracious to your grandparents and everyone there. You'll say please and thank you. No slouching, shrugging or rolling your eyes when you disagree with anything."

"But, Uncle Blake—"

He held up a finger to stop the words. "No arguing. No negotiating. Those are my terms. Yes or no?"

She released a big sigh, rolled her eyes, shook her head and finally glared, but eventually said, "Deal."

"Okay, then. Frankie can stay."

Without a single gesture or word that could jeopardize her pet, and before he could change his mind, Mia left the room with her dog and the door down the hall slammed behind them.

Blake grinned at Casey. "I think I'm getting the hang of this whole parenting thing. Who knew it was so easy to control the kid?"

"She's right about the blackmail thing," Casey pointed out. "Would you really make her get rid of the dog?"

He rubbed a hand over his neck. "I considered it, but did you see the tears in her eyes?"

"Yeah." But she hadn't realized he'd noticed.

Casey realized the man actually had a heart and it was really soft. And she was in a whole lot of trouble. If the sexy five o'clock shadow on his jaw hadn't convinced her, the fact that he wouldn't have followed through on his threat to get rid of the dog would have.

He might be getting a handle on parenting, but Casey was losing the battle to resist him.

Mia stomped into the penthouse foyer after coming home from their counseling appointment and glared at her uncle. "You only think about yourself."

Blake stared angrily back at her. "I don't claim to be an expert in raising kids, but one thing I'm learning, if something I do sends you into brat mode, it must be right."

"I hate you," she said, then turned and went down the hall, the dog on her heels. The next sound was the door to her bedroom slamming.

"Okay." Casey set her purse on the entryway table, wishing for the silence on the ride home, which had been the calm before the storm. "Feel the love."

Blake leveled his scowl on her. "I thought you said counseling would help. Her attitude is worse than ever. For crying out loud, all I said was no to a stop at the mall. Why does that put me at the top of America's Most Wanted?"

Casey folded her arms over her chest and tried to ignore

the fact that in his worn jeans and T-shirt he looked really hot. Not heat hot because it was August and this was the desert, after all. Hot as in she wanted to feel his lean, muscular strength and his manly flesh pressed against her. Preferably while they were both naked. The image did nothing to help her focus on negotiating a peace.

"She's not angry about the mall. It's about painful feelings that were stirred up. You probably already know this, Blake, but counseling doesn't work like aspirin for a headache. It's more like surgery. Open up your guts and take out the bad stuff, with all the pain of recovery and no meds to take the edge off it."

"Gee," he said. "Remind me again why I listened to you and agreed to go?"

"Because I threatened to quit."

"Right."

Still using the medical analogy, she realized there was a reason doctors weren't encouraged to treat family members. It was called losing objectivity due to personal involvement. As if she hadn't known she'd done just that after the first kiss, Casey really got the message when she didn't stop him from getting her naked from the waist up. She should have quit way before Blake agreed to counseling in order to get her to stay.

He blew out a long breath. "Would you like to take a walk?"

*Bad idea. Really bad.* "I should start dinner. And I should be here if Mia needs to talk."

"I need to talk to you." He met her gaze. "I can make it an order."

"Not necessary. You're the boss." Why couldn't she have remembered that when they were drenched in moonlight and his mouth was on hers?

When she returned from telling Mia where they were going, he opened the front door and held out a hand, indicating that she should precede him. After a ride in the penthouse elevator, they went through the building's luxurious lobby and turned right into a hallway, then walked past the his and hers spas and out the door next to the workout room.

The grounds at One Queensridge Place were as impressive as the rest of the complex. An Olympic-size pool was surrounded by chaise longues and patio tables, but there were also cabanas, tentlike areas for a little extra seclusion. Casey glanced up at Blake and the intensity in his profile instantly bumped up her heart rate. Seclusion with him would be dangerous in every way she could imagine.

After they passed the tennis courts, they reached a walking path that was bordered on either side by palo verde trees and vibrant desert plants blooming in red, yellow, pink and purple. It was after six in the evening and the temperature was still in the nineties, but the air was pleasant, as opposed to July's oppressive heat.

At intervals along the winding path, ornate wrought-iron benches had been placed for anyone who wanted to sit and chat. When Blake indicated she should take a seat, she did. Casey didn't want to, but an order was an order. Unfortunately he did, too, and when his leg brushed hers, a quiver started between her thighs that not even an order could stop.

"So, what do you want to talk about?" She folded her hands and rested them in her lap.

"I don't understand why she's so hostile," Blake began. "In the session things started out okay, then went downhill when the counselor brought up her mother."

"Did you talk to her about what happened when her mom left home?"

"I can't."

"Sure you can. I know it's difficult and painful, but you can give her the facts."

"No. I mean, I really can't, because I don't know the facts. I was away at law school when April got pregnant. I didn't witness the events." He leaned back and extended his arm across the back of the bench.

Casey slid as far away from him as she could get and struggled to keep a clear head, what with his nearness scrambling her brain. "So, you're saying that during that time you never spoke with your folks? You didn't call home? Come back for Christmas? Or summer?"

"Of course I talked to them."

"Your sister's name never came up? Patricia and Lincoln didn't dump on you about the crap that was going on with their daughter? Your sister?"

"Yeah, they said she'd taken off. But I was never clear on whether or not she was thrown out or just took off with her boyfriend when she got pregnant."

His mother had implied that Mia's mom had rebelled when she'd been forbidden to see the guy her parents didn't like. "And you didn't bother to find out what actually happened?"

The look he turned on her was filled with dark intensity. "I was up to my ass in law review and classes. My sister never contacted me and I thought she was making a life for herself."

If Casey had been in the same predicament, her brothers would have found her. There was no question in her mind about that. They would never be accused of sensitivity overload, but they'd have made sure she was okay. The Deckers made her family look like communication central.

Casey weighed her options. She could be honest and say that or sugarcoat it and keep from getting fired. What made up her mind wasn't a desire to retain her job, because just a while ago the thought had crossed her mind that leaving would have been best. Telling him anything less than what she truly thought was a waste of breath. She owed it to him and Mia to call it like she saw it.

"I think the truth is that it was easier for you to believe your sister was okay than to get involved."

His fingers curled into his palm. "You have no idea what I believed."

"Not specifically. But I know how you are now, what your priorities are. Work comes first. In my book, family members should look out for each other. You can't phone it in like you did with your wife."

"Wait a damn minute. What does that have to do with anything?"

"It's your pattern and it didn't happen overnight. College, law school and career are all excuses for turning your back on the personal, painful, messy stuff. The stuff you don't want to do."

"That's ridiculous. I wanted to stay married. My wife knew I was focused on building a law practice—"

"You say focused. I say workaholic."

"Whatever. She knew how I was when we got married. Later she changed the rules. She thought she could make me a different man, and when she couldn't, she found another one."

Casey folded her arms over her chest and met his gaze. "Why does that surprise you?"

"What?" He blinked.

"You spent more time with your secretary than you did with your wife, the woman you loved. She wanted to see more of you."

"If she'd told me—"

"Oh, please, Blake. Look at the way you are now. When you hired me, you promised to be here the nights I had a class, and the very first time you broke your word. That behavior started a long time ago."

"Who died and made you the psychology queen?" Anger glittered in his eyes.

"My mother, actually. And I'm no professional. I can only tell you how I felt about it. My dad didn't know what to do with a little girl who cried every night for her mother, so he ignored me. When kids are ignored, they'll do whatever they can for attention and approval. I'm sure you realized that I was the only one of his kids to follow in his footsteps and join the army."

"Yeah, I got that," Blake said.

"Mia wants your attention."

"She hates my guts."

Casey shook her head. "She hates that her mother got cancer and died. She hates that she and her mom were abandoned. Caring and being dumped again would be pretty high up on her list of things not to do. So it's easier to lash out and push you away. It's easier to make you not like her. But hate you?" She shook her head. "I don't think so."

"From here in the cheap seats, I'd say you're wrong about that."

She'd certainly been wrong before. *So wrong,* she thought, remembering the innocent face of the Iraqi teenager she'd befriended. Once before it had been her belief that a sincere desire to help could erase all the bad stuff, but her naiveté had been the means to an unspeakably evil end and innocent people had paid the ultimate price.

And here she was again, going above and beyond the call of duty. For what? Her job was child care, but where did she draw the line? Physical well-being? Or did she try to make a difference by building a bridge from Blake and Mia's past to their future? Was this a hill she wanted to die on?

"Like I said, I can only tell you what happened to me. Rather than deal with me and my grief over losing my mom, Dad hid in his cave. Maybe he handled his own grief that way.

I have no idea, because he never talked to me about it. I'm saying that Mia really just wants an explanation. Your instinct is to fix things and you can't in this case. So you're hiding."

"Whoa. I showed up for counseling—"

She held up her hand. "I'm not saying you didn't. But there are lots of ways to hide from things you don't want to deal with. Work is one. My point is that I can't make you come out. But with Mia under your roof and doing negative things to get your attention, there's no way you can pretend that she's okay."

"Don't hold back, Casey. Tell me how you really feel." He stood up.

"Look, Blake—"

"I think I'm talked out." The look in his eyes was somewhere between angry and confused.

Then he turned and walked away from her without another word. Casey watched until he and his excellent butt disappeared around a curve in the path. Her heart ached for him and his niece.

And for herself.

Apparently what had happened to her overseas hadn't been enough of a lesson to keep her from getting in over her head. The next time she went for a walk with Blake… *Halt. About face.*

There wouldn't be a next time. Heart-to-heart talks were not in her job description. And from now on she needed to remember that this was just a job.

Message received, but following the order would be tougher to pull off.

## *Chapter Nine*

Casey returned to the penthouse after a Sunday visit with her dad and felt as if she were going back and forth between caves. The highlights of dinner conversation with Nathan Thomas had been politics, sports and a rousing debate on whether or not this was the hottest summer on record for Las Vegas.

For her it had been, but that had nothing to do with how many days the thermometer had registered one hundred degrees or more. From the moment she'd met Blake Decker, awareness and heat had ruled her world. And today she'd wished her mother were still alive to talk about things. She'd thought about confiding in her dad. She'd even mentioned Blake and Mia, and he'd said that she looked happy, that working for the guy must agree with her. Reading between the lines, Casey had realized he only wanted the fairy-tale version of her life, not the problems. Yet another way for him to hide.

She let herself into the penthouse, set her purse, sunglasses and keys down, and listened. The underlying hum of the air conditioner was all she heard. No voices. Not even the TV.

That was weird.

The television was Blake's primary defense system in his cave. Whenever he was alone with Mia, he had a gazillion channels of programming between him and an actual conversation with his niece. Casey had suggested he come out of hiding and have an honest-to-goodness conversation about the kid's mother, but there was no historical behavioral evidence to indicate that he would actually do it.

Casey walked down the hall to Mia's room, which was her hiding place. Surprisingly the door was open. That never happened, except when the girl wasn't in there. Like now.

Clothes were scattered on the plush beige carpet and across the pink-and-green floral comforter, along with the iPod that was usually attached to the girl's person. Papers and books littered the white desk. It all looked normal, except that Mia wasn't sprawled across the bed, looking hostile and bored.

There was no indication here of whether or not Casey should be worried, so she reversed direction and headed to Blake's home office, her next stop. But in the family room she caught a glimpse of movement outside and walked to the sliding glass door. In a navy blue tank suit, Mia pushed herself up out of the pool to retrieve a blow-up beach ball. And she had a big grin on her face. Blake was in the shallow end, his broad, bare chest visible above the choppy pool water. He was smiling, too.

This had all the makings of an alternate universe.

Casey opened the sliding door and walked outside. The sun was descending on the other side of the building, leaving the terrace in shade. "Hi."

Mia's smile widened with genuine pleasure. "Casey! I'm glad you're back."

Definitely an alternate reality in which there was no hostility. "I'm glad to be back. What have you two been up to?"

Blake moved from the middle to the side of the pool and looked up at her. "Come on in. The water's fine."

"I'm not wearing a bathing suit."

"Go put one on," he suggested.

"Haven't got one," she lied and the look on his face told her he knew. Exposing her scars wasn't high on her list of things that constituted a good time. There would be questions that she didn't want to answer.

Mia moved beside her. "Uncle Blake took me to Red Rock Canyon. We did the scenic drive and stopped at the visitor center. Then we went to LBS, the hamburger place at the Red Rock Casino, Resort and Spa. The burger was as big as my head."

"Really?"

"An exaggeration," Blake said. "She has a pretty big head."

"Look who's talking," Mia retorted, then threw the ball and hit him squarely in the chest.

*A good shot,* Casey thought, *but what a fabulous target.* The contour of tantalizing muscles was sprinkled with a dusting of hair, which tapered to a place hidden beneath the waistband of his swim trunks. Her palms tingled and the sensation was all about an intense yearning to brush her hands all over him. The oh-so-tempting thought made her back up a step.

She turned her attention to the girl, who'd jumped back in the pool. "So what did you think of Red Rock Canyon?"

"It was so awesome." Mia tipped her head back and wet her long hair to get it out of her face. "The red in the rocks is really pretty."

Casey squatted down by the edge of the pool. "You don't suppose that's how it got its name, do you?"

"No." Mia rolled her eyes in a nonhostile, oh-brother kind of way that was so incredibly normal.

Casey felt a little bubble of satisfaction expand inside her. Blake had taken an interest in Mia and it showed in the girl's softening attitude. He'd taken her advice and come out of his cave. It had made a difference, at least for today, and that made her happy and proud.

"Did you see anything at the visitor center about it being named by a man?" Casey asked, feigning innocence.

"You mean because of the red color running through the rock formations?" Blake asked, eyes narrowing.

"Yeah."

"Are you implying that men have no imagination?"

"Pretty much," Casey admitted. "And I don't mean that in a bad way. It's straightforward. You know exactly what it is. Or where you are. For instance, a street that runs into a home improvement store could be called Home Improvement Boulevard."

His grin made her stomach pitch and roll as surely as if she were on a ship during the storm of the century. Ribbons of desire floated and curled through her, making it a challenge to draw air into her lungs.

"And women are so much better at calling a spade a spade?" he asked.

"Of course. Have you ever noticed how clever the names of hair salons are?"

"Such as?"

"A Cut Above." She tapped a finger against her lip as she tried to think of more. "And A Wild Hair."

"I've got one," Mia said, floating on the ball. "Hair Raisers. And Hot Headz Hair."

"Right. Good for you," Casey said, praising her.

"Figures she'd remember names like that," Blake complained good-naturedly.

"What about Curl Up and Dye?" Casey suggested.

He folded his arms over his chest. "Oh, that's cheerful."

"D-y-e," she spelled out. "Hair Today Gone Tomorrow."

"Creative," he agreed, "But counterproductive."

"Hair Four U," Mia chimed in.

"Hey, two against one," he protested

"So speaks wimp boy," Casey taunted.

"Them's fightin' words."

"I used to be a warrior," Casey reminded him. "Is that a challenge?"

A gleam stole into his eyes. "I'm just saying…"

Casey started to stand and back away, but she wasn't fast enough. Blake grabbed her almost before she saw him move. Strong fingers gripped her hands and tugged her forward, into his arms. Surprise pushed a shriek out of her; with her mouth open, she swallowed water. She came up sputtering and pressed against the world-class chest she'd practically drooled over a few minutes ago.

Laughing, Blake steadied her. "For the record, brute strength trumps cleverness."

"No fair, Uncle Blake."

Mia sneak-attacked him from behind. She grabbed his shoulders and tried to push him under but couldn't manage it. Because he was caught by surprise and thrown off balance, Casey added her weight to the assault, and the girls were able to take him down.

When he surfaced, Casey said, "*That's* two against one."

Retaliation burned in his eyes as he hooked his hands beneath Mia's arms and tossed her into deeper water while she shrieked with delight.

Then Blake turned on Casey. "Cheaters never prosper."

Casey laughed as she eased backward, toward the steps and escape. "That wasn't cheating. It's known in the military as overwhelming force."

"I'll show you overwhelming."

He dove into the water and wrapped his steely arms around her legs as he positioned her midriff on his shoulder. Seconds later he had his feet beneath him and was standing with her hanging over his back. The sudden move surprised her, but this alternate view of his butt wasn't bad at all. Casey wanted to squeal with delight, but her motivation was far different from Mia's.

"Okay, Hercules, you made your point. You can put me down now." The tone seriously lacked conviction.

"Throw her in like you did me, Uncle Blake." Mia was grinning.

"Hey," Casey cried. "Whose side are you on?"

Blake half turned and gave the girl a thumbs-up. "She knows which side her bread is buttered on."

"So it's true what they say." Casey tried to wiggle free but he was too strong.

"What do they say?"

"Blood is thicker than water," she answered.

"Yeah." He shifted her off his shoulder and into his arms.

The early evening breeze in the desert was pleasantly warm, unless you were wearing wet clothes. Casey shivered and he felt it because he was still holding her.

"You're cold."

Without waiting for an answer, he walked to the shallow end shelf and stepped out of the pool and onto the concrete deck, carrying Casey as if she weighed nothing. If that wasn't enough to make her feminine heart go fiddle-dee-dee, nothing would. And then in true hero mode he grabbed one of the big, fluffy towels on the table and dragged it around her shoulders.

"Thanks," she said through chattering teeth.

Mia joined them and he wrapped her in the remaining

towel. Obviously Casey was using his and she didn't miss the thoughtful gesture.

The girl freed her long hair from its terry-cloth confinement. Her thick, dark lashes were wet and spiky and made her turquoise eyes look even bigger and more beautiful. But the coolest thing was the fun shining in them. "You know, Uncle Blake, I've been thinking—"

"That's a dangerous prospect," he teased.

Mia grinned without an eye roll. Imagine that. "Seriously. I've been thinking about the anniversary party—"

He pointed at her and faked a stern expression. "You're not getting out of going, so you can stop thinking."

"A little advice," Casey offered, her shivering under control. "Don't spread that message to the youth of America."

"Will you guys listen?" Mia demanded. "If I have to go, I think Casey should go, too."

"A rousing endorsement." Casey tucked wet hair behind her ear. "It's not in my job description and I'm not part of the family."

"Boring." Mia's mouth puffed into a pout. "At least if you come, it will be a little fun."

"Woo hoo," Casey said. "Way to change my mind."

"You should go," Blake agreed. "My dad likes you."

"Because I'm perky. Or was it plucky?"

"I think he said spunky, but that's beside the point." Blake folded his arms over his chest. "The folks would love to see you."

"C'mon, Casey," Mia pleaded. "Say yes. Don't make me go alone."

Casey sighed. "This is piling on. And I have to say the whole 'blood is thicker than water' thing is darned annoying."

"That means you'll go. Right?" Mia asked.

"That means I'll think about it."

Although she hadn't said a solid yes, Blake and Mia gave each other a high five as easily and naturally as if they'd been doing it for years. That was the good part. The bad? She'd practically agreed to go to a family function that was over and above her regular duties. She tried to tell herself that it was all part of the job, but she wasn't buying that.

She was getting pulled in emotionally as easily as Blake had tugged her into the pool. Her life felt like quicksand, and every step she took, every maneuver, every day with the Deckers made her sink a little more deeply.

If she didn't extract herself from this situation, there would likely be hell to pay.

Three days later, after her summer school finals, Casey stopped by the home office of the Nanny Network president. She'd called earlier to make sure it would be okay and now waited after ringing the bell. Moments later the door opened.

Ginger Davis smiled. "Come in, Casey. It's nice to see you."

"Thanks for letting me come by."

"It's important." She shut the door and led the way through the beige travertine-tiled foyer and into the living room.

The spacious area, with a white sofa and a glass-topped coffee table, was serene with soft lighting. Floor-to-ceiling windows overlooked the lights of the valley but screened out the bustle of Las Vegas far below. The room was luxurious and suited her boss, an elegant woman with an address in one of the city's most recognizable buildings.

Ginger's red-highlighted brown hair was pulled away from her face and restrained with a rhinestone clip. Even dressed casually in crisp denim jeans and a white cashmere sweater with three-quarter-length sleeves, she would have a hard time passing for ordinary. But that didn't mean her life had been easy. Rumors about her past circulated, and the compassion in her eyes hinted at a history full of speed bumps. Right now she exuded welcome and warmth, which made what Casey had come to say that much easier to relate. Then she remembered what Ginger had said moments ago.

"How do you know it's important?" Casey asked, sitting on the edge of the overstuffed sofa cushion.

"Because this isn't normal business hours and you didn't want to discuss it over the phone."

"Right." She folded her hands and settled them in her lap. "Big clues."

Ginger slid back into the plush cushions and tucked her bare feet up under her. "You're stalling, Casey. Just tell me what's bothering you."

So many things, not the least of which was facing the fact that she was a coward. This side trip to see Ginger was what the army classified as running for cover.

Casey took a deep breath. "I can't work for Blake Decker any longer."

"I see."

The words were spoken in a soft, calm voice but did nothing to soothe Casey's concerns, especially when Ginger didn't say more. The silence stretched between them, a management technique to gather information, because a nervous employee felt compelled to fill the silence. Casey didn't bite, mostly because she didn't want to share further information unless absolutely necessary. So they stared at each other until the other woman blinked.

"Is there a reason you want to leave?"

Casey nodded. "It's not working out."

"I'd appreciate it if you could be more specific."

That would mean admitting that she was making the same mistakes after promising herself it wouldn't happen again. She'd vowed to remain objective, but kissing Blake had made detachment impossible. So she only said, "I agreed to take this job on a temporary basis. As a favor to you."

"I'd hoped time with Blake Decker would change your mind." Ginger sat up straight, her eyes widening. "Did he do something to make you uncomfortable?"

"No." That wasn't exactly true, but not the way the other woman meant. And part of the reason Casey wanted out was because of how badly she'd wanted him to kiss her and how much she wanted more. It was wrong and she wasn't sure how to keep from going there if she stayed.

"Did he come on to you?" Ginger asked. She frowned and slid forward on the sofa. "He did. I can see by the look on your face. There are laws against that sort of thing. He's an attorney and should know better than that. The Nanny Network has an attorney on retainer. I'll contact him, and Blake Decker will wish he'd kept his hands to himself—"

"No," Casey said. "It wasn't like that."

"How was it?"

It suddenly became absolutely necessary to share further information.

Casey had hoped to make this quick and easy, but now knew that wouldn't work. Ginger saw too much, and she, Casey, would have to come clean.

"He did nothing inappropriate."

"But he did do something?"

"He kissed me. Twice," Casey replied.

"And if you're taking it out of the inappropriate column, that means you were okay with it."

"Yes." Casey waited two beats, then said, "And no."

Ginger sighed. "What's going on, Casey? Talk to me. I can't help if you don't give me the facts."

"The fact is that I'm attracted to him," she admitted miserably.

*Very attracted,* she added to herself. So much so that he filled her thoughts during the day and her dreams at night.

And she'd never been a starry-eyed, dreamy sort of woman. This was different, something she couldn't seem to control.

"Okay," Ginger said.

"See, that's the thing. It's not okay. It crosses a line. It's a problem."

The other woman looked thoughtful. "Is it impacting your ability to care for Mia?"

"No. In fact she asked me to go along when the two of them attend an anniversary party for Blake's parents. She's not, shall we say, enthusiastic about going and said it will be more fun with me there."

"Sounds like you're bonding with her."

Casey nodded. "That probably happened when I helped her pick out Frankie—"

"Excuse me?"

"The dog. Francesca. We call her Frankie." Casey had to smile at the memory of the ill-fated laptop. "Anyway, Mia was pretty upset when Blake blew off counseling, and she wanted a dog."

"I see."

"He's improving, though," she added quickly. "They attend sessions once a week, and he's home for dinner every night now. He also makes it a point to be there for his niece when I have a class or my weekend afternoon off."

Casey remembered coming back to the two of them having a great time in the pool and pulling her in. Literally. In the beginning she could have walked away unscathed. Now she had feelings for the little girl and the man. If history repeated itself, somehow it was going to blow up in her face, and she was here to prevent that.

"So," she continued, "you can see that it would be best for me to quit working for him."

Ginger looked a little shell-shocked. "What I see is that the

Deckers are making progress in family bonding. Thanks to you, as far as I can tell."

"They're doing better." But Casey refused to make it about her.

"I don't have to tell you that every child needs stability to thrive."

"No, you don't."

The last child she'd befriended had only known violence, and Casey had believed kindness and caring could undo that state of mind. She'd been so wrong and others had paid the ultimate price for her mistake. It was imperative that she get out before anyone got hurt.

"I also don't have to remind you that because of her past Mia Decker needs constancy more than the average kid."

Casey sighed. She so didn't want to hear that. Not long ago Mia had said that her uncle would dump her like everyone else. And there was a very real possibility that leaving Blake's employ would fall into that category for the kid. This whole mess could be filed under the heading "damned if she did, damned if she didn't."

"No, you don't have to remind me of that," Casey finally said. "But the stability she needs comes from Blake, not me."

"I'm not so sure about that."

"If I didn't think leaving was the best thing for everyone, I wouldn't have come here and suggested it."

Ginger nodded thoughtfully. "I just hired someone to fill your previous position with the Redmonds. They're back from their extended vacation, and this seemed like a good time to make the transition since Heidi and Jack aren't used to seeing you every day."

Guilt flooded Casey when she thought about Mia's transition. The girl already had difficulty trusting, and Casey wondered if "Casey Thomas" would go on the list of people who had abandoned her. If only Casey's hormones didn't do a dance of joy every time Blake Decker walked into a room. That reaction showed no signs of letting up and the consequences of allowing the situation to continue could be bad.

No, leaving was the best thing for all of them.

"I'll look for a replacement," Ginger was saying. "But I don't know how long that will take. And I'd really rather not leave Blake in the lurch, without someone to supervise Mia."

"I understand," Casey said.

"So you're okay with hanging in there until I can replace you?"

"Yes."

Casey was surprised how okay she was with postponing her resignation. For one thing it would put off abandoning Mia and the guilt associated with doing that. She was carrying around enough guilt already and wasn't anxious to add to it.

It would also put off the moment when she had to say goodbye to Blake. The thought of not seeing him, not challenging him and, God help her, not kissing him filled her with a bleak, black sadness.

Had she always been this spineless? One minute convincing herself to leave and the next relieved she didn't have to?

Suddenly she could see the appeal of hiding in a cave.

## Chapter Ten

"Uncle Blake said the party is really formal. Like the Academy Awards." Mia was quivering with excitement as she looked in the window of a dress shop displaying ball gowns.

"Yes, he did."

Casey smiled because this was the same mall where little Miss Decker had been caught shoplifting makeup, and that hostile, belligerent, abrasive and unpredictable girl was gone. Or at least taking a break. It made her, Casey, glad she'd agreed to suspend her age-limit rule. If she'd had even a small part in this change for the better, that made her proud.

It also didn't escape her notice that Ginger Davis lived just across the street, and Casey's most recent visit with her boss had been equally as traumatic as that first one with the Deckers, but for a completely different reason. When Ginger found her replacement, it wouldn't be easy to leave Mia.

And Blake.

That was exactly why she needed to get out as soon as possible. In the meantime Mia needed a dress and the nanny needed to provide guidance.

"Your grandparents' anniversary celebration is going to be in a banquet room at the Bellagio hotel."

Mia's eyes grew even bigger. "There's gambling at that hotel."

"Not where you'll be. All kinds of rules are in place to make sure of that."

"I know. But maybe I can peek." Her voice was a mixture of whiny and wistful as she stared into the display window. "With just the right dress, maybe they'd think I'm twenty-one."

Casey put her arm around the girl and eased her out of the flow of mall foot traffic. "Those look kind of grown-up for you."

"I don't want a baby dress."

"That's not what I'm suggesting."

"So I can get a strapless?" Hope gleamed in Mia's eyes.

"First you need something to hold it up." Casey glanced at the twelve-year-old's almost flat chest.

"I've got something. In fact, I've been meaning to talk to you about a bra."

It was on the tip of Casey's tongue to say she didn't need one yet, and especially not for a strapless dress. Two things stopped her. Mia looked completely intense and sincere. Casey knew from her own experience that teasing could be painful. When she'd gone through puberty and her body changed, there'd been no one to guide her. Her older brothers had made fun of her and her dad hadn't had a clue about girls. She'd muddled through on her own. Starting her period. Dealing with excess hormones and mood swings. Growing breasts.

She remembered the shock on Blake's face when he'd

seen the ugly healed wounds. Now her woman's body was scarred because an emotional tug for a kid had grown into seriously misplaced trust and then he'd used her for his violent ends. For the rest of her life, her body would bear the marks, and her heart the pain.

But for now her duty was to this girl. "We'll look for bras. There's a lingerie store here in Fashion Show Mall that advertises an expert in fitting."

"Really?" Mia asked, clearly surprised her request was being taken seriously.

"Really," Casey assured her. "You're twelve. Of course you need bras."

Mia grinned and started to clap her hands like a child, then stopped and looked around to make sure no one had seen her coolness factor slip.

"Wow, that was easier than I thought. Maybe now would be the time to say I'd also like a dress from this store." There was a longing expression on her face when she stared in the window.

"Let's go in and look. Maybe they've got something. But I have the final say. It's got to be age appropriate."

"For, say, a sixteen-year-old?"

"Don't push your luck, kid."

"But, Casey—"

"Have I ever told you that persistence is your least attractive characteristic?"

Mia laughed and slid her arm through Casey's, tugging her body forward and at the same time tugging on her heart. Casey's instinct was to pull back, but this child so rarely acted like a child—a normal, happy, carefree child. No way she'd do anything to stop that.

They walked inside and looked around at the dresses on display and the racks filled with fancy evening gowns. A very pretty saleswoman somewhere in her early twenties approached. Her layered brown hair teased her shoulders, and warm brown eyes welcomed them. "Hi. My name is Ava. Is this your first visit to Special Occasions?"

"Yes," Casey said. "Mia is going to her grandparents' anniversary party and needs a dress."

"Is it a formal event?"

"Very," Mia said. "But I don't want to look too—"

"Old," Casey interjected. "She's twelve going on twenty-five."

Ava studied the girl. "I have quite a few dresses that I think will work for your daughter."

"Oh, she's—"

Mia loudly cleared her throat. There was a gleam in her eyes that was all about teasing mischief. "She's such a *mom*. If a dress doesn't have a mile-wide skirt and pink ribbons, she thinks it's too old for me."

"And my *daughter* is trying to grow up too fast."

"Do you have any idea how many times I've heard this?" Ava smiled, then winked. "Trust me, Mia. I'll find something for you that both you and your mom will absolutely adore." The saleswoman studied Casey, then said, "I've got some fabulous dresses for you, too, Mom."

It took Casey a couple of beats to realize Ava meant her. "Oh, I don't need anything. I'm not—"

"Mom, you have to try on something. It will be a lot more fun if you do," Mia insisted.

Casey knew Mia meant attending the party, but debating in front of a stranger wasn't something she was prepared to do. "We're here for you, Mia. And I'm not much of a girlie girl."

"I can help you with that," Mia offered.

"My job is to help you both. And you've come to the right place," Ava said. "This is a full-service boutique—shoes, bags, makeup. We don't have a hair salon, but I can point you in the right direction."

"But I don't really need the full treatment," Casey said.

Ava held up a hand. "I find dresses. You try them on. If not one of them is something you absolutely must have, if they're not age appropriate, it will not hurt my feelings if you leave empty-handed. You have absolutely nothing to lose."

Casey looked at Mia, who had eagerness written all over her. "Okay, then."

It had started out as a way to make Mia feel more comfortable and escalated from there. Casey zipped and fastened dresses for the girl. They agreed that if the material and strings on a hanger needed a schematic to figure out which parts covered boobs and butt, it had to go on the reject pile.

When Mia tried on something she proclaimed a "Little Bo Peep on steroids" number, they laughed until tears streamed down their faces. Then she tried on a simple, light green, high-necked sleeveless dress that stopped at mid-calf. The color was perfect with her skin and eyes.

Casey stared and caught her breath, but she needed to tread carefully. "So, what do you think?"

"It's not horrible," Mia said cautiously.

"I agree."

"Do you think it's dressy enough?" the girl worried.

"The satin material makes it dramatic and elegant, I think."

Mia nodded as she stood on the round step in front of the full-length mirror and studied herself. "Does it make me look like I'm twelve?"

Casey sat in the chair and tapped a finger against her lips. "Better than that, it makes you look beautiful."

"Really?" Mia's eyes shone with pleasure. "You're not just saying that?"

"When have I ever said something just to make you feel better?" Casey said wryly.

"Good point." Mia looked back at her reflection. "But my hair—"

Casey stood and joined her on the raised area. She gathered the thick curls in her hand and piled the hair on Mia's head. "What if you have a French braid? Or do it up somehow?"

"At a salon?" Mia asked, incredulous. "That might cost a lot."

"As opposed to this dress, which is free?"

"Right."

"Look, kiddo, one of the first conversations I had with your uncle was about getting you whatever you need. And I think you need this dress and a visit to a salon. I've got the credit card, and frankly, this is a charge-worthy occasion."

"Shoes, too?"

"Absolutely." Impulsively the girl threw her arms around Casey and hugged her. Tears burned as Casey brushed a hand over Mia's thin back. "You're welcome."

"Now it's your turn," Mia reminded her. "There's one more dress in your fitting room. The royal blue one."

"I don't think it's worth the energy. Doesn't look like much on the hanger."

"But at least we know which side is front and which is back."

"That's because there is no back," Casey said.

"You don't have to buy it," Mia reminded her.

Finally Casey gave in, went to her fitting room and slid into the gown. The color was perfect for her eyes, and the high neck hid the scars, but the shimmery material clung to her hips and breasts, making her feel incredibly feminine and sexy.

"Come out and let me see," Mia begged through the door.

"Okay."

Mia gasped when the door was opened. "You look gorgeous."

Ava walked over just then and agreed. "It's like someone made that for you. And I'm not just saying that to make a sale."

If the criterion was that she had to have it, this was the one. "I don't know. It doesn't seem right to spend…" She remembered the ruse. "To spend your father's money on something this expensive."

"He said whatever I need," Mia reminded her.

"Your husband won't be able to take his eyes off you," Ava said.

Casey was never quite sure if that was what made up her mind or not, but she was going to the party in this dress. And she took Blake's credit card for quite a spin at Special Occasions. Makeup, silver sandals for both of them and evening bags added up fast. To ease the guilt, she promised herself that she'd pay Blake back. He could deduct some from her paycheck, although that would mean being in his employ for a good portion of the rest of her life.

As they left the store, she remembered what Ava had said. *You have absolutely nothing to lose.* And she realized the reality was that she had *everything* to lose. She was getting emotionally sucked in—by Mia and her uncle. And she couldn't even say for sure which one of them was the most dangerous.

In the banquet room at the Bellagio hotel his parents' party was winding down. Toasts had been made after dinner and now only hard-core partyers were left, small groups standing around chatting. Blake excused himself from several couples, longtime friends of his parents who seemed determined to bring up every stupid and humiliating incident of his youth. This was Lincoln and Patricia's anniversary celebration, not a Blake Decker roast. But he was taking the heat.

And speaking of heat…

In the subdued light of a chandelier on the other side of the room, he spotted Casey. He'd recognize her sexy back anywhere. When he'd first seen her and Mia with hair and makeup done and wearing formal dresses, he'd been in awe. He'd flat out said how lucky and proud he was to be escorting two such beautiful ladies.

Then Casey had turned, giving him an unrestricted view of her naked back—after which he'd been in serious danger of swallowing his tongue. The front of that dress said "sweet" and the other view was all about sin.

How weird was it that he was thinking about kissing every square inch of Casey's back, from the nape of her neck to the spot where her dress stopped, just above her butt? It probably wasn't completely weird, since he was a guy who seriously lacked a social life these days. Having these thoughts while Casey was talking to his mother was what bordered on weird. And then he realized that his mother was looking fairly intense about something, which cleared his mind of everything but the need to rescue Casey.

He made his way through the maze of white cloth-covered tables being cleared of dessert plates and after-dinner coffee cups. On some only the flower arrangements remained. Untouched flutes of Dom Pérignon for the earlier anniversary toast sat on a tray, and he grabbed up three when he walked by.

As he approached the two women, he heard his mother say, "I'm only thinking of you. There are no words to describe my gratitude to you for all you've done. This is a chance to know my daughter's daughter and I thank you for that."

"Hello, ladies." Blake's senses went on full alert with just a hint of scent from Casey's skin. "Champagne?"

"Thanks." Casey relieved him of one glass. It was a challenge not to stare at the way her royal blue dress clung to her firm breasts and the curves of her hips.

"I believe I will, too," his mother answered, looking just the tiniest bit guilty and uncomfortable. She was wearing a long-sleeved, floor-length black lace dress. Very elegant.

He raised his own glass. "In a less public way, let me say again, happy anniversary, Mother."

"Thank you, dear. Your toast earlier was lovely. As was your father's."

"So you're over being mad at Dad?"

"Not completely." Patricia sighed. "We've done more talking in the last few weeks than in the last forty years."

"Aren't you exaggerating?"

"Only a little. The bottom line is that he was wrong."

"But his heart was in the right place," Casey said. "He was trying to spare you more pain."

Patricia's gaze scanned the room and settled on a group of young girls and boys by the door. Mia seemed to be making friends with them. "She looks lovely with her hair done in that simple high ponytail. How did you manage to get her out of those scruffy jeans?"

"Two burly men and a muscle relaxer," Blake teased, meeting Casey's amused gaze. "Actually, that's a question for her nanny."

"Never underestimate the miracles wrought by the judicious use of a credit card," Casey said. "We found a great store and a fairy godmother, otherwise known as Ava, who made Mia over. I figured a little bit of makeup for this auspicious evening couldn't hurt."

Patricia nodded, a wistful sort of sadness in her eyes. "I've often wondered if we'd been more willing to bend with April, maybe she would have reached out for help."

"You loved your daughter and did what you thought best," Casey told her. "The only thing regrets accomplish is making you feel bad. It's a waste of energy that could be more productively channeled into your granddaughter."

"Very wise words for one so young, Casey." Patricia drank the rest of her champagne. "I'll do just that. Starting tonight. Mia is spending the night with us. She agreed to come home with Lincoln and me after the party."

"Really?" Blake glanced at Casey, who looked as surprised as he felt. "Did this miracle include the judicious use of a credit card?"

"No." His mother laughed. "I guess I caught her at a weak moment. Laura Parsons's granddaughter mentioned she was spending the night with her grandparents and I asked Mia if she'd like to do the same. Either she didn't want to turn me down at my party or she wanted to fit in with new acquaintances. Whatever the reason, I'll take it."

"Stroke of genius, Mother." Call him a selfish bastard, but he couldn't suppress the thought that he'd be alone with Casey. "And on the progress front, she's not calling you a dork anymore. At least not to your face."

"Woo hoo," Patricia answered.

Casey was just sipping champagne, and the unexpected comment made her laugh, then choke. He patted her bare back, wanting to help. Really. But the feel of her flesh beneath his fingers sent a burst of heat through him.

"Are you all right?" Patricia asked.

"Fine." Casey coughed again. "But next time I'd appreciate a warning when you plan to say something funny. Just a heads-up along the lines of 'Don't drink' before you cut loose."

"I would have if I had any idea I was funny." Patricia grinned at her. "You just made my evening. And now I think I'll begin what I hope will be a long and illustrious precedent of spoiling my granddaughter."

"Go, Patricia," Casey encouraged.

When they were alone, Blake looked down at her, trying not to be turned on by the way her hair was fluffed, as if a man had run his fingers through it during sex. "You're awfully chummy with my mother."

"Does that surprise you?"

"Since she's not the 'get chummy' type, I guess it does," he admitted. "She can be formidable. Distant."

"That's a defense mechanism. A facade. Clearly she's trying to change because she loves her family."

He watched his mother, who was talking and laughing with Mia and the group of young people. Maybe she was sincerely trying not to make the same mistakes. Or just being in grandmother mode. Her only responsibility was to love Mia and keep her safe. Either way it was a side to his mother that he'd never seen before.

And that made him remember what she'd said to Casey when he joined them—that she was only thinking of Casey. What was that about?

"You've certainly won over my mother. She obviously cares about you."

"I suppose." Casey smiled, but it was tense.

"What's wrong? Don't tell me nothing," he warned, on some level knowing she would.

"Do you really want to know?"

"I wouldn't have asked if I didn't." He set his flute of champagne on the table beside them.

Casey stared at him for several moments, then blew out a breath. "She cautioned me not to be getting monogrammed towels with your initials on them."

"What?"

"She called it the *Jane Eyre* syndrome," Casey explained. Fortunately she added more, because that made no sense. "Nanny falls for boss."

"She had no right to meddle—"

"I don't believe she was. In the most discreet way, she

warned me that your marriage didn't go well. I knew what she meant and told her you'd already mentioned the infidelity to me."

"Infidelity? What a delicate way of saying disaster," he commented.

"That's the same term your mother used." Casey met his gaze. "For what it's worth, Patricia would like to do bodily harm to the witch—although that's not her exact word. However, it rhymes."

"Go, Mom. I wonder how she'd do in prison."

"Never happen. A jury of her peers, mothers whose sons have been cheated on by their wives, would never convict her."

He shook his head. "I can't believe she talked to you about that."

Casey gripped her glass until her knuckles turned white. "For some reason she thought I should know that you really don't like to fail and wouldn't ever put yourself in a position to do it again."

Blake didn't know what to say to that. Patricia had never before interfered in his love life. That stopped him. Is that what this was with Casey? Two hot kisses and even hotter thoughts that were nowhere near in control? Had his mother seen something in the way he looked at Casey? Or the way she looked at him?

That sent the blood surging to points south of his belt. "I'll talk to her."

"No." Casey touched his arm and their gazes locked. Sparks seemed to fill the air and breathing was a challenge. When she pulled her hand away, it was shaking. "She means well."

"That's what you told her about my father. Apparently it's 'defend Lincoln and Patricia Decker' night."

"You might want to cut your parents some slack. It's their anniversary. A commemoration of a long relationship."

"And your point would be?" He knew she had one.

"Your mother was trying to explain what I already know. You're anti-relationship."

"She said that?"

"My words," she admitted. "I assured her I'd already noticed that your career is about extricating people from bad relationships. She was relieved to know that there's no danger of me expecting anything you're unable to give."

"I'm glad the two of you bonded over my disaster," he said sarcastically. "I get that I didn't put enough effort into the marriage. How did you put it? Oh, yes. I spent more time with my secretary than my wife."

"Blake, I didn't mean to—"

"Yes, you did. For the record, it takes two to make or break a marriage."

"I'm aware of that."

"Oh? You've been married?"

"Engaged," she said, shadows in her eyes. "But I found out it takes two and we weren't the right two." She set her glass on the table, beside his. "I'd hate if your mother's anniversary was spoiled. I'm asking you not to tell her that you know what she said."

Blake watched her walk away and suddenly wondered why Casey had related the conversation with his mother. Maybe to put up a barrier? Her own defense mechanism? To push him away? Did she feel she needed to do that after kissing him?

He couldn't blame her. A second or two longer both times and he'd have taken her and damned the consequences. He still wanted her; denying that would be a lie. In fact, he was more curious about her than ever, and all the warnings in the world couldn't make that stop.

He'd finally come to the conclusion that finding out everything about Casey was the only way to put his interest to rest.

# Chapter Eleven

The last time Casey had so badly wanted a night to end, she'd been in a military hospital, her body battered, bleeding and burned. Tonight she was burning, but no one could see. Hopefully. She glanced at Blake, beside her in the elevator as they rode to the top floor of his building. Dark hair fell across his forehead, and stubble shadowed his cheeks and jaw, because his last shave had been hours ago. The effect seemed to make his already potently intoxicating eyes even bluer and so much more intense.

They said there was something about a man in uniform, and though Casey had worn one, too, she knew from frequent exposure that it was true. But Blake Decker in a tuxedo fell into a category all his own.

Sometime earlier the black tie had disappeared and the first button on his crisp white shirt had become undone, revealing just a glimpse of the masculine chest hair. It was enough to make her wish the shirt and jacket were gone. He could easily play movie hero James Bond. She was no martini, but that didn't mean she wasn't shaken and stirred. She was also incredibly grateful when the elevator doors opened and they were back in the penthouse.

She longed for the cool sanctuary of her room, because he was hot. Jalapeño pepper with habañero sauce hot. If she didn't get away from him soon, there was going to be an explosion of heat—and the collateral damage wouldn't be pretty.

Frankie padded into the entry to greet them, her paws clicking on the tile. Casey bent and gave the dog a hug, then laughed when she looked for Mia.

"Sorry, girlfriend, your buddy is doing some serious family bonding tonight."

"I thought she'd back out," Blake admitted, leaning a broad shoulder against the door.

Was he hoping she would? So he wouldn't be alone with Casey? And temptation? She was glad his mother had reminded her that Blake was anti-commitment. And she'd repeated it to him to make sure he knew that she knew that even Patricia was aware that he wouldn't do another relationship. Blake offered no future, and that should have put a stop to temptation, but it didn't even come close.

"I'm glad she went with your folks. This will be good for the three of them." And it would be best if she said good-night to Blake right now.

She scratched Frankie's head and the animal closed her eyes in doggy ecstasy. "Pete said he walked you, little girl, so we're in for the night."

"Would you like a nightcap?"

There was a seductive quality to his voice, making it deeper than usual. The timbre brushed over her nerve endings and thrummed them into vibration mode. A person didn't always know when she was at a crossroads, but Casey knew it now. She desperately wanted to accept his offer, but if she did, there was a very good chance the road would lead to his bed.

"Thanks, but..." She stood and met his gaze. "It's late. I'm tired."

"You're not the only one." He dragged his hand through his hair. "But I'm keyed up. If that makes any sense."

It did, because she felt the same way and was pretty sure she knew the reason. "Then a drink would probably relax you. I'll say good-night—"

"I hate to drink alone." The look in his eyes was one part teasing and two parts pleading, but completely irresistible.

It was hell when you came to a crossroads and took the wrong path, but her reserves of willpower were all used up. "Okay."

Blake shrugged out of his jacket and carelessly tossed it on the sofa in the family room on his way to the wet bar in the corner. He took two small snifters from a shelf, then poured an ounce of brandy into each.

After handing one over, he touched his glass to hers and said, "To sharing."

"You mean, to letting your folks get to know Mia."

Studying her over the rim of his glass, he took a sip. "No, I mean you."

"I don't understand."

"I hardly know anything about you, Casey."

"How long have I worked for you?" Her chest felt tight. "Do you have a problem with my job performance?"

"This isn't about the execution of your responsibilities. No one is questioning how well you've done your job. I want to know more about *you*."

"Like what?" As soon as the words popped out of her

mouth, she wanted them back. She knew what he was going to ask.

"How did you get those scars?"

She set her untouched drink on the edge of the wet bar. "That has no impact on my ability to interact with Mia."

"This isn't about my niece and you know it." He tossed back the rest of the liquor in his glass and set it beside hers.

"If it's not about Mia, then I've got nothing to say."

"This is one friend to another, because I think we've gone way beyond employer and employee. I've talked about my past. You made me face the fact that I didn't put as much effort into my marriage as I should have. Those were painful things I'd rather forget. And if anyone asks, I'll deny saying this, but it helped to talk about stuff. And I've liked spending time with you." Intensity burned in his eyes, a clue that he was remembering kissing her as much as referring to his own personal revelations. "I let you in, but you haven't returned the favor. I intend to change that."

"Or what?"

He shook his head. "I'm not going to fire you, if that's what you're implying. And I'm not letting you quit. Something happened to you and I think it would be good for you to talk about it. Let me be your friend, Casey."

It was his special brand of caring, which was half bullying and half kindness, that broke down her defenses. "It happened in Iraq…."

"I figured as much." When she didn't say more, he said with extraordinary gentleness, "Go on."

"There was this Iraqi kid. About fifteen years old. He started coming around when I was on patrol in Baghdad. My friend Paula—"

"A soldier?" he asked.

She nodded. "Corporal Paula Desiato. She wasn't in favor

of interacting with the people. She was skeptical because the good guys and bad guys have no uniforms to tell them apart."

"I see."

There was no way he could understand fear that never went away. Wondering if death was around the next corner, but having to round that corner, anyway, because it was part of the job. "This kid seemed sincerely sweet and every day we'd wave as the patrol went through town. Eventually I stopped to talk. He told me about his family and asked about mine. His father was a shopkeeper, and his mother a schoolteacher. There were seven brothers and sisters. He wanted to know all about life in America. I showed him pictures and he shared his dream to someday visit New York. I was the one who let him get close. I didn't see the signs—"

He rubbed a hand over his face before asking, "What happened?"

"One day, when we stopped to talk, he blew himself up."

"Oh, God… Casey—"

She backed away when he reached for her. "It wouldn't have been so bad if I'd paid the ultimate price for being stupid and gullible."

"You paid a price. I saw the scars."

"Other soldiers besides me were hurt in the blast." She met his gaze as misery trickled through her. "I'm alive. Paula isn't. Her little boy and little girl don't have a mother, and I'm responsible. I went to see them and her husband after I got out of the hospital. He said they were doing okay. Couldn't have been more gracious. He tried to make me feel better, but nothing—"

Sobs she couldn't control choked off her words, and tears blurred her vision. If she'd been able to see, she'd have evaded Blake's arms, because she didn't deserve sympathy or comfort. But suddenly she was pressed against his solid, warm chest as he murmured soothing words she didn't really comprehend.

"I get it now," he said when she quieted.

"W-what?"

"Why you refused to take assignments with kids over ten."

"I can't ever bring Paula back, but I vowed to make a difference in kids' lives. I regret—"

"What was it you said to my mother tonight about regrets?" He thought for a moment. "Oh, yeah. They only make you feel bad and are just a waste of energy. There was something else about channeling that energy. The thing is, Case, those aren't just words. You live that philosophy every day. You make a difference in kids' lives, too."

"In my opinion that's only possible before they're lost to outside influences. We have to get to them when they're young."

"And yet you've done wonders for Mia."

"Just lucky."

"Just you." He wrapped his arms more securely around her, his hands warm on her bare back.

Awareness seeped through her despair. The strong, steady beat of his heart seemed to pump life into her and suddenly just being in his arms wasn't enough. She lifted her head and met his gaze as something hot and hungry slid into his eyes. It would never be clear who moved first or whether by silent agreement they shifted at the same time, but in a heartbeat their lips touched.

In spite of their dammed-up feelings, the first contact was soft, sweet, seeking. He slid his fingers into her hair, cupped the back of her head to make the connection more complete. He took her top lip and sucked, sending a tingling heat exploding through her. The nibbling kisses he trailed over her nose, cheeks, jaw and neck were soft as fog, thrilling as lightning. When his hand moved to gently and tenderly cover her breast, the touch stole the air from her lungs, partly because she wasn't wearing a bra. He brushed his thumb over the silky material and her nipple hardened with the erotic attention. A muffled moan was clearly audible, but it was several moments before she realized that she'd made the sound.

When he lifted his head and looked into her eyes, Casey realized that his breathing was as erratic as her own. That only turned her on more. She lifted her hands with every intention of unbuttoning his shirt, the urge to touch his naked chest almost unbearable. But she realized there was something in her way.

She traced one of the fasteners and smiled. "I've never been accused of being the fashion police, but aren't these called studs?"

"They are."

His grin took the starch right out of her knees and she was grateful that his arm was still around her. "Oh, my."

"You probably shouldn't make any connection between this and—"

"You?"

He shrugged. "Yeah."

"Okay."

The single word chased the teasing from his expression, replacing it with need. He kissed her again, his tongue sliding into her mouth, taking and giving as heat built inside her and turned liquid. It coursed through her and made her thighs quiver as need pooled inside her.

"Blake, please—"

"Not here. I want you in my bed." The words were spoken against her lips, but when he lifted his head, his gaze challenged her, warned her that now was the time to say no if she wanted.

She wanted *him*. The "saying no" train had left the station when she'd agreed to a drink. When he held out his hand, she settled her fingers into his big palm. He led her down the hall, and it was probably the first time she'd ever thought this place was too big. It seemed forever until they entered his bedroom and she looked around.

The king-size bed butted up against a curved, carved headboard in heavy oak. Two matching nightstands stood on either side. A matching dresser and armoire took up space on the walls, with sliding glass doors in between that led onto the terrace. The curtains were open and lights from Las Vegas illuminated the room, including the tan comforter with black trim. *Very masculine. Very Blake,* she realized, looking up.

Standing beside the bed, he dropped her hand, then took off his shirt in a single fluid movement that didn't include removing the studs. He reached out and slid the top of her dress down, his eyes going dark and dangerous when he couldn't miss the fact that she was now naked from the waist up, too.

He cupped her breasts in his palms, brushing the puckered scars with his thumbs. "You're beautiful, Casey."

"No, I—"

"Trust me. Beauty is in the eye of the beholder. You're brave and beautiful. Take it from me."

"The beholder?" She wouldn't have believed it possible, but she smiled.

"Oh, yeah."

He bent to take first one, then the other nipple in his mouth, and electricity shot through her, straight to that most feminine place between her legs. She pressed her hands to his face and savored the rasp of his beard against her palms. When he straightened, she stood on tiptoe and kissed him.

"I want you, Blake. Now."

"Is that an order?"

"Does it have to be?"

"No."

Without answering, he reached over and threw the comforter and blanket down, revealing beige sheets beneath. In seconds he'd slid her dress and panties off and lifted her into his arms, settling her in the center of the bed. Before her mind had time to register the fact that the sheets were cold, he was beside her, naked and warm and strong. She felt his hardness pressing into her thigh as he pulled her into his arms, kissing her as if he were starving and she were an all-you-can-eat buffet.

He slid his hand over her belly and between her legs, slipping a finger into her waiting warmth. Brushing his thumb over the nub of nerve endings there, he rubbed and gently scraped until pleasure peaked and exploded through her. She came apart in his hands—but his arms held her together.

When the stars behind her eyes cleared, he reached into the nightstand and pulled out a square packet containing a condom, which he used to cover himself. He kissed her again, then nudged her legs open wider as he settled between them and with exquisite gentleness entered her.

Her breath caught as he filled her and her hips lifted to meet him. He thrust into her again and again and she found herself climbing that peak one more time. With one final push, he went still and groaned out his release as she held him as tightly as she could.

For a moment, he rested his forehead against hers, then left the bed. Some part of her pleasure-drenched mind registered the fact that a light went on and seconds later it was off, just before he rejoined her in the bed.

He gathered her to his side and she rested her head on his shoulder. "So—"

"I don't think I can move."

"Stay," he whispered.

And she did.

Casey woke the next morning to the smell of coffee. She opened her eyes and Blake was sitting on the bed—his bed, she realized. Still groggy, she sat up and the sheet fell away, revealing her breasts. Not too sleepy to be embarrassed, she pulled it up to cover herself, although that seemed silly since he'd kissed every square inch of her when making love to her.

Blake, on the other hand, was wearing black sweat shorts, a worn T-shirt and a sexy, self-satisfied smile that reminded her just how she'd managed to get herself in this predicament in the first place.

Good Lord, what had she done?

He handed her one of the steaming mugs. "Good morning."

"Is it?" She took a sip of coffee and realized it had cream and sweetener in it, just the way she liked it.

"What's wrong, Casey?"

*So many things, so little time.* But she figured it could never hurt to go with the obvious. "We had sex."

"Indeed we did." He didn't look the least bit concerned.

"We shouldn't have had sex," she pointed out.

"The last time I checked, two consenting adults were free to engage in intimate activities." One dark eyebrow rose. "I've been known to miss a woman's signals, but I don't think that's the case here."

*Definitely not the case here.* Her body was still humming from their intimate activity. If he wasn't her boss and she wasn't the nanny, she'd be in favor of another round of intimacy.

"No. I was more than willing," she said.

"Then I don't see the problem."

If that were true, nothing she said would make him understand. All she could do was damage control. There was a robe—his robe, because this was his room—on the bed, beside her. She set her coffee down on the nightstand and shrugged into the soft terry cloth as discreetly as possible.

"I need to take a shower."

"Casey, wait—"

"No. I have to go."

Blake rubbed a hand over the back of his neck. "We need to talk about this."

"There's nothing to say, except that it can't happen again."

"You think that will take care of everything? That just the words will make it all go away?"

"I hope so," she said. "That's all I've got. It was wrong and we both need to forget about it."

"Easier said than done. Casey, listen—"

"No. I have to go. Mia will be home soon."

He didn't try to stop her again when she hurried out of his room and to her own. After closing the door, she tossed the soft terry-cloth robe on her bed, the one that showed no signs of being slept in last night, because it hadn't been. She got in the shower and stood under the hot water for a long time, trying to wash away or reason through what had happened. Neither worked. She dressed, put on light makeup and fixed her hair. A last look in the mirror showed a woman who was still confused about feelings for her boss that just wouldn't leave her alone. Peeking into Mia's room, which was beside hers, she noticed that Frankie had been in there tossing around clothes and shoes. She'd missed her buddy last night.

Casey had missed her, too, and not just because nothing would have happened with Blake if she'd been there.

She was in the kitchen when the front door opened and the dog barked an enthusiastic welcome to Mia.

"Hi, you," Mia said. "Hello? Anyone home?"

Casey walked into the entryway. "Hey. Nice outfit."

Mia glanced at her too-big T-shirt and sweatpants. Her dress was on a hanger and covered by a garment bag. "My grandmother loaned me this stuff. She made me hang up my dress and put it in that thing."

"Did you have fun?" Blake asked as he joined them. He'd changed into khaki shorts and a powder blue shirt. His hair was wet from the shower.

Mia sat cross-legged on the marble tile and hugged her dog. The garment bag was on the floor beside her. "I watched a movie with them, and she made popcorn and hot chocolate and stuff. They dropped me off and said to tell you they'd call soon."

Casey refused to meet his gaze, because that would release a flood of guilt, something very distracting when struggling for normal was already a challenge. "Sounds very domestic."

"Whatever." Mia wrinkled her nose. "What did you guys do? Must have been pretty boring without me."

Casey met his gaze then and guilt flooded her, just as she'd figured it would. "We, um—"

"You're right, kiddo," Blake said, looking at his niece. "Boring. We just went to bed early."

Casey winced, even though it was the truth, because he didn't say they went to sleep. Being a silver-tongued legal eagle was a plus in this kind of situation. Twisting the truth was what he did.

But the explanation seemed to satisfy the girl, who barely reacted while she scratched Frankie's head. "Have you guys had breakfast? I'm starved."

"Your grandmother didn't feed you this morning?"

"All they had was gruel. I tried to be polite and eat it," Mia said, looking completely earnest. "But you could use that stuff to stick paper to the wall."

"It's oatmeal." Blake laughed. "And they're watching their cholesterol levels."

"Whatever." Mia's eyes sparkled with teasing mischief. "Until they get some kid-friendly food, I'm not going back."

"Cut them some slack," her uncle urged. "It was a spurof-the-moment decision to ask you to stay. They had no reason to think you'd take them up on the offer."

"Good point," she agreed.

"Give them a list next time, and I'd be willing to bet, they'd accommodate every last whim." He ruffled her loose hair and she jumped up and ducked away.

"I'll fix French toast," Casey offered. She needed to do something, anything, so that she was too busy to think.

"Sounds good." Mia started down the hall toward her room, while Frankie ran ahead of her in that direction.

"Don't forget to hang up your dress," Casey reminded her.

"Oh, right." Mia retraced her steps, bent and grabbed the dress, then was gone.

Casey headed back to the kitchen and started gathering the utensils and ingredients for breakfast. Blake joined her and poured himself a cup of coffee, then leaned back against the counter beside where she was working and doing her best to pretend he wasn't there.

"It's not a crime," he reminded her.

She didn't have to ask what "it" was, but refused to comment. After breaking eggs in a bowl and stirring in milk and cinnamon, she dipped thick slices of bread into the mixture, then set them in the preheated frying pan, where there was an instant sizzle. Three plates waited on the counter next to her.

Blake touched her arm. "The counselor says talking helps."

Before she could respond, there was a movement behind them, followed by the sound of Frankie's paws clicking on the tile floor. Casey looked past Blake and her heart caught.

Mia stood in the kitchen doorway, holding Casey's royal blue gown and one of the silver sandals that went with it. "Frankie found these. You forgot to hang up the dress."

The dog must have wandered into the master bedroom

and brought them to Mia. There was no reason to think the worst. *Just act normal,* Casey repeated to herself. "Thanks for the reminder."

"You left them in Uncle Blake's room." Mia's voice was filled with anger, disappointment and hurt. She glared at Casey and her uncle. "You had sex," she accused.

Blake set his mug down. "Look, Mia—"

"Don't lie to me, because I know you did," Mia interrupted. "Before she got sick, my mom always had guys coming over. Every time there was a new one, she ignored me."

"I'm sorry you had to go through that, Mia," he said quietly.

"Yeah, me, too." Her full mouth twisted bitterly as she looked at them. "And I'm sorry I'm in your way."

"That's not true," Casey protested.

"No? So it's just a coincidence that the first time I wasn't here, you guys hook up? I'm not a little kid. And I'm not stupid."

Casey set her spatula on the counter. "Of course you're not."

"My mom always said that if not for me she'd have had a life." Mia's words were more distressing for the void of emotion in her voice. "And I guess it runs in the family. I'm getting in your way, too, Uncle Blake."

"You're not in the way," he protested.

"Stop lying to me," she yelled. "I don't believe you. And I hate you both."

She threw the dress and the shoe on the floor, then turned and raced from the kitchen. Moments later the door to her room slammed shut.

It would have been quiet as a library if not for the sizzling French toast in the pan. The smell of burning drifted toward Casey and she turned off the heat.

Blake blew out a breath. "Should I talk to her?"

"Yes. But I doubt she'll open the door. You might want to give her time to calm down."

"I could use some, too," he admitted. "Then maybe I could come up with a closing argument, something really profound to make her understand."

Casey wanted to say good luck with that. How would a child make sense of it when the adults involved couldn't?

"Does she really hate me?" Blake looked bewildered. "I thought we were making progress. Was that my imagination?"

"No."

"I thought she missed her mom," he said.

"She does," Casey assured him.

"You wouldn't know it by what she just said."

"Try to see it from her perspective. Her mother repeatedly abandoned her when she was alive, and then she died, essentially abandoning her for good. She doesn't know how to handle the conflicting emotions of loving her mother, missing her and hating that she was always last on her mom's list." Casey understood two out of three from firsthand experience. "Lashing out is her way of dealing with it all."

"I don't know what to do with a little girl who's grieving for her mother, and at the same time resenting the way she was raised." Blake dragged his fingers through his hair. "Is she seriously screwed up? Maybe she wants to live somewhere else. Boarding school."

"The last thing she needs is to be dumped." Casey remembered that first meeting and how Mia had expected it.

The thing was, they had been making progress with her. Now things were back to square one. Actually they were further back than that and Casey blamed herself. It was her fault that another young life had just exploded right before her eyes. She'd failed another kid because she'd crossed a professional line with her boss.

She couldn't imagine how things could get worse.

## Chapter Twelve

The next morning Casey rushed into the kitchen. "She's gone."

"Mia?"

Stupid question. Blake was looking at Casey, and his niece was the only other *she* in the house. His tie was hanging down the front of his gray dress shirt as he poured a quick cup of coffee before rushing to the office. He was late. Oversleeping was the price you paid when a certain sexy nanny kept you awake all night. On top of that, his niece was all screwed up and he didn't know how to fix it. Now Casey was telling him the kid was gone?

"I checked on her last night, before I went to sleep. I was worried because she didn't come out of her room all day."

"What happened?" he asked.

"She refused to unlock her door." Casey's forehead was creased with concern. "She wouldn't let me in. I figured she needed more time to, you know—"

Yeah. He knew. Deal with the fact that her guardian was getting it on with the nanny behind her back. He was no expert, but the way Mia had stared daggers at them yesterday, the rest of her life wouldn't be enough time to get over what she seemed to see as a betrayal.

He ran his fingers through hair still damp from his shower. He'd had no idea that his sister had put her own selfish needs above her own child's until Mia had angrily blurted out the truth yesterday. Apparently the inclination to indulge selfish needs ran in the family. Wasn't that what he'd done? In his own defense it had to be said that he was still new at this parenting thing.

Ditto on sex with Casey. It was great, although there was no such thing as bad sex. But with her it was different, somehow not just a release for the bottled-up need in his body. There was a relief that went clear to his soul—and he'd never considered himself a soul-deep sort of guy. He liked Casey. He liked her a lot and wanted to be with her again. The longing was like nothing he'd ever felt before.

But now he had a kid. He wasn't used to scheduling sex around kids' sleepovers, and having to clean up evidence of the intimacy, which would push buttons he didn't know Mia had.

He took a sip of coffee. "Did you look everywhere?"

"Yes, but feel free to look for yourself," she said. "She could be hiding under the bed, although her past history would suggest she's more of a flight risk."

"You think she ran away?"

"Yes. What worries me most is she didn't take Frankie."

Blake knew how much his niece loved the dog, and for some reason that worried him more. "How did she get out without Frankie letting us know?"

"I don't know, except Mia is good at running away."

Casey bit her top lip. "And she didn't take her cell phone. It's on her desk."

"Chances are she wouldn't answer even if we called," he said grimly.

"But she'd have it if she needed help. What are we going to do?" Casey was more than worried; she was scared.

"The last time she ran away, it was to my folks. If we're going by recent history, that's a good place to start."

"Of course." Hope edged out the fear in her eyes. "Call them."

"Already on it," he said, picking up the kitchen phone. After hitting speed dial, he waited impatiently while the phone rang.

"Hello?"

"Mother?"

"Blake?" There was a split second of silence before she said, "What's wrong?"

*Odd.* He'd never thought his mother knew him all that well to guess from a single word that he had a problem. Clearly he'd never given her enough credit. "Is Mia there with you and Dad?"

"I haven't seen her since yesterday morning, when we dropped her off." There was a mother lode of concern in the words. "If you have to ask, I assume she's not there and you don't know where she is."

"That pretty much sums it up," he admitted.

"What are you going to do to find my granddaughter?" she demanded.

He had to wing it, because there was no plan. He'd hoped there didn't have to be one. That Mia would be with his folks and finding her would be easy. And therein was his biggest problem with this whole thing. His focus had been on giving her a place to live while minimizing the inconvenience to himself. What that said about him wasn't pretty.

"Look, Mother, you and Dad stay put in case she shows up there."

"What are you going to do?" she asked again. "Contact the police?"

"It might be too early. But I know some people. I'll call them and maybe some strings can be pulled. The cops can keep their eyes open. We'll give them a description and what Mia's wearing."

"Don't let anything happen to her, Blake. That little girl has just come into our lives—" Her voice caught, which wasn't at all like Patricia Decker.

"I'll get her back, Mom. Don't worry."

"Like that will happen. I'm hanging up now so you can go find her."

He clicked off, then went to his study to look up the numbers for his Las Vegas Metro Police acquaintance. With Casey's help he gave the guy a description of the clothes Mia was last wearing, her age, height, weight and eye color. The guy promised to pass the word to patrol officers and detectives, all unofficially, and if there was news, he'd call.

"I can't do nothing." Casey paced in front of his desk. "I'm going to look for her myself."

"We'll take my car," he said. "I'll drive."

She met his gaze. "I thought you had a full schedule at the office."

"I'm canceling my appointments today." And tomorrow, if there was still no news.

"But it's awfully short notice."

"Stuff happens." He yanked off his tie. "People will just have to deal with it."

"Are you sure it's okay?"

He rounded his desk and stopped in front of her. Worry and dark circles turned her hazel eyes more green. He wanted to hold her and reassure her that everything would be all right. He wasn't sure about that, and holding her had gotten him into this mess, but he had to touch her. It was a mistake and he vowed the last one he would make, but he brushed his knuckles over the softness of her cheek.

"It's okay. I'm the boss."

"That's the rumor."

After calling his assistant, they hurried to the car and raced out of the complex, even though he had no idea where to look. Actually, that wasn't true. The mall was as good a place to start as any. They checked out Boca Park, which was the closest, without success. There were so many places a young girl could hide if she wanted. And he didn't even want to think about the predators who zeroed in on kids out in public. Mia was young and vulnerable, and he wished she'd taken Frankie with her. He'd never forgive himself if anything happened to her.

For hours they drove around, checking out shopping centers close by, then widening the search. Up and down streets, some upscale, others not so much. With every minute that ticked by, he grew more anxious, less hopeful. The apprehension in his mother's voice gnawed at him, along with her words about Mia just coming to them. There hadn't been enough time to really know her, and Blake hated himself for not even trying.

"Let's try that center on Charleston," Casey suggested. "It's not too far from downtown."

"Okay." Blake knew the way and took the on-ramp to Summerlin Parkway, then merged with the 95 South and headed to Charleston Boulevard.

The sun was going down and they were no closer to locating Mia. He glanced over at Casey. "What if we don't find her?"

"We will," she said. But the determination in her tone sounded forced.

"I'm not so sure. I don't think I ever realized before just how big the Las Vegas Valley really is. And she's just a little girl. It's getting dark."

"There are places to be safe."

"And just as many that are dangerous when the sun goes down. Her pattern might be running away, but being easily found was also part of it. This is different."

She looked over, her eyes huge and haunted in the muted light from the dashboard. "It just means that she's making a point."

As in teaching them a lesson. He prayed that a twelve-year-old girl didn't pay the biggest price of all for that lesson.

He was hoping Casey would disagree with him. He wanted her to say his idea was way out in left field and not even remotely possible. The fact that she didn't meant she agreed with him, and that ate away at his hope and cleared the way for fear to creep in.

"Anything could have happened to her," he said, forcing himself to concentrate on the road.

"There's no reason to go to a bad place." But she didn't look convinced.

"This is all my fault."

"You're good," she said. "But not all-powerful. That would make you God and your résumé doesn't include creating the world in six days."

If this were any other situation, her words would have made him smile, but not now. "We've talked a lot about patterns and mine is failing people."

"No, Blake."

"Want the list?" He glanced over to the passenger seat and saw that her gaze was on him. "I failed my wife. My sister. And I'm well on my way to failing her child."

"You took her in when she needed a place to go. You've given her family."

"Yeah. Some family."

"No one is perfect. The important thing is to try."

"That's my plan. If we find her."

"We will," she assured him.

"I'm going to hang on to that," he promised. "Everything you've said is right on."

"What do you mean?"

"You told me that we have no choice about getting involved with family."

"I remember."

"But there is one thing I *can* choose." He glanced over and saw the question in her eyes. "Mia wasn't the only one I let down by thinking only of myself. I let you down when I slept with you, Casey." She started to protest but he held up a hand. "It's the truth. I see that now. You pegged me right as an anti-relationship guy—a selfish guy. The thing is, I don't want to fail you, too."

"You weren't the only one who made the decision to be close," she whispered.

"I should have stopped it. Hell, I should never have started it." But he wouldn't say he was sorry it had happened. There was only so much he could take and he would never be sorry for having her just once. "Mia has to come first. It can't ever happen again, Casey."

After several moments she let out a sad sigh. "I know."

And he knew the emptiness of it would be his biggest regret for as long as he lived.

Blake had told her he was turning over a new leaf, and Casey soon had proof that it wasn't simply lip service. She'd suggested that she go with him to pick up Mia when the police called to say they had found her. He'd thanked Casey for the offer but said that his niece was his responsibility, which was good news.

And bad.

That left Casey alone in the penthouse. Not completely alone, since Frankie followed as she paced from the foyer to

the family room. The dog looked anxious and confused
Casey almost smiled at the thought, because there was nc
overt change in the dog's expression, but somehow she knew
Frankie was worried about Mia.

Casey had been worried about the girl, too, and about
Blake. Pain and heartache followed when you let yourself
care. And she did, about both of them, which was exactly what
she'd feared would happen if she took this assignment.

Since she'd first arrived at One Queensridge Place, Casey
had struggled to convince herself it was just another assignment
and had failed miserably. Lately it had begun to feel like a
family—at least what she'd always imagined a family was like

If she wasn't *already* in love with Blake Decker, Casey
knew she was in serious danger of it.

But everything was different now because they'd been
intimate. She still didn't know why he'd been the one to make
her take that step. Since the IED—the improvised explosive
device—had blown up her world and scarred her body, she
hadn't slept with a man. More than one had tried, but no one
else had touched her heart. That was more scary than a stroll
through downtown Baghdad without body armor or a steel
reinforced vehicle.

It didn't take a battalion of shrinks to tell her she was feel
ing vulnerable. That had been clear since her first meeting
with Blake and the resulting intense reaction to him. The
question now was what to do about this job, since she'd com
promised it.

Before she could wrestle with a course of action, Frankie
barked and raced to the front door just before it opened. Casey
heard Mia greeting her pet and hurried from the family room
to the foyer. The girl was in the same jeans and green knit
sweatshirt she'd been wearing the first time Casey had met
her, the first time she'd run away. This made number three and

they said the third time was the charm. Casey hoped that was true, because the too-risky behavior had to stop.

After a quick visual examination Casey determined that there were no bruises, scrapes, cuts or any outward evidence of trauma.

"Are you okay?" Casey's gaze jumped from uncle to niece and back again since the question was directed to both.

"She's fine." The look he settled on his niece was rife with anger. "She's also damn lucky."

"Why? What happened?"

"The cops picked her up in a particularly bad part of town with some particularly unsavory people who prostitute teenage girls."

"Oh, no. Did you…" Casey's heart squeezed tight. "Were they—"

"The cops got to her in time."

"Nothing happened," Mia said, hostility dripping from every word. Brushstrokes of boredom painted her face. But what she couldn't know was that the fear lingering in her eyes gave away the little girl still inside her. Or maybe she did know—because she buried her face in her dog's neck and held on tight.

Casey wanted to hug Mia close and two days ago would have without hesitating. But one night in Blake's bed had changed everything.

"We were worried about you," was all she said.

"Right." Mia looked up, then stood and folded her arms over her thin chest, hunched her shoulders forward.

Obviously her body language screamed self-protection, but was that because of what she'd experienced on the street? Because of figuring out what had happened between Casey and her uncle? Or because he'd already lectured her and levied consequences for her actions?

Casey decided to fish for clues. "So you guys had a chance to talk in the car on the way back from downtown?"

"Actually, there was no conversation at all," Blake said. "I was too angry and didn't want to say anything without thinking it through."

This was new. Until now he hadn't been emotionally invested enough to get mad. But Casey was concerned that waiting until tomorrow would mute the impact of anything he said and that they risked going back to business as usual.

"Is there something you want to say to Mia?" Casey asked, nudging him.

"Where do I start?" He ran his fingers through his hair.

Mia dropped to one knee again and put her arms around Frankie, who hadn't left her side. "There's nothing you can say that I want to hear."

"Tough." He put his hands on his hips. He was still in his black slacks and gray dress shirt, wrinkled now after hours of driving around, searching and worrying. His dark hair looked as if he'd run his fingers through it countless times and the shadow of his beard darkened his jaw. His eyes were shadowed, too, and had never looked more vividly blue than they did at this moment.

Casey's heart squeezed tight again, but it had nothing to do with anxiety or relief, and everything to do with an intense feeling of respect and caring.

"This has got to stop," he said.

"You got that right." Mia glared at him.

"What are you talking about?" He folded his arms over his chest when Mia pressed her lips tightly together and slid a glance in Casey's direction. The look said loud and clear what she thought should stop. And Blake didn't pretend to mistake it. "I'm the adult and this is my house. I set the rules."

"So it's a dictatorship?"

"Darn right," he agreed.

"You want me out of the way. I don't get what you're so mad about."

"You took off and put yourself at risk. Casey and I were worried. That's what I'm so mad about."

"You don't care about me," Mia accused.

"I don't *want* to care about you, kid. There's a difference."

Casey realized the words were brilliant, more so because the expression of concern and caring on his face underscored the message. He had protested the situation, tried his best to disconnect from this child who had nowhere else to go. In spite of everything, he *did* care. The best part was that Mia simply stared at him, without a bored, blistering or belligerent reply. He'd rendered her speechless.

"So, here's the deal. You're grounded—"

"I don't go anywhere, anyway," she said, suddenly finding words.

"No mall, movies or outings," he said.

"I'm a prisoner?" she wailed.

He thought for a moment, then nodded. "That works for me."

"This is stupid—"

He pointed at her. "Keep it up. I haven't handed down the length of the sentence yet. But every time you say something, it gets longer. And I haven't even started yet on taking away your phone and computer."

The girl opened her mouth, then shut it again.

Blake nodded with satisfaction. "Wise choice. The thing is, your behavior has got to change, Mia."

It was as if he'd been channeling her thoughts, Casey realized. This was a moment, a really good one.

He blew out a long breath. "I don't have all the answers and I'm winging it, because I've never raised a kid before. What you need to know is that taking advantage of the situation isn't an option for you. Not anymore. If you step out of line, there will be consequences. If you play by the rules, there will be rewards."

"I'm not a dog. That's what I do with Frankie," Mia protested.

"Is it working?" he challenged. Her silence spoke volumes and he nodded. "Running away has got to stop. It's another way of hiding. And it's dangerous."

"You can't tell me what to do—"

"Grounded for seven days," he said. "Maybe without TV. Care to go for two weeks?"

Mia sighed and tried to look bored and angry, but there were cracks in the facade. "No."

"Good answer." He tipped his head toward the hall. "Now go to bed."

Without another word Mia did as she was told, and Frankie followed. The door to her room closed quietly, which was a minor miracle. This was the first time that had ever happened after a confrontation.

Casey looked at him. "Awesome."

"You think?" One corner of his mouth curved up. "She scared the hell out of me, Case."

"Me, too."

He stared at her and she thought there was a yearning expression in his eyes. If anyone ever in the history of the world looked like they needed a hug, it was him. Casey was afraid that if she looked in the mirror, there would be a corresponding expression on her face, so she turned away.

And remembered what he'd said to Mia. Running away is hiding. How many times had she accused him of doing that? Did it take one to know one? Was she the queen of denial, putting rules on the age of the kids she cared for in order to hide from the mistakes she'd made?

"It's late, Blake. You should get some rest."

"Yeah." He hesitated and the air between them was charged. For a moment it seemed like he would say something personal. But he didn't. "See you in the morning."

Her heart cracked just a little more when he left her alone. Since she'd broken her rules on this job, the mistakes had gotten even bigger. What was up with that? She'd crossed a line and now she didn't know where her place was in this household. She still felt like the little girl who couldn't manage to fit in anywhere. She cared too much for Blake to be the nanny, but he'd told her they couldn't be more.

If it didn't feel so much like running away, she'd have given him her notice right then. But she didn't want to punish him for doing the correct thing. She was to blame for Mia's behavior, and he was absolutely right to keep his distance from her.

But why did the right thing have to hurt so very much?

## Chapter Thirteen

"You didn't have to come with me to walk Frankie." Mia's voice was laced with resentment.

"I wanted to. The sun feels good." Casey strolled beside Mia on the condominium complex walking path, with Frankie taking the lead as opposed to taking off, which the dog would have done if she hadn't been on a leash.

"It's hot. You're only here because it's your job to guard me and make sure I don't run away again."

For the last week, during which the girl had been grounded, the two of them had spent a lot of time together, but awkwardness had been like a force field between them. Maybe it was time to get it out in the open, give Mia a chance to air her feelings.

"So, you haven't asked any questions about your uncle and me."

Mia lifted her shoulder in a "so what" gesture. "I don't have any."

"You're not a good liar, kiddo. And you're not in the way. That's the truth."

"Whatever." But Mia glanced over. "I don't believe you'd really answer me if I asked."

"Believe it." Casey's heart pounded but she tried to keep it from showing on her face.

"Okay." Mia stopped when Frankie sniffed a tree. "So what's between you and Uncle Blake?"

"Nothing." Without flinching, Casey met the girl's hostile gaze, because at this moment it was the truth.

"But there was something," Mia persisted.

How did she answer that when nothing about her and Blake was clear? *Keep it simple, stupid.* "What happened that night you were at your grandparents' was nothing more than a brain hiccup. For both of us."

"I don't know what that means." When the dog pulled at the leash, Mia started walking again.

"It means that now we have a respectful working relationship that's all about doing our best for you. Everything is back to normal." That part was a lie, but hopefully there was still enough little girl left in Mia to believe it was possible.

Casey hadn't had a mom to warn her that when a woman gave herself to a man, everything changed and it could never go back to the way it had been. She'd found that out for herself in high school—in the backseat of John Stratton's Camaro. It had been awful and there'd been no one to talk to. Pouring out the story to her dad and brothers had been out of the question, and she'd been too mortified to confess to her girlfriends. So she'd cried alone in her room and publicly pretended to be fine.

She couldn't even claim innocent ignorance for what had happened with Blake. She'd known if she took the step, everything would be different, but rational thought had been no match for the yearning to be in his arms.

It had happened. Now she had to deal with the collateral damage and hope that, at least for this at-risk child, things could go back to the way they were.

Mia mulled over the words for a while. "So you really are here to make sure I don't run?"

Inwardly Casey sighed with relief that the girl didn't seem in the mood for a cross-examination about her and Blake. They were now on to the topic that impacted Mia most—being grounded and losing her iPod.

"Actually, that's what being grounded for the last week is supposed to do."

"If I didn't walk Frankie, I wouldn't get any fresh air at all," Mia complained. "Kids need fresh air to grow and not get curvature of the spine and stuff."

Casey laughed. "That's a little melodramatic. Especially since house arrest is being lifted today. Your uncle is taking you out."

"Like I believe that."

Casey slid her hands into the pockets of her white cotton capris. "He said he'd be home early to pick you up for dinner and a movie."

"I repeat…like I believe that."

"I can see why you'd be skeptical. He doesn't have a perfect record, but he should get points for trying. Give him a break, Mia."

"Like he gave me?"

"You ran away. This restriction is about teaching you that certain behaviors are unacceptable. It's for your own good. Shows that he cares."

"He doesn't want to care about me," Mia reminded her.

Casey was pretty sure the girl understood what Blake had meant, but it was clear that she needed reassurance. "No, wanting to care is guyspeak for he doesn't want to, but against his will, he got sucked in and can't help caring."

Mia rolled her eyes. "I feel much better now."

"I'm serious. If he didn't care about you, no way he'd have gone to every mall in town, looking for you."

"He did?" Mia looked surprised.

"And you know how he feels about shopping," Casey added for emphasis. "He certainly wouldn't have grounded you for a week if he disliked you intensely."

"So you're saying house arrest is an awesome way for me to feel the love?"

Casey laughed. "Someday you'll understand that if he didn't care what happened to you, he wouldn't bother with restrictions. He'd let you do whatever the heck you want, because that would be much easier than putting up with your pity-party prison attitude."

Mia's mouth curved up, and for a split second it looked like a smile would break through the resistance. Then the crack in her facade disappeared. "Am I off suspension when he doesn't show up?"

"He will," Casey assured her.

"But if he doesn't, is the grounding up?"

"Yes." Casey sighed and hoped she wasn't wrong about him keeping his word.

He hadn't been faking the worry when Mia ran away. Casey had never seen him in action in a courtroom and some might say theatrics were part of pleading a case. But Blake's concern for his niece had been genuine. Would sincerity translate to keeping his promise now that the crisis had passed? Time would tell.

Casey looked at her wristwatch and saw that time was perilously close to running out.

They walked the dog back into the building and rode the elevator up to the penthouse. While Mia removed Frankie's leash and got her pet some food and water, Casey looked around in the usual places for the usual clues that Blake was home. She could have shouted, but in six thousand square feet it would have been a waste of breath. And speaking of a waste of breath, she didn't see his briefcase, suit jacket or anything else indicating that he was here.

"Can I have my iPod back now?" Mia asked, her resentful tone clearly indicating she'd come to the conclusion that she'd been stood up.

"Sure," Casey said. "But don't give up. He might still—"

The front door opened and Blake called out, "Sorry I'm late."

The dark shroud of bitterness lifted and Mia smiled. He walked into the family room and looked at Casey, then at his niece.

"You thought I wasn't going to make it," he accused.

"Never crossed my mind," the girl answered.

"You're lying." Blake grinned. "Should I be glad you're so bad at it?"

"Don't answer that, Mia," Casey advised. "It's a rhetorical question."

"I don't know what that means," the girl said.

"It's an attorney trick to trip someone up."

One raised eyebrow and a look from Blake said he could see that a week's worth of tension had eased. A teasing expression made his already handsome face even more appealing and Casey died a little inside.

"So, it's two against one," Blake accused. "In football they call that piling on. Unsportsmanlike conduct. That's a penalty."

"Not me," Mia said. "I'm officially not grounded anymore. This is me officially staying out of trouble."

"That's what I like to hear." Blake walked over and kissed her forehead. "Give me a minute to change clothes and we're outta here. The Deckers are going out on the town. Look out, Vegas. Here we come."

"Okay." The smile Mia gave him was heartbreaking in its hopefulness, a testament to how many times she'd been disappointed. But not this time. The little girl in her positively glowed.

When they were alone, Mia turned to her and said, "I didn't believe he would come for me."

"You were wrong."

"I know." She rubbed the spot on her forehead where he'd kissed her. "He really does care."

"I hate to say I told you so, but I told you so."

"I know." She grinned a very Decker-like grin. There was definitely a family resemblance. "Casey, I'm really, really sorry I was such a brat."

Would wonders never cease? An apology from the princess of pout. As Blake had pointed out, the lesson was learned and there was no point in piling on. "I've seen worse."

"You're just saying that to make me feel better." Mia caught her top lip between her teeth and worried it for a moment. "It's just that I was afraid."

"I know."

"I couldn't help it."

Casey knew that, too. "You're just being silly. Here with your uncle is where you belong. There's nothing to be afraid of."

"You're right. I'm just being an idiot. There's no reason to think that Uncle Blake loves you more, and now I'm sure that he doesn't. He and I are actual family."

Casey's mind filled in the rest. *And you're just the nanny. The hired help.*

Casey kept the carefree mask in place until the two of them left and she was alone. Suddenly her legs wouldn't hold her and she slowly sank to the carpet in the family room, which had never seemed quite so huge and empty before.

She felt as if she'd been slapped. Just because the slap had been delivered with words instead of an open palm didn't make the message less powerful.

Or hurtful.

She knew Mia hadn't meant to wound her, but the arrow had hit its mark with deadly accuracy. The kid was beginning to realize where she belonged and to feel secure enough to say so. Casey envied the twelve-year-old and wished it were possible for her to know what that felt like just once in her life.

Since sleeping with Blake, she'd been caught in an alternate universe: she was neither a paid professional nor his plus one. A verbal slap was just what she'd needed to snap her out of it. Even though he'd made it clear that Mia was his priority, and rightfully so, Casey hadn't quite been able to crush out the hope that she had a ghost of a chance with him.

But Mia had just taken care of that. There was no future here with the Deckers, and the sooner she left, the better off everyone would be.

Blake tried to focus attention on his computer screen, without much success. Something was bugging him and he couldn't quite put his finger on what it was. He leaned back in his chair and glanced at the picture of Mia on his desk. It had been taken a few days ago, on her first day of school—middle school. Before long she'd be in high school, then college. Then what?

Oddly enough he didn't much like the idea of her being somewhere where he couldn't make sure she was okay. That day of worrying about her out in the world alone, of picturing all the bad things that could happen, had made him want to put off her independence as long as possible. The day was coming when she'd push for it, but that wasn't today.

The door to his office opened and Rita poked her head in. His administrative assistant was an attractive woman in her mid-forties with brown eyes and shoulder-length black hair cut in layers.

She put a stack of papers on the desk in front of him. "I've got correspondence ready for your signature."

"Thanks, Ree."

"Cute kid," she said, looking at the photo.

"My niece. Mia."

"I see the family resemblance. There's something stubborn about the tilt to her chin, the determination in the eyes." She put the frame down. "A word of warning?"

"Shoot."

"Exactly." She nodded emphatically. "When boys start showing an interest, make sure they know you have guns and know how to use them."

"I'd be lying."

"Bluff. You're good at that. They'll never know for sure and will be inclined to keep their distance from that sweet little girl."

"Okay. I'll take that under advisement."

After his assistant left, his gaze wandered to the photo and he straightened it on his desk. *A sweet little girl.* He remembered the first few weeks she'd lived with him and the attitude she'd worn like armor. He hadn't known how to strip it away. If not for Casey…

He was pretty sure these last couple of months of adjusting to having a kid around would have been impossible without Casey. Too many times recently he'd had the uncomfortable feeling that life would be impossible without her. The tight feeling in his chest made him frown, because just thinking about her made him want to hold her. It seemed like a lifetime ago when he'd made love to her.

Except he knew his thing for Casey wasn't just about sex. That was pretty awesome. But even that word didn't do justice to the experience of holding her soft curves against him, kissing her sweet lips, loving her until he thought the top of his head would explode.

*Bad analogy,* he thought, remembering the scars on her body from the explosion, for which she blamed herself. He had a feeling that the wounds she carried on the inside were far worse than the ones he could see. He'd read about it: PTSD, post-traumatic stress disorder.

Casey Thomas was a complicated woman and he couldn't stop thinking about her. The intense feelings shook him up. They were deeper and more compelling than what he'd felt for the woman he'd married, the same one who'd betrayed and blindsided him. He'd never expected the bad stuff, and now he couldn't picture himself expecting anything else. A shrink would probably tell him what he already knew—he had his own emotional brand of PTSD going on.

He needed breathing room. He needed—

The intercom buzzed and he pushed the button. "What is it, Ree?"

"Casey Thomas is here to see you, Mr. Decker. She says she's your nanny."

His heart thumped once and he took a deep breath before answering. "Send her in."

Moments later there was a soft knock on his door before it opened and she was there. "Hi."

Her smile released the full power of her dimples, which, he'd found out for himself, were her secret weapon. When they flashed, mass destruction followed, because men would fall at her feet. At least he had. The memory was like a blast of heat that went from brain to gut to groin—the trifecta of turn-on.

"Hey. Come in." It was a major effort to keep his voice

normal, and he wasn't sure he'd pulled it off when she looked uneasy.

That made two of them, he thought, noting the way her white cotton sundress pulled across her breasts. All the skin he could see was tanned and toned, and the toes peeking out of her flip-flops were painted pink. She moved farther into the room, and he held out his hand, indicating the two club chairs in front of his desk. She sat in the one on the right and let her purse in her lap.

He shifted in his chair and sat up straighter, grateful that his desk was between them. That made him realize something else. This was the first time she'd come to see him at the office.

"Is everything all right?" he asked. "Mia?"

"Fine. I just dropped her off at school."

"How's that going?" He was grateful for a topic to take his mind off the disturbing thoughts of him, her, twisted sheets and tangled legs.

"It's the first week, but so far so good."

"By good, do you mean that there have been no phone calls from teachers or the administration?"

"There's that. But I mean she's talking about kids and classes and activities." Casey smiled and the dimples danced.

His gut knotted at the sight, and he wondered if there was a topic of discussion known to man that wouldn't make him think about having her in his bed.

"Good. I'm glad to hear it."

She frowned. "Are you okay?"

*Not really.* This was nice. Too nice. Distracting, but nice. That meant there were fewer hours until it would be time to go home, where Casey would be waiting for him.

*No. Scratch that. She'll be there supervising Mia. Doing her job. That's all.* He needed breathing room.

"I'm fine." *Mostly.* "Happy to hear that Mia is settling into school."

"Yeah. She likes the teachers. By the way, she wants to go to the new restaurant at Encore when you have your next Deckers' night out."

He laughed, which was hard to believe. "She's been a different kid since I grounded her."

Shadows filled her eyes for a moment, before she said, "The transformation has more to do with you showing up for dinner and a movie than with punishment for bad behavior. Setting the parameters and sticking to them are the cornerstones of positive parenting."

"I enjoy spending time with her," he said, surprised he hadn't actually thought in those terms until this moment. "She's fun, funny, smart. She's really a great kid when she's not acting bitter and resentful."

"You pretty much described every kid in the world," Casey pointed out.

"Yeah." He leaned back in his chair. "But in Mia's case it feels like a miracle when I think about how she was at first. She's great to have around and that's something I never thought I'd say."

"You should tell her that."

"Good idea. Which reminds me that I have you to thank for the sheer normalness of her behavior."

"It's nothing."

"Not from my perspective," he said. "Your work with Mia has been exemplary. And to show my gratitude, there will be a bonus in your paycheck."

He was looking straight at her and would swear her face didn't alter, but suddenly it dimmed, as if clouds had blocked out the sun. And since when did he analyze the facial expressions of his employees? Since things took a personal turn, and that was as good an example as any of why he needed to put things back on a firmly professional footing.

"So, what brings you here? I'm guessing it's not about updating me on Mia's first week of school."

"No." She gripped her purse tightly. "I'm handing in my resignation."

That wasn't what he'd expected. "You're quitting?"

"This is my two weeks' notice."

"I don't understand," he said.

"It's my intention not to work for you any longer and I'm notifying you of that."

"That's not what I meant. I get what *resignation* means. It's just that I thought taking care of Mia agreed with you."

"As you said, she's a great kid. I stopped by your office because this isn't something I wanted her to overhear."

His first thought had been about himself, about how much he'd miss her. But Casey was worried about how Mia would react. No one liked change, but a kid who'd been through what she had would take it especially hard.

"She's doing so well. I'd like to see her continue with the forward progress. All those rough edges she had when she first came to live with me have been smoothed out."

"I'm glad. But this is about me. I've got rough edges, too, and they're not smoothing out."

Her eyes said she was dead serious and told him change was in his future. Mia wasn't the only one who didn't like change. "Why, Casey? You're part of the family."

"How exactly?"

"What?"

"How am I part of your family?"

Blake thought about the question. "You take care of Mia."

"Last time I checked, child caregiver wasn't an official limb on the family tree."

"It's the only answer I have," he said.

"Not the one I was hoping for." Her voice was soft and sad. Her smile was sadder and even the flash of dimples didn't restore the sparkle.

Blake realized that this was what had been bugging him, keeping him from concentrating on work. Casey hadn't been acting like herself for about a week, since just about the time Mia got off restriction. Just about the time things with his niece had clicked into place. Personally? He hated the idea of Casey not being there, but that wasn't something he wanted to think about now.

"Is it about money? I'll give you a raise—"

"No. I have nothing more to say." She stood and slid the strap of her purse on her shoulder.

He stood, too, but didn't dare walk around the desk, because he would have pulled her into his arms. "Casey, wait—"

"It's no use, Blake. There's nothing you can say that will change my mind."

"Why are you so determined?"

"You know why." She sighed. "What happened between you and me was an error in judgment."

An understatement, and yet he couldn't regret what had happened. "It's in the past. We can—"

"No. It's not possible to forget. With me there Mia has to try too hard. That will make it much more difficult for the two of you to form a family unit." She met his gaze and determination filled her own. "My bad judgment tore apart the family of my best friend. If I can heal yours, maybe that will make up for it in some small way."

He didn't say anything else to try and stop her. Partly because the knot forming in his chest was cutting off his air, and partly because there was nothing left to say. If he told her he had feelings for her, she wouldn't believe him. Trust was a problem, and she'd think he was using her, like she'd been used once before.

The feelings of anger and loss raging through him were a lot like what had happened when he'd found out his wife was cheating on him. But Casey hadn't betrayed him. She was straightforward, honest and had more integrity than anyone he'd ever met. Case in point: she'd come to his place of business and told him to his face that she was leaving his employ. And why.

Somehow that just made him feel worse.

## Chapter Fourteen

As it turned out, Casey didn't stay for two weeks. Since Mia had started school, she only needed someone at home until Blake returned from work. With that parameter Ginger Davis had easily found a replacement.

He looked in the mirror and concentrated on shaving, because that was something he could control. And it was important to get a handle on something when it felt like his personal life was in free fall. Make that free fall minus one.

Mia was doing great. She'd taken the news of the shift change surprisingly well. Actually she'd shown very little emotion when Casey broke the news. With the mature woman who made sure Mia made it home, started her homework and didn't have wild parties or watch inappropriate movies on TV, the kid's life was very much together.

"One out of two Deckers is still fifty percent," he said to his reflection. He grabbed a towel and wiped traces of shaving cream from his face before shaking his head at the sad-eyed fool looking back. "Pathetic loser."

With a towel around his waist he walked past the bed. His chest felt tight as memories of lying there with Casey washed over him. They'd been as close as a man and woman could be, sharing their bodies and bits of their souls. Since she had gone and no longer shared a part of his space, even time with Mia had been lonely and empty.

"Damn." He clenched his fingers into his palm, wanting to put his fist through a wall as angry frustration expanded inside him.

Deliberately turning his back on the bed, he walked into the closet and pulled out a black suit, a charcoal shirt and a gray-on-gray silk tie. The professional business attire was somber and funeral-like, which was appropriate since he couldn't shake the feeling that someone he cared very much about was lost to him.

There was a knock on the bedroom door, followed by Mia's voice. "Uncle Blake?"

"Just a minute," he called out. What was her problem?

He pulled on boxers, slacks and the shirt, buttoning it as he walked to the door and opened up. "Why aren't you on your way to school?"

"I missed the bus." Wide and not-so-innocent eyes stared back at him.

"Darn it, Mia. You had plenty of time. I'm running late for court."

"I could stay home from school today," she offered.

"No. Why did you miss the bus?" he asked.

"I had to come back."

"What for?" he demanded.

"I had a paper. But when I came back, Frankie—"

He held up a hand to stop her. "Don't even tell me the dog ate your homework."

"Why not?" Mia held up tattered sheets of notebook paper. "She ate your computer."

The one he'd forgotten to close up because thoughts of Casey had pushed everything else out of his mind. "Don't blame the dog. You're the one who's supposed to put things where she can't get at them."

"It's not my fault," she protested. "The new chick put my stuff in the wrong place."

"Her name is Barbara and I'm not sure that having your things in a different spot is an adequate defense."

"Whatever."

There was a word he hadn't heard in a while. "Is that kid-speak for, 'you didn't look for your backpack, to put your homework in it'?"

"It took me too long to find my school shirt. Friday is spirit day and we have to wear the one with the school logo. If Casey was here, it would have been where I could find it."

If Casey were here, a lot of things would be better, but that ship had sailed. "Then from now on we'll have to make sure everything is together the night before."

"I'm hungry." Her voice was just this side of a whine, which grated on his last nerve.

"Did you eat breakfast?"

"There's nothing good."

"You better be wrong. I pay a housekeeper a lot of money to stock the pantry and prepare meals."

"There's just cereal." She heaved a huge, long-suffering sigh. "When Casey was here, she made me eggs and Mickey Mouse pancakes with chocolate chips for eyes and a mouth."

Blake glanced at the clock and struggled for patience. "How about we make some of those tomorrow? It's the weekend and it'll be a fun thing to do together."

Mia nodded but was still making a frowny face. "But I'm still hungry now."

He knew she was being deliberately difficult, and wanted to shake her. Casey would have told him that rattling his cage was Mia's endgame and not to fall for it. He was doing his best, but the strategy would have been easier to stick to if Casey was here for backup. He felt as if he were walking a tightrope over the Grand Canyon and working without a net.

"Why don't you make yourself a peanut butter sandwich? You can eat it in the car on the way to school."

"Eat in the Benz?" she said. "Since when?"

"Since you need a ride to school."

"I thought you didn't have time."

"I don't," he agreed. "But you have to get to school. I'll work it out."

"You wouldn't have to if Casey was here—"

"But Casey isn't here." Blake's voice was louder than he'd intended and Mia's eyes grew wider as she backed up a step.

Blake looked down as he put his hands on his hips. He blew out a long breath, and when the haze of annoyance-fueled anger disappeared, there was a glimmer of understanding in its place. He looked at the girl, who was nervously biting the inside of her bottom lip.

"Look, Mia…" He tried to picture Casey dealing with this situation. There would be honesty, tough love and a little humor tossed in to take the sting out of it. "I'm sorry I yelled at you, even though you deserved it."

"Me?" She pressed a palm to her thin chest. "I forgot stuff. Do you want me to get a zero for homework? It was an honest mistake and you're acting like I did drugs or had sex."

He wanted to recoil in horror at the words but held tough because Casey had taught him not to react to the kid's tactics. "You're smart and capable and organized."

"No, I'm not."

"Look, kid, I'm an attorney. Last time I checked, stupidity wasn't a legal defense. You know better. And both of us are aware that you know better. I'm not as dense as you think."

"Oh, yeah?"

He had her on the run. It was time to get to the heart of what was really going on here. "This is about something else that's out of your control, isn't it?"

"That's just stupid."

Translation: he was on the right track. "No, it's not. You miss Casey, don't you?"

It wasn't so much that he was a mind reader or even an especially intuitive guy. He knew because he missed Casey, too. Her absence left an all-encompassing emptiness, which just couldn't be filled with work or parenting or even the general business of life.

Mia stared at him with a resentment he hadn't seen for a while, but now it didn't work. Full lips trembled as her big turquoise eyes filled with tears. "Why did she leave us?"

Blake pulled her into his arms and murmured reassuring words as he rubbed her back. "I know how you feel."

With her cheek on his chest, Mia nodded. Fortunately she didn't ask how he knew, because he'd have to be honest and he couldn't go there now. The girl's arms slid around his waist and that felt pretty good. It was the only thing about this day that did. When she stopped crying and stepped away, she rubbed a finger beneath her nose.

"Why did you let her go, Uncle Blake?"

"I didn't *let* her. She quit."

"Why?"

"She thinks you and I are having trouble being a family. She didn't want to get in the way of that."

Mia's red-rimmed eyes looked troubled. "Why would she think that?"

"It's complicated," he finally said.

She sniffled. "I told her I was sorry for being a brat."

"It's not your fault." She nodded, but he could tell she didn't quite believe the words. "Now, go make your sandwich and I'll drive you to school."

Without another word, she turned and headed toward the kitchen. Blake finished dressing.

No one was at fault for what had happened except him. He'd finally found a woman who was more interesting to him than anything, someone worth leaving work for, the one who was waiting for him to come home. And he realized the truth: he was in love with Casey and had pushed her away. Some misguided sense of guilt about Mia had convinced him he had to choose. But his niece's behavior just now convinced him that she loved Casey, too.

And he'd let her go.

If he'd told her how he felt that day in his office, there might have been a chance for them. But now she wouldn't believe him; she would think he was using her for Mia, for his own selfish purpose. He'd never be able to convince her that he needed *her.* From the beginning, the one thing they'd agreed on was that trust was hard to come by.

That fact didn't inspire confidence in his ability to get her to believe he was no longer anti-relationship.

Blake's career choice involved keeping his cool when the people around him were losing theirs. Since Mia had come to live with him, his emotions had been on a roller coaster, and he wasn't sure why he'd expected today to be any different. But he had and it wasn't.

He'd gotten a call from Mia's new nanny, who was freak-

ing out because the kid hadn't come home from school on th
bus. He had figured out she was upset about losing Casey, bu
had underestimated her emotions yet again.

He'd been canceling the rest of his appointments for th
day when Ginger Davis had called to let him know Mia wa
with her. Now he was on his way up to her penthouse acros
the street from Fashion Show Mall. This felt a lot like comin
full circle, except for the fact that Casey wouldn't be there.

After ringing the bell, he waited just a moment befor
Ginger opened the door. As always she looked stylish in
deep olive-green-colored crepe pantsuit.

"Hello, Mr. Decker," she said. "Please come in."

"Thanks. Where's Mia?"

"In my office." When he started to walk past her, she pu
a hand on his arm. "Don't be too hard on her."

"Give me one good reason why I shouldn't ground he
until she's thirty-five."

"For one thing you'd never make that penalty stick." Sh
smiled. "And you need to know that she came to me because sh
wants to see Casey and figured I would know how to find her.

"Do you?"

"Yes."

"Then tell me where she is," he wanted to say. But h
didn't. Casey had turned her back on Mia and him. "I'r
aware that Mia misses Casey very much. But I had no ide
she would do a disappearing act yet again. There have to b
consequences."

"And rightly so," Ginger agreed. "I just think you shoul
listen to her before handing down a harsh sentence."

He was feeling pretty raw right now and the kid wasn't th
only reason for it. "I'll take it under advisement."

Ginger nodded. "Follow me."

She led him to her office, a very female space, with it

glass-topped desk, pale yellow walls and floral print-covered love seat.

Mia stood when she saw him. "Uncle Blake, I—"

He pointed at her. "You're in so much trouble, young lady."

"I know. It's just that I had to do something."

"Do you have any idea how frantic I've been since Barbara called?" He studied the contrite expression on his niece's freckled face, and somewhere in his anger-drenched mind, it registered as sincere. "You're grounded from all electronic devices you now own and any that you ever hope to have in the future."

"Okay."

"Okay? No argument?" He hadn't expected it to be that easy.

"I deserve it." She folded her arms at her waist, as if she were hugging herself. "I knew you'd be mad, but it was a chance I had to take. I need to talk to Casey."

"Why?" he asked. "What's so important that it is worth losing your gadgets for the rest of your life?"

"It's my fault Casey left."

"What? Why?"

"I was mean to her," Mia confessed.

There had to be more. Casey had been a soldier, trained to take orders even when no one said please. Obviously she was sensitive, the most caring person he'd ever known. But she wasn't thin-skinned when it came to dealing with kids.

"Tell me what happened," he suggested.

"It was the night you came home from work to take me to dinner and a movie after my punishment was lifted." Mia glanced up at him without quite meeting his gaze. "I—I didn't think you'd keep your promise."

Yeah, he deserved that. "Go on."

"I'm not trying to hurt your feelings, but it's the way things were." It was good she'd used the past tense. "I was so happy to see you and I might have said that you didn't care about her."

Might have?

"What did you tell her exactly, Mia?" Ginger asked.

The kid glanced at Ginger, who was sitting behind her desk. "I was afraid Uncle Blake loved her more. I—I said something about her not being family. Not like he and I are family."

"I see." Ginger's tone was quiet, nonjudgmental.

Blake felt like he was suddenly groping his way around because his vision was fuzzy. "Why would you say something like that to her?"

"I don't know. It's just…" She looked sad and miserable. "I wanted you to love me."

The words were like a punch to the chest and he pulled the girl into his arms. "I do love you, Mia," he said quietly.

"I know. And I'm sorry about coming here without saying anything, but I just wanted to tell Casey that I'm sorry."

"Your heart is in the right place, kid. It's your communication skills we have to work on."

"Yeah." She giggled and nodded.

"Mia," Ginger said, "would you mind waiting in the other room while I speak with your uncle?"

"Sure." Mia looked up at him. "Is that okay?"

"Sure." He kissed the top of her head. "I worry because I love you. I've had my quota of worry for one day, so I'd appreciate it if you didn't take off, like the last time we were here."

"I can do that if you'll let me keep just my iPod while I'm grounded."

"No." He grinned. "But that was a nice try. You've got some negotiation skills going on."

"It was worth a shot, but I wouldn't run away. I'm not that stupid kid anymore."

"Darn right. You're my kid," he said.

"I love you, Uncle Blake."

The words left him with a lump in his throat, so he touched his heart and pointed at her. She smiled, then said, "Maybe you can talk Miss Davis into telling us where Casey is."

"Are you going to ground her?" Ginger asked after the girl had left the room.

"I'll probably give her a suspended sentence." He turned to look at her. "I wonder if Casey has any idea how much she's hurt Mia."

"Mia? Or you?"

"That's ridiculous." But the words had struck a chord somewhere in the region of his heart.

Ginger folded her hands and rested them on her desk. "I think you're in love with Casey."

"I'm nothing more than the guy who signed her paycheck," he said, wincing at the bitterness in his voice, even though he'd already figured that out. "Have you talked to Casey?"

"Yes."

"How is she?" He wanted her to be fine and not fine. He wanted to know that she missed him the same way he missed her.

"She's doing as well as can be expected," Ginger answered cautiously.

All he heard was that she was doing well and something twisted in his chest. "That's because she's the one who walked away."

"Casey cares deeply about you."

He met her gaze and knew the cynicism in his soul showed in his expression. "That's hard to believe. You don't run away from the ones you love."

"Do you know what happened to Casey when she was overseas?" she asked.

"Yes."

"She had two reasons for walking out on you, Blake. The first concerns the trauma she experienced. You know that she saw her friends blown apart. And she believes it was her fault. Because she took an interest in a kid who used her."

"She told me," he said.

"Then you also know that her best friend's death left two small children motherless and that Casey blames herself for tearing that family apart."

"Yeah."

"Do you get that she won't be responsible for ruining another family? One that's just getting on its feet?"

"But she brought us together," he protested. "If not for her, we would be strangers living under the same roof."

"Did you tell her that?"

"I tried, but—"

"That brings me to the second reason," Ginger said. "She won't be made a fool of."

"I wouldn't do that."

"Not on purpose." Ginger picked up a pen and rolled it between her fingers. "But she let someone in once and it cost her plenty. I will not let you call her a coward. She's an extraordinarily courageous woman who would sacrifice herself for the ones she loves. Walking away from you and Mia was her doing that. She would give up her life, but risking her heart is so much harder."

"You think it's easy for me?"

He remembered what Casey had said about his career revolving around destroying relationships. His law practice had actually become more successful following his own divorce, and now he knew that was a result of channeling his bitterness into his business. He was a hotshot attorney who thrived on being alone, but after Casey all he had was loneliness. He could feel himself withering. Suddenly he was tired, weary clear to his soul. And he didn't want to be alone.

"I would never deliberately hurt her," he said. "But I don't know if I can convince her of that."

"Did you make an attempt?" Ginger's expression was kind, sympathetic, and it was as if she'd read his mind. "There's no shame in failing, Blake. Only in failing to try."

"She's not the only one with baggage," he pointed out. "And I'm not accustomed to losing."

"You don't have to be perfect. You just have to show up and do your best."

She made it sound easy and he knew it wouldn't be. But he also knew that if he turned his back now, it would be the biggest mistake of his life.

"Do you know where she is?" When Ginger nodded, he asked, "Will you tell me?"

"She requested that I not *say*."

Blake hadn't become a successful attorney by not paying attention to the fine distinctions of words. His heart picked up speed when she reached for a notepad and jotted something down.

"This is me not *saying* where she is." Ginger slid a piece of paper across the desk.

"Thank you." He met her gaze. "I'm not sure how to do this."

"You've been hurt, too, Blake, so it's not easy to take a chance. But I just saw how easily you told Mia what's in your heart. And I know there's a different sort of risk with Casey, but just tell her what you feel."

Blake nodded as he took the address from her. He knew he was good with words and had delivered successful summations in court because he always wanted to win. It was easier to be rational and emotionally detached when someone else's future was at stake.

This time it was his life on the line. Everything was riding on the argument he was going to make.

"But no pressure," he said grimly.

## Chapter Fifteen

Casey cleaned up her dad's kitchen after cooking dinner. Unlike other evenings in the two weeks since she'd come to stay with him, Nathan Thomas hung around to help. It was kind of freaking her out.

She glanced around the long, spacious room, with its oblong, white tile-topped counter and cabinets below. The refrigerator stood at one end and the nook filled with a maple dinette was at the other. Across from the kitchen was the family room with fireplace, and the adjacent living room had a corner group sofa and a flat-screen TV. Upstairs there were three bedrooms and a railing with glass below it. Her mother had never stepped foot in this house because her dad had moved the family here after her death. That he'd run from the painful memories had never occurred to Casey before.

Maybe it dawned on her now because she was here running

from pain of her own. She desperately missed Blake and hoped that she'd get over him.

Her father dried the small frying pan. "So, when are you planning to go back to work?"

"Are you trying to get rid of me?" She poured cleanser in the sink and started scrubbing.

"No."

"If I'm in the way, just say the word and I'll make other arrangements." She glanced out the window and became aware of the curtains framing it. They were lacy and see through and not at all like her father. "When did you put up curtains?"

"You just noticed?"

"Yeah." She'd had a few things on her mind. Like how much she wished Blake could care about her.

He met her gaze and she noticed that he was a very handsome man. In his early fifties, he had silver in his brown hair and a nice smile when he used it. But what really snagged her attention was the sparkle in his blue eyes. What was up with that?

"So, Dad, lace?"

He cleared his throat. "I've been seeing someone."

"How long?" Casey asked.

"A few months. She works as a receptionist for my doctor."

*Doctor?* A sudden spurt of fear shot up her spine. "Are you okay?"

"Fine. I was there for my yearly physical." He shrugged. "Peg and I got to talking."

"Peg?"

"That's her name. Peg Daniels. She makes me laugh."

"You never told me," Casey accused.

"I'm telling you now. I like to laugh."

"No." Casey sighed. "That you're seeing someone."

"I didn't know how." He rested a hand on the counter, the dish towel dangling from his fingers. "But I figure if you're staying for a while, you should know, because she'll be coming around."

"I can get my own place."

"That's not what I'm saying. But if you don't want to meet her—"

"It's not that. It's just…" Casey rinsed out the sink, then turned off the water. "Maybe it is that. I'm not sure I want to see you with a woman. I guess because I never saw you with anyone but Mom. And you were never the same after she died." She glanced around the kitchen again. "You even sold the house and moved us here because living in the other place was too painful."

"It was hard," he admitted.

That was her dad. A master of understatement. "I guess it didn't help, me being a girl."

"Now why would you say that?"

"It couldn't have been easy for you, not knowing what to do with me after having boys."

Shadows swirled in his eyes. "Are you saying I wasn't there for you?"

"No, Dad. I just meant—"

"Because you'd be right."

"I would?"

"I was in my own world. That wasn't your fault, Case. It's mine. I did what a good soldier should never do. I retreated. The grief eased eventually, but by then you didn't seem to need me. And I didn't know how to be needed."

Casey's throat was thick with emotions she wasn't accustomed to letting him see. Or anyone else for that matter. She'd forgotten how to cry a long time ago. Except that one night with Blake. "It's okay, Dad."

"No, it's not. And it has to be said that you scared the crap out of me when you were hurt in Iraq."

"I'm sorry. And that was my own fault. I didn't see what I should have, because I was so focused on the fact that I was helping."

"You're not a mind reader, Casey. How could you possibly know the evil in that kid's heart?"

"I couldn't. But if I'd just kept to myself—"

"The bad stuff in the world would never get better if everyone kept to themselves," he said.

"I wish my friend's family didn't have to pay the price. Then Paula would still be alive and her kids would have their mom."

"And you know how hard it is growing up without a mom, don't you?"

She nodded. "Yeah, I do."

His eyes were sad. "I was too broken to help you, baby. But maybe Paula's kids have a better dad, one who can be there for them. Help them through it. Help them heal."

"It's okay, Daddy—" Her voice caught and she bit back a sob.

Nathan held out his arms and she walked into them. He held her and rubbed her back. "It's not okay. But I did the best I could. You haven't called me Daddy since right after your mom died."

"I guess I grew up fast."

"You'll always be my little girl. That said, what made you run home and hide with your old man?"

"It's nothing. Just taking a break from work."

He held her at arm's length, studying her. "Seems to me a break from work should make you look relaxed. And I'm not seeing it."

"Not sleeping well." A by-product of too many dreams starring Blake Decker. Sometimes she woke in the middle of the night, so lonely that there was a deep ache in the middle of her heart.

"Being tired doesn't explain the sadness in your eyes, Casey."

"It's nothing. Just burnout."

"I don't think so." Nathan folded his arms over his chest. "What's his name?"

Casey's gaze jumped to his. "How do you know it's a guy?"

"Just a guess."

"I think I liked it better when you ignored me," she grumbled.

"Not an option. There's a new sheriff in town," he said a little sheepishly.

"And her name is Peg."

"You're changing the subject." There was a determined set to his mouth.

Casey sighed. "His name is Blake Decker and he was my boss until I quit. And you know the rest."

"Like hell. What did he do?"

"All the right things." Except loving her. "He took in his orphaned niece and is learning how to be a good father to her."

"So she's all grown-up?"

"No. She's still twelve."

"Then why are you here?" His eyes narrowed. "You're in love with him."

Casey knew it wasn't a question. "He had a bad experience and isn't looking for romance."

"Neither was I, but it happens, anyway. So what are you going to do about it?"

"There's nothing to do. He's making a life with his family. I'll go on to another assignment."

"You've got more of me in you than I thought. And that's not a compliment."

"What does that mean?" Casey demanded, anger pushing away the gooey feeling from moments ago.

"You're running away, just like I did."

"What the heck?" She was no coward. It had taken guts to do what was best for everyone. "I stepped aside so he could concentrate on family. It was the right thing."

"Wrong. You retreated because you're afraid to take a chance on getting close to someone." He pointed at her. "Been there, baby. Done that. You can tell yourself you've got a halo and wings, but it doesn't fly with me. You got jacked up by letting someone close and you're running scared because you just might do it again. And this time no doctor can fix the damage."

He was right, she thought. Her life would be blown apart, not in a physical way, but it would still be devastating. Taking herself out of the game was the best way to keep from getting hurt. Except she was still hurting.

"When did you get so smart?" she asked, smiling sadly at her dad.

"If I was that bright, I'd be able to fix it. Trust me, it hurts like hell that I can't." A gleam stole into his eyes. "How about if I beat him up for you? I may not be good at talking about my feelings, but I'm pretty sure I can kick the ass of the jerk who hurt my kid."

Casey laughed even as sadness seared her heart. "I wouldn't advise that. He's an attorney and wouldn't hesitate to charge you with assault and battery."

"It would be worth it."

"Not to me." She stepped close and hugged him. "I feel like I just found you and I'd rather not lose you again. Besides, you probably wouldn't do well in prison."

"No." His chest rumbled when he laughed. "I'd miss you. And Peg."

His tone was rusty, kind of like his way of talking about feelings. But he did it for her and made her feel marginally better.

"Don't feel guilty about loving someone again, Dad."

"Okay." He rubbed his big hand up and down her back. "On one condition."

"What's that?"

"You don't feel guilty about it, either," he said.

"Deal."

And that was easy for her to promise because she had nothing on the line. She could care about Blake all she wanted and do it without guilt because he would never love her back.

After the heart-to-heart with her dad, Casey went upstairs to her room and grabbed the book on the nightstand, then flopped on the bed. But when she tried to read, her mind refused to take part in the exercise. After going over the same paragraph too many times to count, she quit.

Did her brothers know that her dad was seeing someone? If so, how come they hadn't told her? Or was it classified intelligence—as in "for men's ears only"?

She brushed her hand over the comforter on the bed and just then registered the fact that it was new. Actually she had noticed before but hadn't paid much attention until now, after finding out there was a woman in her dad's life. Casey should have realized something was up because of the homey touches in the guest room. It was all very un-Nathan-like.

The full-size bed still had the brass head- and footboards. The maple dresser and nightstands and the matching bookcase were the same, but there were pictures on the walls. Oval frames. Her dad wasn't an "oval-framed picture" man. On top of the bookcase was a wire birdcage, and the swing inside was shaped like a heart. Her dad didn't do hearts as a decorating touch. But the comforter was really out of character for him, especially because it had purple flowers and greenery, although the background was beige. That was her dad. Only better.

The more the information sank in that he wasn't alone any longer, the happier she was for him. It made her own loneliness even sadder and more pathetic.

When she'd come here after leaving Blake's, what she'd been most aware of was the comfort in this room, which had once been so depressing, and not the details that made it so inviting. She probably hadn't noticed because she was too preoccupied with missing Blake and his niece. Mia was a terrific kid. Casey even missed her abrasive sarcasm. How pathetic was that? And how much longer could this pity party go on?

She needed to get back to work because hanging out with nothing to do gave her too much time to think and play Monday-morning quarterback. To replay every minute at Blake's and wonder what she could have done differently. The fact was that he didn't feel the same as she did, and the sooner she let it go, the better off she would be.

There was a knock on her door. When she opened it, Nathan stood there. "Hi. What's up, Dad?"

"Someone is here to see you."

No one knew she was here except Ginger, who'd promised not to tell anyone. But her father was wearing an intense expression that was so much more familiar than the mooning-over-Peg face she'd seen just a while ago.

"Is there a problem?" she asked.

"That's for you to decide. I was on my way out to take Peg to a show, but I can stick around if you need me."

Her heart started pounding and the hair at her nape prickled with awareness. Blake Decker sensitivity. Something told her that that traitor Ginger Davis had broken her word.

"Is it Blake?"

"Said that's his name." If anything, her dad's expression was even more grim.

"Tell him I'm not here." As soon as the words were out of her mouth, she remembered what he'd said earlier about running home to hide.

"That won't work," he said, obviously willing to help her out. "Your car's parked in front."

"Oh. Right."

"I could tell him you don't want to see him."

If only that were true. More than anything Casey wanted to look at him just one more time. But that was pointless.

"Would you really say that?" she asked.

Nathan nodded. "But I'm not sure it would get rid of him."

"Why?"

"Instinct. A guy thing." He shrugged. "The man is on a mission and something tells me he's not leaving until he's achieved his objective."

Why was he here? It didn't make any sense. He hadn't been able to give her an answer about where she fit into his life, and she'd made it clear that settling for less than she wanted wasn't an option. There was nothing left to say.

Unless this was about Mia. Was there something wrong? Had she disappeared again? Worry gathered around her like a cloud.

She brushed past her father in the doorway. "I'll talk to him."

She walked down the stairs, turned on the landing and saw him standing just inside the front door. He was wearing the look she'd come to know—and love—so well. The tie was missing in action, but the white dress shirt was wrinkled in all the right places from a day at work, and long sleeves were rolled to mid-forearm. It made his already broad shoulders look even wider, and her pulse stuttered. His charcoal slacks were expertly tailored and fit his trim waist and muscular legs perfectly.

She held the railing when her legs started to tremble, and

managed to make it all the way into the living room without tripping.

"Hello, Blake."

"Casey."

His expression gave nothing away, so she had to ask, "What are you doing here? Is Mia all right?"

"Fine."

When his gaze moved past her, she glanced around and saw her father.

"Everything all right, Casey?" Nathan asked.

"Yeah." She glanced between the two men. "I guess introductions aren't necessary."

"No. Do you want me to stay?" her father asked.

She shook her head. "I'm fine. Be sure and tell Peg I'm looking forward to meeting her. I'd like to thank her for all the nice little touches in the guest room."

Nathan shrugged as a small smile played over his mouth. He didn't bother to deny her assumption. "I'll pass that along."

"Have a good time." Casey gave him a hug. "Love you, Dad."

"I love you, too." Nathan squeezed her back and dropped a kiss on the top of her head before walking out the door.

She looked at Blake. "If Mia's fine, I don't understand why you're here."

"You're a coward, Casey."

"What?" She hadn't expected a sneak attack.

"The first time we met, I thought you were straightforward and honest. You had more integrity in your pinkie than anyone I'd ever met. Now I know I was wrong about that."

His words stirred up anger, which crushed her self-pity. "You went to all the trouble of finding out where I was just to insult me?"

"Courage is when you go on in spite of the hard stuff. The bad stuff. But you ran away."

"I quit. There's a difference."

"Semantics," he said.

"What is this? Pick on Casey day? Who do you think you are? By definition, quitting means I don't work for you anymore. If you're determined to evaluate my job performance, you're in the wrong place. And clearly Ginger can't be trusted."

"I'm here to get through to you." He settled his hands on his lean hips and looked down for a moment. "I admit I've been hiding, not willing to take a chance on caring, because getting kicked in the teeth isn't something one willingly signs up for. But that has nothing to do with my career choice. If a couple decides to call it quits, each individual has rights that need protecting. That's what I do."

"Thanks for the clarification. I don't need protecting." Casey could almost feel her heart breaking, and the words were a brazen lie.

"I disagree, but it's hard to prove my case when you won't give me a chance." Intensity glittered in his eyes. "You're too busy punishing yourself for what happened to your friend."

The words slammed her in the chest. "You have no right to say that—"

"Sue me. Someone has to make you see that you won't let yourself be happy." He moved closer and gripped her hands. "She died because of evil you couldn't possibly comprehend. A kid blew himself up and murdered her. If you go on in this half a life, the killer gets to claim one more victim. Don't give him the satisfaction. Paula wouldn't want that."

She didn't know what to say, and even if she did, she couldn't have forced words past the lump in her throat.

Blake gently squeezed her fingers. "So, that's why I came. Every day I see people who turn their backs on love without trying to make it work. And I just wanted to say that if you're that kind of woman, you're not anyone I want to be with."

Then he dropped her hands, walked out and slammed the door.

Casey couldn't breathe, what with the pain in her chest cutting off oxygen. Then suddenly tears filled her eyes and rolled down her cheeks. In that instant she remembered why she had deliberately learned to forget how to cry. It simply hurt too much. She had no reserves to rally her defenses and stop the sob that tore up from somewhere deep inside her. She buried her face in her hands.

She didn't consciously hear the door open again, but the next thing she knew, strong arms gathered her close to a familiar and wonderful warmth.

Comfort flowed as Blake's voice washed over her. "Don't cry, Casey. Please, don't cry."

She lowered her hands and looked up at him in amazement. "You came back."

"Technically, I never left. I couldn't take the chance that you wouldn't come after me." He smiled. "This is me coming after you."

"Why?"

"I love you."

It was like the sun peeking through the clouds. "Really?"

"I guess I deserve that." He cupped her face in his palms and brushed the tears away with his thumbs. "You asked me how you were part of the family and I didn't give you a complete answer. Guess I'm a coward, too."

"Takes one to know one?" she asked.

"Something like that." His smile was fleeting. "You're the heart and soul of my family, Casey. Without you there is no family. I wish I could delete every selfish thing I ever did to convince you I couldn't love you or Mia. The truth is that I love you both. So much. I can't let you go. I won't."

"Really?"

"Really." Determination looked good on him. "Marry me, Casey. Be Mia's mom. Be my wife. If necessary you can consider that an order."

"You can't order me to love you," she said, happiness bubbling inside her.

"I know. That's not what I meant." He shook his head. "This is the worst possible time for words, which I've always counted on, to fail me. I guess it was too much to ask—"

Casey pressed a finger to his lips. "I just meant that I already love you."

"Really?" He blinked.

"I am in love with you and have been for a while."

"The implication is that you just agreed to marry me," he clarified.

"Nothing would make me happier."

He blew out a breath, then lowered his mouth to hers, a coming together of hearts and souls. A promise for the future. It was a while before they came up for air and the two of them smiled at each other.

"So is your father really going to beat me up?" he asked.

"Did he tell you that?"

He nodded and said, "Maybe he'll cut me some slack if I explain that I fell madly in love with his daughter and want to make her the happiest woman in the world."

"That will work." She slid her arms around his waist and rested her cheek on his chest. "And by the way, mission accomplished."

\* \* \* \* \*

# 2 FREE BOOKS
## AND A SURPRISE GIFT

We would like to take this opportunity to thank you for reading this Mills & Boon® book by offering you the chance to take TWO more specially selected books from the Cherish™ series absolutely FREE! We're also making this offer to introduce you to the benefits of the Mills & Boon® Book Club™—

- **FREE home delivery**
- **FREE gifts and competitions**
- **FREE monthly Newsletter**
- **Exclusive Mills & Boon Book Club offers**
- **Books available before they're in the shops**

Accepting these FREE books and gift places you under no obligation to buy, you may cancel at any time, even after receiving your free books. Simply complete your details below and return the entire page to the address below. You don't even need a stamp!

**YES** Please send me 2 free Cherish books and a surprise gift. I understand that unless you hear from me, I will receive 5 superb new stories every month, including two 2-in-1 books priced at £5.30 each, and a single book priced at £3.30, postage and packing free. I am under no obligation to purchase any books and may cancel my subscription at any time. The free books and gift will be mine to keep in any case.

Ms/Mrs/Miss/Mr _____ Initials _____

Surname _____

Address _____

_____ Postcode _____

E-mail_____

Send this whole page to: Mills & Boon Book Club, Free Book Offer, FREEPOST NAT 10298, Richmond, TW9 1BR